'With the expe...,   r, author
Michael Christie carefully and methodically pieces together a
story as intricate as the rings within a tree. The result is a deeply
compelling novel of family and memory ... *Greenwood* is a
towering, profound novel about the things that endure even as
the world seems to be moving on.' ***Bookpage***

'This superb family saga will satisfy fans of Richard Powers's
The Overstory while offering a convincing vision of potential
ecological destruction.' ***Publishers Weekly***

'A lyrical, meditative take on a world in which forests have become
such rare commodities that they are turned into therapeutic
retreats for the very wealthy.' ***New Scientist***

'Christie skilfully teases out the details in a page-turner of a saga
... Beguilingly structured, elegantly written: eco-apocalyptic but
with hope that somehow we'll make it.' **STARRED REVIEW**
Kirkus

'This is one of "those" books. One of "those" books that grabs your
heart and soul and fills you up to overflowing with the immensity
of all that's contained within its pages.' ***NB Magazine***

'Brilliant. Michael Christie shows a cross section of one family's
history, revealing their dark secrets, loves, losses, and the mark of
an accident still visible four generations later. Year by year, page
by page, the layers of this intricate and elegant novel build into an
epic story that is completely absorbing. I had to cancel everything
for this book because I couldn't stop reading.' **Claire Cameron,
author of *The Last Neanderthal***

'[An] eerily real-feeling future.' *Globe and Mail*

'*Greenwood*'s powerful narratives, fascinating characters, and lovely prose full of beautiful specificity take on our contemporary fears for the world. This is one of those novels you thrust at friends and insist: You have to read this!' **FIVE STARS** *Good Reading*

'A literary page-turner that manages to be both nostalgic and modern, personal and political, intimately human and big-picture historical. In an era of so much uncertainty, it is comforting to see novelists begin to work through the biggest issue of our age. And, in this case, convert our collective suffering into brilliant, beauty-filled art.' *Toronto Star*

'At once hypnotic and raging, dangerously real and brimming with hope, *Greenwood* is that most necessary epic that binds our human frailties to our planet's possibilities. Michael Christie tenderly rakes the past and paints a future without flinching. I read this book with my heart in my throat, in my hands, in my gut; I read this book heart-full.' **Katy Simpson Smith, author of *The Story of Land and Sea***

'*Greenwood* is a family story, fractured and often contradictory (as the best family stories usually are) ... bringing together the intimate and the sweeping, the human world and the natural, the past and the future.' *Quill & Quire*

'A dystopian, historical, speculative, multigenerational family saga, this marvellous, generous book is best enjoyed in a forest.' **Sharon Bala, author of *The Boat People***

'Even if you're suffering from what you might call Literary Tree Fatigue, Christie's novel is worth reading, in part because it's a clever mash-up of genres that distinguishes itself from its literary cousins and earns its bulk … broad messages aside, the heart of the novel is a winning and energetic chase story … When do we choose self-preservation, and when do we choose survival in a broader sense? The question has never gone away, but *Greenwood* closes with the message that it's increasingly urgent.' *The Washington Post*

'An impressive ecological novel … From the future, to the present, the past and back again, *Greenwood* is a moving novel of family sacrifice and love for a natural world.' *The Canberra Times*

'Christie dazzles with this richly woven historical tracking five generations of the "trouble-plagued" Greenwood clan and the environmental devastation wrought by its lucrative timber empire … A spellbinding family saga reflecting fiction's intensifying interest in the climate crisis as well as humanity's innate desire to make amends for past wrongs and start anew.' **STARRED REVIEW** *Library Journal*

GREENWOOD

MICHAEL CHRISTIE IS the author of the novel *If I Fall, If I Die*, which was longlisted for the Scotiabank Giller Prize and the Kirkus Prize, was selected as a *New York Times* Editors' Choice, and was on numerous best of 2015 lists. His linked collection of stories, *The Beggar's Garden*, was longlisted for the Scotiabank Giller Prize, shortlisted for the Writers' Trust Fiction Prize, and won the Vancouver Book Award. His essays and book reviews have appeared in *The New York Times*, *The Washington Post*, and *The Globe and Mail*. A former carpenter and homeless shelter worker, he divides his time between Victoria, British Columbia, and Galiano Island, where he lives with his wife and two sons in a timber-frame house that he built himself.

GREENWOOD

MICHAEL CHRISTIE

SCRIBE

Melbourne • London

Scribe Publications
2 John St, Clerkenwell, London, WC1N 2ES, United Kingdom
18–20 Edward St, Brunswick, Victoria 3056, Australia

Published by Scribe 2020
This edition published 2021

Text design by Jennifer Griffiths

Internal images:
chapter openers © https://www.flickr.com/photos/biodivlibrary/10460597646/
pp. viii–ix © Josef Mohyla/E+/Getty Images
pp. 1 and 447 © https://www.flickr.com/photos/biodivlibrary/7064353165/
pp. 41 and 413 © https://wellcomecollection.org/works/c3g45u3g?query=veins
pp. 207 © https://www.flickr.com/photos/biodivlibrary/10460610126/

Typeset in Adobe Caslon Pro by M&S, Toronto
Printed and bound in the UK by CPI Group (UK) Ltd, Croydon CR0 4YY

Scribe Publications is committed to the sustainable use of natural resources
and the use of paper products made responsibly from those resources.

9781912854998 (UK paperback)
9781925713855 (Australian paperback)
9781925693430 (ebook)

Catalogue records for this book are available from the National Library of Australia
and the British Library.

scribepublications.co.uk
scribepublications.com.au

For my family

Trees warp time, or rather create a variety of times:
here dense and abrupt, there calm and sinuous.
JOHN FOWLES, *THE TREE*

There is drama in the opening of a log—to uncover
for the first time the beauty in the bole, or trunk, of a tree
hidden for centuries, waiting to be given this second life.
GEORGE NAKASHIMA, *THE SOUL OF A TREE*

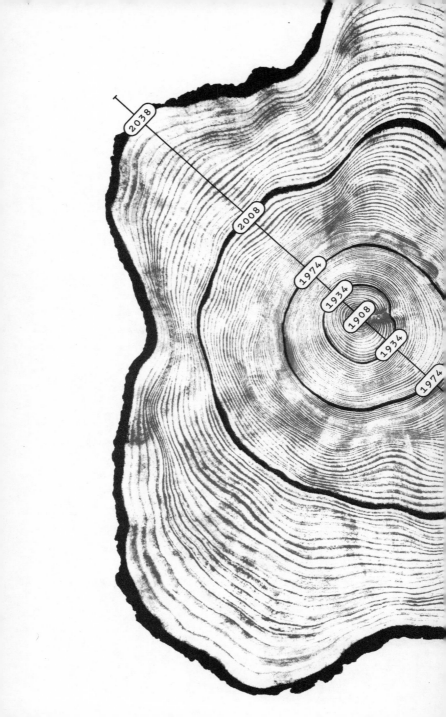

2038

THE GREENWOOD
ARBOREAL CATHEDRAL

THEY COME FOR the trees.

To smell their needles. To caress their bark. To be regenerated in the humbling loom of their shadows. To stand mutely in their leafy churches and pray to their thousand-year-old souls.

From the world's dust-choked cities they venture to this exclusive arboreal resort—a remote forested island off the Pacific Rim of British Columbia—to be transformed, renewed, and reconnected. To be reminded that the Earth's once-thundering green heart has not flatlined, that the soul of all living things has not come to dust and that it isn't too late and that all is not lost. They come here to the Greenwood Arboreal Cathedral to ingest this outrageous lie, and it's Jake Greenwood's job as Forest Guide to spoon-feed it to them.

GOD'S MIDDLE FINGER

AS FIRST LIGHT trickles through the branches, Jake greets this morning's group of Pilgrims at the trailhead. Today, she'll lead them out among the sky-high spires of Douglas fir and Western red cedar, between granite outcrops plush with electric green moss, to the old-growth trees, where epiphany awaits. Given the forecasted rain, the dozen Pilgrims are all swaddled in complimentary Leafskin, the shimmery yet breathable new fabric that's replaced Gore-Tex, nano-engineered to mimic the way leaves bead and repel water. Though the Cathedral has issued Jake her own Leafskin jacket, she seldom wears it for fear of damaging company property; she's already deep enough in debt without having to worry about a costly replacement. Yet trudging through the drizzling rain that begins just after they set out on the trail, Jake wishes she'd made an exception today.

Despite the litre of ink-black coffee she gulped before work this morning, Jake's hung-over brain is taffy-like, and it throbs in painful synchronization with every step she takes. Though she's woefully unprepared for public speaking, once they reach the first glades of old-growth she begins her usual introduction.

"Welcome to the beating heart of the Greenwood Arboreal Cathedral," she says in a loud, theatrical voice. "You're standing on fifty-seven square kilometres of one of the last remaining old-growth forests on Earth." Immediately, the Pilgrims brandish their phones and commence to feverishly thumb their screens. Jake never knows whether they're fact-checking her statements, posting breathless exclamations of wonder, or doing something entirely unrelated to the tour.

"These trees act like huge air filters," she carries on. "Their needles suck up dust, hydrocarbons, and other toxic particles, and breathe out pure oxygen, rich with phytoncides, the chemicals that have been found to drop our blood pressure and slow our heart rates. Just one of these mature firs can generate the daily oxygen required by four adult humans." On cue, the Pilgrims begin to video themselves taking deep breaths through their noses.

While Jake is free to mention the Earth's rampant dust storms in the abstract, it's Cathedral policy never to speak of their cause: the Great Withering—the wave of fungal blights and insect infestations that rolled over the world's forests ten years ago, decimating hectare after hectare. The Pilgrims have come to relax and forget about the Withering, and it's her job (and jobs, she's aware, are currently in short supply) to ensure they do.

Following her introduction, she coaxes the Pilgrims a few miles west, into a grove of proper old-growth giants, whose trunks bulge wider than mid-sized cars. These are trees of such immensity and grandeur they seem unreal, like film props or monuments. In the presence of such giants, the Pilgrims assume hushed, reverent tones. Official Holtcorp policy is to refer to the forest as the *Cathedral* and its guests as *Pilgrims*; Knut, Greenwood Island's most senior Forest Guide and Jake's closest friend, claims that this is because the forest was the first (and now, perhaps, the last) church. Back when air travel didn't command a year's salary, Jake once visited Rome on a learning exchange and saw only curving limbs and ropy trunks in its columns and porticoes. The leafy dome of the mosque; the upward-soaring spires of the abbey; the ribbed vault of the cathedral—which faith's sacred structures weren't designed with trees as inspiration?

Now some of the Pilgrims actually begin to embrace the bark for long durations without irony or embarrassment. In their information packages, the Pilgrims are instructed not to approach the trees too closely, as their weight compacts the soil around the trunks and causes the roots to soak up less water. But Jake holds her tongue and watches the Pilgrims commune, photograph, and huff the chlorophyll-scrubbed air with a reverence that is part performance, part genuine appreciation, though it's difficult for her to estimate in which proportions. Soon they barrage her with impossibly technical questions: "So how much would a thing like this *weigh*?" asks a short man with a Midwestern accent. "This reminds me of being a girl," a fifty-something investment banker declares, caressing a moss-wrapped cedar.

While most of the Pilgrims seem to be tuning in to the Green magnificence, a few appear lost, underwhelmed. Jake watches the short Midwestern man place his palm against a Douglas fir's bark, gaze up into the canopy, and attempt to feel awed. But she can sense his disappointment. Soon he and the others retreat back into their phones for the relief of distraction. This is to be expected. Even though they've paid the Cathedral's hefty fees and endured the indignities of post-Withering travel, there are always a few who can't escape the burden of how relaxed they're *supposed* to be at this moment, and how dearly it's costing them to fail.

The Pilgrims are easily mocked, but Jake also pities them. Hasn't she remained here on Greenwood Island for the same purpose? To glean something rare and sustaining from its trees, to breathe their clean air and feel less hopeless among them? On the Mainland, the Pilgrims live in opulent, climate-controlled towers that protect them from rib retch—the new strain of tuberculosis endemic to the world's dust-choked slums, named after the cough that snaps ribs like kindling, especially in children—yet they still arrive at the Cathedral seeking something ineffable that's missing from their lives. They've read that article about the health benefits of *shinrin-yoku*, the Japanese term for "forest bathing." They've listened to that podcast about how just a few hours spent among trees triples your creativity. So they're here to be healed, however temporarily, and if Jake weren't mired in student debt and hadn't embarked on such a pitifully unmarketable career as botany, she'd gladly be one of them.

When Jake notices a patrol of Rangers creeping through some cedars in the distance, she carefully herds the Pilgrims to the picnic area for their prepared lunches, dubbed "Upscale Logging Camp" by the resort's Michelin-starred chef. Today, it's artisanal hot dogs with chanterelle ketchup and organic s'mores. While watching them photograph their food, Jake's eye snags on a particular Pilgrim sitting apart from the group, wearing large sunglasses and an unfashionable cap pulled low. He's wealthy, some Holtcorp executive or actor no doubt, though Jake would be the last person to know. Because she can't afford a screen in her staff cabin—her student loan interest payments don't leave her enough for internet access—she seldom recognizes the resort's famous visitors. Still, the true celebrities can be identified by that glittery aura they exude, the sense that they've forged a deeper connection to the world than regular people like her.

After lunch Jake escorts the Pilgrims to the tour's grand finale, the largest stand on Greenwood Island, where she hits them with a poetic bit she wrote and memorized years back: "Many of the Cathedral's trees are over twelve hundred years old. That's older than our families, older than most of our names. Older than the current forms of our governments, even older than some of our myths and ideologies.

"Like this one," she says, patting the foot-thick bark of the island's tallest Douglas fir, a breathtaking tree that she and Knut have secretly named "God's Middle Finger." "This two-hundred-and-thirty-foot titan was already a hundred and fifty feet tall when Shakespeare sat down and dipped his quill to begin writing *Hamlet*." She pauses to watch a stoic solemnity grip the group. She's laying it on thick, but her hangover has cleared and she's finally found her rhetorical groove. And when she gets going, she wants nothing less than to wow the Pilgrims with the wonders of all creation. "Each year of its life, this tree has expanded its bark and built a new ring of cambium to encase the ring of growth that came the year before it. That's twelve hundred layers of heartwood, enough to thrust the tree's needled crown into the clouds."

As she's wrapping up, a hand shoots skyward from the back of the group, upon its wrist a thick, dangly Rolex. "A question?" Jake says.

"How much do you think one of these is *worth*?" the celebrity says while kneading his square chin between his finger and thumb. "One tree. Ballpark."

Normally, she'd shimmy out of answering a question of such crudely capitalistic inanity. But coming from that face, from behind those regimentally straight teeth that resemble actual pearls, it nearly sounds witty.

"Oh, I really couldn't say, sir," she says in a serious tone. "These trees are fully protected by Holtcorp's strict preservation—"

"Just toss out a number," he persists.

As a Forest Guide, Jake is routinely advised against making prolonged eye contact with Pilgrims, to avoid interfering with their epiphanies—but she now boldly peers into the greenish depths of the man's expensive sunglasses. "It depends," she says.

"On what?"

"On who's buying. Now are there any other questions?"

"You want a photo?" the celebrity asks her just before they start back. He says it like he's offering an object of great value. She nods and he stands abreast with her directly in front of God's Middle Finger, aiming his phone with a hooked wrist, kinking his neck into the frame. He doesn't know that appearing in photos and selfies are indignities that Forest Guides are contractually obligated to suffer—they're certainly Jake's least favourite part of the job. To think of all the photos she's haunted in her nine years here, a sedately smiling extra, briefly appearing in the brilliant, globe-trotting lives of others.

"What's your name?" the celebrity says, thumbing the screen afterwards. "I'll tag it."

Only because she's required to, she tells him.

His eyebrows crest from beneath the rim of his sunglasses. "Any relation?" he says, doing a little finger twirl, meaning: *to all this?*

Jake shakes her head. "My family are gone," she says. "And even when they were alive, they weren't the island-owning type."

"Sorry," he says, wincing.

"It's fine," she says, forcing a smile. "But we ought to be getting back."

Just as the group rejoins the path, Jake notices that some patches of needles high up on the east-facing side of the old-growth firs have browned. Odd, especially at this time of year. She calls a premature water break and picks her way back through the waxy salal underbrush while scanning the canopy. The Pilgrims wait at the trail, tapping the toes of their Leafskin hiking boots, eager for the private luxuries of their solar-powered Villas, which are in fact secretly grid-connected, because the primeval canopy allows only enough actual sunlight to power a two-slice toaster or to charge their phones, not both.

Upon closer examination, Jake discovers two firs, both directly adjacent to God's Middle Finger, whose needles have rusted to a stricken, cinnamon tinge. And down near the soil, she notes that a few sections of their thick, cement-grey bark have gone soggy. A tree's bark performs the same function our skin does: it keeps intruders out and nutrients in—so any weakening of the bark does not bode well for the tree's long-term survival. With her heart banging behind her ribs, Jake scrutinizes the soggy tissue as though she's peering out a car window at a roadside accident—with curiosity and horror, compassion and revulsion—but the bark seems to be intact, and there's no sign of hostile insects or fungal intrusion. Somewhat satisfied, she takes one last look before hurrying back to the impatient Pilgrims.

To afford her some time to think during the hike back to the Villas, Jake omits her usual speech about the important riparian area that hydrates the forest. *It was only two*, she reassures herself. There were no bugs or funguses, and the surrounding soil looked damp and well aerated, so perhaps the two trees are an anomaly. If they are in fact diseased, it's something she's never observed on the island before.

As a dendrologist—a botanist specializing in trees—Jake knows that many tree species suffered catastrophic die-offs long before the Great Withering struck: the American chestnut in the 1900s, the Dutch elm in the 1960s, and the European ash in the 2000s. Insects, funguses, cankers, blights, and rusts: the enemies of trees are many, and include supervillains such as the emerald ash borer, the Asian long-horned beetle, the dreaded fungus Chalara. But no single organism is responsible for the Withering, and most scientists (including Jake) attribute it to the climate zones changing faster than the trees could adapt, which weakened their ability to defend themselves against invaders. Though formal research has surely been done, somewhere, scientists are no longer freely sharing their findings since the rise of environmental nationalism and the end of the free internet. Jake's personal hypothesis is that Greenwood Island's local microclimate somehow manages to regulate itself, which allows it to remain hospitable to its trees.

But could it be that whatever has protected the Cathedral for so long has now shifted, leaving its trees newly vulnerable to pathogens and intruders? But why would the Great Withering strike now, after all this time? It's more likely something abiotic and noncontagious, Jake tells herself. A nitrogen shortage or a sunscald. Or a good old-fashioned drought-induced flagging. Or perhaps the two firs have simply grown old and, after living in tandem for a millennium, feeding one another through their mycelial networks and conversing through their scent compounds, their plan is to meet their end together, like a couple married for fifty years who die just days apart.

What I really need is a drink, Jake realizes later, while walking to the staff dining yurt after concluding her final tour of the day. But a drink might tempt her to tell Knut about her discovery. Knut's botanical knowledge is vast, but she can't be certain whether he'd help her diagnose the two ailing trees—recording rainfall and gathering soil and tissue samples to examine under a microscope—or whether he might do something drastic. Though he's brilliant, there's always been a precariousness to Knut's sanity, a by-product of a green romanticism that Jake fears can't possibly survive the real world's serial letdowns.

And if the Rangers are now patrolling the old-growth in plain sight of the Pilgrims, then management is clearly already on edge. If they found out about the browning they might do something stupid, like spray the entire island with untested fungicides, or cut their losses and relocate the resort to another of the last scraps of heritage forest that remain—most of them also in Canada, with sprinklings in Russia, Brazil, and Tasmania, the majority on small islands.

For now, Jake decides, the pair of sick firs will remain her secret. The Rangers are private soldiers with no scientific expertise, so they won't notice the browned needles. And since the other Forest Guides have prescribed routes and only Jake's loops around to the east of God's Middle Finger, there's little chance they will see them either. Jake knows that Knut often sneaks into the old-growth during his spare time, so he might spot the damage—but his eyes are going, and it isn't likely he could make out needles that high up. Besides, the soggy bark is impossible to see if you aren't expressly looking for it.

So she has time. She only hopes it's not already too late.

KNUT

"THERE'S SOMETHING TRULY repellant about the notion of reducing what is the very pinnacle of natural magnificence to merely a *therapeutic backdrop* for the wealthy. Don't you agree, Jake?" Knut is warming up his rant-engine, as he likes to do whenever a group of newly recruited Forest Guides arrives. He's giving his unofficial orientation over dinner in the dining yurt, his feet propped on the common table next to their microwaved dinners.

"At least we aren't hacking them all down anymore, Knut," Jake says robotically. Though she is usually happy to play her half of their comedy routine during Knut's orientations, today she's eager to change the subject. Normally, the Rangers' security patrols are focused on the island's coastline, where they repel the ragtag groups from the Mainland that occasionally make landfall to raid the Cathedral's food caches. But lately, Jake has noticed them patrolling more within the resort itself, where they're keeping even closer tabs on the Cathedral staff than usual. If they come anywhere near the dining yurt, there's a solid chance they'll overhear Knut's blasphemous remarks. He's been warned for criticizing the Cathedral before, and if he's caught again, they won't hesitate to send him away from the island and condemn him to huff toxic-dust particulate with the rest of non-wealthy humanity.

"Why don't you tell them about how John Muir singlehandedly convinced the U.S. government to create their national park system?" Jake says, trying to lead him off topic with one of his favourite subjects.

But Knut continues his rant as she goes to the freezer, selects a serving of Turnip and Potato Medley over Creamy Potato Stew—dairy products have always turned her belly into a whoopee cushion—then unskins the plastic from her meal before frisbeeing it into the microwave. Awaiting her food, she checks the yurt's thin plastic windows again, but finds no sign of a patrol. She turns her attention to this newest batch of eight Forest Guides. They're all in their mid-twenties, with trust-funded Ivy League botany or environmental studies graduate degrees, and quite likely haven't inhaled as much as a speck of dust in their entire lives. Most of them will work at the Cathedral for a few years to "gain experience" before embarking on fantastically successful careers elsewhere. Their wealthy parents will visit, shelling out the resort's outrageous fees for just a glimpse of how snappy their offspring look in Forest Guide uniforms, cheering and clapping during their tours. How Jake—with her obscure degree ("The University of *Utrecht*?" they ask. "Do you need a lozenge?")—continues to be employed alongside these gorgeous, superhuman children, who'll work for less money than she could ever possibly survive on, remains beyond her.

"Do any of you appreciate the *unspeakable irony* of elite executives and celebrities travelling here to spiritually replenish themselves," Knut goes on, "only so that they can return rejuvenated to lives that are either directly or indirectly parboiling our planet, thereby further dooming such natural wonders as these very sacred trees they claim to revere?"

As the bubbling pond of her meal twirls slowly in the microwave behind her, Jake watches the young Forest Guides regard Knut—who is approaching sixty, wears a greying mustache, and has wrinkly skin that remains permanently bronzed though he hasn't left the Cathedral's canopy in years—with the wary enchantment one does a newscaster gone rogue. But he's by far the most knowledgeable and best-reviewed Forest Guide at the Cathedral, which is why their boss, Davidoff, has been reluctant to fire him. Despite his insubordination, Knut's online approval ratings are the stuff of legend: always hovering at around 4.9 leaves out of a possible 5. But Jake has seen plenty of Forest Guides and other Cathedral staff expelled for minor infractions like complaining about the microwaved staff meals or even mentioning the Withering in passing.

"But the connection between the Great Withering and carbon emission–driven climate change hasn't been experimentally substantiated," one of the new Guides says, a raven-haired female recruit. *Great*, Jake thinks, *now he's got them talking about the Withering. We'll all be on a supply barge back to the Mainland before dinner's over.*

"Most funguses flourish in warmth, do they not?" Knut queries the recruit, who is young enough to be his granddaughter.

She nods uncomfortably. "Most funguses do, yes," she says softly, unsure if she's being tricked.

"As do insects, do they not?"

Again the girl nods.

Knut takes a theatrical bow. "Consider it substantiated," he says.

"Who are we humble scientists to grasp the mysteries of the universe?" Jake muses fatalistically while carrying her volcanically hot and thoroughly tasteless meal to the table. "Now can we all please just shut up and eat?"

Again ignoring Jake, Knut zeroes in on a particular Guide, a young man whose nametag reads *Torey* who has spectacularly springy, golden hair. "I mean, tell me, how can it *not* cheapen something spiritual when you're forced to watch people pay exorbitant sums to access it?"

Torey shrugs and smiles uneasily, searching for cues from the others.

"*Simony*, that's the English word for it," Knut adds, pleased with himself. "And we, my friends, are the resident desecrators. John Muir, if he were alive, would turn us all out of this temple himself."

Earlier, Knut had informed the new Guides that he was born in Pforzheim, Germany, a city that lies at the rim of the Black Forest, which his ancestors helped clear-cut and raft down the Rhine to the Netherlands to be used as ship's masts, though they later replanted many of the trees, founding some of Europe's first nature preserves. In his spare time he reads Linnaeus in Swedish and he has a religious reverence for John Muir, the first European man to describe the coastal Douglas fir. "And unlike most of you," Knut told them, "I came to Canada *before* the Withering. So remember that."

"At least we're doing what we love," Torey says with unabashed earnestness.

"Yes, my friends," Knut declares, placing a benevolent hand on Torey's shoulder, "the Greenwood Arboreal Cathedral is where good, forest-loving eco-warriors go to die, doing exactly what they love." Knut makes the sign of the cross before he finally shuts up and digs into his prepackaged cake.

Dinner progresses from there in silence, and thankfully without a visit from the Rangers. It's Jake's turn to clean out the staff fridge, so after the meal she remains behind as the others file out.

"Everything okay out there in the trees today?" says a muffled voice behind her sometime later. Jake extracts her head from the fridge to find Davidoff standing at the door with hairy arms crossed. Some Guides claim that, pre-Withering, Davidoff had been some kind of Russian special forces operative, but he's short and flabby with eyes dead as dirty nickels, and Jake has never registered the coiled menace others describe.

"Really positive engagement for my Pilgrims today, sir," she says. "Plenty of great questions. And some bona fide epiphanies too."

"The new Ranger patrols didn't get in your way, did they?" he asks with his chest puffed proudly. "I secured some funding to step things up now that the raids are becoming more frequent. There's concern that the Mainlanders could make it into the resort."

"My Pilgrims never even knew they were there, and I feel much safer just knowing they're around," Jake says with a tight smile. "But I did note a slight anomaly earlier," she adds, as offhandedly as she can manage. "A touch of needle browning on some unremarkable firs near the staff cabins. Certainly nothing to worry about, but it should be examined. With your approval, I'd like to sign out a microscope, some rainfall meters, and a soil collection kit, just to be sure."

"You won't be messing around with any of our old-growth trees, will you?" he asks skeptically. "If the Rangers catch anyone out in the Cathedral with a microscope, they'll be banished before I even hear of it."

"No, of course not," she replies, feeling her stomach twitch with the lie. "It's not the old-growth at all. Just a few trees around my cabin, and only to satisfy my own curiosity."

"I appreciate your interest in our majestic forest, Greenwood," Davidoff says, with a smile that his dead eyes fail to match. "You're cleared to sign out whatever you need from the Maintenance Shed. But I need you well rested for tomorrow. You're booked for a private, bright and early."

"Me?" Jake says. She never gets booked for private tours, most likely because she's ten years older than the other Guides and it's always male Pilgrims who book them. Her thoughts veer to the celebrity in her group today—Corbyn Gallant—whose visit she overheard a few of the recruits mention breathlessly at dinner. "Who with?"

"Not sure exactly," he says. "But some higher-ups at Corporate requested you specifically. So I need you to bring that old Greenwood charm tomorrow."

While hurrying to reach the Maintenance Shed before it shuts down for the night, Jake considers the unsubstantiated tales she's heard of private tours where, following a quick jaunt through the trees, a $5,000 "massage" with cedar-scented oils is provided to a Saudi solar panel prince by an unnamed Forest Guide. And given the fact that by this date next year her ballooning student loan interest payments will swallow her entire bi-weekly salary, she's ashamed to admit that she'd probably do the same. How different things would be for her if she were afloat in family money like Torey and the rest of the Forest Guides. Because there's nothing like poverty to teach you just how much of a luxury integrity truly is.

THE GREAT WITHERING

WHEN JACINDA GREENWOOD is eight years old, her mother, Meena
Bhattacharya—a first-chair violist for the Los Angeles Symphony—
is returning home to New York City from a solo concert she's given
in Washington, D.C., when her commuter train slips its tracks and
arcs forty feet down onto the busy interstate below. First responders
locate her body in the thin greenbelt of trees that divides the interstate's northbound and southbound lanes, her skull crushed yet her
reading glasses somehow still fixed in place. Her mother's death
teaches Jake, too early in life, that the human body is fragile, and that
our brief lives can be halted at any moment, as unexpectedly as a
breeze blowing a door shut.

With her mother gone, it's as though the colour has been sapped
from Jake's world. She seldom eats and speaks only in murmurs. She's
sent to Delhi to be raised by her grandparents, civil servants living
in a middle-class suburb on the city's southern fringe. Immediately,
Jake misses the U.S. The neat geometry of its sidewalks, the splat of
ketchup on French fries—every memory is like a thorn in her flesh
that she can't extract. But worst of all, she misses the sound of her
mother playing her viola in the next room, a soothing warble almost
indistinguishable from her voice.

A week after her arrival in India, Jake finds a cardboard box on
her bed, on the side of which her mother has written LIAM
GREENWOOD. All Meena ever told her about her father was that he
died while working illegally as a carpenter in the U.S. when Jake was
three. Perhaps because she's never seen his face, not even in pictures,
Jake has always imagined him as Paul Bunyan–like, nearly a tree

himself, with a halogen smile, a carpenter's burly hands, a plaid shirt, and sawdust powdering his hair.

As she stares at the name on the box, Jake remembers something her mother once told her while they were riding the subway in New York, her large, unwieldy viola case jammed between them like a bodyguard. "Your father was a troubled person," she said, with the same kindness that she extended to even the city's poorest souls, a few of whom were riding the subway car along with them. "But he was a good person. And he tried to make things right in the end. He left you a few things, which you'll get when you're older, and some money for your schooling, as well as an old farm in Saskatchewan that I haven't managed to sell quite yet."

So this box before Jake is a revelation, a time capsule sent from a distant, unreachable past. She reads her father's name again and imagines all the wonders the box might contain, and how those wonders could send away the dark creature that has lived in her belly ever since her mother's death. Yet when she finally gathers the courage to open it, the box contains no photographs of her father, no stack of letters or diary to explain why he never once took the time to visit her or what her mother meant by "make things right." Instead, it contains the yellowed deed to a piece of worthless farmland, a few old-fashioned woodworking tools, a dozen unlabelled vinyl records, and a pair of work gloves that appear to be unused. She growls and kicks the box deep into her closet. While her grandparents have no turntable to play her father's records, she listens to them a few months later at a friend's house, and is further insulted when she discovers they're not, as she hoped, recordings of her mother playing the viola or of her father reading bedtime stories, but instead a series of droning poetry recitations, all done by the same annoyingly over-expressive man.

Meena was an only child, and because Jake's grandparents had already launched one perfect girl into the world only to lose her inexplicably, they take a reserved approach with Jake, and direct her out into

the large back yard whenever she seeks a playmate. It's there she discovers the great multi-trunked banyan that spreads across the property, thirty-eight trunks in total, which she learns are all somehow a
single living being. Initially, she finds this alien maze of alligator-
coloured leaves frightening, as if it's a monster trying to confuse and
devour her. But because the banyan is the closest thing she has to a
friend, she soon comes to know its contours better than the interior
of her own room. After school, when she's completed her regular
studies, she disappears into the tree with her illustrated botany books
and her tea set, and lies for hours talking to it and imagining its
roots—a many-fingered claw that must reach so far down that it
grasps the very soul of the Earth. After six months, she comes to feel
a kinship not just with the banyan but with all trees, and adores them
with a fervor that other girls reserve for ivory stallions or honey-
voiced Bollywood heartthrobs.

Luckily, the education fund left by her father is just enough to
pay for international schooling, where she takes special lessons in
botany. By the age of ten, she's committed her dendrological ency-
clopedia to memory. By eleven, she can discern images of balsam
from hemlock, oak from dogwood. By twelve, she can make the same
classifications by ear, with only the YouTubed sound of wind running through leaves as her guide.

On her fourteenth birthday, she convinces her grandparents to
let her travel nine hours north on a crowded bus, with not a square
foot of space left unoccupied, to the famed Forest Research Institute
at Dehradun. A sprawling wooded estate established by the British
at the foot of the Himalayas, it's one of the oldest institutions practising scientific forestry in the world. With her clothing shamefully
crumpled from the ride, she meets the Institute's director, Dr. Biswas,
a leading expert on the Bodhi tree, the same species that the Buddha
meditated under at Bodh Gaya. Jake has written many letters brimming with questions for the doctor, who was sufficiently impressed
by their fluency that she offered Jake an informal week-long

residency at the Institute, a time she spends in its laboratories, herbarium, and arboreta, meeting first-hand the countless species she's previously only read about. For the next few years, Jake returns to Dehradun for the week of her birthday, and when she graduates high school, Dr. Biswas recommends her to the botany department at the University of British Columbia in Vancouver, a treed city in which, as Meena once mentioned, Jake's father had lived.

In Canada, aside from a brief engagement to a fellow biology student, Jake devotes herself wholly to tree rings and tap roots, to polyploids and triploids, to pollen dispersion, gametes, ovules, and seed genetics. Daily, her head zaps with fresh currents of insight. She becomes convinced that a true and perfect understanding of the tree's secret workings will provide the intellectual skeleton key to unlock all her questions. That even the impenetrable mysteries of time and family and death can be solved, if only they are viewed through the green-tinted lens of this one gloriously complex organism.

It's while she's earning her Ph.D. from the University of Utrecht four years later—a degree paid for by a complex scaffolding of student loans, scholarships, and credit card sorcery that lingers on the servers of collection agencies to this day—that she first detects the traces of what will become the Great Withering, in dendrology-related periodicals and scholarly reports. As more and more old-growth forests around the globe succumb and die off, the soil dries up without trees to shade the ground from the gnawing sun, creating killer dust clouds as fine as all-purpose flour that choke the land—just as they did during the Dust Bowl, but this time on a much larger scale, burying even the largest industrial farms and strangling entire cities.

It isn't until after Jake has returned to North America and is in Boulder, Colorado, to present a paper on communicative scent compounds used cooperatively by coastal Douglas firs that the world's biggest tree, the Northern Californian sequoia known as General Sherman, splits lengthwise in a moderate wind, and the halves of its trunk, which are revealed to be shot through with fungus, thunder to the forest floor. It's not a great loss in ecological terms—many giant redwoods remain, some just as ancient—but the dark symbolism of the event knocks the economy into a tailspin, kicking off the Withering-induced economic collapse. Farms fail, the stock markets go apoplectic, employment dwindles, unchecked wildfires and shortage riots become commonplace, and utter despair becomes the only rational response.

With her bank card now useless, Jake hitchhikes her way north from Boulder, begging for food, with a dampened T-shirt tied over her face to keep the dust from caking in her lungs. She sleeps in drainage culverts and interstate rest stops, and when she finally reaches the Canadian border, she's shaking with hunger. Luckily, the Withering is still in its early days, and vast stretches of undefended border remain, which means Jake, who is technically one of the first climate refugees, is able to cross unhindered. Just outside a town called Estevan, Saskatchewan, she manages to locate the farm that her father had willed to her. While most of its buildings have been plundered and stripped of their wood, and thigh-deep drifts of dust blanket its fields, somehow the well beside an old willow still pumps clear water and the farm's storm cellar remains intact. Jake holes up there for a month, eating expired canned food, sleeping, and gathering her strength. One evening, she hears the voices of people searching the ruins above. Someone even tries to open the cellar door, but Jake has barred it with an iron rod, and eventually they give up and leave.

The next morning, she walks through the choking dust to the train tracks in nearby Estevan, where she climbs onto a massive rail car carrying new automobiles, all covered in white plastic. Twelve new Mercedes, which somehow there's still a market for, even while people starve and asphyxiate with pale blue faces by the side of the road. She finds a car door that's been left open and sits on the grey leather seats, the new vehicle's smell so strong it gives her an immediate headache. The electronic key is in the glove box, so during her westward journey she's able to play the radio, recline the seat, run the heater, and turn on the wipers when the dust gets too thick.

In two days she reaches Vancouver, only to find her former university shuttered and looted. She picks up the few things she's stored there, including her father's box, and at the bank she's able to access her remaining savings. It's there she also learns that the student debt she planned on paying off with a professor's salary has survived the Withering. She takes cheap accommodations in an old hotel by the water, but food has become unbelievably expensive, and she faces bankruptcy if she doesn't begin to pay down her debt. In desperation, she applies for a job with a vaguely described project located on an island northwest of the city. Though she's grossly overqualified for the duties of Forest Guide at the Greenwood Arboreal Cathedral, she remains convinced that the primary reason Holtcorp plucked her application from what must have been a stack of thousands, thereby rescuing her from a life of rib retch and dust-shrouded destitution—and, worst of all, a life lived without the steadying companionship of the island's trees—is the terrifyingly meaningless coincidence of her last name.

PLANKED SALMON

JAKE REACHES THE Maintenance Shed just before it closes, where she signs out a microscope, three rainfall meters, and a soil collection kit. It would be impossible to take measurements of the sick trees during one of her tours, so she'll have to sneak into the old-growth after hours, which will be risky, especially with the increased Ranger patrols. But she has a private to wake up for tomorrow morning, so she reluctantly decides to leave it for another night, and settles on a quick walk to the ocean to calm her thoughts before turning in early.

The air is breezy and the sky pixelated with stars as she takes the trail to the wharf, where the supply barges tie up. Passing a group of Indonesian chambermaids, she catches the scent of the organic cedar oil they spray the guest Villas with, but only after they've already scrubbed them with eye-flaming chemicals. At the water, Jake stops under an ornamental cherry tree to watch four Salvadoran grounds-keepers silently cleaning a cluster of hot tubs that overlook the bay. While her fellow employees always offer her a friendly nod, she's heard that she's the source of great puzzlement among them. Even though her skin is as brown as theirs, she somehow shares a surname both with the Arboreal Cathedral and the island itself—and yet, she still receives the same measly compensation they do. To them this suggests a downfall nearly impossible to measure.

Jake watches one of the groundskeepers reach into the hot tub with a pool skimmer and scoop out a tree frog from the steamy water. Even at a distance, she can tell that the chlorine has bleached the once-emerald frog to a pale pea green, and the sight of it makes her feel sick. Just as she's preparing to head back, a group of black-clad

Rangers swoops in and surrounds a member of the grounds crew who had been smoking a hand-rolled cigarette, a violation of the Cathedral's strict fire protocols. The man's companions bow their heads and surrender their tools as the Rangers point their snub-nosed guns and pat them all down for contraband. Fearful of being questioned about the scientific equipment she's carrying, Jake slips unnoticed back to the trail, while the Rangers roughly drag the offender off to put him on the next barge back to the Mainland.

It's dark by the time she returns to her cabin to find Corbyn Gallant waiting near her door, his chin glued to his chest as he stares deep into the talisman of his phone. He's left his cheeks unshaven and replaced his Leafskin jacket with an expensively rugged chambray button-up. Minus the sunglasses and hat, his facial structure is impossible not to admire.

"Are you lost, sir?" Jake asks as she approaches.

He looks up from his phone, childlike for a moment as his eyes refocus. "If it isn't the Lady of the Trees," he says as though they're old friends. "I've got a few more important questions that I'd like you to answer."

"I'm not supposed to meet with Pilgrims after hours," she says, glancing around for a Ranger patrol. "How about tomorrow, same time, at the trailhead? We can discuss all the old-growth lumber I'll sell you at ridiculous prices."

"Actually, I was hoping we could talk over a drink at your place, except I doubt that we'll both fit in there at the same time," he says, examining the row of tiny staff cabins. They're glorified sheds really, the shabbiness of which the resort seeks to conceal from the Pilgrims by hiding them on the less majestic half of the island, where the trees are comparatively young and spindly. "But I will say that these trees look like they're closer to my price range than the ones you showed me earlier."

"It's not in the brochures," Jake says in a lowered voice, "but this half of Greenwood Island burned to the ground in 1934. The fire left a single charred ring in the trees that edge the area—which means, I'm sorry to report, only half of the Cathedral is authentic old-growth." It feels good to risk a bit of truth, a small relief after a day of speaking from the script.

"I won't tell a soul," he says, placing his palm to his heart. "Then how about my Villa?"

Jake feels her spine stiffen. Forest Guides are prohibited from visiting the Villas, especially after hours. But Corbyn must be the private that Davidoff told her about earlier. And even if he's not, at the very least Jake can plead ignorance and wriggle out of punishment if she's caught. But going anywhere near the Villas after hours while wearing her Forest Guide uniform would be begging for a run-in with the Rangers.

"Give me a minute," she blurts, ducking inside her cabin to change out of her uniform—a Boy Scout outfit crossed with the technical apparel of a fitness instructor—and into the green Prada dress she took from the lost and found and had been looking for an excuse to wear. She pulls on her Cathedral-issue Leafskin jacket overtop to complete her Pilgrim disguise. After rejoining Corbyn, she takes a deep breath and quickly scans the path for Rangers before they set off for his side of the island.

With its fine timber-frame construction and unobstructed ocean view, Villa Twelve is the most luxurious and coveted accommodation on the island, and is always fully booked years in advance. The Canadian prime minister, now widely regarded as the most powerful human being on the planet, stayed here last year with her family.

"Lately, I've been considering a permanent relocation," Corbyn says as he unlocks the intricately woodworked door with his phone before shoving it open. "So I thought I'd give Canada a little test run."

Jake follows him inside, remembering Knut's rant about how much the U.S. elite used to talk about immigrating to Canada, especially after an election didn't go their way. But since the Withering, and after America's once-mighty aquifers were tapped out like fraternity kegs, many actually went through with it, leaving the immobile and the poor to wallow and retch in the dust. Given Russia's penchant for totalitarianism and the recent coup in New Zealand, water- and tree-rich Canada has become the global elite's panic room. Now it's all movie stars, tech giants, and investment bankers on the streets of such previously ignored places as Moose Jaw, Vernon, Thunder Bay, Chicoutimi, and Dartmouth. "And that's how America's polite and homely sibling," Knut said, "once regarded merely as a country-sized storehouse of natural resources, like some great, unlimited supply chest tucked away in America's attic, became the most sought-after address on Earth."

As Corbyn offers her a quick tour, Jake struggles to conceal her awe. Everywhere she looks is the finest furniture of Danish teak, and there's a real woodstove with an actual fire burning inside, and on the north wall is a giant bookshelf that displays what must be a thousand genuine paperbooks—all surrounded by beautifully intricate old-growth post and beam construction that's surely priceless. There seems to be no end to the luxuries that the Villa contains, but it's the paperbooks that impress her most. Almost all of them appear to be pre-Withering, and they range over every subject imaginable. After the majority of the world's books were pulped for wood fibre to produce such essentials as dust masks, air filters, and currency, the value of the remaining ones spiked. For her birthday five years ago, Jake nearly splurged half her savings on a gorgeously illustrated botany paperbook, but reconsidered at the last moment. Today, the book is worth triple what she would have paid.

"It's got a great retro feel to it, doesn't it?" Corbyn says while he pours two bourbons at the butcher-block island—Basil Hayden's, neat, the brand she'd buy if she ever had money. During the Withering's early days, while catastrophic dendrological data from all corners of the world seeped into her laptop, Jake could do nothing except drink Old Fashioneds and watch pirated video files of BBC's *Planet Earth* series over and over. Those time-lapse shots from space of the once-great deciduous forests rolling through their colours—*green to red-gold to brown to green*—would push shuddering sobs through her whole body until she eventually passed out, whether from dehydration, inebriation, or despair she couldn't say.

Corbyn feeds a few fir logs into the stove and they settle onto the wool sofa and clink glasses as the fire warms their shins. The heat is different than the electric heat she's used to, fuller, deeper-penetrating. "Oh, and I'll need to ask you to power down your phone," he says.

She pats the non-existent pockets of her dress. "Don't have one," she says, nearly adding: *With my credit rating, they won't give me a flip-phone.*

At this, a theatrical expression overtakes him, the kind that could carry the final shot of some sappy movie. "Now *that* is absolutely charming," he says, as though she's a precocious child who's inadvertently said something wise. Then he gestures to the shelves. "You would probably still rather read paperbooks, too, wouldn't you?"

"Guilty as charged," she says.

Corbyn edges closer and discourses upon the perils of technology for a while before he orders them dinner from the resort's bistro with his phone. When their entrees of cedar-planked salmon arrive, Jake hides in the gorgeously tiled bathroom as the waiter, a guy she knows named Ramon, rolls the dinner cart into the kitchen.

When Jake returns, Corbyn has filled two glasses of thin crystal with wine, and they perch on stools at the island to eat. She tastes the salad first, purple heirloom tomatoes and leafy greens as soft as silk. She's neither seen nor eaten salmon in years, not since the Withering dried up all the spawning streams and the ambitious fish were left to languish in the ocean. The fillets are glazed with garlic, balsamic vinegar, and real maple syrup—another outlandish delicacy. The fatty layers of the salmon's ruby flesh are striking, and closely resemble wood grain, she realizes, Douglas fir particularly. The biologist in her loves these parallels of growth. How tenaciously organisms build tissue, layer by layer, year by year.

After they've eaten, Corbyn frowns at his Rolex and escorts her back to the sofa, where they both lean into a kiss. "I'm sorry to bring this up," he interrupts not long after, his wine-sour breath fogging her ear. "I just want us to be straight with each other."

"Sure," she says uncertainly.

"I have something to admit, and it's embarrassing." He takes a deep breath. "But because of a severe latex allergy, I'm on doctor's orders to avoid condoms. You don't want to see what happens when I do, trust me. So I have to ask: Are you clean?"

She almost says: *I could be a walking petri dish of any number of diseases, because even though Holtcorp provides all its female Cathedral staff with free IUDs, it doesn't offer actual health care, so I haven't seen a proper doctor since grad school, so who knows?* But she's having a good time, and can't bear to return to her cramped, gloomy cabin. So she chuckles and says, "Of course. You?"

He laughs. Whether this means "Of course I'm clean" or "Of course I'm not, but you'll do this anyway" is unclear. But barring any major gaffes, she might as well go through with it. Why not? There's something about bottomless indebtedness and churning ecological despair that makes meaningless sex a kind of relief. Sure, she'd prefer a more long-lasting relationship over what is certain to be a brief entanglement with Corbyn, but how can anything last in a world as ruined as this? Where thousands of children cough themselves to death each night, and not even the grandest trees can be expected to survive?

"It must be difficult, as a woman," Corbyn says afterwards, while they're laid out on the sofa beneath an impossibly soft cashmere blanket, "to be so educated and passionate in a field, and have to lead idiots like me through these beautiful trees." He grins, certain that this bit of cleverness proves him to be the very opposite of an idiot.

Jake draws a deep breath. Unlike Knut, she chooses her words carefully, especially when speaking with Pilgrims. "I get to live here," she says, "doing a fulfilling job, and not coughing myself to sleep. So for all that I'm grateful."

"But it must bother you on some level?"

"It's a better life than I or anyone I know could ever reasonably expect," she says. "Except you, I guess."

His smile comes slow, like dawn through the Cathedral's canopy. "You know what? *I* envy *you*," he proclaims with some disbelief, as if he's making a delightfully preposterous statement.

Then give me one hundred and fifty thousand dollars, she thinks. *You can fix my life here and now for the price tag of one of your vacations.* Instead she says: "Oh no, don't say that."

"No, I do! Living here? On this island, in this forest, doing what you love. And reading real paperbooks, with no phone! You lead a good, simple life."

A simple life? Jake almost scoffs. In university, while facing the various thesis defense committees comprised mostly of smug, tweed-coated men, Jake fully realized her loathing of being patronized. "Complete with a simple mind, you mean?" she says now, instantly regretting it.

Corbyn's face contorts into an expression of outsized anguish, like a man in a movie learning of his wife's death. "I've offended you, and I'm sorry."

It's not worth arguing over, so she accepts his apology, then allows their conversation to range over topics that he selects: the great promise of environmental innovation, the dangerous yet irresistible allure of social media, the scrappy resilience of human ingenuity. It seems there's no subject that doesn't interest him, everything layered with the same veneer of boyish enthusiasm.

"So do you still want your private tomorrow morning?" she says an hour later, after they've had sex again and she's starting to plan the route she'll have to take through the trees in order to sneak back to her staff cabin this late at night.

"What do you mean?" he says, checking his watch. "Tomorrow early I'm flying up to Nunavut to join some Inuit elders in a healing cere-mony beneath the northern lights. It's going to be life-changing."

A STORY TO TELL

AT SEVEN THE next morning, Jake arrives for her scheduled private and finds her ex-fiancé haunting the trailhead.

"Is this as weird for you as it is for me?" Silas says, offering his hand.

It's been thirteen years since Jake booked her one-way flight from Vancouver to the Netherlands, but not before mailing Silas's engagement ring back to him without a note or even a single syllable of explanation. So much for Jake's plan to never see him again; and so much for her long-held belief that the Withering had reduced the chances of an accidental reunion to zero.

"This is a surprise," Jake says, taking his soft, well-moisturized palm in hers, which leads them into a hasty, bloodless hug.

No one from her pre-Withering life has ever visited the island before, and Silas's appearance feels other-worldly, as though he's just wandered into one of her dreams. But along with the waterfall of guilt roaring in her ears, Jake also feels a twinge of shame at being found in such lowered circumstances by someone she once admired, as if she's been caught playing dress-up in her ridiculous uniform, hiding out in a silly theme park at the edge of the world.

After their hug they stand awkwardly for a moment, both groping for what comes next.

"Look, Silas," Jake says, interrupting him just as he also begins to speak. "I'd completely understand if you'd prefer we find you another Forest Guide to do your tour."

"Are you kidding me?" Silas says with a dismissive wave of his hand, a wide smile stretching across his face. "Who better than you to lead me through these amazing trees that everyone is talking about?"

"Okay . . ." Jake says tentatively, scrambling to maintain her facade of professionalism. Even if he is the last person in the world she'd choose to spend the next few hours with, he's still a Pilgrim—and her job depends on his satisfaction with the tour. "Then let's get started."

After she performs the first of her canned speeches, Jake lets Silas walk ahead of her on the narrowing trail as they weave through the maze of enormous trunks. An outfit of sleek, black Leafskin, a gym-tended physique, skin so well-maintained it appears lucent—the Withering has been kind to Silas. He's probably a bigwig Holtcorp scientist now, booked for a restorative getaway at one of the company's resorts. But for a fleeting instant it crosses Jake's mind that he didn't appear all that surprised to see her. Did he select Jake intentionally? Just to feel superior for a few hours and to prove to her what a catastrophic mistake she'd made?

They met in an earth sciences lecture during Jake's first year at UBC. A fervent environmentalist, Silas brought her to fundraisers and documentary screenings—unwittingly rescuing her from solitary weekends spent in her dorm, leafing through botany texts, admiring branch structures as though they were fashionable outfits. He was clever, witty without being caustic, and in just a few months they had forged a bond of such intensity it felt as though they were symbioti-cally evolved organisms, incapable of independent survival. Soon, Jake was attending the surfeit of birthdays and anniversaries that Silas's large, wealthy family seemed to celebrate endlessly. Feeling like a drifter who'd accidentally wandered into their ski chalets and lake houses, Jake watched his parents and five siblings collectively prepare elaborate meals, which they then shared at huge, lavishly set tables, amid the din of mirthful conversation. After Jake's lonely upbringing, the fullness of Silas's family life mystified her, and this fascination became impossible to disentangle from her feelings for him. Happily, Silas was intuitive enough never to ask about Jake's past. Their conversations were all carbon credits and ecological devastation and Big Oil's cancerous lobbying—this was the quaint period before the Withering when people still believed that well-intended, measured engagement could avert catastrophe. As graduation neared, Silas's anxiety about their imminent separation grew; he proposed and made Jake vow that they would select geographically compatible grad schools. She agreed, and for a time she was content with her decision. But when she was offered a position with a pioneering researcher at Utrecht, and Silas a full ride at UC Irvine, Jake was faced with a choice: Silas or trees. Her panicked response was to block his calls, texts, and emails altogether, and to depart for the Netherlands with only strangers to see her off at the airport.

In short, Jake chose trees.

"God, I've missed this," Silas says, after the trail has widened and they're again walking side by side. "Sunshine, oxygen, soil, water—the raw material of life."

"Silas," she begins softly. "I know I didn't end things in the best way—"

"Please don't apologize, Jake," Silas says, shaking his head. "It was a long time ago. And you did what you needed to do. I'm just happy to see that you went on to fully develop your talents."

She thanks him, taking a mental microscope to his statement, hunting for trace elements of bitterness or condescension, but detects none.

"To be honest," he continues, "I half-expected you to scream and run the other way when you saw me this morning." *So he did know it would be me*, Jake realizes in a flash. "I'm happy you didn't. It's a relief to know that you've wound up in such a beautiful and secure place."

"And where have you wound up?"

"San Francisco. Or what remains of it anyway. Actually, a gated community in Alameda. But I'm considering a move back to Canada. The dust storms are only getting worse, and with millions of people plunging deeper into poverty each day and all these climate refugees penetrating the borders—"

"Easy there, cowboy," Jake says, careful to keep her tone light. "I'm an immigrant too, remember?"

"Oh, these aren't hard-working strivers seeking opportunity like you, Jake. And they were no doubt good people once. But after a few years in the dust, they're desperate enough to butcher your family and loot your home without even doing you the courtesy of first asking for a handout."

There are plenty of points to argue, but Jake lets them drop because she can't risk displeasing him. "Kids?" she asks, attempting to change the subject and immediately chiding herself for the clumsiness of it. Too premature.

He shakes his head, then returns her the same eyebrow-raised look.

Jake shakes her head. "The Cathedral can't accommodate the children of employees. They even provide free birth control, just to make sure." Jake leaves unmentioned the fact that she'd long ago filed motherhood away in the locked drawer that contains everything that the Withering has made impossible for people like her: her own home, a steady relationship, a research lab, a tenured teaching position. And even if she did have the money, why would anyone willingly bring a child into such a fallen, desolate world? Children require hope and prosperity as trees require light and water, and Jake Greenwood is all tapped out of both.

It's not until she emerges from this quagmire of thoughts that Jake notices they've reached God's Middle Finger. She gives her big speech while glancing up at the pair of sick firs, noting that their browned needles are unchanged from yesterday. Silas asks a few obligatory questions, but despite his attempts at playing the part of a Pilgrim, there's an odd sense of dislocation about him, an impatient clock ticking behind everything he says.

"You mentioned earlier that you were expecting me this morning," Jake says as they walk to the picnic area for a water break. "This isn't exactly a coincidence, is it?"

Silas cracks a sheepish smile. "Jake, you should know that after I got to grad school I abandoned biology for law."

No wonder he's being so forgiving, Jake thinks, *he wants something*. She considers the possibility that he might be there to fire her. Then why wouldn't Holtcorp just send a team of Rangers instead? "And now you're a lawyer for Holtcorp?"

"I work for an independent legal firm that does *occasionally* act for Holtcorp, yes. But I also work for you," he says, his eyes now soft and open, almost wounded. "Or at least I'd like to."

"Just how do you intend to do that?" Jake asks skeptically.

Silas laughs nervously. "This is all going a little fast—my plan was to put this to you over dinner tonight."

"Private tours don't include dinner," she says curtly. "And yours is nearly over."

"Okay, fine," he says, throwing up his hands in surrender. "I'm here because this entire island could be yours, Jake. I mean *legally* yours. And I'm here to help you make that a reality. But to establish whether this is possible, I need you to answer a few questions about your family. Particularly concerning your father, Liam Greenwood."

So he's a vulture, Jake thinks. Since the Withering, she has read about this new breed of lawyer who searches out legal corpses to pick over: unresolved wills, mishandled inheritances, loopholes they can weave into some kind of land-grab or court challenge. But Jake would have expected Silas to be smarter than this. Conditions must really be dire out there if he's aiming to use the flimsy coincidence of her surname as a means to lay claim to a billion-dollar forest.

"Holtcorp named this resort the Greenwood Arboreal Cathedral because it sounded good, Silas," Jake says. "Purely a branding decision. Nothing to do with me. My father was a carpenter who died while renovating a house in Connecticut—I don't even know the exact day it happened. Sound like the kind of guy who owns an island to you?" After mentioning her father aloud for the first time in years, she feels the muscles inside her throat crank as tight as guitar strings.

"I know this is difficult," Silas says with his neck canted sympathetically. "But will you please just hear me out and not run away this time? Don't you owe me that much?"

A guilty knot cinches in Jake's gut. She couldn't feel any lower than she does right now if she slithered under a rock. "Okay," she says, chastened, "you have five minutes before we need to head back."

Silas draws a thick paper index card from his pocket. "Harris Greenwood, the West Coast timber tycoon," he reads, "bought this island in 1934 at the height of the Great Depression—from John D. Rockefeller Jr., no less, who had purchased it from the English, who'd seized it from the Spanish, who'd stolen it from the Haida and Penelakut people following European contact. Harris Greenwood named the island after himself, naturally, though he left it to his daughter, Willow Greenwood, the radical hippie conservationist. She thanked him by donating it—along with the entire Greenwood fortune—to an environmental non-profit, thus dooming her son, Liam Greenwood, to a life of blue-collar toil, and his estranged daughter, Jacinda Greenwood, to the shackles of student debt and tree resort servitude. Over time, however, the non-profit morphed into a green energy company, which faltered in the 2008 crash, and was forced to sell the island for a song to Holtcorp to shore up its losses. Holtcorp then sat on it until the Great Withering, at which time the company recognized an opportunity in monetizing its spiritual appeal—and voila, here we are." He takes a little bow, then offers the index card to Jake. "This was prepared by two of my sharpest researchers. Every bit of it verifiable on the public record. It's yours. A gift."

Jake stands speechless as the blue-green crowns of the giant firs rustle hundreds of feet above. Slowly, she reaches out and grasps the card. The paper is real, crisp, and luxuriously thick between her fingers. She scans the bullet-pointed text printed upon it. *Willow Greenwood.* She can't remember Meena ever mentioning Liam's mother. And there was no trace of her to be found in his cardboard box of useless relics. Yet that doesn't mean she didn't exist. Jake feels dizzy, though strangely elated. After a lifetime of knowing virtually nothing about her family, it's like this unexpected burst of names and history has knocked her clean out of her body. But of course there are layers of life that came before her own, the way trees are held up by the concentric bands of their former selves, rings built up over rings, year by year. How had she never thought to ask questions about her ancestors before? The answer, she realizes, is that there had never been anyone to ask.

"Even if this island *is* named after my great-grandfather," Jake says, fighting to return herself to reality, "Holtcorp owns it now. And if you think we're going to take it from them, then the dust must be affecting your brain. So thanks for the information, Silas, but I've got five more tours to do today, so we should probably get moving."

"But what if I told you that Harris Greenwood *isn't* in fact your blood relative?" he announces with a crafty, self-satisfied expression she had always found grating. "And suppose we can prove that you *do* have a claim to Greenwood Island. Including this impossibly rare and endangered forest that I know you love. Not because you're a Greenwood, but because you're a descendant of the original founder of Holtcorp, R.J. Holt."

Then I'd tell you that if you don't leave me the hell alone to figure out what's ailing these trees, Jake considers saying, *by this time next year Greenwood Island might be a barren rock, and it won't matter who owns it.* Instead she watches him unsling his hiking pack and remove from it a thin, hard-backed paperbook.

"This once belonged to your grandmother," Silas says, holding it delicately with his fingertips. "We considered mailing it to you, until I told my colleagues what a skeptic you are, and volunteered to deliver it personally. Not only is it good to see you again—and believe me, it is—I also hoped that you might still trust me."

Jake takes the paperbook in her hands as a fizzy enchantment spreads through her chest. She parts its hardbound covers, which have a slightly gamey odour and are cracked in places and stained with purple splotches. Bits of dried grass and a fine dust tumble from the soot-blackened pages as she turns them, revealing neatly penned paragraphs of cursive—what must be undated diary entries. The paper itself is the colour of roasted almonds, but has a sturdiness to it, born of a time when trees were an inexhaustible resource, limitless in number. A time when a person soaked up a spill with a whole roll of paper towels, or printed her entire thesis one-sided (as she had) on a fat stack of snow-white loose-leaf.

"I'm leaving tonight," Silas says. "But I've been cleared to entrust this with you until I return. So you don't need to make any decisions about whether to proceed with your claim now—in fact I'd rather you didn't. I want you to read it, mull it over, get used to what it feels like to have a history. Just promise me that you'll take exceptionally good care of it. This is an artifact of tremendous value. Most of all to you."

"I've got a bunch of these on my bedside table already," Jake jokes, attempting to mask her ravenous desire to read the paperbook as she presses it along with the index card against her stomach, "but I'll try to get to it."

Silas shakes his head and grins. "We're currently in negotiations to acquire another critical piece of this puzzle, one that would greatly strengthen your claim. And when we do, I'll be back." He draws close and grasps her elbows. "I looked into your debt situation, Jake, and I know things are dire. But this could fix everything. And I don't just mean the money. You never had much of a story to tell. I always sensed that it hurt you, whether you'd admit it or not. Now all that can change."

Later that evening, Jake returns to her staff cabin, pours herself a hefty bourbon, and curls into the loveseat with the paperbook spread in her lap. After five more tours shepherding Pilgrims through the Cathedral, her eyes are sludgy and unprepared for parsing the book's tricky cursive script. (She hasn't seen anyone write in this antiquated fashion for years, and never learned the technique in her Delhi elementary school.) Just two pages in, Jake's chin begins to dip, thereby unravelling the few narrative fibres that she'd managed to weave together.

It was silly to get your hopes up, she tells herself, rising to place the paperbook in her father's old cardboard box, filing it away with all her other meaningless family heirlooms. Though she understands this journal is something that ought to have great bearing on her life, unfortunately for Silas and his scheme, Jake has always mistrusted the expression "knowing your roots." As though roots by their very definition are knowable. Any dendrologist can tell you that the roots of a mature Douglas fir forest spread for miles. That they're dark and intertwining, tangled and twisted, and impossible to map. That they often fuse together, and even communicate, secretly sharing nutrients and chemical weapons among themselves. So the truth is that there exists no clear distinction between one tree and another. And their roots are anything but knowable.

Jake snaps back her drink and retrieves the paperbook from the box, flipping to the inside front cover, where she finds facing the first page a splash of crudely pencilled words, scrawled in a child's block print:

PROPORTEE OF WILLO GREENWUD

Despite her reservations about Silas's true motivations, and her general bafflement with the book's cryptic entries, Jake's heart takes a little skip at the sight of her grandmother's name, however misspelled it may be. And while drinking herself toward a welcome oblivion throughout the evening, she wonders about Willow Greenwood, about who she was and what impelled her to give her fortune away. She wonders about her father and if he also drank, and whether that's what made him "troubled." If he did, Jake already forgives him. Maybe she drinks because of his genes. Or because of his absence. Or maybe his genes created his absence, which created her drinking. Or maybe he felt just as unwelcome in the world as she does now, and drinking was the only thing that allowed him any reprieve. Or maybe her roots are all too tangled, and there's no single story to be told about any of it.

Deep in the night, just after she's dragged her Cathedral-issue comforter over her body and is preparing to pass out, she lifts the paperbook one last time and fans its grimy, hand-inked pages. How intimately a book is related to the tree and its rings, she thinks. The layers of time, preserved, for all to examine.

2008

TWENTY-SEVEN
AND FIVE-EIGHTHS

IT'S DAY. MURMURS of leafy light on the vaulted walls.

Why am I sleeping during the day? Without a blanket? he wonders as everything around him blurs and ripples. But he hasn't been sleeping. He's suffered something. An unconsciousness. For what duration he doesn't know. Also, his legs are oddly numb and feel as heavy as sandbags. And the most basic facts seem to flit just beyond his reach—even his own name he can only brush with the tips of his fingers.

Laid out on his back, he swivels his head to the side, feels the cool floor against his face. The floor is concrete, buffed to a gleaming, wet-looking finish. Three tiers of scaffolding rise high into the air beside him. *That's what I fell from*, he thinks. Though he remembers nothing about the fall, somehow he knows its height precisely. He'd measured the vaulted ceiling himself and never forgets a measurement: twenty-seven feet and five-eighths of an inch.

He lifts his ringing head, which feels like a bowling ball, and manages to prop himself up on his elbows to look around. The room is cavernous, spare, modern. A living room. Strewn with polygons of austere acrylic furniture. A fieldstone hearth. Arctic-white walls. Old-growth fir beamwork held together by vintage cast-iron fasteners. Custom floor-to-ceiling windows that frame a cliffside view of the ocean, the water like raw denim, flat as slate.

This is not my house, he thinks. It's a rich person's house. A weekend house. Used only a few weeks a year. Summers, most likely. And since he knows the exact height of the ceiling and has a tool belt strapped around his waist, he assumes he's a carpenter, here doing a renovation. And though some deep, essential part of his brain orders him to quit slacking off and get back to work, his head is still too foggy and his legs are still too heavy for him to move. He'll need to get checked out before he can work again.

He scans the end tables of the living room for a telephone he can use to call an ambulance but finds nothing. When he notices a cellphone poking out from a pouch in his tool belt he fishes it out, only to find its glass webbed with cracks, the screen beneath as black as a pupil. He presses the buttons but nothing happens, so in frustration he side-arms the aluminum carcass across the room. But the aggressive motion torques something deep inside his hips and suddenly it's as if someone is holding an acetylene torch to his tailbone. He hears himself scream.

A flock of details rushes in with the pain, like birds returning to roost in his mind's branches. His name is Liam. He's Canadian though he's working in the United States—this he can confirm by the air: warmer with a faint toxicity, like plastic burnt long ago. It's November. He's renovating a house in Darien, Connecticut. He's thirty-four years old and despite his mother's best efforts, he's still a Greenwood.

SUPPLIES

1 Ten-Pound Sack Organic Brown Rice
1 Ten-Pound Sack Organic Chickpeas
1 Ten-Pound Sack Organic Soybeans
5 Cans Krylon Spray-Paint, Chestnut Brown
1 Pair 36" Bolt Cutters
4 Twenty-Five-Pound Bags White Sugar
2 Cartons Menthol Cigarettes

THE HALLOWEEN TREE

LIAM IS TEN years old again and curled in the passenger seat of his mother's sky-blue Westfalia. Willow is driving them south from Vancouver, down the Pacific coast, and riffing on deforestation and acid rain and silent springs and thalidomide and the coming environmental Armageddon as she smokes menthols and shifts with her free hand, steering with a knobby knee. Liam doesn't go to school (he tried a few weeks of it in Ucluelet, where they lived for six months while his mother blockaded a logging operation there, and hated every second), so she's got him some old grade four workbooks from a thrift store to do in the van. But reading exhausts him, so instead he sits listening to the van's diesel chortle, whittling a stick into a lethal point and occasionally checking for pursuing police cars in the side-view mirror.

It's a Sunday, the only day that loggers are known to take off, which means it's also when Willow performs her "direct actions." Early this morning, Liam watched from the van as his mother took the bolt cutters and snipped a thick lock from a gate intended to keep trespassers out of an old-growth forest lot. While Liam's guts clenched with anxiety, she drove them into the trees and parked beside some feller bunchers, monstrous logging machines that have always reminded him of yellow dinosaurs. Then Willow gathered up two of the twenty-five-pound bags of white sugar that she keeps hidden under the van's seats and proceeded to funnel them into the gas tanks of the machines. After that, while Liam begged his mother to come back to the van before the Mounties or the loggers showed up, she spent an hour in the surrounding forest, carefully spray-painting over the markings that the loggers had put on the high-value trees they intended to take down. Liam often has nightmares about the feller bunchers, machines that are somehow powerful enough to devour whole forests. That his mother is insane enough to attack them seems like a heresy that will eventually invite a great disaster down upon them both.

But that's all behind them now. The Mounties didn't come. And since tomorrow is his tenth birthday, Willow is driving him to a beach in Oregon like he's asked so he can try surfing. He'd have preferred California, but Willow has a protest to attend in Vancouver in three days. "So this is the best we can do," she said, tousling his hair.

As a boy, Liam is asthmatic, watchful, and always clutching at his hippie mother's batik-printed skirts whenever strangers are around. Originally, she named him Liam New Dawn, but he'll change it to Liam Greenwood, her legal surname, the day he turns eighteen.

"And here I was trying to give you a fresh start," she'll say woundedly when he tells her, after all the paperwork's filed. "Why degrade yourself with a name like that?"

Willow had him late in life, at forty—*unplanned* is a word he's overheard her use—and she never entirely embraced the project of motherhood. With an embarrassing (for him, anyway) jungle in her armpits and a restless fever to pack her Westfalia and go, she's a Rorschach test of a mother, a shape-shifting cloud drifting across his boyhood horizon. She changes her mind with a swiftness and conviction that terrifies him. A trusted brand commits some ecological sin and she'll swear off their products forever. A lover contradicts her in some pot-warped argument about the military industrial complex and they'll never so much as gas up the Westfalia in his city again. For as long as he can remember, Liam has known that his survival depends upon preventing a similar reversal of feeling about him. So he strains to please her: he repeats her phrases, wears the tattered clothes she finds in thrift shops, and marvels at the same sunsets and the same trees.

But mostly the shape Willow assumes is that of a wandering monk, fuelled by weed and chickpeas and the soymilk that she presses herself. Her true religion is Nature, trees especially. Her belief in green beings is as pure and fervent as any self-immolating Buddhist's. This is why Liam fears her environmentalism above all else—he knows that it's the thing that could someday steal her from him completely.

After hours of driving, they park at a forested pull-off near a river in central Washington to camp for the night. Willow simmers brown rice on the van's propane burner while reading *Swallows and Amazons* aloud, a book she loved as a girl despite it being "terminally bourgeois." Later, Liam lies sleepless in the Westfalia's rooftop tent, nauseous with worry that the State Patrol will knock on the van's fogged-up windows with their chrome flashlights, find the weed and the bags of sugar, then drag his mother to jail and whisk him off to some American orphanage where the kids all carry switchblades. Willow's worries, however, assume a wider focus. She makes flashlit notes about her newest ploys to halt the ongoing genocide of the great heritage forests of the Pacific Northwest while drinking her fancy tea.

Outwardly, his mother is ecologically devout, but Liam knows her secrets. Her weed and mushrooms are kept mostly in the open, but she has caches of opulence squirreled around the Westfalia. A bottle of Chanel No. 5 tucked into a slit in the mouldering seats. Bags of fine English teas buried deep in the glove box. Little do her fellow eco-warriors know that his mother was raised rich: an estate; a live-in gardener; equestrian classes; private schools; tartan uniforms—the works. Her father, Harris Greenwood, founded Greenwood Timber in 1919 and amassed a fortune in the manner fortunes were amassed in Canada in those days: by chewing up the natural world and selling the spoils at great profit. Though he died when Liam was a baby, Harris is a person Liam has admired from an early age, if only secretly. At least he built real, tangible things, rather than Willow's goal of "building awareness"—a phrase that Liam has never understood.

Despite their strained relationship, Harris left his entire fortune to Willow when he died: a mountain of cash, a mansion in Vancouver's exclusive Shaughnessy neighbourhood, and a private island—all of which his mother then proceeded to donate to an environmental group concerned with global forest protection. Willow often re-enacts this selfless gesture for Liam in the Westfalia over tin bowls of her lightly sea-salted chickpeas: "Will that be all?"—*gulp*—"Ms. Greenwood?" she'll say, impersonating the shell-shocked bank manager who drew up the drafts. "Yes, that's it," she'll reply, playing the character of herself with a bland smile, before she bursts into manic laughter.

When Liam wakes the next morning, he finds a birthday present wrapped in newsprint on the table in the van. For a moment he pretends it's from his father, who went by the name Sage and who hailed from Oceanside, California, and was some kind of surfer poet who trolled the Oregon coast, converting women like Willow to a religion he'd invented while listening to the album *Pet Sounds*. But Sage was left in the Westfalia's dust long before Liam was born, and Liam has never met him.

Liam takes the gift in his hands. Because money is always tight, he knows not to get his hopes up. To finance their lean existence, they harvest wild chanterelles once yearly. In late summer, they hike to Willow's secret spots—her "faerie farms"—hidden in the deepest old-growth woods. Liam is always amazed whenever they come upon hundreds of chanterelles, entire orchestras of miniature yellow trumpets poking up amongst the roots of the trees. How Willow remembers their location each year, with neither map nor compass, baffles him. They fill five baskets each, then thread the mushrooms on fishing lines hung around the van to cure. Afterwards, she fries some in butter and serves them on a bed of brown rice, but Liam always picks his off. Chanterelles taste too much like the forest, too much like how his mother smells—of faint peach and nuts and dirt. When the curing is done, Willow drives to high-end French restaurants in Seattle, Vancouver, and San Francisco and sells them by the bagful at cut rates to the elated chefs who meet them in the alley during their cigarette breaks. But after they buy food and replenish Willow's sabotage supplies, there's never much left over.

Liam tears the paper back to reveal a dream catcher, identical to the one he got last year, woven by Willow with colourful threads crisscrossing a few thin boughs of cypress. Noting his limited enthusiasm, Willow launches into a familiar tirade on modern toys and comic books, "Which were invented by media corporations and plastic death merchants." Liam mumbles his thanks and sets about packing the van. Before they set off, he claims he has to pee and sneaks off into the trees, where he viciously stomps the dream catcher to bits upon the mossy forest floor.

It's his first betrayal. His first rebellion. One she doesn't even notice. Though she talks constantly of Liam's bright future and worries aloud about whether there'll be any unspoiled woodland left for him to enjoy as an adult, he counts weeks between the times that she actually focuses her green eyes on his face or listens to what he says. For this reason, every Halloween (a holiday she actually observes, dragging him to the same party at the Earth Now! Collective house in Vancouver each year) Liam has dressed up as a tree—a Douglas fir, in fact, her favourite species, wrapping himself in grey cardboard bark and branches, adorning himself with pinecones carved from her wine corks and with construction-paper needles that he's painstakingly cut out himself. He wears the costume in the hopes that his mother will finally see him. It's never worked.

And so that year, Liam decides to start dressing up as a lumberjack.

LIVE AUTHENTICALLY

TO HIS RELIEF, a noise rescues him from the quicksand of memory: his air compressor, set near the scaffolding ten feet to his right, roaring to replenish its tank pressure. It's his machine—this Liam confirms by its unique patina of dents and scuffs. *But why is it here?* he thinks. *Did I bring it?* Yes. He and his helper Alvarez carried it from his van to the house this morning. Then where's Alvarez? Hadn't they raised the scaffolding together? Put rubber booties on its feet to protect the floor's finish?

When the compressor shuts off, Liam's eyes follow the scaffolding up to the patches of exposed insulation high above him. He and Alvarez had been tearing out the teak tongue-and-groove ceiling—just imagine the jokes carpenters make—and replacing it with Liam's signature reclaimed boards, despite the fact that the teak was flawless and only ten years old. Once every spring Liam places a small ad in *The New Yorker*—one of the strange, ill-designed ones near the back:

> GREENWOOD CONTRACTING:
> RECLAIMED WOOD. CUSTOM WORK.
> LIVE AUTHENTICALLY.

Eight meaningless words that are enough to keep his phone buzzing as constantly as a pair of barber's clippers. Who knew that the Olympian-rich crave the A-word as desperately as they do, that they want their houses to look like spaceships on the outside and Depression-era factories inside. Regardless of their reasons, Liam happily obliges them, and reclaimed wood has become his bread and butter. He's strapped on his tool belt for 406 consecutive days, no days off, and sleeps on a thin foam mattress in his contractor's van (his home since losing his house in Fort Greene in the lead-up to the housing market crash), which he parks near his current job site. Perhaps it was his rootless upbringing in Willow's Westfalia, but Liam is most content in this itinerant state, living one step ahead of his past. And carpentry—with its endless measuring and hammering and cutting and sanding and moving on to the next job—leaves little opportunity for his memories to intrude upon him, which is just how he prefers it.

The reclaimed boards piled against the nearby wall are sun-silvered and scribbled with the marks and checks of age, and Liam remembers pulling them from the old barn at his great-aunt Temple's farm outside of Estevan, Saskatchewan, where he spent a summer as a boy. Temple and her partner had no offspring, so Liam inherited their worthless land after they died. Because he couldn't sell it and he isn't the farming type, Liam has been pulling its structures apart over the years, board by board: the house and its miles and miles of fences, which were all rebuilt in 1935 after a cyclone razed the property during the Dust Bowl. Liam will invoice the owner of this house— a distant descendant of the Rockefellers—twenty grand for such premium material, and the guy won't bat an eye.

Except Liam won't be billing anyone if he doesn't get himself fixed up and finish the job. Mercifully, the burning in his tailbone is gone and much of the fog from hitting his head has cleared, though his legs are still unresponsive. But he takes the prickling sensation in his hamstrings as a sign that the damage isn't permanent. Probably a cracked tailbone or at worst a broken pelvis that's pinching nerves— two injuries he's witnessed other guys suffer on the job.

He rests on his back for a moment and tries to assemble a plan. The radiant heat that would normally warm the concrete floor has been set to a minimal temperature for the off-season. And this house sits upon a fifty-acre headland of oceanfront property, perched on a cliff that's three miles from the main road, so the mail is likely delivered to a rural box somewhere. Which all means that nobody will be turning up here to save him anytime soon—probably not until spring. Liam lifts his head again to examine the room, and the large heap of off-cuts jumbled next to his DeWalt mitre saw tugs at his memory: Alvarez wasn't looking well today, his eyes livid with wormy pink veins. All his cuts were off by a good eighth of an inch, sometimes more. He was wasting good wood—wood Liam drove to fucking Saskatchewan to get—so he sent Alvarez to the van for the rest of the day.

Whenever Liam requires a carpenter's helper, he places an ad in a free weekly and contacts the guy who sends him the most crudely written email. He hires drunks, ex-cons, addicts, headcases. Most last only a few weeks, until they get money in their pockets and disappear. This practice of charitable hiring is at least partially attributable to some hippie do-gooderness inherited from Willow—or from Temple, who once ran a kind of soup kitchen out of her farm. Sometimes he wonders if it's also his attempt to atone for his own wasted years. Whether he's benefitting these hard-luck cases or simply offering them more money to destroy themselves with, Liam isn't sure. But he prefers the company of those for whom life hasn't been a cakewalk. They say more interesting things—and seldom comment upon the scorched mess he's made of his own life.

Alvarez has been with him for six months and he's a good worker. He's a gambler, though. Does it on his phone, which is even worse than in a casino because it's always with you, beckoning from your pocket. Some paydays Alvarez has already lost his week's wages in the van before Liam drops him off at his mother's house in Queens. Which means he's in the van right now, waiting for Liam to finish work and drive him home. So all Liam needs to do is crawl out of the house and down the driveway to his van. Liam even has another phone in his glove box, a prepaid one that he uses whenever he goes to Canada. That settles it. While he fears that crawling could cause the burning to return and knows moving around could make his injury worse, he has no other choice.

Liam sucks in a ragged breath, flips himself onto his stomach, and slithers a few feet on his elbows, the claw of his titanium hammer— a gift from Meena during the early days of their relationship— screeching against the concrete, his steel-toe boots like barbells laced to his feet. Already breathing hard, he shucks the tool belt from his waist to ease his progress, and a few strings of brad nails spill out across the floor. He vows to pick them up once his legs come back, because no matter how sloppy his life has become, he's always left his work sites immaculate.

Since the house is embedded in a low cliff that overlooks the Atlantic, the living room is sunken, so he'll need to ascend two flights of shallow concrete stairs, a dozen steps in total. His arms are already weak from nailing reclaimed boards to the ceiling all day, so he barely climbs six steps before he's sweating and gasping for water. The pipes will surely be dry, and if he ventures down into the basement to flip the water main he may never climb back out. Of course Liam has a few flats of Red Bull in his van. He drinks nine or ten daily because he despises black coffee and his stomach can't digest lactose—Willow was the same, with her homemade soymilk and goat cheese crumbled over kale salads. The fact that Liam escaped five years of wanton drug use only to be left with an unquenchable thirst for these ridiculous caffeine-loaded sugar bombs seems half blessing and half curse, depending on the day. His old Narcotics Anonymous group was rife with such secondary addictions: most of them were pack-a-day smokers, or at the very least they drank coffee like air-traffic controllers. There was a tacit agreement among them that these lesser vices didn't require kicking, because people like them would never really exist free of need.

Liam manages to climb the last six stairs on his elbows, and after much struggle he flops onto the front landing of the house. He rises onto one hand, arching his back, and strains for the handle before dragging the heavy plate glass door open. The late fall air is frosty, almost viscous, and it's later than he thought, the frail sun sinking below a tidy congregation of rare elm and magnolia that some top-dollar arborist planted around the house.

He drags himself out along the brick path, his bare elbows digging into the freezing pavement. When he reaches the rust-coloured octagonal paving stones of the driveway proper, he can see his white contractor's van parked about a hundred yards in the distance, near the maintenance shed. Liam calls out for Alvarez but none of the van's doors come open. Maybe he's sleeping. Or, more likely, gambling on his phone with his headphones in.

The sight of how much farther he needs to crawl with only his arms to propel him forces Liam to lay his face on the cold ground for a moment in despair. In his spent shoulders and buzzing spine, the years of toil, labour, and hard living are finally settling upon him. He's never been so exhausted in his life. While he rests, he senses a curious wetness in his pants—a ticklish trickle. He spins onto his back, reaches down, and slips a juddering hand under his tool belt, behind the fly of his Carhartts, and his fingers emerge slick, pungent with the sour reek of urine. He hasn't wet himself since his days of chasing a dozen oxycodone with an eight-pack of Lucky Lager.

He needs to keep moving or else he'll start remembering again, so he flips back over and continues his excruciating commando crawl through the half-frozen leaf mulch. He's always treated his past like an enormous trailer that he's towing behind him, one that will overrun and crush him if he ever dares come to a stop. But even though he's crawling as fast as he can, he can feel his mind begin to sputter and slow, and soon he has no other choice but to get run over.

JOURNEYMAN

WHEN LIAM TURNS sixteen, Willow treats him to a rare dinner at an actual restaurant. "It's time we get serious about your career plans," she says, while he regards her skeptically over the steak he's ordered just to disgust her. "You don't want me dragging you around forever, do you?"

His mother has always hoped he'll be an artist, a nature poet, or a hippie mystic like the wide-eyed men she entangles herself with. Or better yet, a fire-breathing academic: a Marxist sociology professor or a bearded tree biologist, or, best of all, a mad-dog environmental lawyer, dedicating his life to pro bono skirmishes with lumber conglomerates and Big Oil. But Liam has never cared about politics. Or art. Or immaterial thought. From an early age he admired working people, especially those who live by their own labours like his grandfather Harris and his great-aunt Temple. Liam has considered logging, just to piss Willow off, except he knows the feller bunchers do all the work now, and a whole forest can be levelled without anyone so much as touching a piece of bark with their hands. So when Liam informs her of his plan to apprentice with a journeyman carpenter and take classes to earn his ticket at the local community college, Willow's face falls and she asks for the cheque.

"I just don't know why you feel the need to assume this working-class identity," his mother says two months later, while he's studying provincial building codes by flashlight in the van after they bed down.

"I need to *work*, Willow," he says exhaustedly. "What part of that is an assumed identity?"

"There are many kinds of work, you know," she says. "What I do is work. Important work. Maybe the most important work there is."

"If you count ruining other people's livelihoods as work," he replies, flicking off the flashlight, "then sure, you work plenty."

At eighteen Liam earns his ticket, leases a half-ton truck, and starts his own skylight installation business, which immediately booms. Within a year he's putting in skylights all over British Columbia. He expands, hires guys twice his age, buys trucks and fills them with lockboxes of the finest German power tools. At twenty-two he buys a five-bedroom house in a Vancouver suburb called Langley and riddles its roof with skylights, while out back he installs a barbecue as big as a grown man's coffin.

Luckily for Liam, very few contractors do skylights because the insurance is a killer. The truth is that all skylights leak, eventually. Liam does five hundred rushed jobs in a two-year period, leaving a trail of leaky—or soon to leak—installations littered across the province. But if nothing else, Willow taught him how to excise himself from complication, how to drive off and never look back. When Liam tears his rotator cuff and won't let himself take any days off to let it heal properly, one of the injury-addled old-timers on his crew offers him oxycodone.

Perhaps it's another dark inheritance from Willow, but there has always been this screaming greed in his neuroreceptors, this proclivity for chemical rapture, and, worse, repetition of that rapture. First came the sugary corporate sodas that his mother outlawed, which he'd steal from service stations when they stopped to fill up and sip secretly while she drove; then her weed, which she offered freely once he turned the ripe old age of thirteen; then, for a short time, cigarettes and booze, both of which she denounced, though she used them copiously herself. Nothing, however, could compare to the glorious melt of an oxy in his stomach, its warmth spreading through him, leaving him soothed and forgiven and secure in a way he'd never been before. It's like falling in love. Or how love is advertised to feel but never actually delivers. Liam is soon taking a few pills daily and working eighty-hour weeks without any discomfort at all.

But when the insurance adjustors finally catch up with him and repossess his house, his fleet of trucks, and every tool he owns, Liam tips into a spiralling, unbounded addiction that burns through his remaining savings like a wildfire. Dopesick and broke following a short jail stint for possession, Liam moves back into the Westfalia. By this point, Willow is in her early sixties and has settled into more benign forms of activism: printing pamphlets at Kinko's and leading email-writing campaigns. She drives Liam to one of her faerie farms, and for the first week of his detox he's completely mute with shame. Fortunately, she leaves unmentioned her previous warnings about the perils of free-market capitalism as well as his unwise choice of career.

To keep his mind occupied, she plays him some old records she has of a man reading poetry. "These were your grandfather's," she says with an uncharacteristic solemnity. "I've had them for years, but I never put them on for you as a kid because I thought you wouldn't like them." Though the poetry is mostly unintelligible to him, the lilting rhythms of the man's voice soothe his shredded nerves, and in time Liam's minute-to-minute existence grows nearly tolerable. After a month of Willow's nettle tea, her chickpeas, her soymilk, her sandalwood incense, her bland hippie wisdom, her poetry records, and, most restorative of all, many evenings spent among the trees, Liam is himself again. When he's strong enough, they go chanterelle picking and earn enough money to buy him a pair of steel-toes and a good tape measure, and he signs on to a condo construction crew in Vancouver, building foundations. It's belittling work, the lowest circle of hell as far as carpentry goes: wallowing in muck five days a week, hammering together forms that will only be ripped down after the concrete has set, his fingers and toes permanently pruned like those of a kid who never leaves the bath. All to erect glass towers of a thousand designer closets, not one of which Liam could ever afford.

Still, his mother's furtive taste for luxury has left a lasting impression, and the guys on his crew jeer when Liam returns with his daily ten-dollar brie baguette purchased from a chic downtown bistro. That is until the owner of the bistro takes a liking to Liam and hires him to fabricate a reclaimed wood counter. In a panic, Liam hurries to the public library after work, where he pores over every book on fine woodworking in their collection. The best of them is written by George Nakashima, a master woodworker raised in the forests around Spokane, where Liam himself spent some time as a boy. Liam decides to simply rip off Nakashima's designs and throws himself into the job, beginning by illegally dragging an old-growth piece of windfall fir out of Stanley Park with Willow's van. It's from Nakashima that Liam first gets the idea to "book match" his boards, by taking two successive slabs sawn from the same log, and then attaching the nearly identical pieces side by side, in mirror image, creating the almost uncanny effect of the spread pages of an open book.

After he's joined the live-edged planks with butterfly keys and applied numerous applications of tung oil and two coats of polyurethane, the wood's unique figuring, burl, and honey-tinged grain pulse with life, like a solar system that has been frozen for centuries within the wood and is only now being revealed. It's a piece of delicate yet bomb-proof beauty, and the bistro owner claims that the installation doubles his business. Certain design bigwigs view Liam's work on their computers, and a month later he's got his own apartment and has quit foundations to do fine woodworking full time. He remodels restaurants, craft breweries, and cafés, outfitting them with reclaimed lumber: old, forgotten wood previously left to languish. He dumps his earnings into an account he can't access without his mother's co-sign, and quells any chance of relapse through incessant toil.

Soon after, he's flown to New York by a group of investors to redo a popular café in Park Slope. While he works, he overhears the café's young patrons lament their student debts, their failing indie bands, their useless Ph.D.s, their unpaid internships, and at twenty-eight Liam already feels ancient, like some mythical Canadian forest creature that has errantly wandered into a metropolis. The café's employees—with their old-time canvas aprons, linen work shirts, perfectly distressed boots, and beards aromatic with organic detangler—look as though they've stepped from the pages of a Steinbeck novel. Still, Liam doesn't judge them. Times *are* hard. Not hard like they were in the 1930s, when his aunt Temple ran a soup kitchen on her farm, but hard differently, even in a wealthy place like New York. And during hard times, people crave the consolations of other hard times, whether those of the past or of an imagined ruined future, to ease the pains of the present they're stuck with. He's no expert, but in his opinion these young people have been left to pick over the table scraps of Willow's generation, and if Liam didn't have a trade and hadn't been born a Greenwood with tree sap running in his veins, he'd be just as lost as them.

When the café is finished, he's contracted to build several book-matched conference tables for various corporate offices in Manhattan, including Holtcorp, Shell, and Weyerhaeuser—companies that Willow warred against all her life. It isn't until he's been living in New York for two years, and he's renovating yet another Brooklyn craft brewery with some expensive old-growth redwood, that he meets Meena Bhattacharya, who's helping the owner, her long-time friend, make decor decisions. Though they've been introduced, Liam buries his nose in his work whenever he sees Meena, who is lovely in a hundred ways previously unknown to him.

"Shouldn't you be wearing gloves?" she asks Liam one day while he's bent over his table saw, preparing to make a finicky cut. "What if you touch the blade? You won't make any more beautiful things without fingers."

"This thing eats gloves for breakfast," Liam says, pointing at the saw blade. "And gloves can make you careless, so it's better to work without them. Also, I like to be close to the wood."

The next day she asks him to meet her for coffee after work, and they sit in a busy café cramped together at a counter that Liam once built, though he's too shy to mention it. It's the first time he's properly sat down—other than to shit, drive, or fly—in months. "I'm happy to see that your hands are still intact," she says, prompting him to examine hers, which are similarly callused and corded with sinew. He learns that she's the first-chair viola of the Los Angeles Symphony, and has been booked for a six-month stint of performances at Lincoln Center. She's clever, funny, and outspoken, though all her political views seem perfectly reasonable, or at the very least grounded in fact. She grew up as an only child of aspirational parents in a suburb of Delhi. "I chose the electric guitar, and my parents chose the cello," she says dryly. "My mother actually called the viola a compromise."

The next weekend, Liam takes Meena to the Museum of Natural History to see the cross-section of a giant sequoia that was cut from a forest where he and Willow often camped. During the subway ride he tells Meena about his mother for the first time, making her activism sound more idealistic than fanatical, and her distracted parenting more eccentric than hurtful. But at the museum, he's disappointed to discover that the sequoia has been varnished over, so they can't smell the rich tannins in the naturally rot-resistant redwood that he'd been describing. Meena is impressed nonetheless, and afterwards invites him back to her apartment for the first time.

Each weekend over the following months, Liam and Meena take drives upstate to fetch reclaimed materials for his jobs. They pay farmers for weather-beaten planks or beams, then load them into the van while the farmers regard them like they're escaped mental patients. At first, she's game enough to take up a nail-puller and help bring down some old fences and stables, but after she gouges her thumb sufficiently to require a tetanus shot and nearly has to cancel a performance, she's content to perch on a fence rail and watch him work.

"I'm not a big fan of the term 'reclaimed wood,'" Meena says one Saturday as they're headed back to the city.

"Here we go," Liam says, reaching over to squeeze her knee to show he's only kidding.

"It begs the question: reclaimed from what? Or, more specifically, from who? The answer is from people who are using it wrong. Poor people. People with no taste. People who don't deserve it."

People like me, Liam thinks but doesn't say.

"Why is it that the rich always want to buy back the few things they've allowed the poor to have? Is it to remind them that nothing is theirs, not truly?"

Yet despite Meena's strong opinions, she couldn't be more different than Willow: she's disciplined, rooted, slow-moving, thoughtful, and chemically conservative—a single glass of white wine the most reckless inebriation she'll ever submit to. Liam loves how, immediately upon entering his van, she always plugs her phone into his stereo and floods his ears with music. Despite her classical training, she can't bear to hear orchestral pieces on her personal time. Her great love is sixties soul, which she belts out while shimmying in the seat beside him. "Be My Baby," "Baby Love," "Baby I Need Your Loving." For someone who claims to be delaying motherhood until her career is established, he teases, it's an unsettling amount of babies.

It's during these drives that he first gets the idea to build his own studio, somewhere rural and away from the city, where he'll make custom furniture of his own design, just like George Nakashima had in New Hope, Pennsylvania.

"Your counters and tables are beautiful, Liam," Meena says, touching the back of his neck after he shares the idea with her. "But I can't imagine the miracles you'll work in a proper shop of your own, without some snotty corporate decorator peering over your shoulder."

Liam adores the uncondescending interest that Meena shows in his carpentry, as though both their vocations are of equal cultural value. To his surprise, she views her own musicianship as a kind of hard labour, submitting herself to a grim practice regimen that trumps all else, including spending time with him. And as a result, Liam already hungers to spend every waking minute that he isn't working in her company.

After six months, Meena's New York engagement ends and she gives up her apartment in preparation for her return to Los Angeles. Because Liam still lives in a tiny room above an auto shop in Crown Heights, he can't possibly host her while she's in town, so he withdraws his entire savings to put down on a semi-detached house on the "up-and-coming" edge of Fort Greene. Thankfully, Meena appreciates the boldness of the gesture, and promises to divide her time between L.A. and New York.

Yet her obligations prevent her from visiting as often as planned, and half-time quickly turns into quarter-time. While Liam knows he's possibly being insecure, he grows convinced that because she's so accustomed to fine hotels and opulent concert halls, his house displeases her. So in his off time he strips the walls to their studs and performs a complete renovation, all in meticulously finished old-growth Douglas fir and redwood. The raw materials alone nearly double his debt, and though Meena marvels outwardly at the job, she still doesn't visit as often as he'd hoped. And when she books a two-month engagement in Prague, Liam trips into a black and airless cavern, and dreams of Oxycontin for the first time in years.

A QUESTION

"DO YOU LOVE the forests more than you love me?"

His mother shifts in the lawn chair she's pulled from the Westfalia to sit by the ocean, running a hand through her salt-tangled hair. They've finally made it to the Oregon coast for his tenth birthday, except the water here is black and freezing and the waves are squat and impossible to surf. Liam has spent the afternoon in a funk, crushing between two rocks the purple mussel shells that he finds on the beach. The cold hasn't stopped Willow from skinny-dipping all morning, bobbing out there with an armada of bull kelp. He wishes she'd wear the bathing suit he prudishly bought for her with his own money at JC Penney, but she hasn't even removed the tags.

His question hangs in the air unanswered as she slowly quarters an orange with her Opinel and then bites into a wedge. He's asked this question before and knows it annoys her, but he repeats it anyway. He needs her answer more than he needs anything else, and perhaps because it's his birthday, this time he gets one.

"You're a good person, Liam. One of the best. But you're just one person," she says, sucking pulp from her teeth and spitting it into the sand. "Nature is greater than us all."

THE VIOLA

DURING MEENA'S TWO-MONTH trip to Prague, Liam manages to beat back his cravings for Oxycodone by throwing himself into a series of complex contracts: huge gut-jobs for which he refuses to hire a helper. And when she finally returns, things are good for a while. That is, until she first brings the Stradivarius home.

"Officially," Meena tells him excitedly that night over Korean takeout, "it's known as 'the Russian Viola' because it was once the property of the Soviet state. But after glasnost, it fell into the hands of a woman named Tanya Petrov, an oil oligarch's wife who's since fled St. Petersburg and now fancies herself a patron of the arts. She heard me play in Prague, and has loaned it to me for the weekend while she's in New York."

"Wow, that's great," Liam says, stretching for enthusiasm. In truth, he hates all this talk of Europe and rich patrons loaning Meena irreplaceable items, favours for which she'll be indebted forever.

After dinner, Meena lifts the viola from its military-grade Kevlar case and plays it for Liam as he does the dishes in his wood-shrouded kitchen that still smells faintly of varnish. His eyes well up at the instrument's lush yet precise sound, though after she's finished the piece, he claims to prefer the sturdy resonance of her regular viola.

Later, while Meena showers, Liam takes up the Stradivarius in his rough, splinter-ridden hands. Though his first instinct is to criticize it, he can't resist admiring its magnificent workmanship. Some species of spruce on top, what looks like willow for the internal blocking and lining, then rigid old-growth maple for the back, ribs, and neck. Everywhere the grain, joinery, and finish are impeccable.

Covertly, he snaps some reference photographs with his phone while memorizing the object's every texture and nuance. When Meena emerges towelling her hair, he expresses his unease at having such a priceless object in their home. "This thing's worth more than everything we've ever owned or will own in our entire lives," he says.

"Oh, it's insured," she says nonchalantly.

Still, he has trouble sleeping, especially given the wretched souls that patrol his *up-and-coming* neighbourhood—people sunk to a hopeless impoverishment he seldom witnessed in Canada. Much to his relief, Meena returns the viola before flying back to L.A. that Monday for a concert. Yet the next weekend she appears with the case in tow, and after that comes a semi-permanent loan. As Liam feared, with Meena now associated with the Russian viola's mystique, there's a flood of new bookings, including solos and lucrative guest gigs overseas with prestigious quartets. When Tanya Petrov invites Meena to perform at a party she's hosting at the Waldorf Astoria, Liam claims he doesn't have a suit and spends the evening at home, running some oak cabinet fronts that have warped through his planer.

After what feels like just a few weeks at home, Meena leaves again for a one-month European tour. To keep himself from asking the neighbourhood crackheads to score him some oxys, Liam reads up on the viola's construction. He hurls himself into the research—he hasn't read this much since cramming for his carpentry ticket—and unearths obscure theories about how Stradivari achieved his iconic resonance. It's believed that he first treated the wood with mineral solutions—sodium, potassium silicate, borax—and then coated it with a lacquer of *vernice bianca*, egg white, honey, and acacia sap. Whenever Liam's questions linger unanswered, he phones experts on the subject, fusty professors at universities in Vienna or Florence, who sigh at his intricately technical queries but answer them nonetheless. Liam learns that while some assert that Stradivari used only reclaimed wood salvaged from ancient cathedrals, perhaps even from crosses themselves, tree-ring dating has proven these theories false. "So they could be made from modern wood, you're saying?" Liam asks, and the professor replies: "Oh yes, of course."

Liam orders the clearest slabs of the required wood from online dealers and builds a steaming rig in his basement. Like Stradivari, he constructs his instrument by way of an inner form, rather than the copyists like Vuillaume, who used outer forms to approximate the shape. Even after Meena returns, Liam remains immersed in the project, forbidding her to go down to the basement, where he plays his music loud to cover the whir of his band saw as he cuts the instrument's curves. For finer scrollwork he breaks out the hand tools—carving gouges, knives, scrapers, and tiny finger planes that he inherited from his great-uncle, who'd made chess pieces in his later years. Liam knows that if the viola is out even a tenth of a millimetre, the sound will be off, and though Meena may claim to love it, she'll secretly sense its imperfections—an outcome too crushing to contemplate.

In all his years of woodworking, Liam has never before made something so alive, with the shape of a human form and the timbre of a human voice. And after he finishes sanding the joins and is applying the last coat of precisely concocted varnish with a sable fur brush, he's struck by the realization that perhaps his mother had been right: maybe trees *do* have souls. Which makes wood a kind of flesh. And perhaps instruments of wooden construction sound so pleasing to our ears for this reason: the choral shimmer of a guitar; the heartbeat thump of drums; the mournful wail of violins—we love them because they sound like us.

At the end of nearly three months of toil and frustration, the viola is ready. And when Meena is in New York over her thirty-second-birthday weekend, they have dinner at an expensive restaurant Liam once renovated in Red Hook. After they've returned home and made love for what will be the final time, he goes down to the basement then returns to the bedroom with the viola.

"What's this?" she says, setting her wine down on the nightstand.

Proudly, he lays the instrument in her hands. "It's a gift."

"It's exquisite," she says. She sits studying the instrument with tentative fascination, feeling its smooth neck, testing the action of the strings with the thick pads of her fingers. "Where'd you get it?"

"I made it," he says, trying but failing to swallow the sour paste that has inexplicably begun to seep into his mouth. "For you."

Suddenly she lays the viola down on the quilt, as if it's grown hot and painful to hold. "Oh, Liam," she says, covering her mouth with her hand, her unfocused eyes casting around the bedroom. Then she rises to stand beside the bed. "I can't accept this," she says, shaking her head. "It's too much."

"You need to play it first," he says, feeling a kind of cold desperation grip him—something he hasn't felt since those days detoxing in Willow's van. "I did hours of research. It's the exact replica of a Strad."

Without another word Meena darts into the ensuite, latching the pocket door behind her. He goes and stands with his forehead against it, listening to her sob quietly inside.

"I don't understand," he says, forcing a laugh. "You just need to play it. It sounds just as good as the real one, I swear. Better even. I did tests."

"I'm sure it sounds wonderful, Liam," she says through the door, and for a moment he recalls hanging it, performing the many fine adjustments that ensured the door slid freely without scraping against the frame—which means he could take it down in a hurry if it comes to that.

"I just can't believe that this is what you've been doing down there all this time," Meena goes on. "I thought you'd finally made that studio you always wanted—like George Nakashima—and you were making furniture. I thought you were doing something *you* cared about, Liam—for yourself. Not just for other people."

"Why would I want to build anything for myself?" he says, his diaphragm tightening like a reef knot. "I already have everything I need."

"I'm so sorry, Liam," she says, before expelling a sad sigh. "I'm so sorry that you don't understand what I mean."

"But I *did* build the viola for myself," he says, his eyes burning with tears, and even to his ears his tone is embarrassing in its childishness. "I built it so you won't have to do whatever Tanya Petrov says anymore. And you won't need to travel so much. You can play shows in New York and be around more."

"I travel and perform because I want to," she says with audible exhaustion. "Not because someone tells me to. And definitely not because I want to escape you."

"Well that's not how it fucking *feels*," he barks as he punches the thin door, punctuating his last word with the blow, leaving a three-knuckle indentation in the wooden panel.

Looking back, Meena's reaction to the viola is exactly what the deepest, least rooted part of him had expected all along. Over the ensuing years, her refusal to accept it will come to embody all the mysteries he'd never grasp about her, all the things she wanted from him that he could never hope to offer. And while building the viola is surely the most satisfying thing he's ever done, it also taught him that Meena would never be with him, not completely. And just like Willow, she'd always be ready to abandon him for something she loved more.

Liam backs away from the door, retrieves the viola, and carries it outside. In his driveway, he gets an orange extension cord and ties the instrument by its perfect maple neck to his van's trailer hitch, leaving enough slack that the body of the viola rests on the ground. Then he puts his van in gear and drives around Brooklyn all night with his windows down, until he can no longer hear the sound of woody scraping behind him.

The next morning, Meena wakes early and packs up the belongings she keeps at his place and calls a cab to the airport. That day, Liam works for fourteen hours straight. He does the same the following day. And the day after that. Three months later, his house sheds half its value in the housing crash and he defaults on his mortgage payments. After the foreclosure, he moves into his contractor's van full time, parking at a state campground at Montauk, where he sleeps as wintry ocean gales lash the van's thin steel walls.

Luckily, the bank allows him to keep his tools and his van, so instead of getting high, Liam takes out his first ad in *The New Yorker* and accepts as many carpentry contracts as can possibly be crammed into a calendar. After that, alongside guys like Alvarez, he renovates vacation homes seven days a week, fifty-two weeks a year.

Those who claim that rage is counter-productive need only consider all the wondrous things that Liam Greenwood has built in his thirty-four years of life to understand that the opposite can also be true: that rage is perhaps the most productive fuel there is.

GAPS

HE DOESN'T REMEMBER how he made it to his van. But it's dark now, and the night-triggered driveway lights have popped on. He can see his own body's drag marks snaking through the frosty sludge of decaying leaf mulch all the way back to the house, which is now just a series of distant glass cubes, glowing expensively in the distance.

He pounds loudly on the van's side panel to get Alvarez's attention, but there's no response. Jaw clenched, shoulders shaking and nearing collapse, Liam hauls himself up into the driver's seat, drawing up his legs manually before cramming them beneath the wheel. Despite the clawing cold, it feels good to be upright, to have the seatback against him.

"Alvarez, you in here?" Liam says, scanning the cargo area of his van by swivelling the rear-view mirror around in a circle. "Alvarez?" Nothing.

Liam rests a moment, watching the white bouquet of his breath assemble before him then float up to cling to the windshield. When some sensation returns to his hands, he rifles through the glove box but can't find his extra phone. Alvarez must have been so pissed after Liam kicked him off the site that he called his cousin for a ride, then offered him the phone for gas money. But instead of anger, all Liam feels for Alvarez is pity. He'd been a good employee, and Liam hopes he finds peace, perhaps in an online casino, or perhaps elsewhere among all the world's shattered people.

His molars chattering, Liam digs his keys out from the pocket of his Carhartts and gets the van started. There's over a half tank of gas left so he lets it run, and soon the heaters blow hot. It doesn't take long for the piss that had frozen stiff in his pants during his crawl to melt into the seat. It looks like he'll have to drive the van to the hospital himself. When he's ready, he'll press the gas pedal with the baseball bat that he keeps around in case thieves come for his tools while he sleeps. And if that's too difficult, he'll just let the van creep along in idle to the main road, which could take a while, but better late than never.

You grew up in a van, all your life you've gone to work in one, and now here you are dying in one, too, he mutters to himself and then laughs until he coughs, which conjures a quick stab in the small of his back that nearly makes him black out. Willow's gone now, he thinks after the pain recedes. Then why does he feel—even after years of her absence—that she could pull up beside his van in her Westfalia right now and he wouldn't question it for a moment?

Lung cancer took her. Bong hits, menthol cigarettes, and organic gardening—that was Willow. Had Liam visited her when she was sick? He had. He went to Vancouver and cared for her and eased her discomfort. At least he'd done that.

Though in truth, there are few mistakes that Liam has avoided in his life, few decisions he doesn't regret. And as a result, there are so many gaps in what he permits himself to think about, so many things he's left in his own personal rear-view mirror—just like Willow had taught him.

He ought to get driving, but he's not ready yet. He reaches down and kneads each of his thighs with the palms of his hands and feels nothing. His body has served him so faithfully until this day. It has wrenched and torn and built. It has lifted and pushed and pulled. It has pounded a million nails and driven a million screws. It has shed itself of a thousand pounds of toxins and cut a million pieces of wood to exact lengths. It has risen for him on a thousand dark mornings and endured enormous discomfort in order to survive. All to fail him now.

He sits warming himself and gathering his strength. It's been so long since he's sat idle like this without the numbing distraction of work, and the longer he sits, the harder it will be to keep his mind from filling in certain gaps that he's left in the story. Each passing minute inches him closer to the chasm of what he's been running from, the memories that he's so vigilantly trained himself to avoid, and just as he's about to tumble over the edge and let her into his thoughts—his daughter who he's never met—Liam closes his fist and strikes the van's rear-view mirror, breaking it off, leaving only a circular crust of adhesive on the windshield. The ferocity of his movement causes a vise to clamp down on his lower back, which cranks tighter and tighter with every short, gasping breath that he takes. He feels his eyelids flutter.

And all the gaps begin to fill.

1974

WILLOW GREENWOOD

NOTHING—SHE DECIDES, AS she shows her driver's license and signs the visitors' register at the discharge desk of the Edmonton Correctional Institution—bothers her more than this word: *GREENWOOD.*

The mere sight of it is enough to pollute her with shame. How could such a natural construction (what two more pleasant words are there, really?) have become a shorthand for rapacious greed, treasonous betrayal, and serial Earth rape? And how could this colonial stain, this symbol of all that is clutching and parasitic and short-sighted about the human species, possibly have attached itself to her?

After signing in, Willow is escorted into a waiting area, where outdated magazines blanket a Formica coffee table and a water cooler gurgles nearby like a giant blue stomach. While outside the prison aspen leaves tremble in the sun and bearberries hum sweetly on bushes, there is neither a plant nor a scrap of natural light in this windowless crypt. A prison is the opposite of a forest, she concludes. Designed to sink the spirits and deaden the senses, to disconnect a human being from all that is crucial to life. If there is a fate worse than incarceration, she can't imagine it.

She sits chain-smoking menthols, shivering in the air conditioning, her dress stuck to her like cling wrap, the sweat from her sun-baked journey pooling in the cavities made by her collarbones. And because there was quite likely dairy in the muffin she bought in desperation at that gas station, her stomach churns.

She drove her Westfalia, alone, for fourteen hours east from Vancouver to get here, over mountains that her father's now-dissolved company clear-cut decades ago to amass his grotesque fortune. After reaching Alberta's rolling grasslands, she passed cancerous oil derricks and freight trains that stretched across the entire horizon, dragging off the spoils of cut-and-run capitalism: wood and oil, factory-farmed grain, and coal. She's heard it said that Greenwood Timber has brought down more North American old-growth than "wind, woodpeckers, and God—put together," a joke repeated by every cigar-chewing captain of industry and every snivelling member of Parliament who ever came calling to her father's Shaughnessy mansion.

While Willow knows that the cops bustling past the waiting area are merely incarcerators, and not investigators, she's still careful to avoid eye contact. Two weeks ago, deep in the forested interior of British Columbia, she poured ten-kilo bags of white sugar into the gas tanks of three MacMillan Bloedel feller bunchers, permanently crippling the million-dollar machines responsible for murdering thousands of hectares of old-growth Douglas fir that had grown peacefully for millennia. It was her first direct action, her first attempt at sending a palpable message to the timber conglomerates and slowing the desecration of irreplaceable life—and it was like drinking a glass of pure adrenaline. Yet afterwards, while fleeing the cutblock, she passed a timber crew's truck on the logging road. She'd removed her license plates before entering the forest, of course, but the road was narrow and her van passed close enough for the loggers to get a good look at her face and make a few obscene gestures in her direction. After returning to Vancouver, she immediately painted her yellow Westfalia a sky blue and bought a blonde wig and some large sunglasses. Still, she was certain that a black sedan had been following her during her usual supply run over the past few days. Perhaps it was Sage, the lover she broke it off with a few months back when he got needy. More likely it was RCMP investigators waiting for her to return to the Earth Now! Collective's house in Kitsilano, where she's been living for the past five years. Since joining the collective,

Willow has written manifestos, done sit-ins, organized protests, and set blockades—all worthy forms of resistance, sure—but the group balked when she first suggested ratcheting things up to direct action. Sometimes she thinks the Earth Now! members would rather be shouting a clever slogan on the news than actually saving a living tree. But if she goes home now, she'll risk exposing the others to police scrutiny—and everybody knows cops are in the pocket of industry, and would love any opportunity to break up the collective— so she's been staying in her van ever since. Besides, Willow has never felt at ease in groups, with their quibbles and egos and petty dramas. And the best sacrifices, she believes, are always made in solitude, with not a camera in sight.

While a maximum-security federal penitentiary is the last place she wants to be right now, the deal she brokered with her father was too good to pass up. They hadn't communicated for a year when she found his cryptic message waiting in the post office box she keeps in Vancouver. And though they pre-arranged to meet in the remote corner of Stanley Park where Willow planned to hide out until the heat dissipated, when his black Mercedes pulled up alongside her van, she was certain the Mounties had tracked her down.

"You're not an easy person to find," Harris said as his driver assisted him out of the car, an infantilizing act she once saw him fire a man outright for.

"Hard to find is how I like it," Willow said, watching Harris orient himself to her voice and start toward her. Her father was born at the turn of the century, though he claims his exact birthday is a mystery to him (his way of avoiding parties, she's long suspected), and despite his blindness, he's always stayed physically strong—due to his insistence on cutting the firewood for the estate himself, even after the mansion's baseboard electric heaters were installed and the fireplaces all bricked over. But his balance looked off, and his once-sandy hair had gone a duller, snowier white. After Greenwood Timber was dissolved, for years Harris did nothing more than track his land holdings and investments from his home office. And when he officially retired three years ago, he began spending half his time in San Francisco, where each morning he would take a taxi into the redwoods along with a guide to listen for birdcalls that he'd note down in a little book. But given this rapid physical diminishment, it was clear her father was not made for idle time.

Then, when he got close, he did the unthinkable: he reached out and embraced her. "You smell like a bunkhouse at one of my lumber camps," he said after releasing her.

"And you smell like a retirement home," Willow said, still perplexed by the gesture. "To what do I owe this honour, Harris?" Throughout her childhood, he had forbidden her to use the words *dad* and *father*, though naturally there was a phase in her teens when she made a point of sneering, "Anything you say, *Daddy*!" But he seemed to be making an effort at civility, so she decided to spare him her venom.

"Your uncle is due to be released in two days," he said, exercising his long-standing distaste for small talk. "And given your unique relationship, I thought you might like to retrieve him." She could almost detect a trace of jealousy in his voice, as if Harris wasn't the one who'd engineered—and financed—their "unique relationship" in the first place.

When Willow was six, Harris promised her a quarter for every letter she wrote her uncle, Everett Greenwood, and even left a stack of pre-stamped envelopes in her desk drawer. Eager to buy her own Arabian jumper like the other girls at her private school, she wrote a letter every day, sometimes several. For ten years they corresponded from their respective penitentiaries: Everett from his maximum-security cell, and Willow from her father's mansion. Initially, his letters came in a childish script, rife with grammatical errors and misspellings that she could identify even then. But over the years she watched his writing improve, like a slide projection drawn into focus, and in some sense they became literate in tandem.

Willow believed from a young age that even if her father's sight were restored by some miracle, he still wouldn't *see* her, not how a daughter needs her father to. Strangely, it was through her correspondence with her uncle that, along with enough money to buy her first thoroughbred Arabian, she gathered the kind of recognition she'd long thirsted for. Often reaching thirty single-spaced pages, and penned in a claustrophobic block print, Everett's letters never delved into prison life. Instead, he discussed such riveting subjects as the proper method for tapping maple syrup, or old movies he'd watched, or his readings of Homer, Emily Dickinson, Henry David Thoreau, Marcus Aurelius, or the pulpy novels of the prison library, from which he gleaned an overabundance of meaning. Willow treated her uncle more like a diary-by-correspondence than a real, living pen pal. She confessed her regret at not having a mother to braid her hair (her mother had been a wash-woman at one of Harris's lumber camps and had died at Willow's birth), and detailed her rare trips with her father to Greenwood Island, as well as her deep longing for a horse. When eventually, at sixteen, Willow's life cluttered with friends and equestrian classes and boys, she ceased writing altogether. Everett sent three more unanswered letters before stopping as well.

It wasn't until much later that she clued in to the oddity of paying a six-year-old to write to her incarcerated uncle, especially one serving out a thirty-eight-year sentence for some offence never spoken of. Any of her questions concerning the details of Everett's crime would always erect a rampart of silence across the dinner table, or send Harris fleeing to his study, where he'd latch the oak door behind him, locking himself in with his Braille editions and LPs of recorded poetry. In her twenties, Willow asked a law student friend to look Everett up, and discovered that the particulars of his conviction were sealed by the Crown—a circumstance, her friend suggested, that implied an offence concerning a child or children. Willow left the matter alone after that. She'd always imagined the Greenwood family as a house built of secrets, layers upon layers of them, secrets encased in more secrets, and she'd long had the suspicion that to examine them too closely would be to pull the whole edifice down around her.

Her final conclusion was that Harris was too emotionally stunted to correspond with Everett himself, so he'd outsourced the task to her, which was typical of her father: he was adept at paying people to do his dirty work.

"Pick him up yourself," Willow told him. "He's your brother."

Her father shut his sightless eyes for a moment and took a steadying breath, like a seasick man trying to overcome a resurgent bout of nausea. "I expect he'd prefer your company to mine," he said in a muted voice.

"Well, I just stocked up for the rest of the summer. And I'm quite busy hugging trees right now, can't you tell?"

"Ah yes, you and your trees," Harris said, swivelling his neck, as though he could actually see the intricately needled cedars and firs intermingling high above them. "You've come to know them even more intimately than I ever did. Then why the self-deprivation? What you need to do is finish your degree. Get into government. *Policy-making*, Willow. I know that's a dirty word to you, but it's only if you get your hands on the real levers of power that you can create some actual change."

How, Willow wondered, could anyone possibly believe in old-fashioned political change in an era like this? An era when the president of the United States is a lying ghoul, the rain melts your skin, the food is laced with poison, wars are eternal, and the world's oldest living beings are being felled to make Popsicle sticks. "This whole sick system is in its death throes, Harris. And in my opinion, those holding the levers of power ought to be the first to get dragged down with it."

"Oh, people said the same thing back in the thirties," Harris said, waving his hand dismissively. "And they'll be saying it forty years from now, mark my words. Time goes in cycles. Everything comes back again, eventually. You learn that at my age."

Willow felt his dismissal harden her voice: "What you've destroyed will never come back, Daddy."

Such a brazen insult would normally have jump-started one of his rages, and plunged their relationship into the ice water of another multi-year silence. But instead his lips pursed and his cheeks reddened, and if it hadn't been Harris Greenwood standing before her, Willow might have thought he looked hurt. He turned away without another word, and she stood watching him scuttle to his car. The combination of his unexpected restraint and his geriatric gait prompted in her an odd sensation of pity.

"What's it worth to you, Harris?" she called out.

Her father stopped and turned back toward her with narrowed eyes and a devilish half-smile. "Name your price." Negotiation had always been his native tongue, the only language that ever truly reached him.

"The deed to Greenwood Island," Willow said.

Harris laughed soundlessly; then, after he realized her sincerity, crumpled his grey eyebrows. When Willow was a girl, and only after a scorched-earth campaign of dogged lobbying, Harris would sometimes agree to take her on two-week retreats to the remote cabin on his private island—just the two of them, that was the deal, no assistants or employees. They took daily walks through the old-growth, Willow craning her neck in wonder and Harris listening carefully for birds. In the evenings they discussed botany and books and the war in Europe, and then listened to his poetry records before bed. Away from his office, Harris was a changed man. He never scolded her for chewing too loudly or lectured her on the critical importance of industry, and even made the occasional joke. Those trips were everything to her then: her only escape from the slow suffocation of their mirthless home; the only time she ever saw her father approach some form of contentedness.

Then came the Inquiry. She was eleven at the time, but she still remembers conclaves of slick-haired lawyers in the house at all hours, her father yelling into telephones with his eyes pinched shut. In the end, a special committee convicted him of collusion with the enemy for selling vast quantities of timber to the Japanese just before the Second World War broke out. Not only were many of his assets seized and divvied up among his bitterest competitors; he was—and here was his greatest defeat of all—entirely cut out of the enormous reconstruction profits to be had in post-war Europe. It was then he truly disappeared: as though to complement the loss of his vision, he lost his ability to be seen, to occupy space in the world. He became the phantom haunting their house, and they never set foot on Greenwood Island together again. If it hadn't been for her horse and the letters from her uncle, Willow would have perished of loneliness.

"I'm impressed by your audacity, Willow, though I must admit that the island still holds some sentimental value for me," Harris said. "It was one of the only bits of land those wretched cowards allowed me to keep. And it was quite a chore to acquire in the first place, you know. I had to arm-wrestle John D. Rockefeller to buy it!" The story was new to her, and she didn't know if he was joking or if his mind was declining as rapidly as his body.

"So while I can't give it to you," Harris continued, "how about I let you stay there for as long as you like?"

It was wishful thinking to expect to bargain land away from Harris Greenwood, especially old-growth forestland. And because she'd been such a thoroughly uncooperative and disrespectful daughter, a wellspring of frustration and disappointment, he'd informed her years ago that he'd entirely written her out of his will. This small concession was better than nothing. And besides, the island would be the perfect place for her to hide out from the cops.

"Fine," Willow had said, walking over to take her father's hand and shake it.

It wasn't until hours later, as Willow was preparing her simple dinner over the van's propane stove, that she realized she'd just witnessed a legitimate miracle: she and her father had agreed on something.

IT'S GOOD TO MEET YOU

SHE HAS ALWAYS pictured her uncle as a wizened, tottering thing with an ankle-length beard. Who else but Rip Van Winkle could be expected to walk away from a thirty-eight-year prison sentence? Yet the figure who emerges two hours later from the holding cell, a mint-green chamber bounded by riveted, buzzing doors, is a surprise. Despite a mild limp that seems to originate somewhere on his left side, Everett is tall and solid like her father. He wears cheap, elastic-waisted pants, prison-issue Velcroed shoes, and an impeccably white T-shirt, still creased from its package. His angular face is handsome, if that isn't odd to say, and his hair, an intermixed grey and black like iron ore, has been close-cropped to his neck—a style nobody wears anymore except cops and squares.

"It's good to meet you, Willow," he says, with his eyes glued to the floor.

Willow knows that given their years of correspondence, she ought to hug him, yet despite her father's recent spasm of sentimentality, the Greenwoods aren't huggers. So she shakes his hand, perfunctorily, as though she's just sold him a used car. "Let's get the hell out of here."

After some parole instructions from the discharge clerk, they collect his duffle and walk out into the sunshine. Willow exults in her liberation, though she can't even fathom the ecstasy her uncle must be feeling at this moment. Still, his gaze remains fixed on the pavement a few steps ahead of him as they head toward the parking lot.

"This is some vehicle," Everett says after they reach her Westfalia, examining the van's roof-embedded tent. "Can you set up a camp in there?"

Willow nods proudly. "I call it my getaway van. It keeps me close to nature."

"I could've used one of these in my time," he says wistfully.

"Well, it leaks exhaust, so you have to drive with the windows open to keep from getting woozy, but it's been good to me." As they climb inside, she tells Everett about how she bought the van with money she earned tree planting the land that her father clear-cut in the twenties, and how she hasn't accepted a cent of his death-trip fortune since she dropped out of college. She describes the month-long solo camping trips she takes each summer, bouncing from national parks to secret plots of land, swimming holes, and hidden hot springs. "It's just me, a few sacks of rice, soybeans, and chickpeas, my sleeping bag, and the great North American forests as my own personal rec room."

"That sounds real nice," her uncle says in a flat tone that suggests he's not one for the outdoors.

"So where to?" Willow asks after the van coughs to life, realizing that she and Harris didn't discuss where to deliver Everett once she'd retrieved him.

He shifts on the beaded seat cover. "There's something I need to do in Saskatchewan," he says, almost bashfully. "And I plan to hop one of those airplane flights to get there."

Willow shakes her head. "Saskatchewan's close. You'd be better off just taking the train east from here."

At this, she swears he shudders. "I've had my fill of trains," he says with a masklike expression. She remembers her father mentioning one Christmas after he'd drunk too much sake that Everett had been a hobo during the Great Depression, a train-hopper, and a veteran of the First World War before that, details that seemed utterly prehistoric. "And besides," Everett adds. "I need to check in with my parole officer in Vancouver before I go anywhere."

"Be warned: flying has got expensive since the oil crisis with the Middle East."

"That's fine," he replies. "I did some carpentry work while I was in there. I probably built ten thousand birdhouses, and some shelves for the prison library. So I was able to sock some money away."

"Vancouver it is," she announces, with no small amount of dread at the idea of returning to the big city and once again exposing herself to the scrutiny of law enforcement. She lights a menthol and coaxes the Westfalia from the penitentiary's parking lot, the ominous black sedan that was following her still creeping through the back alleys of her mind.

ALL THE YEARS IN BETWEEN

USUALLY, THE ENVIRONMENTALIST in Willow detests the fact that she finds the act of driving so profound, that such joy can be decanted from something that lays so much smog on the biosphere. Today, however, the drive is a drag. She's unaccustomed to having a co-pilot, and it doesn't help that Everett's prison stint seems to have atrophied the knack for conversation he displayed in his letters. He's too stiff. Too cordial. Too unwilling to meet her eyes. In the flesh, it seems that her mysterious outlaw uncle is about as much fun as her father. So after a few hours of silence—Everett staring with wonderment at the scrolling landscape like an acid-tripping freshman—Willow's eyelids grow heavy. It's then she remembers the white crosses in the glove box, leftover pills from that decadent final week with Sage. To perk herself up—and to compensate for Everett's miserly way with words—she discreetly pops two.

"Thanks for doing this," he says finally, after they've watched the highway's lines arc and stutter for another hour, while Willow sucks down menthol after menthol, her smoke-scorched eyes darting to the rear-view mirror every few seconds to check for the black sedan. "I never learned to drive myself."

"It's my pleasure," Willow says, trying not to grind her teeth.

"So how is old Harris holding up?"

"He and I don't practise what you'd call regular contact," she says, and for a second she's forced to ponder once more the unprecedented sentimentality of their most recent interaction. "He's fine, though, I suppose. He's slowing down now that he's retired. At least he's not a full-time forest murderer anymore. He listens to birds now."

"And that friend of his? What's his name—Feeney?"

The question seems loaded in ways she can't decipher, though the name is unknown to her. "Must be before my time," she says. "Harris never had any friends. He prefers assistants. They're much easier to order around."

But her response only saddens her uncle, whose face clouds over, and he remains quiet for some time. "At least he has you," he says.

She laughs bitterly. "I think I've been more of a headache to him than anything, especially since I dropped out of his alma mater." With her tongue racing from the speed, she describes her brief stint at Yale—a final gambit for Harris's impossible-to-attain approval— and how initially she loved the field trips to the woods of upstate New York and Maine, and the classes in "forest management," which, she later realized, was just a euphemism for determining which trees to destroy first. It wasn't until the end of her second semester, under an enormous chestnut tree outside the campus chapel, that she read a book called *Our Plundered Planet* and her entire world caved in. The exploitation, the waste, the destruction of the land and its indigenous peoples were all laid bare, and, worse, it was people like *her* who'd perpetrated these crimes. "I dropped out that week and went tree planting," she says. "I'm not boring you with this, am I?"

"Not at all," he says. "I could listen to you all day."

After they've left the grasslands behind and climbed up into a wooded valley of tall lodgepole pine, Willow notices a dark sedan in the rear-view mirror. *How long has it been there?* she wonders in a panic. "I need to pee," she says, and pulls onto an old logging road, feeling great relief when the car carries on down the highway. She parks in a patch of gravel near a cobalt-blue mountain stream and goes off into the woods. Returning, she watches her uncle limp out to a lone cypress that bends over the stream's bank, leaning against its trunk and tearing off some new-growth needles from its lowest branches. He proceeds to crush them in his hands, then cups the needles to his face and inhales deeply—an act of such strange intimacy, Willow feels guilty being witness to it. Every culture has its tree-related myths: from the ubiquitous trees of life that quite literally hold up the sky, to the monstrous trees that eat toddlers or drink human blood, to the trees that play pranks or heal the sick, remember stories or curse enemies. And watching her uncle, who has time-travelled here from a different age, she's reminded that trees are also capable of resurrection.

When he returns to the Westfalia, his hair is slicked back with stream water, and the citrusy aroma of pine floods Willow's nose. "Thanks. I needed that," he says in a markedly enlivened tone while meeting her eyes for the first time. Willow remembers the oppressive concrete and steel of the prison, how its designers had avoided using wood in a way that felt vindictive.

"They move you around when you're in prison for that long," he says, as she tentatively steers them back onto the highway, but not before checking both directions for black cars. "First I was in Stony Mountain. Then the Kingston Pen. Some years I couldn't see any greenery at all from my cell window. Other times, it was just a few scrubby black maples out on the yard's perimeter. For a while it was a nice stand of south-facing birch, and I could watch their bark peel back like parchment. Those were the best five years."

"You know, your letters were very important to me growing up," she says. "Sorry I just kind of trailed off and never thanked you."

"I always knew it would end. And I should be the one thanking you. I'm not sure I would have made it through those early years without your letters to look forward to."

"What was it like?" she asks, instantly regretting the question. A child's question.

"Oh," he says. "It was like riding a train car that doesn't go anywhere. Riding it with some of the worst and some of the best people you ever met. And doing that for decades."

"The longest they ever kept me in jail for trespassing on a forest lot was overnight, and that was more than enough," she says, silently wondering what kind of time the destruction of three logging machines worth a million dollars each will fetch her if she's caught.

Everett flashes a quick smile, his first. "You get used to it. You find ways to handle the time. I went in during what they're calling the Great Depression—and even after I learned to read I stuck to novels and never followed the news. I figured it'd all just be different by the time I got out. I miss anything important?"

"The stock market's just crashed again and lost half its value," Willow says. "Not as bad as it did in your day, I guess. And as I said there are gas shortages, because oil prices have gone crazy. They've lowered the speed limit in Oregon to conserve fuel." She lights another menthol and continues her lecture on the festering rot of human greed and consumerism, while also stressing how Mother Nature is pushing back with acid rain and resource depletion and desertification, and how a global environmental apocalypse will be the only way people finally learn their lesson. While listening to herself talk, she wonders if it's cruel to describe the world's imminent end to a man who's just regained it after so long a time away.

"There were some good years in there, though, right?" Everett asks after she's talked herself out. "Other than that Second Great War?"

"Sure, things were fairly comfortable for a while after that."

He nods. "Sorry to have missed it. Not the war, I mean. But all the years in between."

I WON'T MENTION IT AGAIN

AT DUSK, THEY pull off at another logging road for dinner. To settle her persistently gymnastic stomach, Willow brews nettle tea on the van's propane burner. Everett accepts his clay cup, clutching it intently, like it's brimming with liquid gold. She picked the nettle herself with cowhide gloves from one of her secret spots, and the tea is rich with tannin and chlorophyll, almost creamy.

"I prefer simple foods," she says later, stirring tahini into the chickpeas that she's boiled before ladling a scoopful over his brown rice. "Hope you don't mind."

"I can't imagine a meal I'd rather sit down to," he says, taking his bowl.

"When we depend less on industrially produced food and live in the world's quiet spaces," she says, quoting something she read in the *Whole Earth Catalog,* her mouth still turbo-charged by the pills, "our bodies become vigorous. We discover the serenity of living in sync with the rhythms of the Earth. We cease oppressing one another."

"Makes sense," he says, slipping his fork into his mouth. She still can't tell if he's capable of sarcasm.

For dessert she offers some of the soymilk she makes, heated with honey stirred into it. Everett sips approvingly as she details the process: boiling the beans, blending them, and straining the mash through a muslin bag.

"Even when you were just a little thing, you never could stand cow's milk," he chuckles after he takes an approving sip, his voice suddenly alight with the past. "I used to give you goat's milk, whenever I could find it. But this bean milk is a fine alternative."

"Funny, Harris never mentioned you being around when I was a baby. When was that, exactly?"

"Oh," Everett says, a hesitant gaze cast into his cup. "I'm getting things twisted up. Sorry. Your father was right. I wasn't around. All that about the goat's milk was something Harris once told me." Still, the warmth of his recollection moves Willow, even if he invented it. Harris never reminisced fondly over the past, and especially not over memories of her childhood.

After they finish, Everett insists on washing the dishes in the van's small basin while the sun's salmon light falls fast behind the mountains.

"So why do you choose to live this way?" Everett asks as he scrubs. "I imagine you could afford to live otherwise, if you wanted."

"I don't live in my van full time," she says. "I used to stay in a communal house in Vancouver during the winters, except now I need to figure something else out. But out here in the forests, I'm constantly reminded that I'm no more important than any other organism, and that nature is the greatest force of all."

Everett nods affirmatively. "As a younger man I never had much use for proper houses, either. Or people."

"Do you know that there were once six trillion trees on this planet?" she replies. "And now there are three trillion? How long do you think they'll last at the rate we're going? So I guess I'd rather be with them before they're gone. And maybe even save a few in the process."

By the time the dishes are done it's dark. But Willow is still too high to sleep, so she declares it best for them to keep moving. She's eager to get to Greenwood Island as quickly as possible; it's the only place she'll be safe from the black sedans, including the one that followed them briefly on the highway. She's realized there could in fact be many sedans, because their surveillance could be part of a coordinated investigation. She climbs behind the wheel, and though the engine starts fine, when she flicks the headlights nothing happens.

Given that she rises and sleeps with the sun, it's been ages since she's driven at night. And with no moon, the winding mountain roads will be suicidal without lights.

"It's going to take a little longer for you to get where you're going," she says after explaining their situation.

"Doesn't bother me. Time and I have come to an understanding," Everett says, his eyes fixed on the blackening trees. "This is a fine place to camp."

While she reaches to set up the rooftop tent, Willow's nipples inadvertently rub against her polyester shirt, which suddenly feels like sandpaper. Then, while she's changing into her pajamas in the woods, she checks her underwear with a flashlight and finds evidence of spotting. Her period is quite probably late, but she doesn't use calendars, which are unnatural, invented by railroad operators and bean counters. Not that she needs a calendar to tell her that another presence has entered her belly, another flutter of the future. In Willow's thirty-nine years of life, eight of these flutters have come and gone like uterine eclipses. Yet each one ended quickly, always during the first trimester. *So I won't be putting much stock in you either*, she thinks.

She returns to the van to find Everett reading a book in the van's dim interior light.

"What's that you've got there?" she asks while laying out their bedding.

He holds up the cover of the *Odyssey*. "The prison librarian let me keep it after I borrowed it so much. I like books where people go places. Especially when they go home. It's an inmate thing, I guess."

Then, just as she's drawing the curtains, a gorge of chickpea bile crowds her esophagus and she thrusts her head out the sliding door to spew it onto the gravel. "Don't worry, it's not the food," she says through a cough when Everett comes to her side.

She brushes her teeth then proceeds to roll a neat little joint of indica on the van's fold-out table. As she hoped, the smoke eases her nausea, and out of sheer habit, she holds the roach out to Everett, who to her surprise pinches it in his fingers and purses his lips.

"I'm happy to sleep outside if you'd rather be alone in your vehicle," he says, exhaling a great ivory plume and gesturing to the fold-out hide-a-bed she's set up in the van's lower section.

"It's freezing at night this high in the mountains," she says. "You'll be better off in here." She climbs up into the rooftop tent, kills her flashlight, and listens to the wind sigh through the mesh screen just as the joint hits her in earnest. Weed has always been her shortcut to tuning into the sweetest natural frequencies, a way of assuming her rightful place in the great cosmic scheme. She lies there, feeling the contours of time warp and expand, listening to the great symphony of grass and wind and tree.

"It's been a while since I've been with anyone who isn't locked up with me against their will," her uncle says from below, just as she's beginning to drowse.

"So why don't you and my father speak?" she asks sleepily.

Everett lets out a long breath. "He did something to me," he says, his voice croaky and philosophical from the dope. "It wasn't a good thing that he did. But I understand why he did it. He was protecting something he cared about. Something he lost in the end anyway."

"Let me guess what he was protecting," she says. "It's what you keep in a bank."

"Something like that," he replies.

"Harris has a talent for leaving devastation behind wherever he goes. Just ask all those acres of stumps and slash piles. I will say, though, that it seemed very important to him that I come get you. He offered to let me live on Greenwood Island in exchange."

"That was very kind of him," he says. "And it's a fine place."

"You've been there?"

"Oh, no," he says. "That's what I've heard."

"Yeah, well, most of all Harris likes to get people to do things for him. It makes him feel powerful."

"You know, I was so nervous at first, when I heard you were coming. I didn't know what to say or how to act," Everett says, his voice suddenly thick with emotion. "But I can't tell you how nice it is. Just to see you. It's been so long. And you've grown even more beautiful than I imagined, Pod."

Willow bolts upright, smacking her head on the tent's aluminum struts, a surreal sense of recognition overwhelming her. "What did you call me?"

"Beautiful?" he stammers. "I'm sorry. I didn't mean anything by it. I'm out of practice with talking. And this stuff has my head all twisted up."

"No, the name. *Pod?*"

"Oh," he says nervously. "That's just a nickname I made up when you were a baby. You were really something then. Just a little package, so stuffed with life."

"I thought you said you never knew me as a baby," Willow says coldly.

"Yes," he stammers again. "That's right."

All at once she feels the heaviness of the day: the oppressive prison, the flutter of the future, the dead headlights, her grinding anxiety about the black sedan. And now she's grown sufficiently weary of her stoned uncle's weird prison fantasies about their shared history.

"Just do me a favour and keep the nicknames to yourself," Willow says, lying back and re-cocooning herself in her sleeping bag. "That's not the trip I'm on, okay? I'm not a baby anymore. And I'm definitely not anybody's pet."

A long silence.

"You're right," he says, almost too quiet for her to hear. "You're not. I won't mention it again. Good night, Willow."

SUMTHING THAT
COULDNT BE MINE

THEY RISE WITHOUT words, the exchange that concluded the previous evening weighing upon them. They drink hot black tea and eat the steel-cut oats that Willow soaked overnight to save time, then it's five more wordless hours of driving through a grey fog that clings to the road, down from the mountains and into Vancouver.

In the city, she parks in an alley behind his parole office with curtains drawn over her van's windows, and sits smoking menthols, wearing her wig and sunglasses. When Everett comes back out, she drives him to the sea-level airport and stops in the unloading zone as he gathers up his penitentiary-issue duffle. Willow climbs out to stand amid the ruckus of cars—many of them are black sedans, but that's to be expected, isn't it? Her lungs burn from the toxicity of the exhaust as she watches her uncle flinch like a doe each time the white belly of a jet screams overhead.

"You sure you have enough money?" she asks, even though she doesn't have any to spare him, but it seems the proper remark to spur things along.

He nods, once again unable to look at her. "I'm fine in that department."

"Just remember to be back in time to check in with your parole officer next week. I'm not driving all the way out to Alberta again," she says, somewhat jovially, trying to superficially lighten the mood enough for her to escape without another emotional incident.

He nods again. "I don't imagine this will take very long."

"I never asked—what's so important in Saskatchewan?"

"A woman I knew. I mean, well"—now he actually blushes—"it's partially that. But it's more that she's got a book of mine. One I left with her years ago for safe keeping."

"You're going to fly to Saskatchewan and potentially break your parole because you loaned her a book? Must be some woman."

Everett nods. "She is. And the book is important," he says. "Of particular interest to you, I expect. In fact, if I can retrieve it, I'd like to give it to you. As a keepsake."

"I lost my taste for books some time ago," Willow says. "These days the forest and the sky teach me all that I need to know."

"Your father always had plenty of books around. Braille and otherwise. I'm sure those will go to you eventually."

"You mean Harris Greenwood's collection of relics full of square wisdom that nobody needs anymore? No thanks. I'll pass. I mean, what's a bookshelf's purpose, other than to quietly remind one's guests of one's superior intellect?"

"Suppose I *do* find this particular relic I'm talking about. How can I get ahold of you?"

"I'll be unreachable for a while, I expect," she says. "I'm going to set up on Greenwood Island, and there's no phone or mail delivery there, just a shortwave radio. So send it to my father. I visit him every decade or so. I'll pick it up then."

Now Everett lifts his chin and their eyes catch the way people's do before they part ways. Already he appears different than when she picked him up yesterday, wearier, hurt somehow. He's swallowing a great deal and his eyelashes are damp. Could their years of correspondence possibly mean so much to him? This was how it had been with Sage, who professed a sudden, syrupy love after just a few months together. Perhaps her uncle is simply deranged, Willow concludes as she cordially shakes his hand, then watches him disappear into the terminal, a mere speck of life in a churning sea of being. Cut from the same cloth as her inscrutable father.

After she merges her Westfalia, turtle-like, back into the hurling tumult of the midday rat race, she decides to terminate it—the flutter—if this time it somehow persists. Acid rain, rampant inflation, police firing on students, mindless conformity, looming economic collapse, overpopulation, suburbanization, species extinction, wanton deforestation—the last thing this world needs is another resource-sucking human showing up to ruin it further. Not to mention the fact that she's quite likely under police investigation and there are still about three trillion or so trees left to defend. Those bags of sugar were just the beginning, and she doesn't need a dependent to slow her down.

She lights a menthol and steers toward the harbour, where she'll hire a barge to carry her van to Greenwood Island. As she smokes, a memory rises up, the first written exchange she'd had with her uncle, one of the handful of letters that she kept, stuffed in a shoebox somewhere in her van along with a few other trinkets from her childhood. She was six when she wrote it, and still possessed the child's nerve to question why Everett couldn't come to her birthday party and ride the pony her father had rented, why the judges and police wouldn't let him.

I tok sumthing, was his near-illegible reply.

What something? she wrote back.

Sumthing that couldnt be mine.

Sure, he'd been kind to her, her strange, convict uncle. And there was a time when reading his letters was the only way for her to feel noticed as a child. But now that he's rejoined the world and she's felt the full brunt of his puzzling attachment and this fictional intimacy he believes they share, which comes complete with strange books he wants to give her and nicknames he's invented for her without her knowledge, she doesn't care if she never sees him again. In the end, it turns out that her mysterious uncle is just another Greenwood, needing her to be someone she isn't.

1934

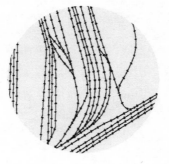

THE CRY

THAT NIGHT, A sound reaches Everett Greenwood's shack. Wheedling, incessant—impossible to ignore. Some nights, especially when it's raining, he might hear the chuff of trains dragging coal to the scows at port in nearby Saint John, or the shriek of an animal either giving birth or facing death in these woods. But this sound hails from another world.

Twice he nearly takes up his kerosene lantern to go search out the sound's source—to do what then, who knows—though mercifully, it drops off after an hour and he returns to sleep.

Just before sun-up, Everett sets out amid the last dregs of spring snow to prepare his taps, and he's relieved not to hear it again. If he were questioned by some authority—some Mountie or judge—he could perhaps identify it. But another, more cowardly part of him maintains that it was nothing more than two maples rubbing in the wind, or a red fox caught in one of his rabbit snares.

It's nearly April, and the maple woods are leafless and fresh with meltwater. Any day the sap will begin to run up from the deepest roots, and Everett's taps must be set to bleed the trees of their sugar. He knows a wealthy man owns this forest, but he seldom visits his property, and only ever to hunt grouse and fox with his guests, their bugles blaring, their hunting vests clinking with rounds ten times the calibre required for small game. So it's nothing for Everett to keep hidden.

He discovered these woods a decade ago after rolling off a train in a drunken stupor and waking up here. He spent years on the rails following his return from the War, a stretch of his life he prefers to forget; mostly he was drifting, blind drunk, robbing other hobos for pocket change, knocking at porch doors for food in exchange for splitting some firewood. During those years he'd often find himself standing on high railway trestles that swayed in the wind, daring himself to jump, imagining the relief he'd feel after his head came apart on the serrated rocks below.

But the solitary enterprise of his sugarbush has been his salvation, and he hasn't touched a drop of liquor since finding it. Along with woodcutting and carpentry, Everett taught himself to tap syrup as a boy, and during the War he even fashioned some spiles from empty .50-calibre shell casings, hammering them into a few black maples during a cold snap near the Somme. Though the villagers had inhabited the place for thousands of years, their eyes flew wide when a thick, pungent sap came running. In Everett's view, syrup is one of nature's few gifts, a true benevolence, offered with no expectation of repayment.

Now he takes a deer path that runs along the belly of a wooded gulch, his boots sucking in intermittent stews of mud. He finds his first sugar maple, its silver-grey bark scarred by years of his tapping. He draws his auger and bores a fresh hole into its south side. The bark gives way and threads of blonde sapwood peel from the bit's grooves. He takes a wooden mallet and knocks a steel spile into the hole—too deep or too shallow and he'll miss the sap completely. He hesitates to admire his work before hanging a collection bucket and moving on.

He's always preferred trees to people. Their habits and predilections are much easier to discern. And these trees are as good as they come: a thousand acres of the finest sugar maples that ever reared from the soil, with leaves that spread as wide as a giant's hand, all running with a caramel-like sap so rich it requires minimal boiling. This year, after the sap runs dry, he'll bottle his syrup, then exchange it in Saint John for oats, lard, sugar, flour, and a small roll of bills. A month's work, at most. For the year's remainder, he'll laze by the brook, entertaining half-thoughts, watching seed pods and whirlers drift on the slow water. It's lonely living at times, yet peaceful—and after a long life of toil and struggle, he feels deserving of such leisure.

He taps ten more trees then builds a small fire to fry breakfast: oat-cakes dredged in last year's syrup. He washes up then fords the brook and taps twenty more along its eastern bank. He's just nearing the end of his circuit when he spies it: a bolt of brocade cloth, hung by a nail driven into his last maple, a grand, stately tree he's tapped for years, one of his best producers, stout enough to take four spiles. As he approaches he notes the strained way the cloth hangs, and shoos away a greasy crow eyeing the bundle from a branch of the same tree. With a retch the bird settles on a slightly higher perch, unwilling to cede more ground than it must. Up close there's a faint wriggle to the cloth, which could be from the breeze. Then a soft snuffle.

Just leave it, he thinks. *The forest will take care of this itself.*

Reluctantly he parts the folds and slides his leathery hand inside. There he finds warmth, breath.

He whispers: "Shit."

HARVEY BENNETT LOMAX

ON THE MORNING of the big day, Harvey Lomax drives his employer over the frost-spangled streets of Saint John in his newest Packard Straight Eight. Because the rear seat is loaded with gifts, Mr. Holt has been forced to sit up front. For today's occasion, he's selected a pin-striped suit of modern cut—not the conservative tweed he normally wears—and has stuck a feather in his derby, plucked from a grouse he once shot in the woods that surround his country estate, the very place they're headed. Despite Mr. Holt's cheerful attire, after twenty years in his employ Lomax knows a sour mood when he sees one—something tense and roiling around the eyes—so he makes no chit-chat, and smokes his Parliaments in silence. Though they're not long into the drive, his back begins to trouble him, a radiating numbness that prompts him to squirm and shift his gigantic frame behind the wheel.

"And how is your condition this morning, Mr. Lomax?" Mr. Holt asks, his stony eyes fixed straight ahead. "Those medicinal cigars my doctor prepared for you aren't helping?"

"I haven't sampled one yet, sir," Lomax says, wincing as a swarm of fresh spasms begin to assault his spine. "I know what those medicines can do to a man. And I'd rather not go the route my father did."

"Very stoic of you," Mr. Holt replies. "But there's no need to suffer."

Harvey Lomax was a large baby, a massive toddler, and a down-right mammoth child. One morning when he was eleven years old, he confessed to his father that he couldn't get out of bed without lightning shooting through his back and forking out into his limbs. His father brought Harvey to a doctor, who tapped his joints with a tiny hammer and shined a light in his eyes, then claimed that other than his unusual height, there was no physiological cause for his discomfort. "Money well spent," his father said bitterly, dragging Harvey roughly by the elbow back to their apartment.

But over the years, as Harvey grew ever bigger, the lightning sensation only worsened. Soon it was torturing him not just in the morning, but throughout the day. It became the kind of suffering that can't possibly be described, the kind that drills into you a little deeper each day, the kind that makes you mean. He tried every remedy: heat and cold, balms and tinctures. And when all had failed, he learned to accept the fact that a body as large as his can't possibly exist without a good dose of suffering, and that his lightning is just the tax he must pay in order to survive.

Yet size does have its advantages. When faced with his cabbage-sized hands and his hulking, nearly seven-foot frame, people veer from his path like sailboats from a freighter. And given the few vocational options available to men of his physiology, he's been lucky to serve R.J. Holt personally for the past twenty years, handling his most sensitive matters. Whether it's a tenant owing back rent on a Holt building, or a miner who's snuck a raw diamond out of a Holt mine, or one of Mr. Holt's girls acting indiscreet—it falls to Lomax to set things right. And at this function he has yet to fail.

"I've always wanted to be a father," Mr. Holt muses gaily, after they've driven for an hour and the pavement has submitted to the gravel track that winds through the vast woodland surrounding his estate for fifty acres in every direction. "But my wife just isn't up to the task. God knows we've tried. Of course yours doesn't suffer from any such malady, does she, Mr. Lomax? What's the latest count? Six?"

"Seven, sir," Lomax says, clearing his throat. "The first was unplanned. And when we married, we hoped for just two more. But it turned out that Lavern and I have no trouble in the miracle-making department. If we as much as use the same soap we're in the hospital nine months later."

Holt offers a rare chuckle, which pleases Lomax, though speaking of his seven children also puts him in mind of the deep financial hole they've dug him into—a debt only recently consolidated into a sizeable mortgage on his house, a mortgage Mr. Holt has been generous enough to provide interest-free.

"Do you have any advice for me?" Mr. Holt asks. "One father to another?"

"Don't have more," Lomax says flatly. "And don't spend money that isn't yours."

"Well put, well put," Mr. Holt says, then he gets that fierce, faraway look that settles over him whenever he discusses his business affairs. "Yet I may soon share your financial woes, Mr. Lomax. If this Crash continues to have its way with my companies."

Lomax knows it's unlikely that the Crash poses any real threat to his employer. He inherited his vast fortune from his father, R.J. Sr., and despite Junior's philandering preoccupations, he's since grown the business and now owns half the province of New Brunswick: coal, steel, oil, both newspapers, banks, service stations, Automats, grocery stores, and shipping. It's said that you can't go for a Sunday stroll without inadvertently stuffing fifty cents into Holt's pocket by the time you get home.

"And the child? You're certain it's well formed?" Mr. Holt asks.

"It is, sir," Lomax confirms. "The mother is still recovering from some complications. But the little girl is as healthy as can be."

"Good, good. Girl, boy—it doesn't matter to me. I'm going to need someone to leave all this money to, aren't I? If I manage to keep it?"

"You certainly will, sir."

"And the mother?" Mr. Holt says some seconds later, in the lesser tone of afterthought. "She's fully recovered, you said?"

Like many of Mr. Holt's conquests, Euphemia Baxter began as his employee. After she caught his eye while cleaning one of his banks, he asked Lomax to install her in an apartment that he keeps for such purposes, and for six months he visited her regularly while his wife played bridge. Mr. Holt's infatuation eventually flagged, as it always did, and he'd already moved on to another girl when Euphemia announced she was pregnant. Mr. Holt was unexpectedly pleased, both because of the prospect of an heir and because the pregnancy proved his theory correct: it *was* his wife's defect that had so far prevented him from siring a child. Immediately a deal was struck, with Euphemia agreeing to receive a sum of money to carry the child, which the Holts would then adopt. To avoid scandal, Mr. Holt suggested that Euphemia remain sequestered in her apartment until the birth. So over the course of her pregnancy, it fell to Lomax to bring her groceries, books from the library, and the ten-cent magazines she liked. Then, four weeks ago, mere days before the baby was due, Mr. Holt insisted that Lomax relocate her to his isolated country estate in preparation for the child's arrival.

"She's not entirely recovered, sir," Lomax says. "There's been bleeding and cramping, and she's running a high blood pressure, but—"

"Dear Christ, Lomax," Mr. Holt interrupts, waving his hand in front of his face to dispel the image. "Spare me the gory details."

"She's been resting for three weeks now. And she's regained some of her spirit. The doctor said she'll be fine as long as she stays in bed and doesn't move around."

"Good, good. You'll see to it that she does, won't you, Mr. Lomax?"

"Certainly, sir."

"And when Mrs. Holt returns from her mother's in Connecticut next week," Mr. Holt goes on, "we'll formalize the adoption papers and bring the child home with us to Saint John."

Lomax parks the Packard on the cobblestones of the country house, which sits amid a picturesque expanse of trees, brooks, and knolls that Mr. Holt pays a game warden to keep well stocked with fox and grouse for him and his guests to shoot each summer.

Lomax stifles a groan as he lifts himself from the car, a cascade of low-grade voltage spilling through his back and running down into his thighs. He stifles a second groan when he stoops to gather the gifts from the rear seat.

"The cook isn't up quite yet, sir," Lomax says while examining the darkened main floor windows as they approach the house.

"We'll be quiet," Mr. Holt says, his eyes flickering as he brandishes a bouquet of purple daffodils. "Let's go greet the future, shall we?" He throws open the door and strides to the master bedroom near the back.

As they approach the door, Mr. Holt removes his hat and tightens his tie. "Euphemia, darling, it's R.J.," he says in a softened voice, his ear pressed against the wood while rapping it with his chunky class ring.

Silence.

"She and the child may be sleeping, sir," Lomax says softly.

"Oh, there's no harm in just a peek," Mr. Holt says, delicately trying the knob, which is locked. He raps again.

After the tenth unanswered rap, Mr. Holt's good mood fouls, like a boy who's run joyfully out into a field with his new balloon and immediately let go of its string. "Where's the damned key?" he asks, examining the lock.

"The locks in this place are old, sir; every door has a different one."

"Oh for God's sake!" Mr. Holt shouts. "What do I keep an ogre like you around for? Certainly not for conversation, I can assure you of that."

Lomax sets down the gifts and aligns his shoulder so that it will connect squarely with the door. He takes a short, awkward run and strikes the oak panel, which is sturdier than expected, and a screeching noise sounds out as the jamb pulls away from the frame. Exploding into the room, Lomax feels an awful ripping sensation run up his spine, and immediately collapses, nearly vomiting from the lightning that's now crackling up his vertebrae and forking into his brainstem.

"They're gone," he hears Mr. Holt say.

On all fours, Lomax forces his eyes into focus. The bed where he last saw Euphemia nursing the child is now empty. Beside it, the French doors that face the back woods yawn open.

"Women can behave curiously after a birth, sir," Lomax manages to say while rising with tremendous difficulty to his knees. "They do odd things. Lavern saw ghosts. But Euphemia is likely just out for a walk in the woods."

"In the snow? With a newborn?" Holt yells. "This isn't one of your twenty worthless whelps, Mr. Lomax! This is my only child she's stolen!" In a rage Mr. Holt demands an immediate search of the grounds, and Lomax limps for the telephone.

While they await the search party, which Lomax raised by claiming that one of Mr. Holt's guests has gone missing, Lomax hobbles to the servants' quarters to question the cook and the maid, who both haven't seen Euphemia since early the previous evening. It's just shy of noon by the time the groundskeepers and groomsmen arrive from Mr. Holt's mansion in Saint John, as well as a handful of trusted men from the Holt steel mill. After the party is assembled, the game warden leads them into the woods carrying a silver bugle. They search throughout the afternoon, and much to Mr. Holt's annoyance, Lomax's injury prevents him from joining them for any duration. Just as the dark starts to filter into the trees, Mr. Holt approaches Lomax on the second-floor terrace that overlooks the property.

"You visited Euphemia last night, did you not?" Mr. Holt says.

"I did, sir," Lomax replies. "Around seven. To check on her condition."

"Did she mention any second thoughts about our agreement?"

Lomax feels his heartbeat stutter to a stop. "No, sir. Nothing like that," he says tightly. "Why do you ask?"

"No reason," Mr. Holt says, nodding. "But it turned out to be clever thinking on our part, didn't it? Bringing her here?"

"It did, sir," Lomax replies, his heart kicking into gear once again. When Mr. Holt first insisted that Euphemia give birth at his estate, Lomax knew that it wasn't just for its privacy—it was because Mr. Holt had calculated that if she *did* reconsider their arrangement, there would be nowhere for her to go.

"And she can't possibly get far in her weakened condition, sir," Lomax adds. "Especially not with a child weighing in her arms. I expect we'll locate her shortly. She'll come through this just fine."

"I'm sure, I'm sure," Mr. Holt says. "And has there been any sign of her book?"

"Book, sir?"

"That journal she was always writing in," he says with bald disgust. "It wasn't in her room—I searched it myself. Have you seen it?"

"No sir," Lomax says. "She must have taken it with her."

At this, something in Holt shifts: his eyes lower and he acquires an unsettled expression, as though he's reading some chilling passage written in the grain of the terrace's woodwork. "I'm not sure you understand, Mr. Lomax," he says in a hesitant, shrivelled voice, "that while writing in that book of hers, Euphemia could have recorded certain . . . acts. *Intimate* acts, if you gather my meaning, that we engaged in—quite willingly, I should add. But it could be very damaging for me if the journal made its way into the wrong hands."

Lomax now recalls the bruises that have occasionally appeared on Mr. Holt's girls, including Euphemia—especially during the early days of his infatuations with them. Faint rainbows edging out from under the cuffs of their long-sleeved dresses, or nosing up their necks from under the otter-trimmed collars of the coats he's bought them. But since none of the girls has ever complained, Lomax has known better than to ask.

"We'll find her, sir," Lomax vows. "And the book."

"Of course we will, Mr. Lomax," Mr. Holt says darkly as he stares out into the fast-blackening trees, a trio of bats hurtling through their branches.

THE BUNDLE

IT KEEPS SILENT while Everett lugs it back through the woods. The faint tremble ceases as he walks—a development he finds encouraging. Maybe the quandary of what he'll do next has already been solved for him, and all he'll need to do now is dig a hole.

He reaches his shack and feels a great relief when he sets the bundle down on the floorboards near the stove. Not that it's heavy—his arms had flown upward when he pulled it from the tree, like when you lift a plank that appears to be solid walnut yet is in fact only cheap veneer—but holding it made him uneasy.

He didn't take up the bundle out of pity. He did it because if he let the forest take care of the child, as he'd planned, and its remains were discovered hanging from one of Everett's nails, the Mounties would search the woods, and it would just be a matter of time before they found his shack. He'd done time for vagrancy during his tramping years, so it would be nothing for them to pin the child's fate on him. And even if they didn't, he'd certainly be turned out from his home, and the good life he'd assembled here would be lost forever.

Everett builds a fire with some hot-burning ash logs and soon the stove splashes red with heat, which pulses outward in slow-rolling waves. For a moment he considers the small amount of effort that would be required to swing open the stove's door, ease the bundle down upon the seething embers, and shut it again. Though he'd mostly served as a stretcher-bearer in the War, he'd fired upon his share of Krauts, many of them mere boys. And during his subsequent hoboing years he'd left numerous souls stabbed and beaten all over the interwoven rail lines of North America. So what difference would this little pile of ashes make in the grand scheme of things?

But after deeper consideration, Everett worries the act could haunt him. Perhaps even worse than what he witnessed in France, which to this day can infect his dreams with visions of the shredded creatures he carted in his stretcher, their viscera dangling out and dragging in the mud, their tortured voices screaming for their mothers, as though they might appear with their sewing kits and stitch them back into something human.

Everett leaves the bundle near the stove and beds down. Just as he begins to doze, the child starts wailing like a stepped-on cat. The cry, up close this time, pumps blood into his temples and rattles his skull. He knows what might make it quit: songs and rhymes about birds and stars and fairies and celestial things. Yet all he knows are infantry marching songs, bawdy blues tunes, and filthy limericks. When the cries intensify, Everett fetches the beeswax he rubs on his hands after they crack in winter and pushes two dollops into his ears. Still the racket is audible, so he heads out into the frozen dark in just his red drop-bottoms to milk his remaining goat, an old, taupe-and-white nanny he acquired for a few pints of half-fermented syrup. Even though her last kid died of dysentery during the winter and her milk has dwindled since, she manages a cupful, and he scratches her twitchy ear in gratitude.

Inside, he dumps the milk into an old teapot and presses its chipped spout to the infant's tiny mouth. "This better do," he says while purposefully looking the other direction, his voice hoarse after years of disuse. "Because there isn't anything else, other than syrup, and that I need."

The baby quiets as it suckles and chokes with clenched eyes, and Everett permits himself a momentary examination: nostrils whorled like seashells, skin the tint of an unripe strawberry—a creature specifically designed to elicit sympathy, he realizes, before briskly averting his gaze. When the teapot empties, he re-bundles the child and dumps it back near the stove, vowing never to regard it directly again.

Pity is the barbed hook that children catch you with, so it's pity he'll guard himself against until he rids himself of this curse.

Tomorrow morning, he decides. He'll take it into Saint John and leave it somewhere for someone else to find. Or maybe, with some luck, the child won't survive the night. Or even better, he'll wake to it vanished—just the solitude of his sugarbush and its velvety maples cloaking him once again. Stranger things have happened. It's his experience that such curses can dissipate as unaccountably as they arrive.

THE SLIPCASE

HARVEY LOMAX'S BRICK bungalow in West Saint John is where he's most untroubled, most serene, most himself. Since Lavern's father first helped the newlyweds with the down payment—this after the accidental conception of Harvey Jr.—the house has been more than a dwelling. It's Lomax's oasis of meaning in an increasingly meaningless world, a monument to his steadfast dedication to his family. And it remains his only possession that he'd protect with his life.

Tonight, after they get seven mouths fed and seven bodies bathed and tucked into seven beds, Lavern retreats to her radio serials, and Lomax to his study to smoke Parliaments in his favourite chair, the thickly cushioned one that offers his tortured spine a modicum of relief. Mere strangers when they married, Harvey and Lavern have forged a sturdy domestic alliance over the years, like two factory workers who've toiled elbow-to-elbow on the same assembly line for so long they no longer require words to communicate.

Throughout the evening Lomax checks in with the game warden by telephone, and so far the search has turned up nothing. When Lomax calls Mr. Holt with an update, he sounds inebriated, and orders Lomax to search Euphemia's apartment immediately. But since battering down that oak door earlier, the lightning strikes to the apex of his spine have been unrelenting, and he can barely take a breath without a wince. Desperate to carry out his employer's wishes, Lomax pulls from his desk the box of opium-laced cigars that Mr. Holt's doctor gave him. While they aren't exactly legal, the doctor didn't mind making a special preparation for such a valued employee. Lomax rips away the paper seal, takes a cigar, and runs it under his nose: scents of orchid, clove, manure. And beneath that a vivid memory of his childhood: the strange pipe of his father's that he kept hidden in the coal scuttle.

Also a large man, Walter Lomax was a drinker, an opium smoker, and a part-time magician with pockets full of marked cards and a wandering eye for women. "Our vaunted guest," his wife would proclaim when he'd skulk home for Sunday dinner and slump in his armchair, tie loosened, guzzling water like a prizefighter in his corner.

When he finally left them for good when Harvey was twelve, to make ends meet the boy was forced to take a job collecting on milk accounts for the Holt Dairy Company. As the youngest collector, the most hopeless cases in the foulest neighborhoods fell to him. Most collectors went in for intimidation, threats—overt or implied. Some squeezed the woman a little if her man wasn't around. But Harvey didn't need to. Even at twelve, already he struck an intimidating figure, and after his first month he'd recovered more than the firm's best collector. Soon he was drawing a dollar a week in commission, money that kept him and his mother from destitution. Then, twenty years ago, Lomax was recruited by Mr. Holt himself. Violence is a language Lomax learned to speak early, from the drumming cadence of his father's fists, and he quickly discovered the thrill to be had in roughing up a thief or a cheat—someone who'd gleefully shirked his responsibilities in a way Lomax would never dream of. Life had already dealt him so much pain; why shouldn't he redistribute some back out into the world, if the situation warranted? And while the frequent violence has exacerbated his condition, the job has allowed him to provide for his family and prove that he's cut from a markedly different cloth than his deadbeat father.

So what harm could one measly cigar possibly do? Lomax thinks now as he snips off the end then lights it, taking only a modest puff. As the smoke spreads languidly through the fleshy closets of his lungs, he feels nothing—no euphoria, no life-altering rush—so he takes another puff of equal measure. Wary of overdoing it, he places the extinguished cigar back in the box and sits in his chair, waiting. Slowly, almost at the speed of a sunrise, he feels a balmy relief come over him, a bright sensation that hums sweetly through the length of his spine like water through a pipe.

Feeling more limber than he has in years, Lomax drives to the low-rent apartment near the docks that Mr. Holt provides for Euphemia. He uses the landlord key to let himself inside, and just as he expected, she isn't there. Though her mind is meticulously well ordered, she has always kept her place a terrific mess: a blizzard of fruit flies rear upward from food-ridden plates in the basin; jewellery dazzles in heaps around the dressing mirror; books lie splayed open on every surface, some stacked a dozen high, nested face-down like Ukrainian dolls. He touches the silk dresses and nightgowns that dangle in her wardrobe, and on a nearby shelf he spots framed photographs of her family, headed by a proud, coal dust–blackened man standing rod-straight beside a grinning, middle school–aged Euphemia, gap-toothed and already lovely. Lomax momentarily entertains the notion of his eldest daughter, Hattie, moving to the big city with even bigger aspirations, only to end up as the bruised plaything of a rich tycoon—a thought that upheaves his stomach. Then, tucked inside Euphemia's flip-top desk, he finds the slipcase she keeps her journal in. Upon its spine is written:

THE SECRET & PRIVATE THINKINGS & DOINGS
OF EUPHEMIA BAXTER

But the slipcase is empty.

Perhaps she somehow managed to make it back here to the apartment to collect the journal and has already skipped town? But she was always sentimental about her family, so why leave her photographs? Suddenly, the irrefutable absence of the journal, coupled with Mr. Holt's inevitable disappointment at Lomax's failure to find it, launches him into a frenzy. He yanks out drawers, flips the mattress, drags boxes from the closet, and tips over the desk, toppling a sewing kit and spraying needles and notions across the floor. Ignoring the clawing jolts in his back brought on by his savage actions, he pulls back a few loose pieces of wall panelling with hooked hands in case she's tucked the journal in behind.

Breathing hard, with blue sparks crackling behind his eyes and nearly unable to stand, he eventually finds his hat, takes up the empty slipcase, then locks the apartment door and limps to his car. There he opens his glove box and pulls from it the half-smoked cigar he'd brought along just in case his back acted up. But after imagining his father's meaty face sucking on his opium pipe, Lomax pitches the cigar to the pavement and drives off.

While tossing in bed that night, he worries that if the wrong person gets hold of the journal and blackmails Mr. Holt, it will be all Lomax's fault, given that the affair's concealment was his responsibility. And so he reassures himself that the search party will locate Euphemia and her baby by tomorrow afternoon at the latest, and that she quite likely has the journal with her. It will be a chilly second night for them to spend in the woods, yet not fatally so. Mr. Holt will be furious with her for running, though his relief at recovering his child will win the day. And before the dust settles, Lomax will take the journal, unite it with its slipcase, then promptly dump them both in a roaring fireplace where they belong. And this whole irritating matter will be put to rest.

BLANK

AT FIRST LIGHT, Everett scoops the child into his wool coat, cinching his belt overtop to suspend it against him, before setting out for Saint John. The baby fusses some, then goes slack after a half-mile's walk through the trees. He makes this trip as seldom as possible, and never overnight. The city always disturbs him: automobiles backfiring like German artillery; hard-browed loggers coming to blows outside taverns at midday; over-pruned trees living stunted lives on the boulevards. Usually, after trading his syrup at the general store, he'll see a moving picture. Many times he's sworn off the extravagance, yet during each visit to town he becomes fatigued by people, by their gawking and talking, and the shadowy theatre is a welcome relief, a place where people are his to examine, not the other way around.

As he walks up Broad Street, everywhere he looks seems as good a place as any to abandon the child: the crook of the dogwood near City Hall, an old crone's washbucket, a well-swept doorstep, the front seat of a polished silver automobile. But there are too many people about. Though literacy escapes him, he scans the dailies on a newsstand for images of a missing baby and finds nothing. *Nobody wants this child, you dolt*, he thinks. *It was hung in the forest to die.*

Everett walks to the Catholic Charities on Waterloo Street, where a long queue of derelicts snakes out front and down the block. It's there the nuns tell him that they don't accept orphans from men. After that, he can't just leave it on the street with so many onlookers, especially men who may recognize him. So with no other options, he veers crosstown, dodging some destitute boys hawking cigarettes rolled with aspirin and greasy napkins of roasted peas, and knocks on the door of a man familiar to him from his tramping days.

When it opens, Everett finds that Howard Blank is just as ugly as he was ten years before. Blank also served in the War, though it wasn't until after demobilization that they met, in a hobo jungle somewhere outside of Oakland. Blank had caught a squib round in the barrel of his Ross rifle during training exercises in England, and when he imprudently squeezed the trigger a second time, the gun exploded pressed tight to his cheek. He returned from the War without firing a single shot that wasn't at his own face, and the shame of it left him nasty.

"Greenwood. Pee-wee Morton said he heard you'd settled down somewhere," Blank says with a mystified expression. "Sugaring near the old Holt place. That true?"

Everett says it is.

"He also said that you turned into the kind of man that parents tell stories about to scare their children. He wasn't kidding."

"I sell Pee-wee a jug of syrup from time to time," Everett says, tugging at his tangled beard for effect.

On closer inspection, Everett notices that the years have been kind to Blank's scars, smoothed them, his bad side now more like the texture of a cucumber than the cauliflower it once was.

"Well, come on," Blank says, cuffing Everett's shoulder and pulling him inside. "In the old days you'd come knocking for one of two reasons: to bum money for whiskey, or to bum whiskey. So which is it?"

"Neither," Everett says, before sitting in a ramshackle chair worn shiny in places like a mangy deer.

"Good, because I only stock seltzer these days. So if you've a problem with that you get out right now."

"I'm all done with drinking too," Everett says, impressed that Blank has likewise managed to correct his doomed trajectory. Everett can recall mere scraps of the booze-flamed weeks he'd lodged in this house that Blank inherited from his father, an Anglican minister. Mostly, they drank and quarrelled to avoid the subject of the War.

When Blank returns with two green jars, he spies the fleshy bulb of the child's head at Everett's neckline. "What you got there?" he asks.

As they sip, Everett relates how the little curse came to him, and how he'd walked in to Saint John to be rid of it.

"You see anybody in the forest who could've left it?"

Everett shakes his head.

"Some seamstress with a flock of kids already and empty cupboards," Blank says. "Take it to the nuns. They're looking for lambs to corrupt."

"Just tried. They don't accept them from men," Everett says impatiently. With the weather warming, the sap will run any day now, and if he doesn't empty his collection buckets, they'll overflow to the ground. The first sap is always the sweetest, and just a short delay will mean half his year's income forfeited. By the time the maple branches nose with green buds, the caramel flavour will be spoiled completely. "Can you help me find a place for it?" Everett says. "I don't care where. But I need to be rid of it by tonight."

"I ain't taking it, that's for sure," Blank says. "How about that brother of yours? The lumber millionaire out West? Maybe he could?" This Blank relates with a glint of mockery, recalling to Everett's mind how cruel he so often was, how vindictive he could be with your private details.

Though he regrets much of his past, he regrets most of all that time he let slip that his estranged brother is Harris Greenwood, *the* Harris Greenwood, and that the sole person he'd shared this confidence with in his entire life was Howard Blank. "We haven't spoke for eighteen years."

"Brothers are brothers."

Everett shakes his head. "Not after what he did. Not anymore."

"What kind is it?" Blank asks.

"What do you mean what kind—"

"A boy or a girl, you lunk!"

Everett shrugs. "Don't know."

"He don't damnwell know!" Blank declares to the dingy pine ceiling.

"It's no business of mine."

"Well, if I'm going to help you, I need to know what we're deal-ing with," Blank says, extending his hands. "Come to Uncle Howie, little nipper."

Everett extracts the child from his coat and hands it off.

"Looks like a girl to me," Blank says, picking apart the cloth with his fingers. "But hooey!" he says, waving a hand at his nose. "She's made a real mess of herself. You need to bathe them, you know? Change their flannels?"

Everett shakes his head. "Not my concern."

"You'd best make it your concern. She'll be a lot harder to get rid of in this condition." Blank starts unwinding the brocade cloth, and from its folds he pulls a book. "How about this?" he says, setting the child down and flipping open the hard-backed cover. "An operator's manual?"

"What's it say?" asks Everett, sidling up beside him.

"Still an ignorant son of a bitch, huh?" says Blank, thumbing the pages. "Remember when we'd bum a few bucks for a meal and I'd have to read you some greasy dive's menu?" Everett does—and also remembers Blank once trying to charge him a dime for this service, an offer for which Everett blackened both his eyes.

Blank moves his lips while examining the words. "It's a diary, judging by the entries. Woman's penmanship."

"Will you just hurry up and say what it says?"

"She's trying to be clever, using plenty of two-dollar words." Blank taps his temple proudly with his index finger. "But I know most of them."

"You think the mother wrote it?" Everett asks.

"Looks that way."

"Any addresses? Maybe I could return the child to her."

"Nope, but hold on . . . there's a name here."

Everett follows Blank's index finger down the page, which to him is nothing more than a soup of curlicues and sticks.

"*R.J.,*" Blank says with wonder, as though invoking a bit of scripture. "You figure it could be R.J. *Holt*? That's his estate you're squatting on," he says, nodding excitedly at the baby.

"I don't care if it is," Everett says. "Whoever had it doesn't want it anymore. And neither do I."

Blank slaps the book shut and takes a long, thoughtful belt of seltzer. Everett can hear the carbonation sizzle in Blank's mouth as he makes some kind of calculation.

"Now see here, we need to consider this whole thing from multiple angles," he says with a shrewd look. "Maybe I *could* take her in, seeing how she's so abandoned and everything."

Everett's mind flashes to the time he and Blank beat a pair of wine-heads who owed them a dollar over some dice toss, kicking them until they wet themselves. Which makes Blank about as suitable to care for a child as Everett is.

"You said yourself you don't want her," Everett says, rising to his feet. "I'm going to just find the busiest corner in Saint John, plunk her down, then run like hell."

"Whoa now, you can't do that! This poor little lamb? What if a cart horse stepped on her?" Blank says. "They'd blame you."

"I'd never know. I'll be back on my sugarbush. Happy as a clam."

"Now Everett, you're just lucky you came to me when you did," Blank says warmly, clapping a hand on Everett's shoulder. "Even after the Crash, I know plenty of good folks who are looking for a healthy tyke still wet behind the ears."

TO THE TREE

BEFORE SUNRISE THE next morning, Lomax drives out to Mr. Holt's country estate to check on the search party. The game warden meets his car in the driveway with a pale, stricken expression. He's carrying an electric torch and wearing an oilskin slicker though it isn't raining.

"We discovered something in the trees," the warden says. "We were waiting for you to confirm it before we woke Mr. Holt."

Lomax follows him into the woods, a white moon singing in the dark branches. While they walk, the trunks of the trees seem to draw closer and closer together, like a herd of grazing animals facing a predator.

Soon the warden swings his light across the trees to illuminate what appears to be the form of a woman kneeling against a big maple, her arms outstretched to embrace its trunk, as though she's begging it for help. Lomax kneels beside her, in an almost identical posture, he realizes, the thawing ground dampening the knees of his trousers. She's shoeless, wearing only a nightdress. And when he draws back her pageboy haircut, he finds that animals have already been at her face. Her nose half gone. Cheeks chewed at. Eyes out. Flown away. Perhaps stashed somewhere in this same maple, watching him now. When Lomax drops his gaze, he sees rivulets of army ants marching down her arms, which are as pale as cod—and empty. The baby and the journal are nowhere in sight.

"Any sign of her child?" Lomax asks, fighting to ignore the hot bolts in his spine that will only worsen the longer he kneels.

"No. But there's a good amount of blood soaked into the ground around her," the warden says grimly. "And it appears she was crawling before she ended up at this tree. Some of our foxes must have done that to her and then carried the child off."

While the warden speaks, Lomax fits the story together in his mind: After having second thoughts about giving up her baby, Euphemia had fled the estate late the previous night. And as she ran, her bleeding returned. When she grew too weak to go on, she crawled up against this maple to gather her strength and bled out with her child against her breast.

Oh, what a curse it is to live in these wretched times, Lomax thinks, as a blade of abject sadness pierces the thick armour he's built up over the years working as Holt's collector. He feels a sudden fatherly urge to comb Euphemia's hair, to retrieve the fugitive parts of her face and reassemble them somehow. All that vivacity and intelligence—where has it gone? Into the tree? With a zap of fright, Lomax suddenly perceives this maple as a living being. A reaching, petrified soul. A witness perhaps. More alive than Euphemia or her child ever will be again.

He groans while lifting himself to his feet, feeling a shard of regret for having deliberately left his cigars at home—a few puffs would have rendered all this so much easier.

"I want the child's remains found," Lomax says.

"There'll be nothing to find," the warden says, shaking his head. "The teeth of an adult fox can grind bones. Especially small ones."

"I don't care, keep searching," Lomax says. "And if she dropped anything while she was crawling, I want it found, too. Also, do me a favour and don't tell Mr. Holt. I'll speak to him myself once I fetch the child's gifts from inside the house. We don't want to make this any worse than it needs to be."

"What a way to go," the warden says as he escorts Lomax back through the green-black woods to the house. "All alone like that."

Though Lomax agrees that this forest is indeed a lonely place, for a moment he's heartened that at least Euphemia and her child had a sturdy tree to die against. He hopes it gave them some comfort.

THE HOUSE

FROM A GROVE of stick-thin poplar, Everett scans the butter-yellow, one-storey woodframe with its cedar-shake roof gone punky, the head beam already sagging, a rotten droop to the whole affair like a scolded dog. Inside, a shape swims to and fro behind dingy chintz curtains.

"You got that child with you?" says a man's voice from behind a rattling storm door as Everett approaches.

"I do. An infant. Just a few weeks old," Everett says, guessing.

"Doesn't have fleas or a cough or nothing, does it?" the man says through the screen, with skeptical grooves carved into the forehead of an owlish face.

"She's fit as a fiddle as far as I can tell. Got a good solid wail to her, too."

The man opens the door and invites Everett inside. He's short, nearly a dwarf, his stubble is flaked with snuff, and he's wearing shabby pinstriped bedclothes. Everett draws the child from his coat and cradles it awkwardly in his arms as the man regards her dozing face.

"Look at that," he says admiringly, and his joy reassures Everett. After he'd refused Blank's offer to take the baby himself, Blank had contacted a couple he knew who'd recently lost a child while the woman was birthing it and had been wounded by the process, making another impossible.

"Go on, give it here," the little man says, extending his arms.

As Everett goes to pass her over, one of the infant's raccoon-like hands pops free and yanks at his beard. He can't avoid feeling stung by this final reproachful gesture, after all he's done for her. Immediately, the man presses the child tight to his chest as though they're old pals.

"I'm sorry for your loss, sir," Everett says, removing his hat. The floor is threaded with animal hair and peppered with grit, almost filthier than that of his shack. Hadn't Blank claimed the couple was well off?

The man mumbles something affirmative that Everett can't make out. Though he's greatly relieved to be rid of the baby, he isn't quite ready to make his exit. "Your wife ought to sew her some new suits," Everett says. "I don't think she cares for the wool one she's got. It's itching."

"Mmmhmm," the man says, kissing her downy head. "I'll take real good care of her. Clothes and food and such."

"I imagine you will," Everett says noncommittally. Then he points upward with his hat. "And your roof leaks something awful. You should fix it before this place comes down on you."

The man's eyes get hard. "Plenty of suggestions from a man who can't be bothered to keep his own child."

Everett sets his jaw and breathes hot through his nose. This is why he avoids people. "Just care for her properly," he grumbles, stifling his anger by turning to go.

"Sure, I'll care for her just fine," the man says.

"What about your wife?" Everett says, turning back. "You keep saying 'I'?"

"She'll care for her, too," he says flatly. "Hey, wait, where's the book? Blank said the baby had a book with it."

"I nearly forgot," Everett says, pulling the journal from his coat and pressing it into the man's free hand. "If an airplane wrote my name in the sky I wouldn't know," he says, intending to lighten matters. "But I imagine this will be important to her someday. It may tell her about her kin or maybe her momma."

"Every child needs a keepsake," the man says, snatching the book from Everett.

Everett avoids taking one last look before he slips from the house.

He can't set out for home in the dark so he wanders downtown and into an opulent restaurant beneath a hotel. Seated at a chestnut-panelled booth, he orders a steak and a Bavarian beer to celebrate his regained freedom. The beer is served in a fluted glass that towers over his table and embarrasses him. He accidentally orders another when he tries to wave down the waiter to ask where the outhouse is located. After ten years of teetotalling, the beer hits him fast. He sits watching the waiter lay out the twinkling silver cutlery as though the various forks and spoons are the most precious artifacts in the world.

But his meal is disturbed by thoughts of the little man and his house, which is even more dismal in retrospect. The powder of dried mud in the hall. The wallpaper dappled with mildew. The precariously saggy beams. And the man himself: callous, unkind. Why wasn't his wife there? Especially in the evening? Was she still in the hospital? You'd think there'd be some excitement, securing a new child and all? And what if, Everett muses while sawing his bleeding steak, the little man didn't intend to keep her at all? What if his true aim was to get the child for Blank, who'd then sell her back to Holt himself?

Pity is a sentiment long lost to Everett Greenwood. Extinguished by those ruined men he carried during the War, by his brother's betrayal, by the scrabbling nature of life—like a bright coin dropped into a black lake.

But here it is again, back from the muddy bottom, shining in his palm.

A CALLER

AT FIRST, LOMAX pegs the caller for a crank, telephoning him at home on his day off, forcing Lavern to rouse him from a nap on the davenport in the living room.

A baby, says the caller, who identifies himself as Howard Blank. *Maybe a month old.* Discovered in the woods by some illiterate hermit.

"What baby?" Lomax says, trying not to telegraph his shock. He squashes the receiver closer to his mouth so Lavern won't overhear.

"Don't worry, I'm already fixing to return her to Mr. Holt personally," the man says with false mournfulness. "For the reward."

"Under no circumstances will you contact my employer," Lomax growls. "And Mr. Holt has offered no reward for anything of the sort, Mr. Blank," he adds. "But tell me: Who found it again?"

"Like I said, a hermit," Blank answers. "I used to run with him after the War until we parted ways. A disturbed bastard. He taps maple trees for a living. He lives in a squatter's shack on Mr. Holt's estate. Just yesterday he found the child hanging from one of his nails." Blank then goes on to describe an area a mere mile from where Euphemia's corpse was discovered. Lomax had occasionally walked those woods before, and he dimly recalls seeing nails driven into some of the maples, which he'd thought nothing of at the time. "And now that he's come to Saint John to sell the poor child into slavery, I've arranged to relieve him of it."

"The hermit wasn't, by chance, also in possession of an object?" Lomax asks. "Perhaps discovered along with the child?"

"A journal," Blank declares proudly. "Wrapped in her blankets. It even mentions Mr. R.J. Holt in there. Seems like personal matters.

That's how I knew to call you, sir. You once collected a Holt debt from me—which I gladly paid, if you'll recall—so I just knew you'd be concerned about someone sullying your employer's good reputation. I might even remember the hermit's name, if I had a proper meal."

"You give me a name," Lomax says evenly, "and you've got yourself twenty dollars."

After miraculously summoning the name Everett Greenwood to his lips, Blank tries to chisel off another fifty by feeding Lomax some story about the hermit being the brother of the West Coast lumber tycoon Harris Greenwood, but Lomax cuts him off. One thing the years of debt collection have taught him: in their minds, these lowlifes are all inches from royalty.

"But I'll pay a hundred if you get both the child and the book to me by tomorrow afternoon," Lomax adds.

After Blank agrees to the deal, adding that he expects to have them both in his possession by this evening, Lomax retreats to his study and sits for a while with his head in his hands. He ought to telephone Mr. Holt immediately with an update, yet he knows better than to get his hopes up needlessly. Mr. Holt was devastated when Lomax informed him of the loss of his daughter this morning. So what if this turns out to be a scam? Lomax would never be forgiven.

All that day, while awaiting Blank's call, Lomax's eyes stray to the cigar box that sits on his desk, but he refuses to surrender to the temptation. His self-discipline is the only thing that's set him apart from men like his father and this Blank character and all the other addicts and lowlifes that he runs down to make his living. So Lomax sits on his thick-knuckled hands, and waits.

THE HOUSE AGAIN

THRUMMING WITH BAVARIAN pilsner, Everett is back out front of the dingy yellow house, whacking its tin door with an open palm.

"I'm sorry, but I need her back," he says when the little man comes to the door in the same filthy bedclothes, the child nowhere in view.

"I thought you didn't want her?" he says angrily.

"Still don't, but I can't leave her with you," Everett replies. Even to his own ears, his inebriated voice is distant and faint, a sailor calling out from a trawler foundering at sea. "Not without speaking with your wife. And even then I don't know."

"And what about the money Blank promised me for holding on to the baby and the book until he collects them?"

"Blank?"

"Ten even. And a jug of wine."

"Well, that's between you two," Everett says through gritted teeth. Now the infant's wail commences from somewhere deep within the house, though the chilling sound seems to originate right up close, like an icicle shoved in Everett's ear. The shock disables something in his brain, and already he's shoving the man aside and clomping down the hallway.

"You're that hermit who sugars trees," the man hisses while tailing Everett into the back room with the aggressive air of a terrier. "Blank said. Your name is Green-something or other. Greenland. Greenleaf."

Everett tracks the sound to the rear of the house, and finds her tangled in a mess of stinking blankets upon a wrought-iron bed.

He lifts the screaming baby to his chest, her face purple, her eyelids clenched as tight as clamshells. She gains an octave and Everett itches to leave except he's forgetting something. He whaps his ear with his fist. How can anyone reason things out in such pandemonium?

"Where's the book?" Everett demands, the baby now wriggling in his grip like a landed trout. The man says nothing so Everett boxes him on the side of the head. The swing surprises Everett just as much as it does its target. Not since finding his sugarbush has he struck another man. But the beer made the act easier, as did the baby's shrieking.

"I trashed it," the man says with shifty eyes, so Everett cuffs him again. "It's under the mattress," he says finally, cowering on the floor.

Everett flips the bed, pulls the book free, then pins the baby to his ribs and kicks the rear door from its flimsy leather hinges. With the book stuffed down his trousers and the child against him, he scrambles through the alley. From a window the little man is yelling for the constables, and Everett dashes through a junkyard and then some private lots. After a while he rests in some rose bushes, where he vomits steak and lager foam onto their roots. When he's done, he hears men hollering some blocks over. Frantically, he tries the doors of several automobiles until one flings open. Though he's never driven a car before, he sets the child on the rear seat and manages to depress the start pedal and the ignition button, and the engine catches. Driving without lights, fighting the steering, he bumps over curbs and rebounds off fences.

No doubt Blank was fixing to make some deal with R.J. Holt, so Everett certainly can't return home to his shack now. Probably never again. Men will be waiting. There'll be questions. And Everett would sooner steer this automobile over a sea cliff than be caged again in a prison.

When he reaches the rail yard near the port, he kills the engine and checks behind him to find the rear seat empty. For a moment, he fantasizes that the baby has opened the door, crawled out, and latched onto some other poor sap whose life needs ruining. But she's only toppled to the car's floor, and is now fast asleep. In the car's trunk he finds a good, thick-napped trapper's blanket as well as a couple of four-quart jars of blackberry preserve, one of which he empties and fills with water from a hand pump behind a filling station. After bundling the baby in the blanket, he pushes the automobile into some brush to conceal it from the road and scales the wire fence before scampering out over the gleaming tracks.

He hides behind a wintergreen shrub as stars pinprick through the blackening sky. Soon a passenger rig grinds through the yard, hooting and rumbling. It's slow enough to hop, except Everett never rides passengers. While they're faster than freights, they involve more cat-and-mouse with the crew. He's always preferred boxcars—more space, though riskier, on account of the miscreants you can get penned up alongside. And now, after the Crash, they'll be more crowded than ever.

When a freight passes, a goliath of cinder and smoke, its brakes pealing and hissing, he sprints with the baby jouncing against him, letting two coal hoppers go by before he lunges for a boxcar with its door ajar. The whistle blasts and the child bleats in fright. His final pull up into the door nearly unsockets his arms. Inside, the car is vacant, except for a pile of hay that seems halfway fresh and a bale of feed sacks. He drags the door shut, leaving a crack for air, then tucks himself and the infant into the hay. The train accelerates after clearing the yard and he's grateful for the rail's seams, the ceaseless bum-*bump*, bum-*bump*, bum-*bump* that jiggles the child's cheeks and mesmerizes her into sleep.

As a blur of hill and forest whips past the door's crack, the scent of evergreen fills the car. Everett had vowed to never jump another freight for the rest of his life. But despite his best efforts, this cursed creature has steered him back into the restless, scrounging life he thought he'd given up.

Before long the boxcar falls into absolute blackness. *What is the dark to a baby like this?* he muses. And though it always vexes him to think of his brother, he finds himself remembering how Harris's sight began to fail when he was sixteen, like a great, black wedge pounded between him and the world. He recalls Harris setting his water glass down directly into his soup, or holding the newspaper upside down, or gashing his fingers with a hatchet while chopping the kindling they sold. Over the years, Everett has spotted what he's sure is the *G* of his brother's company stencilled on towering packets of lumber riding the rails from the west, and has always felt a guarded pride at what he went on to accomplish. Yet even though the occasional fond memory can creep past his defenses, his outrage at his brother's betrayal has not given an inch over the years. And it isn't about to start any time soon.

THIS ISLAND, BURNING

THREE THOUSAND MILES to the west, just off the opposite edge of the continent, on a small and nameless forested island set like a green jewel in the sea near Vancouver, a cream-coloured Bentley carries Harris Greenwood along a rutted logging road between cloud-grazing spires of Douglas fir, none of which stab less than a hundred feet into the sky. Though it's clear and midday, Harris knows that the trees gather darkness about them, plunging the island into permanent shadow. While he's lived sightless for the last eighteen years, he still orients his face toward windows, to taste the air and to feel scraps of warm light waltz over his cheeks. Fragrances of red cedar and kelp sweep crosswise through the car as its undercarriage grinds and bangs against the rocks and roots that surface between the ruts of the road—a road that, to Harris's fury, he did not construct.

"I won't have my pocket picked by a gang of tree poachers," Harris mutters. "How long have we leased cutting rights to this island?"

"About five years or so, sir," Baumgartner replies.

"And how much have we bled out to Mr. John D. Rockefeller for the honour? All told?"

"I'd have to consult Milner, but I'd say five grand or so. Give or take."

"Yet the poachers who built this road believe they can cut my sticks while I still hold the rights to them and I won't notice?" Harris says. "Maybe they figure I won't *see* them?"

"Here's their camp," Baumgartner says, drawing the car to a halt. Probably the finest lumberman that Harris has ever known, Mort Baumgartner has stood by his side since the beginning. He and

Harris met while studying forestry at Yale, and though Harris has never actually laid eyes on him, they'd once embraced—after signing a lucrative contract with the Royal Air Force for aircraft-grade Sitka spruce—and Harris took his measure then. Short, strong, and stumpy, with a bad knee and a musky, woodsy odour that persists even after a week of supply chain meetings in Vancouver.

Harris pops his door without waiting for Baumgartner to open it, and finds the ground springy with moss, the forest pleasantly silent. "What am I looking at?" he says. "Are they MacMillan's?"

"It's like one of our setups from the old days, sir," Baumgartner answers. "Stables for oxen. Canvas shelters for the men. A cook-shack floating in the bay. Double-bitted falling axes, crosscut saws, Gilchrist jacks, and a donkey engine for dragging sticks into the water. They're just creaming off the high-value trees—some of the stumps here are as wide as supper tables. But there isn't a soul about. They must be floating a boom to the mainland today. And they are too ragtag to be MacMillan's men. Locals probably. We'll radio the Mounties from the schooner and make sure they confiscate their gear and run them off before another tree drops."

Harris shakes his head. "No need to overreact," he says, tracing the Bentley's roofline with his fingers around to where he unhitches the trunk. He feels for the slick crocodile leather of his briefcase, and from it he pulls a jar he'd had prepared, which he carries out into the trees.

Harris Greenwood is six feet tall, with wavy hair the colour of wet sand. Despite his visual limitations, he possesses a ropy, wood-cutter's physique, thanks to his stubborn insistence on chopping all the firewood required for his sprawling mansion. Now, as always when he's walking in a forest, he feels his jaw loosen, his muscles slacken, his unease dissipate, and soon his rigid stride gives over to an easy stroll. In the city, corners may strike like cobras and hard shoulders may thump him aside, but trees he can sense long before he reaches them, from the aura of quiet they emit and the way the ground rises up before them. In his boyhood, Harris and his brother, Everett, lived alone on a woodlot, selling windfall firewood and fending for themselves, and even after all these years forests remain the landscape of his most inner self.

Last night, Harris dreamed his sight had been restored, though the faces of those he encountered were blank as eggshells, all except for the single face he still knows by heart: his dead brother Everett's. During the last days of the War, Harris wrote to Everett, who was nearing the end of his deployment in France, and offered him a large stake in the then-fledgling Greenwood Timber Company. Though Everett agreed, after he shipped back to Canada he didn't return home as he'd promised. Harris was livid. He was convinced that his brother's time overseas had accustomed him to life without the burden of having to care for a blind invalid who could no longer pull his weight in the forest. And though Everett was always the least ambitious of the pair, it was clear to Harris that he now saw better prospects for himself alone. But Harris proved him wrong—him and anyone who'd ever doubted him.

Despite the betrayal, during the years of his company's post-war success, Harris hired a barrister to track his brother's whereabouts. He learned that Everett had been convicted of various offences since his return, including vagrancy, public inebriation, and petty larceny, and had done time in prisons across North America. When the frequent charges and misdemeanours halted abruptly a decade or so ago, it was the barrister's assessment that this did not signal that Everett had mended his ways, but instead indicated that Harris's wayward, illiterate, criminal brother had finally met his end. Harris viewed this outcome as a kind of mercy. It's always better for a diseased tree to be felled quickly, rather than to dwindle slowly with rot and decay.

Now Harris reaches a massive cedar—this he knows from its velvety bark and tea-sweet smell. "You asked why I insisted we bring the Bentley today," he calls back to his assistant, unscrewing the jar.

"It's because we'll need something that can get us back to the boat at a good clip." Harris douses the bark with coal oil and its fumes invade his nose. He then lobs the empty jar into the woods, where it thuds against a pillow of moss and does not break.

"If we're lucky, we might roast a few of the poaching bastards in the process," Baumgartner says cruelly.

"At the very least, I hope they're in the mood for a swim," Harris says, fishing a strike-anywhere from his coat pocket.

"Makes no difference to me, sir, but it's been a dry winter, and this island's a tinderbox," Baumgartner says. "That'll be ten thousand acres of virgin stand put to ashes."

Over his career, Harris Greenwood has overseen the clearance of over five hundred million acres of old-growth forest. Some of the thickest, tallest, most glorious trees this planet ever nurtured have toppled at his command. But in just three months his lease to this island will expire, which will likely trigger a bidding war, no doubt to be won by Harris's better-moneyed rival, H.R. MacMillan's timber syndicate. And though this waste of timber will pain him, the thought of either poachers or MacMillan logging these trees is too much for him to accept.

With a flick the match gasps. As the flame passes from warm to hot in his hand, Harris inventories all that was required to birth such a forest: whole oceans of rain and centuries of sunlight. The same sunlight that glinted upon the helmets of the Romans. The same winds that carried the first explorers to this continent. Here are trees taller than twenty-storey buildings; trees that had already attained immensity when the first printing press rolled. Baudelaire called them "living pillars of eternity" and Harris agrees. Yet ask anyone who's spent a life among them, and they'll tell you that while trees are unimpeachably impressive, they're also just weeds on poles.

"They'll grow back," Harris says, tossing the match. A bulge of heat presses against him as Baumgartner seizes his hand and pulls him toward the car. After an even bumpier ride back to the small jetty, the crew quickly loads the Bentley onto his schooner and they lift anchor.

Out on the bay, Harris reclines on the deck in his ladderback chair amid the half-wondrous, half-ghastly smell of an entire forest ablaze. He detects notes of charred moss and boiling pitch, the perfume of torched wood. Then comes the sound of fist-sized fir cones roasting like cobs of corn and the screeches of deer blundering about in the smoke, just audible over the growing crack and rumble of fire. Soon a powder-fine ash dusts his skin and he imagines the curtain of flame drawing around the island, the great dirigible of smoke and cinder wafting upward, and he wonders what it looks like. Baumgartner does his best, but like most loggers, words to him are crude tools. If only Harris had someone to properly describe this island, burning. He's sure there'd be some beauty in it.

It's something to consider. A brand-new position. A fresh pair of eyes. *A describer.* He's still mulling the notion over as his schooner pulls from the bay and the fire's deep rumble dissolves into the more general roar of the ocean.

THE HERMIT

"HE GOT SPOOKED and ran off with the baby," Howard Blank says the following afternoon, at the lunch counter that Lomax frequents despite its diluted ketchup and dish-pit coffee, which he always takes black. "But I *did* manage to secure the journal, like I promised," Blank adds, waggling his eyebrows. "Which I'll gladly return for a partial reward."

Though he's disappointed about the child eluding him, some relief settles over Lomax as Blank—a cretin with a half-demolished face that's already put him off his clubhouse sandwich—digs through his satchel to produce a hard-backed journal. As Lomax takes it in his hands, a dose of contentment spills across his chest.

But just as quickly the contentment drains away as he flips through the journal's pages, only to find a mere handful of entries, penned in a crude, mannish script, very unlike the precise penmanship that graces Euphemia's slipcase. Lomax frowns and with an open hand he clubs Blank to the restaurant's sawdusted floor and walks out.

Near dusk, Lomax drives to the Holt estate and spends hours limping through the surrounding woods. After the long car ride, he feels as though the marrow of his spine has been siphoned out and replaced with acid, so he allows himself a few good-sized puffs of a cigar, just to his ease his search. The relief is immediate. In the secluded area that Blank had described to him that afternoon, Lomax discovers a tin bucket hung by a nail, overflowing with a golden sap that drizzles onto the forest floor, yielding a thick sludge that nearly tugs the loafer from his foot.

After examining the adjacent trees for some minutes, he finds a big one with only a nail and no bucket, and figures Euphemia must have made it here just as her muscles became too starved of blood to carry her child any further. He tries to imagine how difficult it was for her to decide to bundle her baby up with the journal and leave it here, hung up high to protect it from scavenging animals, while she crawled back to the estate for help.

Lomax finds more buckets hanging not far away, and follows their trail to a well-hidden clapboard shack that skulks amid some hawthorn bushes, walled in by a copse of ash. Outside the shack a goat lies dead in its pen, its protruding tongue as pink as candy floss. Inside, Lomax discovers little human imprint: a hefty woodstove—cold; some greasy cooking utensils. An archaic flintlock rifle. Rabbit snares. Sacks of cornmeal. No journal.

Despite its poverty, Lomax feels a stitch of envy at the hermit's spare existence. Often, on days when his fatherly duties are particularly taxing, he's imagined himself disappearing into just such a quiet, wooded place, free from both debt and responsibility. No wonder Greenwood is scrambling to rid himself of the infant. Anyone living this well has no need to spoil it with parenthood. Still, the absence of clothing and money suggests he's left for good. Surely he's running by instinct, too ignorant to grasp that he hasn't done anything illegal.

Knowing he can no longer keep his employer in the dark, Lomax trudges back through the woods and drives to Mr. Holt's mansion in the city, where he finds him in his drawing room, drinking brandy and frowning at the financial papers. When Lomax tells him about a baby found in the woods by a hermit who has now very likely skipped town, Mr. Holt leaps to his feet.

"And you think this baby could be my child?"

"It could, sir. It was found on your property the morning after Euphemia went missing."

"And the journal? Does he have it?"

"That has yet to be determined. But it's been reported he does."

Now Mr. Holt reaches up to rest both of his fine-smelling hands squarely on Lomax's shoulders. "If you return them to me—my child and this journal—then the entirety of your mortgage on that nice little brick bungalow of yours will be wiped clean, Mr. Lomax. You have my word. Every penny.

"But if you fail to do so," Mr. Holt adds, brushing some invisible lint from Lomax's shoulder, "and this louse makes off with both my daughter and the material sufficient to ruin me with, then your house will be the least of what you'll lose. In fact, you'd be better off not returning to Saint John at all."

To shore up his employer's confidence, Lomax describes his plan to check train stations and flophouses down the line. The task will be made easier because he'll be seeking a single derelict with a child, surely an unusual sight. "After I locate him," Lomax says, "I'll offer a reasonable sum in exchange for the child and the journal. No need for theatrics. And certainly no need to involve the Mounties in such a sensitive matter."

Just as Lomax is preparing to leave, Mr. Holt turns to him with a frosty smile and says, "Mr. Lomax? If at any point you are faced with the choice of which to recover, the child or the book, choose the book. Is that clear?"

As the father of seven, Lomax knows that while a child's memory is an impermanent, malleable thing, paper is another story.

"Perfectly clear, sir," he says.

NO BUSINESS

SINCE HE'S STUCK with the baby—at least until he can find a semi-respectable place to rid himself of her—Everett has vowed not to speak to her directly. He applied a similar rule on his sugarbush: no talking to trees. He'd seen it in the War, men talking to things that couldn't answer back: guns, trucks, trenches, mud, even their boots—and it was always their first step down into the root cellar of madness. In Europe, with his brother—who'd always been their spokesman—absent from his side for the first time in his life, Everett found conversing with his fellow soldiers arduous, and managed to avoid them by taking odd jobs. When his superiors discovered he'd been a wood-cutter, he was tasked with replacing the rotting trench planks that kept the men raised above the fetid mud. Everett preferred this to regular soldiering, though it felt bizarre to work with wood in such a wasted, treeless landscape, with planks brought in from Scandinavia, or even Canada, because there wasn't a single living tree around for fifty miles.

After his carpentry was done, Everett volunteered as a stretcher-bearer, for which his youthful footspeed served him well. As bullets tore through the air, he'd dash out into the corpse-strewn patch that lay between them and the enemy to drag the wounded back, travois-style. After a year his regiment was transferred to the Somme. Then Vimy. Then Arleux-Fresnoy. Then Passchendaele. Each battle more gruesome and barbaric than the last. From mud as thick as suet, he pulled stray limbs dangling skeins of yellow fat and grey skin. He watched a man's head get cut clean from his neck by a blade of shrapnel the size of a garbage can lid. He saw severed hands in the mud, stiff and contorted like great alabaster spiders. It was as though the horrors he witnessed were being stored in a reservoir inside him, rising a little each day, until the reservoir was full and its poison began to seep into his bloodstream. In the War's last days, he was hospitalized for a bout of tremors and confusion that left him unable to tie his boots, and then he was shipped home.

Tonight, however, Everett sleeps untroubled and wakes in the boxcar at dawn, the baby curled in the hay beside him. They ride in silence until the train sidetracks around noon to let an express pass and an old tramp joins them in the car. He's starved and skinny, red crescents hanging below his eyes like wounds, and given his frailty Everett pays him little mind and allows himself a nap. But he wakes later to find the man gone and his right foot naked as a whelp. Though his other boot remains, its laces have been sliced through and half yanked out.

"What kind of weasel steals one boot?" Everett demands of the sleeping baby, cursing himself for breaking his rule against speaking to her.

Everett sits grumbling about his misfortune until her eyelids crack open. Immediately, the corners of her mouth bend downward and she starts up again. He unfastens her sleeper to find a foul paste rimming her flannels, accompanied by a staggering stench. With held breath, he peels the fabric back. He's never examined the female region so directly: that simultaneous absence and presence. Everett dampens a jute sack and wipes her clean as she squalls ferociously, nostrils flaring, tiny ribs heaving. With no spare flannels, he wraps her in a feed sack after shaking out the weevils, then scoops out some blackberry jam with his finger and pushes it into her mouth. Luckily, she shuts up, smacking her lips and pumping her legs like a bullfrog.

Later, when the freight grinds to a hard stop in a stretch of orchard land, he looks ahead and sees the spout of a water tower lowering to the locomotive's boiler. Any hobo knows there's always a water source near a tower, so he leaves the sleeping baby in the straw and hops down to the trackside gravel. Nearby he finds a small, purling creek that wanders through rows of white-blossomed apple trees. He submerges the soiled sleeper and flannel in the water, dragging them over the pebbly bottom, filth tumbling downstream in clots. He pins down the baby's garments with rocks to let the creek do its work, then walks upstream to replenish the jar with water.

"You have no business on my land," a voice declares suddenly from behind him. Everett whirls around to find a hefty man of about fifty, a wide straw hat over sunburned ears, a pair of thick pruning shears in his hands, the kind used for lopping large branches.

"Just washing up, sir," Everett says amiably, cursing the creek's babble for disguising the man's steps.

"Well, you're washed, so get moving."

"I'll be doing that shortly. There aren't any local statutes against cleanliness, are there?"

"No, but there are plenty against you getting back on that train over there," the man says, pointing to the tracks with his sharp shears.

"You got it wrong, sir. I came from the road," Everett says, taking the opportunity to check the train: the tower's spout is retracted but the cars remain still. "I've been hitching rides. Seeking work."

"Which way's the road, then?" the man asks.

Everett scans around for what he knows is an incriminating duration. "Over there," he says, pointing beyond the man's left shoulder.

"Then you won't mind walking *over there*, will you?" he replies.

Everett hears the distant *crunch-rasp* of the fireman's shovel, and the locomotive whistles fiercely. Fireflies of cinder and bone-white steam lift from its stack. Almost imperceptibly slow, the wheel gearing starts to move. "Okay, okay, you're right, sir," Everett says, putting up his palms. "I came on that freight. But there's something I need to retrieve from it first. Then I'll be on my way."

The man points the shears at Everett's one naked foot. "You're going to have to get a boot somewhere else."

"It isn't just my boot," he pleads. "Everything I own is on that boxcar. My bedroll, my life savings, snapshots of my family. I'll just grab them and jump off. You can watch me the whole way."

Agonizingly, the train gathers momentum and whistles again. Soon it will be about as fast as a man of Everett's age could ever hope to sprint. His mind flashes to the infant, stark naked, wrapped in a rough jute sack, about to be ferried off into a lonesome Hell of dehydration and death.

"You don't belong on that train," the man barks. "And I'm tired of you hobos shitting in our creek."

"I'll be straight with you," Everett pleads. "I've got a child over there. A baby. If you don't let me go, she'll ride off alone."

"Oh pigshit," the man snaps. "By the time I count to three you'd better make for that road," he says, edging in Everett's direction, pruning shears raised. "One . . ."

Everett feels the old poison in his bloodstream—the brutality he'd cultivated protecting himself and his brother on the schoolyard, which had further concentrated inside him while watching all those boys butchered for no reason during the War.

"Two . . ."

He rotates away from the shears, angling the man into the sun. When a full squint eclipses the man's face, Everett lunges the tip of his elbow into it. The man staggers, gore zipping from his nostrils, then drops to the creek bed as Everett breaks for the train.

While he runs there's no cover, and the sun is high and his footfalls stamp noisily on the trackside gravel and the train's crew will surely spot him. At full sprint and barely keeping pace, Everett manages to reach what he guesses is the correct boxcar and attaches himself to its iron rung just as he can run no farther. He throws his chest onto the car's wooden planks, still only half hoping to find the baby waiting for him inside.

A DESCRIBER

THE GREENWOOD TIMBER Company operates out of the east wing of Harris Greenwood's sprawling private mansion in the exclusive Shaughnessy neighbourhood of Vancouver. Harris knows that the local business community finds it eccentric that he doesn't purchase a floor of offices in a ritzy building downtown, but he prefers to keep his company and his personal life enmeshed, and he deflects any inquiries concerning the arrangement with a rehearsed joke: "Why would *I* pay for *a view*?"

At seven a.m. Harris sits at his desk and readies his mind for the day's tasks, itemizing the mill managers, timber buyers, and high-profile accounts he'll converse with today. His office is both his war room and his sanctuary, a place as familiar to him as the crooked log cabin that he and Everett built together as boys. While he's at his desk, in the midst of his steadying routine, he never falters, never bumps walls or topples shelves, never ends up calling for help like a child lost in the woods.

Harris summons Terrance Milner, his long-time clerk and accountant, a trustworthy man and steadfast wizard with figures, who proceeds to read him documents that require his signature. Long ago Harris had Baumgartner bolt an inkwell to his desk—a foot forward, a foot to the right—and Harris feels a predictable trill of gratification as he pokes his pen into the well, which is exactly where he expects it.

Beyond his desk hang the cages of three dozen exotic birds—his one enduring pleasure, excluding his routine. Milner sends off for catalogues and Harris places orders by telegram with cranky British dealers, who ship the birds back on his returning freighters. Diamond doves. Cinnamon-wing budgerigars. Bengalese finches. African silver-bills. Any client unfortunate enough to speak with Harris Greenwood during morning hours seldom hears him over the squawks and twitters of his collection. For many years, this birdsong has been enough to dispel the fits of lethargy and low mood that can sometimes seize him. Yet his current collection has afforded him decreasing pleasure in recent weeks, and to counteract this Harris makes a mental note to place a new order soon.

After he signs the day's meagre stack of shipping manifests and correspondences, he's left crestfallen by the relative emptiness of his desk. Here, purchase orders were once stacked neck-high—it seemed the whole world needed rebuilding after the War: public buildings, houses, railways, bridges. He logged his first thousand hectares by the time he was twenty-five, and earned his first million by twenty-seven. Many claimed that blindness gave him an advantage, made him shrewd and impossible to swindle, and his nose for timber became legendary.

But since the Crash has choked off all North American railway development and mining starts, including residential and commercial construction, Greenwood Timber has begun bleeding like a bow-shot deer: fifty thousand dollars monthly in operating overages, mostly due to a rapidly depreciating overstock—clear beams and boards rotting and twisting in the weather—as well as to rising labour costs, paid to men who threaten to strike every other week as though they're a bunch of wheedling toddlers. And it doesn't help that the Soviets are using what amounts to forced labour. Their prime lumber is just as good as his own: full-dimension, unlike the inch-and-a-half by three-and-a-half sticks that most producers pass off as two-by-fours.

Without newsprint and paper, Greenwood Timber would already be dead in the water. He supplies all the Canadian periodicals, and half the major U.S. book imprints. But soon he'll be forced to pulp trees that would have once served as the bones of palaces, which to a lumberman is akin to grinding up prize tenderloin for breakfast links. All so people can do pointless crosswords and read inane dime-store paperbacks.

Harris pushes through his low mood by busying himself with telegrams, letter dictations, and telephone calls, before taking his usual pheasant lunch at his desk while Milner reads him the *Globe*, which has declared that despite the Crash, the economy's fundamentals remain sound. Harris, however, needs further convincing.

"A tree will tell you everything you need to know about the variations of prosperity," Harris muses to Milner through a mouthful of pheasant. "Dark, thin rings indicate dry years. Thick rings, bountiful wet ones. And the lumberman in me suspects it may be thin rings for a while yet."

If he was smart he would have shifted to steel long ago and been done with logging altogether. Timber is a brutish business, and requires brutes to harvest it. He attended Chicago's world's fair last year, and never heard the word *lumber* spoken once—it was all alloy, glass, and plastic. Steel-girded buildings that will survive any fire or flood. While Harris had a brief opportunity years ago to buy some Bessemer steel mills from R.J. Holt of New Brunswick, he'd deemed the numbers too risky and backed out. But any man with a head on his shoulders could predict lumber's inevitable decline. "The future ain't made of no wood," he once heard a pole-jack from one of his lumber gangs declare, words that have wormed into him ever since.

At two o'clock Baumgartner knocks and Harris orders him in.

"We've received a report that a rain came and only half of that island you set on fire was burned," Baumgartner declares. "And you'll be happy to know there were no corpses to get rid of, either."

This pleases Harris. Both the rain and the lack of casualties. After his rage at the poachers had subsided, he regretted the squander of good timber. And now the island's plucky knack for survival has charmed him even further.

Harris works through supper, opting again to dine at his desk, his napkin tucked uncomfortably behind the silk Windsor knot that he refuses to loosen until he quits for the day. Just as Harris is clearing his desk and preparing to retire to his room, a telephone call comes from a sales agent who's received a cable from Japan's largest railway company.

"The word is they're sniffing around for lumber for a massive project," the agent says. "They're considering Douglas fir sleepers, and need nearly a million of them. This could be considerable, sir. Like the old days."

"Have they mentioned the Russians? Are they at the table?" Harris demands, bolting to his feet.

"They hate the Russians," the agent says. "They wouldn't buy a cord of Russian firewood if their hands were frozen to their dicks."

"And the Americans?"

"The Yanks don't have any good timber stock left. Especially not Doug fir in these quantities. They already hacked all theirs down."

Even before he hangs up, Harris's mind blazes with calculations. He'll travel to Japan himself to negotiate the deal, yet already he can sense the enormous emptiness of the ocean, the disorienting absence of his routine, and the humiliating confusions of a foreign land: unfamiliar accommodations, unfamiliar food, unfamiliar architecture, unfamiliar voices warbling in an unfamiliar tongue. He won't be able to bring his birdcages, so what if his low moods and lethargy afflict him in Japan and he can't overcome them? Once again the idea of a visual assistant returns to him. Someone to illuminate his dealings, energize his spirit, brighten his days with well-chosen words of observation, and brighten his nights with readings of the finest literature. A *describer*. At this juncture of his long, solitary life, Harris Greenwood is weary of darkness.

THE COAT PEG

WHEN THEIR TRAIN slows for a curve and whistles for the next junction, Everett spies automobiles ahead, five or six, near the tracks at the interchange, including a handful of Mounties in blood-red tunics sheltering themselves from the slanting rain under the lamplit eaves of the station. Which means that he hurt the man in the orchard even worse than he thought.

With the infant tucked into the crook of his elbow, Everett dips his chin and throws himself from the boxcar door and out into the sheets of eye-stinging rain. He takes a few strides on the wind-flattened meadow beside the tracks before tumbling into a ditch, going ass-over-head until he skids to a halt. Regaining his wits, he draws away the jute sacking to examine the child: eyes wide, a look of utter shock, one soon eclipsed by a slow-blooming grimace that commands her entire being—all while sucking a great quantity of air into her lungs.

Then it starts.

"I'm sorry, dammit," Everett growls amid the passing train's roar as he pushes into a copse of birch that runs alongside the track. He jogs and walks for half an hour, hugging the treeline, checking periodically for pursuing Mounties, the infant shrieking as though she's on fire.

When the rhythm of their march eventually settles her, he stops to get his bearings and rain funnels off his hat directly into her eye, pooling there, and she resumes wailing. Everett clears the water from her eye socket with a coal-black thumb. "Oh come on, you little bugger," he says. "You were born wetter than this."

After her baptism the baby turns sulky, her eyes slitted like a cat left lonesome for weeks. And it's only then Everett spots it: a dent, dead-centre at the apex of her fuzzy head. Horrified, he presses his thumb into the gruesome depression and finds no bone, just the throb of blood and squish of brain. He yanks back his hand and checks her pupils, but they're aiming correct and she's breathing fine. It must have happened when they tumbled in the grass. Everett curses and punches the bark of a nearby birch. In a scramble for something to soothe her, he opens his sack to find the jam jar smashed, purple paste slathering the bag's lining and the journal, its rear cover now snapped in half. He takes the book, shielding its pages from the rain with his body, and wipes the gobs of jam on his trousers.

After an hour's walk the clouds disperse, and with no sign of Mounties or the yelps of bloodhounds, he risks crossing a hayfield to approach a farmhouse. He leaves the baby out near a half-toppled fence and proceeds to the porch. Everett hasn't sought charity like this in years, and the shame of it already claws in his chest. A gangly farmer with a napkin tucked into sky-blue overalls appears, speaking French. They've ridden into Quebec, it seems, farther than he figured. When Everett communicates his willingness to work for a meal, the farmer wags his head and closes the door.

Everett takes to the farm road, listening for automobiles. When one passes he lies prone in a ditch, ready to cover the infant's mouth if need be. After more hours of walking his calves pound and he's lightheaded with thirst. The baby is crying again, and this time her face is nearly blue, her screams growing more ragged by the minute. For all he knows she's bleeding in her brain and is inches from the grave, so when he spots another farmhouse, this time he approaches with the baby hollering against him like an air raid siren. Hearing this, a woman ceases pinning sheets to a line strung between some cottonwoods next to the house and comes toward him.

"This child needs a doctor," Everett calls out. "I can't quiet her. And I think I put a hole in her head."

Calmly, the woman takes the baby from his arms to inspect it. She's wearing a cotton pinafore, neatly hand-sewn, her black hair drawn loosely back by a ribbon. He watches her kiss the fluffy down of the child's indentation.

"Is okay," she declares in a thick Québécois accent. "The head isn't fully make yet."

Relief washes over Everett. Already the woman's presence and the gentler reverberations of her voice have calmed the baby, who is driving her nose into the woman's chest and rubbing her eyes with the backs of her wrists.

"See how she root," the woman says. "Is just tired and hungry." It shames him to watch, so Everett drops his eyes. The woman follows his gaze down to his naked foot, black with soil, then invites him inside.

Her house is light-filled, well ordered, the airy kitchen's bead-board walls recently whitewashed. A wooden crucifix stands sentinel over a sturdy maple table. She sets a copper kettle on the cookplate and carries the child to the icebox. She takes out a pitcher of but-termilk and pours some into a small jug, but when she tries to feed the baby, it gets a defiant look and screams some more and won't suckle at the spout.

"She likes goat's milk?" Everett offers. "She only had it the once, but she was pleased by it. You keep any goats here?"

The woman nods, fetches a bottle of goat's milk, and refills the jug, which the child soon slurps at greedily.

When the kettle boils, the woman sets a galvanized tub on the table and adds the hot water. She peels away the jute sacking to reveal the baby has fouled itself, except the woman seems unbothered.

"This why she cry," she says, pointing to the red welts in the seams where her legs attach to her impossibly tiny body. In the tub, the woman buoys the child with one hand and scrubs with the other. Afterwards, she applies yellow suet between the baby's legs. "Should keep the rash down," she says. Then she swaddles her in a dishtowel, carries her into the adjacent bedroom, and shuts the door.

Alone in the kitchen, Everett examines the entranceway and finds no little shoes, just two pairs of shiny black loafers—one man's and one woman's—probably only worn to church. The woman is near Everett's age. There'd be a child by now if there could be.

After some minutes, the woman tiptoes from the bedroom, latching the door softly behind her while putting a single finger to her lips. She prepares him a cottage cheese sandwich and a glass of milk. The bread is seeded and soft, the curds salty and rich. Everett eats in silence and has to restrain himself from dispatching the sandwich in a single bite. Soon there's clomping on the porch and a man enters, wiping his hands with an oilcloth. He's tanned, with thick eyebrows and a lethal-looking nose, and wears the same overalls as the farmer who'd shooed Everett away. The couple speak to each other in low voices, the woman pointing with unmasked glee to the next room as the man nods seriously, with neither displeasure nor excitement.

The man shakes Everett's hand and joins him at the table. He pinches his nose between finger and thumb and offers a lengthy grace before eating in silence, occasionally refilling his and Everett's glasses with milk.

"I appreciate the meal, sir," Everett says afterwards. "I'm eager to work if you have anything that needs doing."

The woman translates and the man returns from the cellar with a pair of old toe-capped boots. Everett pushes his filthy feet inside, which knock around a little, but they'll do, and the two spend the afternoon slopping hogs and shovelling out stalls. With good food in him the work passes easily. The farm boasts thirty head of dairy cattle, goats, hogs, mules, a coop of chickens. Everett spots some sugar maples edging the pasture, over-tapped for their size, the collection buckets all hung too high, yet he holds his tongue regarding the error for fear of appearing ungrateful.

At day's end they find the woman in the porch swing, its brass chains creaking in time with the French tune she trills for the baby, which is wrapped in her lap, clutching a sock critter the woman must have stitched, and suckling from a bottle with a red rubber nipple. "From the neighbours," the woman says of the bottle. The men remove their sweat-stained hats and sit listening to her sing, as the maddening aroma of home cooking seeps through the window. After a while they retire inside and hitch their clothes over the stove to dry. Everett accepts the clean trousers and shirt the man offers, and it's while he's changing out on the covered porch that he notices it. Mounted low, beneath their coats. A single wooden peg. Set just two feet off the floor, eye-level for a small child.

Everett returns inside to find the smiling woman setting out plates of hamburger steaks, boiled vegetables, and drop biscuits. Again the man prays, this time for longer. The woman touches her penny-brown forehead to the child's ear and murmurs along. *So this is a home*, is all Everett thinks during the incomprehensible recitation.

After dinner the woman keeps the baby at her hip while she washes up one-handed, and the man invites Everett to a checkerboard. They play silently until the man speaks without lifting his eyes from the pieces: "Bap-tize?" he says, miming a sprinkling motion over his own bald spot.

"Surely is," Everett assures him while throwing the game on purpose. Afterwards, the man guides Everett upstairs to a spare room, where a nightshirt is laid out beside an old shaving kit. Everett changes and beds down, full-bellied and content, though he's unused to the sensation of the rag-stuffed mattress, which is like being swallowed by a huge, mushy mouth.

But how the baby gurgles and coos whenever the woman picks her up! And what a bountiful farm this is. The man is a trifle severe, though what does an orphan like Everett know of the ways of fathers? After an early bath and a shave tomorrow morning, he decides, he'll make this transaction easier for everyone and sneak off in the direction of the tracks.

ALL FREIGHTS

LOMAX RETURNS HOME from Mr. Holt's mansion to find Lavern asleep in the living room with the radio on. He carries her to bed, sleeps fitfully beside her, then wakes early the next morning, packs his valise, and leaves a note on the kitchen table. He's performing a crucial errand for Mr. Holt, he writes, one that could remedy all their financial woes if he succeeds. And he'll be back before the twins' birthday in a week.

He boards a first-class passenger coach bound for Montreal, a private compartment with emerald walls of crushed velvet. Normally, Mr. Holt is tight-fisted with respect to expenses, but he's offered a generous stipend as well as his personal railway and hotel account for Lomax to charge to.

He'll search Montreal first, check the rooming houses, ask around about a single man with a baby, and then improvise from there. If he'd been thinking straight, Lomax would have left at first mention of the hermit's transient past, but Howard Blank's shenanigans have cost him valuable time.

Though it's only mid-afternoon, Lomax is already exhausted and his spine is crackling with a low-wattage pain that makes it difficult to sit, so he has the porter make up his berth. He'd intended to leave the box of medicinal cigars at home, but after he learns that his cramped berth was built for a man of half his size, he's happy to note that the box found its way into his valise after all. Lomax lights up and smokes a whole cigar, blowing its sweet beige haze from the compartment window, and soon phosphorescent beetles of relief scamper through his body.

He settles into the train's gentle rocking, the unfathomable soft-
ness of the sheets cool against his skin. He closes his eyes and slips
into a memory of Euphemia: Three months pregnant, she is poised
over her roll-top desk, her short hair tucked behind her ears, writing
in her journal with that deep-diving focus that comes to her so easily.
When finally she hears him enter her apartment to bring her several
bags of books and groceries, she looks up and smiles, a bright flash
like sunlight hitting water.

"More grist for the mill," she says breezily, coming over to clear
some space on the cluttered counters for what he's brought. Her belly
is plump and rounded, forcing her back from the counter, just slightly.

After Lomax sets his delivery down, she takes up a short stack
of library books, lifts them to her nose, and inhales deeply.

"Is there any better smell than this?" she asks. "And why do you
think library books smell so completely different than the ones we
own? Do they use a different paper for them? Or is it because so
many people have touched them? Or maybe it's the smell of all
the library books on the shelves combined? Or is there some other
reason?"

Lomax says he doesn't know because he's never had a reason to
think about something like that before, which makes her laugh. She's
always finding an odd delight in the things he says—but there's never
any meanness to it, so it doesn't bother him. In fact, there's very little
that doesn't invite her curiosity, especially if it involves something
written down: odd phrasing on a food package he's brought; a poorly
worded funeral notice in one of Mr. Holt's newspapers; an advertise-
ment with curiously inserted quotation marks. There's always something to trigger her rippling laugh.

"Why don't you stick around for a while?" she says as he's preparing to go. "I'll put on some coffee. I'm going batty just sitting around
here all day with no one to talk to."

"Another time," he says.

"Why don't you ever want to stay anymore?"

"You know why," he says curtly, then tips his hat and leaves, locking the door behind him.

He opens his eyes to find the blue glim of morning filling the small window of his berth. With the cigar's help, he's managed to sleep straight through to the next day. He climbs down from the bed with no lightning sensation whatsoever in his spine, feeling better rested than he has in years. He dresses, and over breakfast he questions the train's porters and stewards about any single men travelling with an infant. Afterwards, he goes to the front of the train and asks the fireman and brakeman about a hobo with a baby. Both shake their heads. Next he checks the car's outside baggage area; tucked among the suitcases in the raw, rushing wind, he finds an old Indian man, crouched down with a worn bowler pulled low over his ears.

"I've got a question for you, fella. Earn you a nickel."

"Shoot," the man yells warily over the engine's roar.

"Say you were hopping trains, and you had a baby in tow."

"Hey, what's the big idea. I don't have no baby—"

"Just listen," Lomax interrupts. "Say you *did* have a baby with you—nobody's saying you do—but you didn't have much money, so you were train-hopping. Where would you ride? Would it be right here?"

"Well, I wouldn't ride no passenger coach."

No wonder this man is destitute, Lomax groans inwardly; his mind is about as flexible as glass. "No, I'm not being clear," Lomax adds with belittling clarity. "I'm saying *if* you were riding this train. Where would you be?"

"Like I said, I wouldn't ride this train." Fed up, Lomax grips the handle and prepares to throw the door shut. "I'd ride freight," the man says. "Boxcar, if I could find one open. Safer. Less chance of getting pinched by the bulls or dropping the little one into the rails. Plus, wood planks are much warmer for a child than an iron floor."

"And where would you go exactly?" Lomax says, grinning, hunching down to tuck a dollar into the band of the man's filthy bowler. "Riding one of those freights?"

"Toronto," he says, as though the answer is obvious. "All freights run through Toronto. Spur lines radiate out from there."

LIAM FEENEY

NORMALLY, HARRIS WOULD delegate such a task to his subordi-
nates. After all, Milner excels at identifying fools, and Baumgartner,
layabouts, while together they boast an exemplary record of fishing
industrious employees from the teeming sea of human incompetence,
a sea rising daily since the Crash. But for such a unique position, it's
imperative that Harris performs today's interviews himself, without
distraction or interference.

So far, however, the applicants have been uniformly lacklustre:
dim-witted, uninspired, charmless. Yet he retains high hopes for
the final man, recommended by one of his regional mill managers:
an Irish poet of some repute who'd come over to log the great
Canadian forests. Along with his literary aptitude, he's touted as one
of the finest tugboat pilots anywhere.

A minute before the man's arrival, Harris knocks over a drinking
glass and clips his elbow on a bookshelf that has been there for years,
blunders he attributes to too much tea at lunch, or perhaps to the
disorienting absence of his bird collection—he had Milner temporarily move the cages into the boardroom so they wouldn't hamper
the interviews.

Usually, Harris avoids face-to-face meetings with strangers. Over
the telephone or through the telegraph, people rely on neither facial
expressions nor gestures. They fill silences and choose their words
carefully. They *describe*. To Harris, meeting a stranger in person is
akin to opening a zoo cage at random. One must be ready for a tiger
or a peacock. A rabbit or a wolverine. And it's often too late in the
game before you figure out which you're dealing with.

At the appointed time, Milner escorts Liam Feeney in. They shake hands across Harris's desk. Feeney's grip is cool, the pads of his fingers thick as felt. He smells of fir pitch, skid grease, the sea, and perhaps—or is Harris's nose off?—a touch of French cologne.

"Pleased to meet you, Mr. Greenwood, sir," Feeney says. Other than his Irish accent—knife-sharp *t*s and *l*s that unfurl like a carpet from the back of the tongue—nothing seems overwhelmingly poetic about his voice. Yet it's a clean register with the resonance of an instrument that Harris can't place, a voice that could fill an entire theatre with a whisper.

Because one of the other applicants may have moved it, Harris resists gesturing to the chair while asking Mr. Feeney to take a seat. Straight away Harris leaps into an account of his impending journey to Tokyo, where he'll be negotiating a contract to supply sleepers to the largest railway company in Japan.

"This involves sea travel, naturally," Harris says. "Does that suit you, Mr. Feeney?"

"Sea travel is my specialty, sir."

"I will also be bringing along my assistant, Mr. Baumgartner," Harris goes on. "Who, in addition to being the best faller on the West Coast, is good for a crude appraisal. 'The sky is grey'; 'These trees are straight'; 'The sun is out'—that kind of thing. But what I require is a keener sensibility. Someone who recognizes subtlety, humanity, beauty"—this last word wrong-foots him and a near-cough momentarily stops his airway—"with an eye for detail. Do you figure yourself to embody these traits, Mr. Feeney?"

"On my good days, sir."

Was that flippancy? "Your primary role will be to provide me with descriptions," Harris hears himself continue. "To be my eyes. In English, I can negotiate the stripes off a zebra. But with this Japanese nonsense to contend with, I'll be lost. Translators only scratch the surface. I need someone to watch faces, track mannerisms, read situations."

"I've always been an observer, sir, since I was a boy. It's the poet's curse."

Was there a smirk to how he said that? More flippancy? Harris needs to get him talking. "Have you much experience with the blind, Mr. Feeney?"

"Not much, sir. Only the few relations who temporarily drank themselves there, I'm afraid."

"That's fine, I don't need a nanny," Harris says, comforted by the man's witticism. "You'll see I'm quite independent," he says, resisting the temptation to mention his insistence on cutting his own firewood and shaving his own face. "So perhaps a bit more about me," Harris soldiers on. "I'm a lumberman, through and through. I've no family. Neither wife nor children. No time for such frivolities. I live for my work. And my work is trees," he says, before summarizing further a few more of his accomplishments.

When he's done, Feeney makes no remark and Harris dangles over the abyss of silence, regretting bitterly the absence of his bird collection. And why is he telling this man all of this? As though *he's* the one applying for a position, and not vice versa? He's already offered up more personal detail to this stranger than he has to Baumgartner over their many years together. All this about a lack of a wife and being a "lumberman, through and through." Nonsense.

"You've family yourself?" Harris asks, clutching at the cliff's edge.

"Not to speak of, sir. An auntie back in Cork. A sister who passed before I left. That's the sum of it."

"Good, good." Why would his not having a family be good? "And so what would draw an Irish poet to the woods of Canada?"

"My homeland wasn't agreeable to me, sir: too small-minded and cloistered. And working in the forest puts you closer to the heart of things. The money beats poetry, besides," Feeney says tightly, and this time Harris can hear the smirk.

"Too true," Harris says knowingly—why is he addressing him as a fellow poet? What does Harris know of their finances? "You know, in my time studying forestry at Yale, it was said that I had a 'facile pen.' And despite my obvious limitations, I did deep readings of the classics. Does this surprise you?"

"Not in the slightest. You seem a classical type of fella."

Harris risks a gesture to his bookshelf: "I've accumulated a good collection of literature, though I find Braille cumbersome, slower-paced than the nimble mind. I prefer the music of the human voice."

"Who doesn't, sir."

"Much information is contained in the voice, Mr. Feeney; more than the vulgar import of words. There's tone, a person's background, and emotion." Another pause and Harris has no inkling whether his remarks have landed. Is he being pedantic? Of course a poet knows the subtleties of voice!

"Along with a describer," Harris continues, "I require a man who can breathe life into language. One who can hold my interest. Have you done much public reading as a poet, Mr. Feeney?"

"Here and there," he says noncommittally.

This settles it. Harris has grown sufficiently chaffed by the glibness of his tone, the lack of snap to his responses. "*Here and there?*" Harris retorts. "I asked if you've performed many public readings, Mr. Feeney."

"That's right, sir, you did. And following that, I replied 'here and there.' Glad we're all caught up."

Another toe-curling pause. Harris recalls how Everett, as a boy, met the world with a similar glibness, and how it always infuriated him. Now he draws a deep, volcanic breath. "I advise you to be careful, Mr. Feeney. Perhaps because you're an artist you think you're somehow my intellectual superior? That I'm playing the role of the crude indus-trialist, and you, the noble, carefree poet? In my experience, artists often elect to ignore the ironclad fact that without the aid of my lumber they'd be freezing in the dark with nothing to read but the anguish on their children's hypothermic faces. Shakespeare himself would've been a shivering loon writing on the walls of a damp cave with his own urine if it weren't for men like me."

Now he's certain that Feeney snickers, which half enrages him, half invites his own laughter. He *is* being over-dramatic, isn't he? 'His own *urine*'?

"Or perhaps you suspect a blind man is incapable of running an outfit like mine?" Harris asks menacingly, leaning forward, his hands pressed to his desk.

"*Outfit*, sir?" Feeney says. "Three million in annual revenue hardly qualifies you as an outfit. I'd say you're doing just fine."

Harris is so unaccustomed to being addressed with such frankness, he's nearly enjoying it. "Those are pre-Crash numbers," he says, resting back in his chair and shoving his thumbs into his armpits. "But it seems you do know a little about me after all."

"Only the important bits, sir."

"Such as?"

"Well, that you lost your sight in the War, and were decorated for your trouble."

"Outright rumour and exaggeration. Anything else?"

Another pause.

"I require honesty from my employees, Mr. Feeney."

"That you pay your oxen better than your men. Regardless of their honesty. Sir."

Harris considers firing him at once, and having Baumgartner turf him to the sidewalk on his ear. Yet it was a well-constructed jab. True in a sense. And it took panache.

"I've yet to hear an ox complain," Harris says. "Even so, I assure you, if you perform your duties to my satisfaction, you'll be well rewarded, much better than for hauling booms to my mills. Now does *that* interest you?"

"It does," Feeney says, chastened by the almighty dollar.

"That settles it, then," Harris says, clapping his hands. "But before I tender my final decision, I'd like you to select a volume from my bookshelf and read a verse of your choosing."

He hears Feeney rise and shuffle about. For a moment Harris fears he's leaving the office, until there's a leathery sigh from the chair and the sound of leafing pages. Then, without preamble, Feeney commences.

Harris identifies the verse instantly: some Tennyson, a fine and unusual choice of Tennyson. But more than the words it's the voice—a sweet, exalting instrument—that ensnares him. It's a mere cousin to the man's speaking voice, though an elevation of it. The clean tone of a stringed instrument—a cello, yes, that's it—yet more expressive, sopping with life, his vowels and consonants fitting together as neat as a joined wooden box.

Baumgartner often checks prospective lumbermen like livestock before he hires them, examining their teeth and gauging the tint of their eyes beside a sheet of white cardstock. And while Harris knows that the blind often pass their hands over a person's features to gather a sense of them, he's never performed such an imposition on anyone. It's always seemed like such a vulgar act. A groping admission of his enfeeblement. Yet for the first time in his life, Harris wishes he could feel the face of Liam Feeney, this man whom he's picked to be his describer, this bearer of a voice more arresting than anything he's ever encountered.

"You're hired," Harris says brusquely after Feeney's reading is done. "So don't you ever speak to me like that again."

A CAKE OF SOAP

HE'S HEARD IT claimed that maple syrup's minerals will grow a person's hair twice as quick, and Everett believes it. In the lavatory early the next morning, he undoes years of such growth with the woman's shears, pulling away handfuls of beard like the pelts of small critters, tossing them from the dawn-lit window for the jays to nest with. After he shaves close with a straight blade, he shears his hair tight to his neck, as it was in the 116th Canadian Infantry Battalion, then draws a bath. It's been a good decade since he's bathed anywhere but a creek, and the experience is serene, especially with his troubles so nearing their conclusion. Without a baby to hinder him, the freights will have him back in Saint John in two days, where he'll gather up his buckets and other sugaring implements and go find a place to start over. Perhaps he'll even chisel a few bucks from the couple for a rail ticket so he can ride home like an upstanding citizen.

He scrubs his body then brushes out his toenails, and has just laid a washcloth over his face and shut his eyes when a hard thump sounds on the door downstairs. The husband speaks French with other men. Two of them. Then the woman speaks. After this conversation the door closes and the couple whisper awhile. Then whisper and yell. Then yell outright. Before long the woman is gasping and crying, and the man shouts a final command that puts ripples in Everett's bathwater. Lastly, the woman clatters about the kitchen, speaking only through the rough treatment of dishes.

Everett returns to his room to find his clothes boiled and folded on the bedspread. He dresses and slips downstairs to discover his rucksack packed near the door beside the toe-capped boots the man gave him. The man stands rod-straight in the hallway, brow hardened. Beside him is his wife. "The neighbours," she says. "The same I got the bottle from. They say the Mounties search for a man with . . . a baby."

The man in the orchard must have recounted Everett's claim about his child being on the train. Either that or the Mounties pulled the soiled flannel and sleeper from the creek and pieced it together. "Now wait a minute," Everett begins, "That doesn't mean we can't—"

"You go now," the man says firmly, stepping forward.

"I packed things," the woman says. "Some food. And new flannels I stitch for . . . for her." She disappears into the bedroom while Everett laces his boots, and returns with the sleeping baby, its cheek mushed against her bicep, releasing a long dangle of drool that sparkles in the morning light. The woman passes the child over with her face averted, as though it's some gruesome accident that's best not looked at.

"I appreciate your hospitality," Everett says in the doorway. "And I'm sorry for any trouble I brought here."

The man purses his lips and nods.

"Wait," the woman says, extending her palm; in it is a cake of homemade Castile soap, scented with lavender. Years later, Everett will recall this cake of soap—along with the low-set coat peg—as among the most sorrowful sights he's witnessed. That peg. That soap, there in the woman's open palm.

He sneaks from the house and clambers back through the field, avoiding the road until he reaches the birch woods. The going is faster in daylight and he listens close for hounds, but hears only birdsong spilling through the trees and the sift of wind over grass. After a brief wait at the rail junction they catch an empty freight—until they're promptly ditched by an apologetic brakeman. They hole up to wait in an abandoned telegraph relay station, Everett nibbling at the jerked hog that the woman packed, along with two egg sandwiches and five silver dollars balled up in a pair of fresh socks, as the baby slobbers over the sock creature that the woman sewed. When the infant gets hungry, he feeds her some milk from the nippled bottle—not goat's milk but buttermilk, which the woman must have packed by accident in her hurry. But this time the baby is hungry enough to accept it, though it isn't long before she's thrown into a bout of explosive flatulence that startles her and makes her cry. "No wonder you prefer goat's milk," Everett says, smiling at the rudeness of it.

Near suppertime they jump another freight without detection. The car is half-filled with crates of flapping hens, the air swirling with motes of down, and the sulphurous stench of excrement is unpleasant, though tolerable. Everett fixes the door shut from the inside with some chicken wire so that no tramps join them. But the baby cowers whenever the hens flap and squawk, and when Everett goes to offer her the sock puppet for comfort, he realizes that in the rush to jump the train he'd forgotten it back where they'd waited.

"It's gone, little one," he says, patting the warm melon of her head. "Your puppet. Those people. That home. All of it. Gone."

She wails for hours.

THE CITY

ON MR. HOLT's dime, Harvey Lomax takes a suite on the fifteenth floor of the King Edward Hotel in Toronto, high above the wide, cobalt-blue lake. It's luxuriously outfitted, including a sitting room and a private lavatory with a clamshell tub. Typically, Lomax wouldn't dream of incurring such an expense, but Mr. Holt has assured him that he can't be expected to conduct his important search while sleeping in cramped, unwholesome quarters.

Lomax knows he'll give himself away if he's wearing his usual tailored three-piece, so he purchases some worker's dungarees and a canvas shirt from a street vendor. He pulls them on, then takes a fistful of earth from the lily bed out front of his hotel and rubs the soil over his face and clothes, drawing curious glances from the valets. Properly disguised, Lomax makes enquiries at flophouses, especially those near the rail yards. To each clerk he slips a dollar bill with the name of his hotel written on it, instructing them to keep an eye out for a derelict with a baby. "Most are running away from them," one remarks skeptically. "Not carting them along."

"That you, Everett?" Lomax says to a pram-pushing, dark-haired man of the correct height. Of all the identification gambits he's employed while collecting debts over the years, this is the most effective by a mile. Yet the man doesn't flinch, and on closer inspection, Lomax sees that his pram is full of empty tin cans and machine parts.

That night, Lomax cables Mr. Holt and regretfully informs him that his first day in Toronto has been unfruitful. His employer's reply is swift:

IVE PUT MY TRUST IN YOU MR LOMAX STOP DONT
LET ME DOWN STOP RJ

Each day, Lomax completes a circuit of hotels, flophouses, and taverns. The hours of pounding the pavement are murder on his back, and by day's end the lightning coils and snaps, nearly doubling him over on the street. To make it back to his hotel, he's forced to smoke up the last of the cigars, judiciously, taking only a few puffs at a time. Once they're gone, he's too ashamed to ask Mr. Holt to send more. So he knuckles down, buys a pair of good loafers, and soldiers on. But the city grows ever more gloomy around him: iron-clad clouds drag their grey bellies across the roofs of brick tenements; a cripple pulls himself around upon a scrap of automobile tire; a woman thrusts her head into a trash can and screams. The city is a maze of sorts, he realizes, where souls wander and collapse, damned either by something they've done or by something they're unable to do.

Each night, before soaking his ravaged muscles in the clamshell tub, he dutifully cables Holt with the same disappointing report. And although he notes a compounding curtness to his employer's replies, Lomax assures himself that with some persistence, his break will come. At the end of his first week, while Lomax is eating at a lunch counter, a Mountie who'd been schoolmates with Lavern takes the stool beside him. The Mountie mentions in passing that the brother of a senator was recently attacked by a tramp in an apple orchard in Ontario, and that the tramp claimed to have an infant in his care. "CN Rail detectives are rounding up vagrants all down the line," the Mountie says, "raiding hobo jungles, checking dive-hotel registers. A hundred bums have been dragged in. So far no baby's been found."

Lomax hurries back to his suite, where he paces the carpet. If Greenwood, the baby, or the journal are taken into custody by railroad detectives, it will be disastrous for his employer. But if the beating took place in Ontario, then that means Greenwood was indeed on his way west. So Lomax cables Mr. Holt, delicately offering up the news as a positive development, and he's relieved when Holt seems pleased. Lomax vows to triple his efforts to find Greenwood before the Mounties do.

After dinner that evening, a bellhop brings another telegram to his door:

BEEN OVR A WEEK STOP TWINS BDAY COME AND
GONE STOP HARVEY JR HAS CROUPE STOP ANGIE LOST
TWO TEETH STOP NO COINS TO PUT UNDER PILLOW
STOP OUR GEN ACCNT NEAR EMPTY STOP LOVE
LAVERN

After reading it, Lomax sends the infuriating card spinning from the high window of his suite, watching it flutter to the street like a crippled dove. It's unlike Lavern to be impatient, and this is the last thing he needs with Mr. Holt breathing down his neck for results. And besides, he knows very well there is plenty of money kicking around the house for groceries, as well as coins to put under Angie's pillow. Lavern should be grateful that their children know their father at all, not to mention the fact that they eat to their hearts' content and needn't work like Lomax did as a boy. Still, to keep the peace, he telephones down to the hotel operator and wires his wife a hundred dollars of Mr. Holt's stipend money, as well as cabling to say that he loves her and he'll likely be back home in the next few weeks. Though he's beginning to suspect that this matter may draw him farther from his beloved home than he's ever been.

THE CITY

EVEN IN THE dark, Everett knows from its particular bouquet of greenery—beech and balsam and huckleberry with a hint of white pine—that his freight train is passing near Kingston, and the wood-lot where he and his brother spent their boyhood with Mrs. Craig. And it surprises him that after all this time, he can call to mind every shade of green contained in that forest. How the stream tasted of copper and of the trees it ran through. And he wonders if Harris can still picture it himself, or if the remembrance withered away after he lost his sight, like a plant shut away in a closet. Harris's mind has probably become too clogged by greed for him to call up the chestnut that overhung the log cabin they built, the one that dropped its conkers on their tin roof, which always made them bust up laughing.

By the time the train arrives in Toronto, both the bottle of buttermilk and the egg sandwiches that the woman packed back in Quebec are gone. Everett collects the baby, leaves the boxcar, and trudges through a sprawling stockyard of steaming cattle into the city. The first two rooming houses he approaches declare full occupancy, though he suspects that the cinder burns on his coat, his raccoon mask of coal soot, and the odd, wriggling bulge at his stomach aren't helping matters. Everett ventures into a more run-down area of the city, where sun-heated trash cans stand putrefying on the sidewalks and custard-yellow undergarments flap in alleys. A trolley bangs over a puzzle-board of tracks and the baby shudders at the noise. A nightpan is dumped from above and a torrent of filth misses them narrowly.

To his eyes, the Crash has hit Toronto even harder than Saint John. It's as though an artillery shell has gone off, loaded not with gunpowder but despair and squalor. On benches and stoops, atop overcoats, waxed cardboard, and crosshatched sticks, people sleep. They wake with bird droppings blotching their coats, pavement pock-marking their cheeks, newsprint blackening their skin. Everett spots a woman no older than twenty run aground in a park—either unconscious or never to be conscious again—a dark stain blooming in her crotch, a fresh flower in the buttonhole of her lapel.

Finally, the clerk of a decrepit rooming house allows Everett to sign a fake name to the register. "No booze, no girls, no children," the man says, pointing to the sign behind him that must indicate the same. He guides Everett up to a large communal room, where a grid of thirty mattresses is arrayed on the floor. At the washbasins filthy men cup water-filled hands to their faces, making loud sputtering noises. When the clerk exits, Everett turns his back to the others at the corner basin and unwraps the baby before scrubbing her with the woman's lavender soap.

That evening, the baby nestles against him as shadowy shapes sweep in to fill every mattress, the room roiling with their animal stench and nocturnal emissions. Deep in the night, a man drags a girl to the adjacent mattress, jostling and hissing at her for an hour. Momentarily, the child wakes to the scene and Everett stops her ears with his palms until the man groans and tells the girl to leave.

Later, Everett wakes with the baby's fingernail fish-hooked painfully in his nostril. Most of the lodgers are already off begging, working, or some combination of the two. After the week's deposit on the rooming house and this morning's pint of goat's milk, the woman's silver dollars are nearly spent. Out on the street he hears a man calling from a truck with an electric megaphone: "The Holt coke mill requires fifty men in Fredericton! A buck thirty-five a day! That includes free rail transport!"

"I can't go working for that nasty old Holt, now can I?" Everett says to the child. "Seeing how he hung you out in the cold like that?"

After an hour spent hunting for work, Everett feeds the baby on a park bench where a number of unemployed men have gathered to share loose newspaper pages and scavenged cigarettes. Before long, a man riding on an inoperable Model T being pulled by a piebald mare calls from the road: "Seeking work?" None of the reclining men stir, and though Everett knows this disinterest is perhaps an ill omen, he approaches the wagon.

"I am," he says. "But I've got an infant that needs minding."

"That's fine," the man says. "I know a woman, though I expect she'll charge half the daily rate I'll give you."

"Doesn't bother me. What's the job? Freighting?" he says, gesturing at the wagon hitched to the horse-drawn car, which is constructed mostly of salvage wood banged together crudely with threepenny nails.

The man shrugs. He's portly, oily-faced, with mossy teeth and sludgy lips. His eyes are cloudy and small, and look like they've been spooned out, fried in bacon grease, then shoved back in. "There ain't never no one job," he says. "Not during hard times. We'll do a touch of everything. Some hauling. A little tinkering. Tear-downs. Build-ups. Bit of pick and shovel work. Mostly moving some shit from somewhere to somewhere else. That suit you?"

Everett hops up beside the man, who introduces himself as Sinclair Monahan. He drives the buggy to a three-storey red-brick tenement, where out front a thin Mediterranean woman of about forty kneels on a patch of grass, spoon-feeding two toddlers.

"What I call her?" the woman, Mrs. Papadopoulos, asks Everett when they've settled the terms of the baby's care.

"Call her anything you like," Everett says, climbing back onto the wagon. "Won't bother her."

"Yessir, these hard times will make a saint spit on the cross," says Everett's boss as they set off, his loose suspenders slipping from his round shoulders as he speaks. Everett ascertains early that the hardships of the age will be his primary oratorical subject. Not that he minds the chatter. He prefers someone else doing the talking, and Monahan's back is strong and he's smart with his horse and knows the city.

From behind a boathouse they load some planed boards into the wagon bed and cart them to a nearby lumberyard. Next, they haul three claw-foot tubs out of a condemned hotel, each heavy enough to flood Everett's head with sparks when they lift them. By midmorning, the clouds have burned off; the two sop their brows with their shirtsleeves and the draft horse lathers under its collar as it drags the tubs to the salvage yard. Apart from the work he did on the Frenchman's farm, Everett has been stuck playing nursemaid for too long, and he's cheered by this job's physicality. While it's not yet clear whether they're stealing, repossessing, or donating these things they're hauling, Everett knows not to ask.

"During hard times nothing is nobody's," Monahan says, as if reading his mind while sharing his onion sandwich with Everett as he drives. "Not really. Not forever."

After lunch, Monahan pilots the buggy to a foreclosed orphanage down near the western lakeshore. "Happy days are here again," he sings while they're carting out dozens of children's cots from a warren of dingy rooms. "Don't carry them too close," he says as they bump through the hallways. "Not unless you're fixing to open yourself a lice hotel."

Peering from the building's shadowy nooks are youngsters with flea bites spangling their faces, their bodies stunted by hunger. In the yard, a girl skips rope with an electrical cord; her dress is moth-eaten and there are at least four fresh-looking holes punched in her belt. Everett has always avoided children, but since finding the baby, he's been noticing when their coats are ripped at the armpits, or when their pants are more patch than pant, or when their rickets are so bad they're chewing their palms for the texture of meat.

"My stepsister works in city records," Monahan says during the ride home. "She says people aren't getting married since the Crash. No new licenses. Even fewer birth certificates. The future's only going to be dust and scarcity from here on out, and don't people know it. I've no idea why anyone would procreate during times like these, no offence."

"None taken," Everett says.

"And who can blame them? See those banks over there? Empty. Every one. Not an ounce of bullion to be found. No sir, I bury my money. Got a fine spot for it. You'll bury yours, too, if you're smart."

When the day is through, Monahan returns Everett to Mrs. Papadopoulos and the baby doesn't cry when he takes her up. During her bath in the washbasin later, he checks her milky body for chigger bites or bruises and finds neither. After supper, with the money he earned he buys himself a work shirt and some copper-riveted trousers, as well as a new creeper in blue, because pink will soil too easily, and two more flannels so he doesn't have to wash daily. After working with Monahan for a week, Everett purchases some horsehide gloves and a suitcase that he keeps packed in case the Mounties come knocking and they need to skip town in a hurry.

Each day, Monahan's jobs grow more and more obviously illegal. They cut a crude tap into a city gas line, then hook it up to the cookstove of an old drunk with a lacework of busted capillaries in his nose. They wire around the electricity meter for a Negro family of ten, all with grey teeth that look like things pulled from a fire, the little girls in flour-sack dresses, their shack so small they must sleep in shifts because there isn't floor enough for all of them to lie down at once.

In the park after quitting time, and after the baby's had its goat's milk and Everett eats his ham sandwich and his apple, he heeds Monahan's advice and wraps both his savings and the journal up in an oilcloth and buries them at the root of a wide-spreading magnolia. Back at the rooming house, other lodgers have noticed the child but keep it to themselves, given that she never cries or fusses. After she's asleep, Everett scrubs her flannels in the sink and hangs them to dry from a line over the alley before lying down beside her, the bed surprisingly warmed, the baby like a fresh loaf of bread that never cools.

Though the child has grown on him, he doubts he can maintain this caretaking much longer, and his new plan is to sock away enough money to pay Mrs. Papadopoulos to accept her outright. After he works a little more, he'll purchase new spiles and buckets, then go hunt out another sugarbush somewhere on the city's outskirts and start over. If there's anything that the Dominion of Canada has, it's an endless supply of trees that nobody's using—that is, if his brother doesn't cut them all down first.

Everett works another week until Monahan gives him Sunday off while his carthorse is being shod. He considers taking the baby to a moving picture, then worries the phantasmal screen will frighten her. Instead he cuts over to a duck pond in a nearby park, where he tears some of the last blossoms from a cherry tree and brushes them along her cheek. Her eyes track the swallows darting through the canopy, and she points at the ducks that patrol the pond and squeals.

Who knows, once she's living with Mrs. Papadopoulos and he's established his new sugarbush, there might even be some money left over for her education. He could be her benefactor of sorts. Like in some old story. Money was never much use to Everett anyway. And since she seems to like natural things so much, perhaps he'll visit occasionally and take her to this park to smell the blossoms and chase around the ducks. She may even grow into a person of value, of refinement and intelligence and dignity. Just the kind he isn't.

THE LEAST OF
WHAT YOU'LL LOSE

LOMAX CIRCUMNAVIGATES HIS room, bedevilled by a restless agitation, the muscles in his back tugging like a ship's rigging in a storm, as the breakers of a headache crash against the shore of his skull. He's been checking in with the Mountie who eats his lunch at the same counter each day, and, thankfully, the vagrant with the baby has yet to be captured. But in yesterday's cable, Mr. Holt remarked upon Lomax's mounting hotel bill, suggesting he move to a less extravagant room in the same hotel. Another sign of his displeasure with Lomax's failure to locate the child or the journal, especially after he'd been so confident the matter could be resolved quickly.

Your house will be the least of what you'll lose, his employer had said. And Lomax shudders now to contemplate what his threat actually portends. If Mr. Holt called in the mortgage on Lomax's bungalow, his whole family would be tossed out and condemned to the poorhouse—an outcome nearly too catastrophic to contemplate.

And now Lavern has requested more grocery money, and Lomax is nearing the end of his stipend and can't possibly ask Mr. Holt for another. Lomax feels a sudden constriction in his chest and worries that he might weep. He hasn't done that since his father left. But over the course of his long, pain-ridden life, he's learned that if one were to give over to weeping, there'd be only tears. Seas of them. And seas of tears will neither complete his task nor secure his family's safety. Instead he draws a hot bath, which does nothing to ease his back or quell his mental agitation. Angrily, he dresses and leaves his hotel to patrol the sidewalks, eyeing faces, watching for single men with babies, the same mind-numbing task that's occupied him now for weeks. When the lightning in his spine stalls him out front of a Chinese laundry, he locks eyes with a skinny man clearing the sidewalk of litter with a wood-tined rake. The man flicks his head toward the alley, and in some deep region of his mind, Lomax registers his meaning. He follows him around the corner, where the man holds out his palm. When Lomax passes him some money, the man fetches a small, butcher-wrapped package from the hollow of a nearby drain.

Lomax can't suffer the miserable march back to his hotel without some relief, so he ducks into another alley, this one next to a flophouse he's already checked countless times. Not without some shame, Lomax twists the tobacco from the tip of one of his Parliaments and crams into the hole a kernel of the oily opium he's just bought, an operation learned while watching his father during his rare visits home. Lomax lights it and inhales lily, licorice, and creosote, his every capillary extending its arms for the restoring smoke. He fights against exhalation for as long as possible, while divine chimes peal in his ears and his spine sluices with gratification. This opium is twice as potent as the doctor's cigars, leading Lomax to wonder whether the drug's power will only grow the farther west he ventures—which might then be the sole consolation of this so-far disastrous expedition. He finishes the cigarette, his entire body softened like butter in a pan, and the urge to recline overcomes him. He spies some relatively puffy bales of trash and curls into them, his blood purring.

An uncountable duration of time passes before the softened sensation crests and begins to fade. As it does, Lomax opens his eyes to a curious sight: a white cotton bird soaring against the alley's cloudy sky. Dangling from a wash line in the foul breeze, puffing, contracting, nearly breathing. And despite his initial bewilderment, Harvey Lomax recognizes this bit of cloth for exactly what it is. He ought to. As the father of seven, he's been changing flannels for what seems like his entire life. And while he's spotted numerous flannels hung from laundry lines throughout the city, none were outside the window of a skid-row flophouse.

THE RAILWAY
COMMAND GROUP

AS THE TRANSPACIFIC steamer *Empress of Australia* departs from Victoria, Harris takes great care in unpacking his dressing case, arranging his effects, and memorizing his stateroom's unfamiliar contours. When everything is to his satisfaction, he dons his finest silk jacket and dismisses Baumgartner, who seems surprised and even perhaps a little affronted as he goes off in search of a bridge game. Harris then summons Feeney to accompany him to the steamer's topmost deck, where he leans at the rail and takes several salty draughts into his lungs. "All right, poet," he says. "What am I looking at?"

"The Olympic Peninsula, sir," Feeney replies. "A wall of hemlock, cedar, and the odd madrone. And there's a fine stand of second-growth fir, all good and straight, but too young to cut. Beneath them is a rocky shore, graded well to drag the logs into the water."

"Oh, come on, man!" Harris says. "If I want a logger's take I'd have asked Baumgartner up here with me."

Because of Feeney's quip about Greenwood Timber's habit of paying its oxen better than its men, Harris made a point to offer him an initial salary double that of Baumgartner's. "I'll never publish another poem again in my life," Feeney said after they inked the agreement. Yet now Harris worries that he's overestimated the man's value.

Feeney laughs. "Fine, keep your knickers on!" he says. "I must say I've never been *paid* to be a poet. Which is a tremendous sacrilege in itself, I might add. But I'll have a go."

Harris waits in anticipation, and overtop of the steamer's great chuffing he hears his describer draw a breath. "Fog seeps between the brindle stalks," Feeney begins, "and the sun, hooded with sea-borne mist, burns among the striving arms of branches . . ."

In Harris's mind a vivid panorama assembles, accompanied by an overwhelming sense of relaxation. Of goodness, rightness, and exactness. For the remainder of their voyage to Japan, Harris has Feeney conjure more of these seascape descriptions—"my postcards," Feeney calls them—at set intervals throughout the day. Though the poet's usage is at times a touch overblown, Harris enjoys himself all the same.

It's six days to Yokohama, then another day to Tokyo, during which they're driven below deck by a sleet-smattering gale. They pass the time with readings of Wordsworth and Yeats—both Feeney's suggestions. Harris prefers poetry above all else, for how it sets like concrete in his mind, as opposed to the short-acting fireworks of the novel, long, agonizing yarns concerning people and families he'll never know.

From the Tokyo wharf, they're escorted by a profusely apologetic government agent to what he says are merely their temporary accommodations while their proper accommodations are readied. Feeney describes the guesthouse as a low-lying house that sits next to a bog. A curious supper of sea creatures is served along with much bell-ringing and burning of acrid incense.

Harris wakes in the middle of the night to the stirring of the paper walls by the breeze. He can hear Baumgartner's grizzly bear-like snoring somewhere nearby, but also Feeney's soft inhalations in the room immediately adjacent. With some shock and revulsion, Harris realizes that they're all separated, essentially, by nothing.

There once was a pair of swampers employed at one of his logging camps who were discovered one morning naked and whiskeyed-up in each other's arms beneath an overturned skiff. The other loggers beat them with the butts of their axes and trampled their naked flesh with spiked boots. With some glee, Baumgartner had informed

Harris that the bodies were dumped out in the cuts, while the Mounties were told that the men had gotten drunk and wandered off. Though the event revolted him, Harris knew better than to interfere with logging camp justice.

But here in Japan, Harris reminds himself, this thin sheet of paper is defined as a wall, legally speaking. And no one could possibly deem it indecent for one man to hear another man breathing in his sleep through a wall. Relieved, Harris puts his pillow over his head and rolls over.

In the morning, Harris, Baumgartner, and Feeney are brought to the Imperial Palace, where they wait in the garden. It's here they learn that the meeting isn't with a private railway company at all, but rather the Japanese High Command. After an hour of idling, Harris's mounting frustration quelled only by Feeney's detailed account of the garden's exotic birds, they're led to the negotiating room. Feeney describes a vaulted chamber of clear beams, all fit without nails. It's Harris's experience that the Japs know timber better than anyone. He sold them boatloads after their earthquake in '23, and they're always first to snap up his best quarter-sawn logs. A translator introduces twelve uniformed men as the Railway Command Group, and they all kneel at a low table, which Feeney says has a sword placed at its centre.

"What kind of sword?" Harris says from the side of his mouth.

"Ceremonial," Feeney replies. "Blunt as a tin can."

"I should've brought my ceremonial rifle," Baumgartner grunts as he squats uncomfortably on his bad knee. Though he's never cared for international travel, Baumgartner is particularly ornery this morning, and has been since they left Vancouver.

"Do they seem ready to give us their money?" Harris whispers to Feeney.

Feeney puts his mouth near Harris's ear, which electrocutes something in his stomach: "Not quite."

There's much introduction and ceremony, including recurring talk of the "Emperor's will" and more bell ringing and tea that tastes of sodden pine. By the time they break for lunch, the negotiations haven't even reached preliminary stages, and Harris's legs are completely numb, and Baumgartner's knee has seized so badly they've fetched him a cot to lie down in. After they eat, maps, plans, and technical drawings are brought forth, which Feeney does his best to describe. Engineers come forward with complex inquiries about wood species and their deflection ratings. Through the translator, Harris does his best to allay their skepticism concerning the use of Douglas fir for railway sleepers, extolling the tree's sturdiness and rot-resistance, assuring them that Canada's own Board of Railway Commissioners chose it for their continent-spanning line for good reason.

After five days of deadened legs and bizarre lunches of sea urchins and fish roe, which Baumgartner refuses to eat, it's related by an agent that the Railway Command Group doesn't actually have purchase authority for the newly nationalized railroad, and that the real negotiations will begin with the Imperial Railway Purchasing Group the following day. Baumgartner nearly strangles the man and has to be restrained. To keep a lid on things, Harris asks his gruff assistant to return home to Vancouver to settle a labour dispute that's cropped up at their Chemainus mill. It isn't until Harris tells Baumgartner that his strong hand is the only thing that can resolve the matter that he agrees to go.

The morning he departs, Baumgartner suggests that because the Japanese are most likely using the paper-walled guesthouse to listen in on their conversations, Harris should leave immediately and move into the Imperial Hotel. "And don't scrimp, Mr. Greenwood," he says insistently. "Make sure you get two suites. One for you, and one for Mr. Feeney. I'm going to call them now to ensure they accommodate you properly."

"A fine suggestion, Mort," Harris replies, roughly slapping Baumgartner's back. "Two suites it is."

When they arrive at the Imperial Hotel that evening, Harris, still a bit puzzled by Baumgartner's odd parting request, skips his nightly poetry reading and elects to eat alone in his suite, leaving Mr. Feeney to fend for himself.

A FLANNEL

LOMAX RISES FROM the trash heap, brushes away any refuse sticking to his trousers, and rechecks the sky for what was indeed no phantom: a baby's flannel hung high in the alley's foul air.

His spirit quickened, Lomax slaps his cheeks and drags his fingers through his oiled hair, then he enters the building to which the line is attached. This time he pays the clerk to escort him upstairs to a single mattress that smells of sour cream. Since the large room has no chairs, Lomax sits on the mattress with his back to the wall and waits, smoking Parliaments, reading scraps of yesterday's *Star*. But none of the men who enter match Greenwood's description. Too derelict. Too young. Too old. Too destroyed. Too blonde. Not woodsy enough for a hermit. Then, after a few hours: a lean, hard-looking man of about the correct age, though he's beardless with close-cropped, dark hair. Lomax watches him draw some horsehide gloves from a suitcase, stuff them in his back pocket, then go to the window on the opposite side of the room, where he reels in the flannel and begins folding it with the care of a housewife.

"Everett, that you?" Lomax calls out warmly.

Though Lomax could swear there's a tremor in his cheek and a subtle stiffening of his composure, the man continues folding.

"I said that you, Everett?"

"You've got the wrong fella," the man says, tucking the folded flannel into the suitcase without glancing over.

"My mistake, friend," Lomax says. Then, so as not to appear over-eager, he lights another Parliament and takes a long inhalation. "See, I've got an old War buddy named Everett Greenwood," he begins.

"We go way back. And you know he's your spitting image? The thing is, he's recently been placed in a tight spot. He had a child fall into his custody, for which I don't imagine he was prepared. To his credit, he's managed quite well so far—"

"I got no idea what you're talking about, mister," the man interrupts.

"Oh yeah, then what's with that flannel?"

"I'm washing it for a girl I'm sweet on."

"That's real friendly of you," Lomax says, realizing that the man is now loading the last of his few belongings into the suitcase. "But this girl of yours," he adds delicately, "she *does* have an infant in her care? Does she not?"

The man hesitates. "She does," he says carefully. "She takes fine care of it, too, despite everything she's facing."

"Well, I work for a powerful man who wants to express his deep gratitude to your girl. And he's eager to relieve her of her burden. Which could include a patch of woods where a quaint little shack was accidentally constructed on his property. I have his assurance that the land could be made available in perpetuity, as well as a tidy sum of money. Especially if a journal were also recovered." Lomax notices the man's jaw tighten at the journal's mention.

"What would become of the baby," the man says measuredly, "supposing all this played out like you said?"

It's him and he still has it, Lomax thinks, and his pulse jumps like a cricket. He considers lunging to his feet to take a run at him, but Greenwood is far across the room and there's a good chance Lomax's back will seize up. Besides, Greenwood seems amenable to a deal, which is always the quietest way to do things. "I would personally see her returned to her safe and rightful home," Lomax says.

"Her mother?"

"Sir," Lomax says, putting his hand over his heart. "I'm sorry to report that she's deceased. An unfortunate accident. All the more reason for her father to want the baby home. He's just sick over the whole thing, and he's eager to put it behind them."

"The same father that was looking out for her when she got lost? The one who allowed her to end up with some stranger?" Greenwood says sharply. He buckles his suitcase, hefts it, and darts across the room to the door.

"Things can get real mixed up following a birth," Lomax says, trying to buy time as he strains to heave his great body upright. "People aren't always themselves."

Greenwood pushes open the door. He's twenty paces away and light on his feet. There's no way Lomax can catch him now. Especially not chasing him down three flights of stairs.

"Be sensible, Everett," Lomax says in his warmest tone. "With the Mounties hunting you for that man you beat, this is the only chance you'll get to slip away to some quiet place where no one will bother you again. My employer Mr. Holt feels no need to involve the authorities. He simply wants his lost child returned."

"A little girl ain't no ring of keys that gets lost, mister," Greenwood retorts, preparing to step through the door. "Seems like a hard thing to misplace, especially if you aren't trying to. Someone hung that baby from one of my tapping nails on purpose. At first I thought they wanted to be rid of her. But now I figure they were trying to protect her. And after meeting you, I suspect they'd good reason to."

"Don't throw away your entire life over this!" Lomax roars, trying to frighten him, anything to keep him in the room.

"You're mistaken there," Greenwood says, unfazed. "Because there was nothing to throw away to begin with."

YOUR LITTLE HELL

"IN YOUR VIEW, Mr. Greenwood, how do you see this arrangement playing out?" asks the chairman of the Imperial Railway Purchasing Group, by way of the translator.

"Frankly, sir, Mr. Greenwood doesn't have *a view*," Feeney remarks with thorny frustration. "But what he *does* have is trees. Trees that he'd like to cut up into neat little strips and sell to you at a fair market price, so you can go and build your Emperor's little toy railroad."

With Baumgartner back in Vancouver, Feeney has expanded his role beyond Harris's describer into more of a co-negotiator, and so far he's done well at curtailing the irreverent candour he displayed during his job interview. But clearly his restraint is beginning to fray.

Now the chairman himself replies in crisply spoken English: "It is the Emperor's wish that we proceed according to the guidelines—"

"Why don't you tell your Emperor," Feeney says, "to stop all his wishing and pull a reasonable per-foot price out of his—"

"That's enough, Liam," Harris interjects.

Feeney is clearly overstepping—Baumgartner was never so bold—but it cheers Harris to have someone battling at his side, the way he and Everett used to throw their fists while standing back to back in the schoolyard when the other boys teased them for being orphans.

"Look, can someone please explain to me what it is we're doing here?" Harris asks the room. "My lumber crews are at the ready. The saws of my mills are spinning. I'm fixed to deliver you these sleepers. And all you want to do is hide behind your translators and ring your bells. Why don't you go cut down your own trees and save us all this trouble? You have a garden outside that is full of them!"

"Our trees are sacred to us, Mr. Greenwood," the Chairman says.

"Our trees are sacred to us, too, sir," Harris replies. "We just have a billion more of them than you do. So all I need is your fucking per-foot price."

"Mr. Greenwood," the Chairman says in a flustered tone, "perhaps in your rough country it is customary to speak this way to—"

"Gentlemen! It's nearly lunch, and you all look famished," Feeney interrupts, before dragging Harris from the room, past the dining area, out through the main palace doors, and into the ornamental garden.

"I'm sorry for losing my cool in there, Harris, but I hate the belittling tone they take with you," Feeney says as they walk. Sometime after Baumgartner's departure, Feeney started calling Harris by his Christian name, and Harris has yet to correct him.

"And I'm still unsure if it's in our best interests to go through with this deal," Feeney continues. "Japan has invaded Manchuria and withdrawn from the League of Nations. They talk about this Hirohito as though he's Jesus Christ's older brother, and you couldn't throw a baseball into the harbour right now without hitting a warship. Looks to me like they're itching for a fight. Guess who with?"

Harris shakes his head. "We can't walk away now, Liam. This is too important. If they buy our lumber, they can do whatever the hell they like."

That evening, at the bar of the Imperial Hotel, Harris strikes up a conversation with a man from the Ford Motor Company. When Harris relates his negotiating troubles, the man says: "They gave you the whole guest house-and-translator routine, huh? You just need to shove a hot poker up their asses. It's the only play they respect."

The following morning Harris cables the Imperial Railway Purchasing Group, claiming that the Indian government has ordered a significant number of railway sleepers and he needs Japan's answer by noon or he'll sell his timber to India instead. An hour later, an agent arrives at their hotel with a draft purchase agreement for three shiploads of sleepers, at a board-foot price better than expected. The Imperial Railway Purchasing Group will pay ten per cent up front, and the remaining ninety upon delivery.

To celebrate, Harris and Feeney share an opulent meal of various creatures plucked from the sea, a cuisine which both have come to enjoy. "It's zippy, tastes of licorice and camphor," Harris says of the warmed liquor they bring to the table. Amid the afterglow of their monumental agreement, one that will cement Greenwood Timber's long-term prosperity, this sake tastes to Harris like the distilled nectar of victory.

Following dinner, partly out of the silliness imparted by the drink and partly out of his compulsion to test Feeney's skills of description, Harris expresses his desire to "view" a Japanese film. They find a theatre and sit elbow-to-elbow in the dark to the clatter of the projector. Even after weeks abroad, the scent of the forest—fir sap and cedar tannin—still clings to Feeney, and suddenly, sorrowfully, Harris yearns for the early days of his career when he oversaw his sawmills personally, cruising the woodlands of North America for new timber. How did he wind up craving his office routine and the confinement of a desk, he wonders, caged there like one of his birds?

Despite his scant grasp of Japanese, Feeney does his best to describe the samurai story, a talkie, paying particular attention to the lead actor's face: "Like the expressions of an entire troupe of actors," he says, "melted down then re-formed into one man." As the film nears completion, amid the blare of trumpets, the deafening clash of swords, and the guttural battlefield grunts, Feeney's mouth draws nearer and nearer to Harris's ear.

"You never said whether he's handsome," Harris says in a low voice.

"Who?" Feeney asks.

"This samurai fellow. The lead man. The one you mentioned." Harris clears his throat. "In a universal way, of course?"

A pause. Harris worries Feeney didn't hear him and decides he won't repeat himself if he didn't.

"Well, yes," Feeney says. "He is. Quite."

"And me?" Harris says, nearly inaudibly, keenly aware of his inebriation yet allowing its belligerent momentum to carry him.

"Sorry?"

"Handsome, would you say? In the same fashion? If I were up on the same screen?"

"Of course, these things are subjective," Feeney answers.

"Of course. Quite correct. A silly question," Harris says, his face heating like a woodstove. "Disregard it."

"And besides, I'm unsure you want me to say."

"Think no more of it. A misfired joke."

Suddenly, Harris feels his breath in his ear. "Yes," Feeney says. "You are. Profoundly so."

Without turning from the screen, Harris reaches over to feel Feeney's unshaven cheek with his palm, finally allowing himself to take the measure of its shape—though he's instantly petrified by how improper this gesture may appear to those in the theatre, even after he reminds himself that they're all foreigners, with no power to wield over him.

"You as well," Harris says, drawing his hand back. "Universally so."

"If you must know," Feeney says. "Like all true poets, I'm ugly as a pug. But thank you."

"I apologize for the intrusion," Harris blurts, horrified as much by his impulsivity as by the odd riptide of sensations crashing around inside him. "I have a hell in me. A little hell. I hide it. But when I take alcohol, it rises up."

"Oh, don't be so hard on it," Feeney says, patting Harris's trembling knee. "Your little hell." Then he collects Harris's damp hand in his own. "We may need it."

THE BIG MAN

WHEN EVERETT HAD returned to the rooming house to fetch his horsehide gloves, he'd noticed the unfamiliar lodger smoking on one of the mattresses. Initially, he thought against collecting the flannel with the stranger present; but it was threatening rain, and the big man's clothes were sheened with filth and he seemed too haggard for a Mountie. But he was Holt's man, no question. Though he'd remained polite, there was a dangerous note in his voice, and a grim menace coiled in his colossal body, his hands like sledges riveted to his arms, surely enough to ragdoll Everett around if he ever caught ahold of him. Just the way he spoke of the child and the journal was chilling. And his pinpricked pupils—as though the man had spent the past week staring into the sun—and his burnt voice. *Demonic*. There's no other word for it. He intends her harm, Everett can feel it.

After he and Monahan quit for the day, Everett retrieves the baby from Mrs. Papadopoulos and rents them a new private room, for which he's gouged more than triple his previous nightly lodgings. That evening, with streetcars rattling the room's thin windows, it requires hours of rocking and fourteen limericks to convince the child to even lay down her head, which she's recently started lifting. Once she's finally out, he transfers her to an ersatz bassinet he's made on the floor and trudges to his old rooming house, hat pulled low. At the desk, the clerk, a bald man with misaligned eyes, passes him a message.

"You mind reading it for me, sir?" Everett says, thumbing a shiny nickel onto the desk. "I've misplaced my spectacles."

The clerk frowns, unfolds the paper, and raises his glasses on a stick:

Everett, it isn't safe riding freights or staying in dives like this with a little baby. She isn't yours and you don't want her. We just need to talk this through. We want the book AND the child. No need for the law. If you knew me you'd know I won't let you go. Not ever.

– Harvey Lomax

"Are you thick?" the clerk sneers, scooping Everett's nickel into his vest pocket. "No children allowed."

"Fine, fine, we're already gone anyway," Everett says. "But I paid up for a week. So I'll have that back."

"If you could damn well read you'd know what this says, wouldn't you?" the clerk says, pointing with his glasses to the sign behind him.

Everett keeps his eyes trained on the man. "I can read it fine. It says you'd be wise to return my money and mind your business."

"No—" the clerk snarls, banging out the syllables with his fist. "*Chil*–dren!"

"I didn't have a damn child!" Everett yells back. "It was an infant that didn't cause anybody a stitch of trouble!"

The clerk's eyes narrow. "Infants *are* children, you son of a bitch."

"Now, if your sign said *No Infants*, that'd be a different story," Everett says. "But it doesn't, does it?"

The clerk starts groping beneath the desk, probably for a club or a pistol. Everett feels the old poison in his blood cry out to slug him, but that would only land him back in a penitentiary and maroon the baby in that dingy room, so he makes his exit. He cuts through a lightless graveyard to ensure Lomax isn't trailing him and returns to find the child asleep, the room stagnant with her breath.

Everett sticks to his savings plan and works into mid-June, always careful to wear his hat low when he's out on the freight wagon because he knows Lomax is still hunting him. But the added cost of the new room combined with the child-minding means Everett is socking away just two bits for a full day's labour. And maybe it's the rattling windows, or the lack of snoring drunks, but the baby combats sleep in their new lodgings as one would drowning. After many nights of this, Monahan gives him a rum-soaked rag for her to suckle before bed, which does the trick, though she's sluggish in the morning, so Everett quits the practice. When he waters down her goat's milk to pinch pennies, she stops taking the nippled bottle altogether, and cries until she vomits across her blankets.

"Quit your snivelling!" he yells at her contorted face. "I'm doing my best!" Half-mad with sleeplessness, he carts her out into the cool night air for a walk, letting her wail in his arms, Lomax be damned.

"No mistaking that sound," a woman in tight satin slacks and high heels says from under an awning as he passes. Her short curls are lacquered to her cheeks and pencil lines are drawn where her eyebrows once grew.

"She won't take the bottle anymore," Everett confesses.

The woman steps closer to scrutinize the child. Her eyelashes appear to be dipped in crude oil. "Feed her myself for a dollar," she says.

It takes a moment for Everett to grasp her proposal. "Will that settle her?"

"No guarantees," she says. "It might. They all give up sometime, in my experience. Better sooner than later."

Everett agrees and follows her up some stairs to a bare-walled room, where the only traces of domesticity are a chair, a table, and a naked light bulb dangling above an old bedroll. Beside a basin on the floor is a large rubber-bulbed syringe. The woman perches in the chair and takes the infant in her arms, cooing to it softly. She scoops a hand into her brassiere to free her breast, which is large and under-painted with blue veinwork. Everett's face grows hot.

"You going to just stand there and gawk?" she says, folding her plum-coloured nipple in half and pressing it into the child's tiny mouth.

"I'm sorry," he says meekly, turning away. "How will I know you're feeding her?"

"I grew six babies this way," she says. "It's impossible for me not to. But if you're watching, that'll be double."

Everett goes into the hall and waits uncomfortably, until the woman emerges and passes him the infant, now comatose, her breath sweet as honey. That night she sleeps more soundly than ever, and wakes as cheerful as a puppy.

For the next several weeks, even though Everett and Monahan work into the evening hours, his wages still can't cover the child-minding, the private room, and a nightly feeding from the street-walker. "How am I going to be your benefactor if I don't have anything to benefit you with?" he asks the baby over their dinner of boiled oats.

By the first of August, Everett is forced to dig up what's left of his savings. And although he promised the child that their days on the rails were over, and it pains him not to thank Monahan for taking him on, Everett walks to the rail yard with a pack of meagre provisions and a woollen blanket draped over his shoulders. His only comfort is the notion that despite Harvey Lomax's threat—*I won't let you go. Not ever*—he will eventually relent. Because if there's anything that Everett Greenwood has always excelled at, it's his ability to go deeper into the gutter than anyone else will go.

PERHAPS A RELATION?

AT THE REFERENCE desk of the Archives of Canada, Lomax requests the military records of Everett Greenwood. The librarian—who regards him as if he were something recently dredged up from a grave—tells him to wait while she pulls the file. He picks a secluded carrel and stuffs himself into its tiny armchair, which constricts his wide hips painfully.

After Greenwood gave him the slip at the flophouse, Lomax staked out Toronto's rail yard for a week but came up empty. But how could he possibly admit to Mr. Holt that he'd been just ten feet from Everett Greenwood and yet failed to capture him? So Lomax has kept the encounter to himself. And with no other developments to report, a week ago he halted his daily check-ins with Mr. Holt completely. Now a small stack of unopened telegrams from his employer awaits him back in his hotel room. (Along with some from Lavern, who likely wants more money he doesn't have.)

No doubt Greenwood has fled Toronto and has again taken to the rails. But Lomax can't just go traipsing around the country hunting him, especially not with Mr. Holt's stipend nearly exhausted. Which means if he doesn't drum up something soon, Mr. Holt will ruin him. So it's a testament to Lomax's desperation that he's travelled to Ottawa to confirm Howard Blank's claim that he and Greenwood had both fought in the Great War.

To settle his jangled nerves, as well as to render the cramped armchair more tolerable, he smokes an opium-laced Parliament, hoping that none of his fellow scholars have travelled widely enough to place its odour. To mitigate the stresses of his hunt,

Lomax secured a small brick of the drug from a Chinese bathhouse, and has been smoking a measured amount daily. He has yet to experience any of opium's negative effects, and feels only a warm and predictable relief from the lightning in his back. Even still, he remains steadfast in his conviction to cease the practice the second he returns home to Saint John.

He must have drifted off because he wakes with a start to find the librarian standing over him. "No Everett Greenwood ever served in the Queen's Own Rifles," she says dispassionately. "Although I did pull a *Harris* Greenwood. From Kingston?" she adds, brandishing a manila file. "Perhaps a relation?"

Snatching the file from her hand, Lomax dimly recalls Blank's outlandish assertion that Everett was related to the famously blind West Coast lumber tycoon. Though military terms are foreign to Lomax—Mr. Holt had a knack for securing draft exceptions for his friends—it appears Harris Greenwood enlisted voluntarily through the Kingston detachment and returned from Europe in 1919, after earning the Mons Star and the Canadian General Service Medal. The file states he was uninjured, with no record of his being blinded in combat. Then, paper-clipped to the rear of the folder, Lomax finds Harris Greenwood's service photograph: a soldier with dark hair standing with chin raised and helmet clutched against his ribs—the very likeness of the man who escaped him back at the flophouse.

Lomax pockets the photograph and hops a train back to Toronto the next day, elated by this fresh development which he can use to appease Mr. Holt—only to discover that the lock to his suite now refuses his key. He rides the elevator down to the concierge, who politely informs him that his hotel account has been frozen at the request of Mr. Holt. "We require a cash deposit if you intend to remain with us this evening, sir," the man adds. Lomax hands over the remaining bills in his wallet and is given a new key.

Back in his room, he tears open the topmost of Holt's telegrams.

AS WARNED YR EXPENSE ACCNTS FROZEN STOP
DETECT MCSORLEY OF CN POLICE NOW HNDLING
SRCH STOP RETRN TO ST JHN IMMED TO AVOID
FURTH DISCIPLN

Since Holt Steel built much of the CN railroad, Mr. Holt sits on
its board of directors, and in the past he's used a railroad detective
named Art McSorley to run down any fugitives who've bolted from
Saint John. Lomax knows McSorley to be a cunning, brutal man,
and if he gets his hands on the baby and the journal first, it will be
irrefutable proof of Lomax's total incompetence. What Mr. Holt
means by "FURTH DISCIPLN" isn't clear, but it could involve some
sort of harm being visited upon Lomax's family. In Lomax's experience, if Mr. Holt becomes sufficiently enraged, there's no cruelty that
is beneath him. So for the first time in his career, Lomax decides to
disobey his employer. He won't return to Saint John as instructed.
Instead he'll go to Vancouver, find Harris Greenwood, and wait for
Everett to show up there. Detective McSorley surely has no idea
about Everett's powerful brother, and in Lomax's experience it's
always easier to greet a fugitive at the place they're headed than to
catch them along the way. If Lomax can secure the child and the
journal and return them to Mr. Holt before Detective McSorley, he
might still be able to hold on to his job and his home.

But trips require money, so the next morning Lomax tramps
downstairs and informs the concierge that he's just returned from
breakfast to find his room disturbed. When the man accompanies
him back upstairs, they discover the dresser overturned and large,
fist-sized holes driven into the plaster walls. Areas of the bathroom
tile are shattered and a wide chip has been knocked from the sink.

"We are very sorry for this, Mr. Lomax!" the concierge says in
shock. "Is anything missing?"

"Yes," Lomax replies, after he checks the empty billfold tucked
in the bedside drawer.

"What exactly, sir? I'll prepare a report. Of course our hotel will reimburse you for your lost articles."

"Four hundred dollars," Lomax replies. "Cash."

After completing the hotel's forms and writing up an account of the incident, Lomax receives his money from the cashier's desk that afternoon, and immediately wires two hundred to Lavern back in Saint John. The remaining sum is more than sufficient for a first-class berth to Vancouver.

JUDGMENT

FOR GOOD LUCK on their return voyage, Harris Greenwood secures for Feeney and himself the two very same cabins on the very same steamer, the *Empress of Australia*. During the daytime, the passage is pleasant: trade winds soft from the southwest, the flat ocean a deep blue-green that Feeney describes as "normally only found upon an artist's palette." In the evenings, however, the sea roughens, and Harris and his describer dine in the first-class lounge beside a baby grand bolted to the floor, while the maître d' spritzes their crisp white tablecloth with water to keep their plates from skating around. They eat mostly in silence, like children sharing a conspiracy, as Harris takes great pains to discuss only business matters and to avoid smiling or laughing altogether. When Feeney reveals that a cabin boy gave him an odd look up on the observation deck during their third day at sea, Harris insists they henceforth take meals separately.

Still, Feeney sneaks across the hall into Harris's cabin to perform a nightly poetry reading, his delicious cello-like voice sweetening the air as they recline in leather chairs. When the reading is over, Feeney dims the lamp and they lie parallel in the narrow, sea-lolled bunk, Harris riveted in place with fright. At Yale, he occasionally saved up his scholarship per diems to go off campus and visit one of many brothels with his fellow students. But never did he enjoy himself the way his classmates professed to. For the act's duration, he worried that they'd passed a lesser woman off to him, some homely crone that any sighted patron would flatly refuse, and as a result, he was often unable to properly conclude these engagements.

But after many minutes of fighting to remind himself that no eyes are upon them—not God's, not Baumgartner's, not the loggers who'd stomped those two swampers to death—Harris draws Feeney against him. Eventually, he even allows himself to run his hands over Feeney's shape to discover that, other than his curiously hairy calves and small paunch, his body is like his face: lithe and smooth-muscled as a seal.

At first, Harris sought to keep the incidents at the movie theatre walled off within him, as he had the "little hell" he'd always sensed was there. He could have easily blamed the indiscretion on the sake, the cultural disorientation, the stresses of deal making, or the eels and urchins they'd been eating. Yet how can he possibly discredit this unimpeachable joy he's found in his describer's company? So much like the joy his bird collection offered him in dribs and drabs over the years, except in this case compounded a hundredfold.

"You failed to mention in your interview, Mr. Feeney, that your teeth are quite crooked," Harris says after they've been kissing for an hour, an act that he's still not able to perform without an undertow of nausea.

"The subject never came up," Feeney says, nibbling the bulb of Harris's nose, delicately, the way a horse takes an apple. "You were too busy prattling on about your beloved timber company."

Over the duration of the voyage, Harris finds that beneath his describer's prickly honesty is a seam of doting sweetness. While growing up, Feeney tells him, he had an elder sister who was incapacitated in both mind and body, a girl he'd cared for himself, dressing her and feeding her each day. Feeney had honed the knives of his wit to defend her on the sidewalks of Cork, and her death of heart complications when he was twenty was what had prompted his move to Canada. Not that Harris requires any such defense; but there's a bone-deep loyalty in Feeney that Harris values. He describes things as they are, not as Harris wants to hear them. And his poet's eye gazes into the very essences of things, whether the observation conforms to popular opinion or not.

Despite the deal with the Japanese they've secured, Harris seldom considers his business affairs during the journey. His thoughts centre mostly on the threat of discovery by the steamer's crew, and on the rare birds he wants to show Feeney, and the hidden places he wants them to escape to upon their return.

Still, Harris is no fool. He knows exactly what awaits them in Vancouver. Unlike the anonymous movie theatre, people will be watching at home. Baumgartner, who was even more ill-tempered than usual during the trip, and who'd had the gall to insist that Harris take two suites at the Imperial Hotel, might already suspect something. If word ever got out, both Harris and the company he built could be destroyed.

But who more than Harris is prepared for the ruthlessness of the world's judgment? And who knows better that some force will eventually snatch away this sweet gift he's been given so late in life, just as his sight was taken from him on the cusp of manhood by a pitiless disease, just as his brother was taken from him by his own selfishness and stupidity?

Even so, Harris is not afraid. The blind, by their very nature, already operate as outcasts. And ever since he was a boy, he's excelled at both concealment and self-preservation. As orphans, he and Everett managed to protect themselves by building that crooked log cabin on Mrs. Craig's woodlot, and Harris's arrangement with Feeney will be no different. If life has taught him anything, it's that you must be more secretive, more protective, and more pitiless than the next man. Either that or everything you are, everything you've built, and everyone you love, can be trampled in an instant.

THE SALT RHEUM

SICKNESS COMES TO their hay-packed boxcar as they fly westward out of the black heart of Ontario. Each time the baby slips into sleep, she fails to draw air through her rheum-clogged nose and snorts herself awake. This is followed by a series of hacks that loll out her tongue—an impossibly tiny thing that recalls to Everett a tinned oyster. He keeps her head tipped back to drain her airway, which does little good, and the whole ordeal is repeated endlessly. At last he gives up and they sit awake, her eyes slick with mucus and flashing in the dark like gemstones, as they *clickety-clack* past pole-straight evergreens interspersed with inky lakes, the child clutching pitifully at his shirt as though he's fixing to drop her.

Everett has given her a temporary name: Pod. He avoided doing so thus far, the way a farmer leaves the pigs bound for his smokehouse anonymous. But Pod is still just a placeholder. A road name, a hobo moniker—something to be sloughed off the moment she settles into her real life, wherever that may be. He knows that trees often use birds and squirrels to spread their seeds, along with various flying contraptions like whirlers or cottony fluff that can blow great distances. Much of creation works this way: living things send versions of themselves out into the great puzzle of the future. And like a seed, this girl is in dire need of a hospitable place to land. And it's his job to find it.

At sunup the next day the salt rheum has mostly dried up, though Pod still hums with a low fever, her skin unnaturally shiny. She refuses the biscuits he's brought, even after he soaks them in water, and when she does sleep at last, she wakes to a thick green crust sealing her eyelids, which provokes a thrashing yowl. Everett holds his wetted shirtsleeve to her grimacing face until her eyelashes come unglued. By the afternoon her cough has worsened, and she burns to the touch and stops taking water. Everett turns down her sweaty creeper to cool her, and when she still refuses to drink, he plugs her nose, pries open her jaw, and pours water down her gullet as she gurgles and screams.

Fearing the hay dust is aggravating her condition, he climbs out of the boxcar and over to a lumber gondola so they can ride out in open air. They tuck in beneath the woollen blanket as Pod tracks the landscape's scroll with woozy interest. They roar past frizzy fields, slow-winding rivers, fall-down barns, grown-over paddocks, chicken pens, and groves of every tree imaginable. When dark falls, Pod's eyes brim with starlight, and the moon, white as a sliced radish, floods the whipping forest. For an instant, they spot a wolverine sharpening its claws on a stump, then two deer, ears perked, frozen as though caught at some criminal act rather than chewing clover in the middle of nowhere.

To distract the child Everett begins speaking freely, even if the practice is bound to turn him crazy. "Your name's Pod," he says. "*Pod*," he repeats, patting her creeper, and she replies with a gurgling, lamb-like bleat that sounds nothing like the word whatsoever. "And this here's a *gondola car*," he says, pointing everywhere. "It's attached to other *cars*, which are all pulled by a *locomotive*. Whole thing's called a *train*." Though Pod listens with gaping eyes fixed on his lips, his words make little lasting imprint on her understanding. Because when he asks her later to point to the *gondola car*, she merely grunts and soils her flannels. "How am I supposed to teach you the words for things if all I have to do it is some other damn words?" he says, tapping the nub of her nose with his fingertip.

After he runs dry of definitions, he stumbles into a telling of his own life. Speaking with a candour he'd only ever employed with Harris when they were boys, he begins with how they became brothers and how they started out as woodcutters, and carries on from there. At times Pod regards him knowingly, as though it's a story she's heard a thousand times before, and Everett grows convinced her head is already larded with knowledge, not just of his own life and history, but all things that ever happened to anyone. Still, the story soothes her, whether she knows it already or not, and soon her limpid eyes dip shut.

The next morning her fever has broken and she guzzles up most of their water. The train runs fast all day and never sidetracks to let others pass—it may be an express, carrying something like freshly slaughtered steers or urgent mail, which, Everett knows, could pose a problem if they run out of provisions before it gets where it's going. The train climbs squat, rocky shelves of rusty-tinged granite, dashing west past cut-over forests, mines, and gravel quarries—land that men like his brother Harris have already despoiled to pave their personal roads to riches.

He and Pod nestle between the stacks of fragrant lumber until the sun drops and the sky over Lake Superior is shot through with fuchsia spokes of light. Everett removes his boots and hangs his feet from the car's edge. Pod lies splayed on his belly, her warmth boring into him. As they near the outskirts of Port Arthur, a sensation of wide-open liberty overcomes him, as though he and Pod are themselves the breeze and the world is theirs alone to blow through. He wriggles his toes in the leaf-sweet wind like a boy.

1908

HEARTWOOD

ONE IS SUBJECT to much talk nowadays concerning family trees and roots and bloodlines and such, as if a family were an eternal fact, a continuous branching upwards through time immemorial. But the truth is that all family lines, from the highest to the lowest, originate somewhere, on some particular day. Even the grandest trees must've once been seeds spun helpless on the wind, and then just meek saplings nosing up from the soil.

We know this for certain because on the night of April 29, 1908, a family took root before our eyes. We awoke to the apocalypse itself. The tremor flung the dishes from our cupboards and unhitched the frames from our walls. Two twenty-car passenger trains had collided head-on a mile east of our township. The westbound locomotive's tender caught fire and the flames passed from one train to the other and hours went by before we could push our water wagons deep enough into the oily coal smoke to douse the blaze. The fire left a gruesome scene: skulls studded with black teeth; indistinguishably charred appendages intermixed with twists of contorted iron and torched garments. A proper accounting of the dead was impossible, but of the sixteen passengers thrown from the train's windows on impact, the sole survivors were two young boys, both left barefoot by the tremendous force of the crash, one discovered tangled deep in the brush, the other floundering in a nearby brook. Both were near nine years of age, by our reckoning, and even after hours of hunting, we never found a single shoe.

Our town physician determined that it was their small statures that saved them, the way a squirrel can plunge from a tree and skitter off unharmed. Either that or, as was claimed by the more speculative among us, something evil and unkillable resided in them both. Still, that the boys escaped such a cataclysm seemed as much a miracle then as it does now.

We sent word of the two survivors to the CN Railway Company, who maintained they had no record of any children riding either train, so they bore no responsibility for any that happened to be found in the vicinity of the accident. While it was upsetting business to face the young victims of such tragedy, it was our rail junction—and our octogenarian switchman—who'd effectively orphaned them, so after our failed efforts to locate any surviving family, we appraised the boys as our responsibility and assumed their charge. Matters were handled differently in those days, and lost people circulated as unnoticed as slight gusts of wind.

Though the ordeal had rendered both boys mute, it was immediately clear that the mysterious pair shared no blood. One was slightly shorter, with dark, wavy hair and almond eyes that always avoided your own; and yet he had an easy, almost carefree way of moving about the world, despite what he'd suffered. The taller one had long fingers and thick, honey-coloured hair; that one would meet anyone's gaze with a shrewdly appraising glare, as though even our rescue had been some kind of trick, a further continuation of the disaster that had befallen him. Yet despite their outward differences, we figured those two boys were better off kept together, and billeted them with several charitable homesteads in the area while we waited futilely for someone to claim them.

It's well established that the recollections of youngsters are about as reliable as rainbows. This is especially true, we learned, of the recently orphaned. When after a week the boys finally spoke, the difficulty wasn't that they'd forgotten their names, it was that they drummed up too many: a junk shop of surnames and given names all mumbled and jumbled together—Tommy, Mackenzie, Buck, Smith, Jacob, Finnegan, Seymour, Gordon, Aaron. Perhaps the impact had scrambled their heads, or perhaps their true names had become too painful to utter now that their families were dead, but our only remedy was to jot them all down on scraps of paper and pull two from a coffee can and get on with it. Concerning their pasts, the blonde one, for whom we pulled *Harris*, could recall only fragments: sheep, five or six sisters, an uncle, rain pattering a metal shed roof, a smoky hearth. The darker boy, for whom we pulled *Everett*, recalled slimy fish knives, a barking man with no hair at all, a sickly mother, a wireless that never worked.

Beneath the overpowering stink of burnt horsehair cushions and immolated flesh must have lingered the traces of their lost homes and families, still caught in the fibres of their sweaters and the linings of their nostrils. Yet each passing day must have left those traces a little weaker, further confused, less distinct. Soon their pasts withered away completely, and all that remained was haze and hearsay.

It was shortly after we named them that we began discovering their beds empty in the night. Our townspeople took up naphtha lanterns and tracked them into the woods. We found the boys cowering and clutching each other in the bedclothes we had given them beneath a wide-spreading tree, muttering in an unsettling shared tongue. When this was repeated over several nights, we were near ready to shove those boys back on an outbound train and be done with it. And given how things turned out, lately we can't help but wonder if it was a mistake we didn't.

It was Parson Brennan who took note that whenever the boys absconded, it was often to one particular woodlot, an otherwise vacant plot officially owned by Mrs. Fiona Craig. We still can't say why this was. Perhaps they were drawn to the old trapper's hut they discovered there, a rotted windowless shack once used, it was rumoured, to harbour runaway slaves from the United States. Or perhaps it was some comforting aspect of the woods themselves, which were thick with oak and maple, foxglove and trillium, elderberry and chokecherry.

Especially after they started taking to the woods, there was something otherworldly and haunted about the pair. So while many of us could've used some extra hands around our properties, none volunteered to take the boys on a permanent basis. As a last resort we proposed to Mrs. Craig that she allow their habitation in that hut on her woodlot. The township would provide her with a yearly sum to house and feed them until they came of age. And though the old widow had no offspring of her own, and wasn't what you'd call the caretaking type, we were pleasantly surprised when she agreed.

MRS. FIONA CRAIG

SHE AND HER husband, James Craig, a lantern-jawed physician, arrived in Canada at the Halifax harbour in 1893. The transatlantic relocation had been wholly his idea. Fiona, a slight but attractive girl raised in Glasgow's tenement slums, met James while he was there studying the spread of pulmonary consumption among the poor. As he often went unmasked, even when performing autopsies on the most wretched corpses, he contracted a case of his own shortly after their marriage. This was Fiona's first taste of James's foolhardiness, which would frustrate her to no end, especially after she'd struck the kind of marital gold unheard of among those of her low station.

When James took ill, his ears pricked to the beckoning New World, with its healthful air, economic opportunity, and abundant greenery. Fiona knew her husband was always romantic about woodlands—too much Burns and Wordsworth in his youth perhaps—and he even viewed his consumption as a kind of poetic affliction, a deepening of the senses. They would leave the bleak moors of Scotland, James decided, a land of too few trees and too many people, with its grimy smoke and vagrants and urchins spitting in the gutters, and establish a country practice in the wooded province of Ontario, near the city of Kingston. Eventually, James aimed to travel on the newly constructed railroad even farther west to British Columbia, where the marine air was said to be moist and sweet and the trees grew as high as clouds and could be chopped at for weeks before they'd so much as wobble.

When the couple arrived in "the Land of the Trees," they found the thirty thickly wooded acres they'd petitioned from the Canadian

Land Registry already occupied by a band of roving Mohawk, who'd been displaced from their traditional trapping grounds by a local lumber concern. Despite his compassionate ways, James Craig bought a rifle and raised a local militia to drive the band from his property, a brutal yet necessary act that many of us had once performed ourselves. Some of the Mohawk refused to vacate and grew so uppity there wasn't much to be done except shoot them as examples and burn their women and children out.

A well-appointed house was constructed in the fire-cleared section. There, James accepted as his clientele the local lumberjacks and axemen who'd also been lured by the Dominion's great woods, fleeing famine or, for many, their own spotty pasts. Irish, Norwegians, Finns, Germans, Danes, Swedes, Frenchmen, and fellow Scots of low birth—they were degenerates all, in Fiona Craig's vocal estimation, outcasts well beneath her husband and the bucolic life she'd envisioned for herself. Fiona kept to her chambers whenever the men frequented her husband's office.

The restorative country air did little for James's health, however, and when his condition turned and the bloody sputum and sweats beset him, he shed half his weight in a fortnight. In just a month he lay dead in their marital bed at the age of thirty. The shock of her husband's departure left Mrs. Craig unstable. She'd been duped, that was her view—by whom she wouldn't tell Parson Brennan when she described to him the feeling—by false promises of prosperity and a new life. Many said she resented this forested continent itself for the trickery. In the end, Fiona Craig was left shrill and embittered with the Devil's rage.

James had provided a good-sized nest egg, it was rumoured, allowing her to maintain the ways of a woman of means. She kept the house to herself and surprisingly took no boarders. She had the house painted a blinding white, the kind of white that tarnishes after just a year. With her nearest neighbour four miles distant, she rarely attended church and was seldom seen in town, though whenever she was, she'd always be well turned out: corsets, bustles, and frilly dresses she must've sewn herself or mail-ordered. She'd purchase odd items at the general store, like needles and thread, noxious chemicals, and bolts of French lace. All requested with a belittling shriek that some of the less generous among us compared to that of a diseased eagle. Our children feared her as a witch, and told stories of the dead doctor's ghost and the cursed fortune that Fiona kept buried somewhere on her woodlot.

While none of us figured her a kind woman, when she agreed to harbour those two orphans our opinion of her improved, if only slightly. Many of us were convinced that she'd soften on those poor wretches over time, that they'd be a remedy for her loneliness and strange ways. And after they'd suffered a few miserable weeks out in that dreary hut, she'd take them into one of the many bedrooms of her big white house, and given the chance, perhaps would even come to love them as her own.

But on the day we brought them to her porch, she slapped Everett, the cheerful, dark-haired one, for slouching, then did the same to Harris, the skeptical, blonde one, for posing too many questions. Then she made them both swear against ever entering her house for as long as they lived, even if she invited them inside herself. In retrospect, it's clear to us now that we overestimated the pliability of Mrs. Craig's heart.

THOSE BOYS

AFTER THEY TOOK up residence on the Craig woodlot, mere days passed before the plunder of our vegetable plots began in earnest. Turnips, peas, carrots, and lettuces vanished as soon as they ripened. We'd leave our shotguns racked and wait up late to hurl handfuls of stones at the two shadowy figures fleeing into the woods. Small stones, mind you. This was charity then: small stones. It's a notion that's not understood anymore, charity. If we'd fed those boys outright, they'd conclude that the world owed them something, which, as we all know, it doesn't. So we made inquiries with Mrs. Craig to ensure she was providing for them as she was required, and she insisted she was, though we had no means of verifying it. Despite her assurances, and our stones, those boys continued to raid our gardens and trespass on our land with impunity. They stole apples and chickens and eggs and women's undergarments from our laundry lines. They even kidnapped one of old Gord Campbell's prized lambs, dragging it bleating back to their hut, and were fixing to roast it when we had some of our older boys lead an expedition to rescue the creature and put a modest licking on the pair.

Many blamed Mrs. Craig, contending that the only mind she ever paid those boys was to rouse them at dawn by kicking their shack's flimsy walls before leaving outside their door a bucket of the daily provisions that our contract required her to furnish. It was widely held that Mrs. Craig could scarcely stand the sight of them, and only took them in to sock money away for more finery, or her own private castle in Scotland.

Still, no one had the fortitude to discipline the boys as they ought to have been. Instead, when we heard that their hut was leaking and their clothes were rain-rotten, we left a roll of good tarpaper by their door. Then it was a bushel of apples when they looked scurvy. When we heard coughing from the direction of the woods, we'd leave jars of fish oil and some old blankets, and some fresh cream cooling in the shafts of our wells for them to find and pilfer.

Throughout that first year, the boys would often come knocking on our doors so that Harris, who'd by then assumed the role of spokesman for the pair, could ask odd questions, such as "What time is it?" or "How high are the clouds?" And while some of us suspected the true purpose of this was to assess our houses as potential targets for robbery, the more sympathetic among us figured it was so they could sample the smell of a legitimate home—of baking things and detergents, fruit and coffee—if only fleetingly.

Whenever the boys came into town, it was always an event. In light of the frequency with which things fell into Everett's pockets, shopkeepers either followed them around or shooed them off. Harris would always stride a few steps in front of his brother upon the plank sidewalk, Everett merrily trailing just behind with his bemused smile and easy gait. In their Sunday best our children would follow the two primitives just to watch them scale the tall elms that our township's founders had planted in the square, jumping branch to branch like a couple of howler monkeys, rising so high the limbs could scarcely support them. Some Sundays all you'd see of those two boys were the soles of their boots, and it was up there that they often practised their swearing.

"Peckerwood!" Harris would yell at the top of his lungs.

"Pisswidget!" Everett would yell in reply. And this scatological one-upmanship would play out for nearly half an hour, the two almost tumbling to the ground from the riot of their laughter that shook the elm's uppermost leaves.

Bedding our own youngsters down in the evening, we'd remind them: "At least you aren't out there on that dark woodlot by yourselves with the bears and the wolves to sing you to sleep," and they'd hold us tighter and sit up straighter at the table the next day and take to their chores with greater zeal.

Over the boys' second summer on the woodlot, Everett managed to construct a pair of four-foot bows from windfall alder, along with arrows he fashioned from dogwood shoots and fletched with jay feathers. The boys soon became proficient at shooting hares, which kept running in the dirt even after they were skewered through the ribs. They learned to scrape and tan the hides, and, it was rumoured by our children, slept in each other's arms beneath a heap of rabbit pelts.

We applauded this bit of self-sufficiency—that is, until they shot and skinned the town alderman's prize terrier. It was then decided that the boys required something more productive to fill their days. They were too uncouth to cut it as domestics, so we had them slingshot pigeons from the stone sills of town hall. Next, they harrowed our fields, dug up stumps, and caught nuisance squirrels by the grey plumes of their tails.

The boys were enterprising—Harris especially so, often demanding exorbitant payments for even the smallest tasks—and both took handily to manual labour. Some said they must have been born of good working stock from Germany, England, Ireland, France—or even Yankees. But the jobs were all of limited duration, and afterwards the two would relapse into delinquent pastimes: hunting foxes, kicking beehives, and hooking the fish in our private brooks. We called an emergency town meeting and agreed to procure for them a set of steel files and a whetstone, the expense justified as an investment in our township's collective well-being and security. These implements appeared outside their shack the following day.

THE GREEN WOOD BOYS

THROUGHOUT THE WINTER of 1910, we brought them our dullest plow blades and knives and axes and saws. When those edges were freshened, we brought our longest-abandoned implements: bucksaws, picks, awls, hatchets, adzes, froes, files, and barking irons—all dull as marbles and gone tangerine with rust. Which the boys returned as sharp as scalpels, edges bright and silver with mineral oil. When there was nothing left to sharpen, they mended axehandles and taught themselves to shoe horses and rebind tack. And when that was all done, for hours they'd straighten used nails with hammers on flat rocks, in a race to be the first one to complete a whole bucket.

Their thieving and troublemaking were curtailed thereafter, and with all those saws and axes about, the boys couldn't avoid familiarizing themselves with their usage. When Taisto Maki, a Finlander and the town's finest woodcutter, was crushed by a great white pine he was felling, his widow allowed the boys to keep his tools, given they'd cared for them so well in the past. Though they were only eleven at the time and lacked the brute strength for proper logging, they managed to buck up the plentiful windfall littering their woodlot, which they'd sell by the cord out beside the road. It was then Harris's entrepreneurial streak truly emerged, as he hollered out to our wagons and haggled over prices like he was born doing it.

Over time they refined their axe strokes—more hips than arms—and soon knew exactly where a whorled grain would prove troublesome, and how to let the maul's weight do the work for you. Still, none of us had the heart to mention to the boys that they were supposed to first dry the green wood for a minimum of a year—and ideally, two or three. And because we suspected that the funds we paid to Mrs. Craig weren't entirely making their way into the boys' stomachs, our townspeople were charitable enough to purchase the green wood at full-cord price, then season it ourselves so our stove-pipes wouldn't plug with creosote and burn our houses down.

So this is how it came to be that instead of what we'd previously called them—either "those poor boys" or "those goddamned boys," depending on what they'd done that week—the pair came to be known as "the green wood boys."

As years passed, the name settled upon them and rooted them in place. With it, they seemed less like ghosts or demons and more and more like regular boys. It became difficult for us to say whether they hadn't always carried the Greenwood name, even since before the train crash. Some swore that despite their differences of physiology, those two even grew to look more alike, so much so that many of us forgot that they'd each been thrown from separate trains. It entered popular remembrance that the poor brothers had been found clutching each other, barefooted but dressed in matching outfits, the name *Greenwood* stitched into the labels of their coats.

With their woodcutting earnings the boys bought coloured pencils, maple candies, and some proper clothes, which they ruined immediately with pine pitch. Most of the spoils, however, went toward presents for Mrs. Craig, including some fine perfume and a smart beaver hat, which they left on her porch. It was rumoured that she never brought the gifts inside, and that it was never long before some tramp came from the railway and carted them off.

NUMBERS AND LETTERS

OVER TIME WE watched the ligatures of brotherhood thicken between those boys. We heard it claimed that they shared everything: even a trifle like a boiled duck egg they took great pains to split dead even with their sharpest jackknife. Yet despite this mutual reliance, all wasn't peaceable. As it goes with siblings, their relations were part love, part rivalry, with wrathful annoyance making up the remainder. Scripture reminds us that brother has always warred with brother: Cain with Abel; Isaac with Ismael; Esau with Jacob. While it's said that God gave trees their towering height in order for them to compete for the sun's attentions, it seemed to us that brothers came up in a similar competition, elbowing and bickering with each other for the same patch of light.

Though Harris remained taller than Everett, the boys were of near-equal strength, wits, and fleetness of foot—this verified by the unending games of push-over, boxing, and sprints they engaged in daily. In a contest to raise the highest welt, they pelted each other mercilessly with crabapples, and with Mrs. Craig holed up in her house, there was no authority present to settle their disputes or drive them apart.

"Mrs. Craig prefers me," we once overheard Harris proclaim with a sigh, carrying on another of his one-sided conversations as the boys sat eating the boiled peanuts Everett had lifted at the annual fall fair. "I'm sorry to tell you this, Everett. But it's a plain fact. Last week she brought a nice pastry she'd baked out to the shack—you were off cutting wood or something—and she pecked me on the cheek while I ate it."

"She didn't give you no peck you damn liar," Everett declared, except in a joyful tone, as though the sheer preposterousness of the lie delighted him.

"What'd you say?" Harris muttered, his face bright crimson. Though he always spoke for the pair and for this reason seemed older, Harris was easily wounded, and lived constantly on the verge of either tears or an angry outburst. Most infuriating to him of all was his brother's habit of viewing him as ridiculous, and the world as one enormous, inconsequential joke.

"Which part bothers you more?" Everett replied nonchalantly, still grinning. "Me calling you a liar? Or that Mrs. Craig wouldn't kiss a filthy rat's ass like you 'cause her lips would rot clean off afterwards?"

Harris reared back, hurled a handful of peanuts into his brother's face, and tackled him. After that the pair wrestled around in the grass for a while, the scrum quelling Harris's rage. "Well, if I were a clumsy little dwarf like you," he grumbled when they were done and he was straightening the collar of his torn shirt, "I wouldn't expect no pastry either."

By age twelve, the woodcutting had already piled muscles under their pitch-stained shirts, and their young bodies grew ropy like the boughs of white pine they cut daily. Their bloody skirmishes could last days: a series of ambushes, counter-ambushes, and retributions that would make a Trojan proud. Soon they were loosening teeth, nearly tearing the other's ears off, and tugging out whole handfuls of hair. It was as though the brotherly bond they'd forged had pooled the ownership of their bodies, including the God-given right of self-destruction.

"Those boys are going to kill each other," we'd say, but no one had the gumption to do much about it except the parson, who left a songbook of old spirituals at their door, hoping Christ's more peaceful teachings would sedate them. Since neither could read, however, the songbook's pages were used as fire starter.

Though the boys were clearly simple-minded, the school principal suggested his institution may be of some benefit. They could attend on a trial basis, and perhaps gather the basic accounting and literacy skills required to properly run their woodcutting business as adults. And, we suggested, a bit of schoolhouse discipline might well keep them from maiming each other permanently. So a few of us, along with the town constable, ventured to their shack to inform them of their mandatory enrolment. Harris met us at the door with that same appraising, suspicious look he'd worn when we first found him.

The principal asked whether they'd attended school as youngsters, before they were orphaned, and Harris claimed they had no recollection. "We're too busy working for any school anyway," he said, cluing in to the purpose of our visit. "Are you gentlemen certain you're well stocked for the winter? The rumour is that it's going to be a cold one, and we've got some nice—"

"Don't you boys want to learn to read?" the constable interrupted.

"No," Harris said flatly, and made to shut the door.

"Aw, come now," the constable said, stopping it with his boot. "What about your brother? You don't speak for him. Doesn't he want to learn to read?"

Harris turned to his brother. "Everett, do you want to be cooped up in some musty old school all day so you can learn to read?"

Everett, while taking a spoonful of the rabbit stew that always bubbled on their stove, just shrugged his shoulders.

"My brother says he doesn't want to go to any damn school," Harris said. "And if you keep coming around here, he'll bury a hatchet in your back."

We couldn't send them to an orphan home or the town jail, which left us no choice but to inform them that it was Mrs. Craig's personal desire for them to get their numbers and letters, and if they attended school regularly she'd agreed to consider taking them into her house as her sons. Which was, admittedly, false, yet it was all to their benefit, and we were pleased when the boys took our bait and agreed.

As a surname for enrolment purposes, we wrote *Greenwood* for want of another, thereby rendering it official. Little did we know it would be a name we'd be glimpsing on lumber packets and in shameful newspaper headlines for years to come.

Looking back, we ought to have forced the Greenwood boys to walk to school on Whalen Road with the other children, rather than allowing them to trek through the forest. Because when they emerged from those trees into that play yard, with their tattered clothes and pitch-stained hands, how could they not have enshrined themselves as outcasts?

"You don't look like no brothers," some of our rougher boys said to them that first morning.

"We're brothers. Because we say we are," Harris declared as Everett balled his fists.

If the Greenwood boys fought face-to-face at home, at school it was only back-to-back. Everett, who quickly cast off his good-natured disposition, was especially brutal and efficient in battle, and the brothers won five separate fistfights on their first day alone.

In the classroom, however, they fared less well. They'd been in the forest too long and couldn't sit still. Their eyes strayed to the greenery in the windows, and they'd be paddled daily for various infractions, which always just made Everett laugh and Harris purple with fury, no matter how hard Ms. Miller swung. She'd call in the principal, who, at double her size, still couldn't squeeze a single tear from either of them.

While they were already miles behind, academically speaking, the boys gleaned what they could from the curriculum, and both made modest progress. But after just six months, Ms. Miller and the school principal had reached their limit and could withstand no more disruptive squabbles with the other students.

And so it was suggested that if only one of the Greenwood boys attended school, the benefits to their fledgling business could be reaped all the same. And though Harris was the more temperamentally

volatile of the two, he was also more outspoken and entrepreneurial—
not to mention slightly less dangerous—so we selected him to do the
learning. Since that day we've often argued over how Everett was just
as clever as his brother, and was perhaps the more level-headed and
studious of the two; and we can't help wondering what would've transpired had it been him we'd chosen to remain.

But we picked who we picked. And the following Monday morning Everett Greenwood was expelled, and made a much-relieved
return to the quiet, leafy labours of the woodlot.

THE LOG CABIN

WITHOUT HIS BROTHER to distract him, Harris Greenwood turned his combative spirit to his schoolbooks, and managed to complete his grade eight by age fourteen. When Harris finally rejoined his brother at woodcutting, he was no longer just their spokesman—he was their leader. He decided which trees they'd take and where they'd drag them to be chopped, a responsibility the easygoing Everett relinquished gladly.

When the lot's windfall was exhausted, Harris decided they were strong enough to fell trees themselves. After some close calls, the boys learned to fashion proper back cuts rather than hacking straight through, and soon they could drop a tree right between a man's eyes. Their thirty acres were a good mix of hardwoods and white pine, and they could fell, de-limb, buck, and split a tree in a single day. It was said that Everett could tell red oak from black oak or birch from poplar just by the music of their leaves, and that Harris could gauge a cord of wood with just a passing glance at some standing trees. Before long they had enough money to buy a horse team and sledge to skid logs out to the road during winter.

"Behold, the mighty woodcutters!" the town's working men jibed when the two passed by, axes flung over their shoulders.

"BEST FIREWOOD IN THE WORLD" announced their new sign, carefully painted and meticulously lettered by Harris, and it wasn't far from the truth. At five dollars a cord, the Greenwoods couldn't be beat, and buying from the boys was no longer an act of charity. Their wood was always well split and bone-dry, and it burned hotter than coal and came in full cords, not like the three-quarter bundles that the Bonnevilles had passed off on us for years.

As their business grew, Harris, still the taller of the two, tired of clocking his skull against the low rafters of the trapper's shack. Given that Mrs. Craig wasn't about to allow them into her house anytime soon, the boys set about constructing a proper dwelling. Everett made sketches while Harris selected the finest corner of the wood-lot, with a view of the creek. They felled trees and made a clearing, limbing the pine logs, peeling their bark with a drawknife, squaring and notching them, then capping them with tar. They used horses to drag and pulley the dressed logs into place, then chinked the gaps with creek mud and hemp. After the roof was on, they began con-structing some crude furniture. They still bickered occasionally but no longer came to blows, and anyone who watched them while they worked would say that it was as if they were in a shared trance, and that they moved as though they were two hands of the same body.

The finished log cabin was a primitive structure, crooked as a politician's ledgers. So crooked, in fact, that chairs and tables wobbled no matter where you put them in the room. On the happy occasion of the cabin's completion, the boys managed to coax Mrs. Craig—who'd recently been ailing, we'd noticed, coughing constantly into her lace hankies—out to inspect it. The man delivering their wood-stove that day claimed that though the Greenwood boys had dressed up in ties to receive their guardian after preparing her a fine meal, standing there on their porch with their bushy hair slicked with skid grease and combed flat, their chests puffed like a couple of conquer-ing generals, the old widow wouldn't even set a foot inside.

"You could've done with some more windows," she said with a pursed expression, electing to address them from the porch. "Too dingy for me in there. I'm afraid you'll have to eat that supper yourselves."

A CONDITION

WHEN THE GREENWOOD boys neared sixteen, Fiona Craig's health took a malign turn. Her cough began doubling her over the counter at the general store, and her ankles swelled unnaturally beneath her fine hosiery—though she always sent Doc Kane away with choice words whenever he inquired after her well-being during her increasingly rare trips into town.

Soon she stopped coming altogether. And after her accounts with the general store and the hairdressers went unsettled for weeks, we decided to petition the boys to check in on their guardian. Everett and Harris insisted they knocked on every window and every door of her house for a full hour before giving up. Her firm rule prohibiting their entry was still about the only one that those delinquents had left unbroken.

A few of us accompanied Doc Kane to the house the next day. We forced the door and found her corpse in the parlour, gruesomely bloated and half putrefied, her flesh blue as the April sky. Consumption, Doc Kane concluded after examining the body. Likely caught from her husband, a disease that'd eaten at her over time, until her lungs had degenerated into nothing more than liquid sloshing around in her chest. "This poor woman drowned in herself," Doc Kane said. "And didn't once complain about it."

It was a pitiful, painful death, and we couldn't bear to inform the boys that she'd suffered the way she must've. We also concealed from them a certain speculation ventured by the most generous of us: that the reason Mrs. Craig kept them at arm's length for all those years wasn't that they displeased her; it was to protect them from contracting the affliction that had consumed her husband and, eventually, herself. Even if this notion were true, it wouldn't have put food on those boys' table, or replaced the many losses they'd already suffered. The woman was gone now. And it's common wisdom that we're all better off not dwelling upon the sacrifices of those who came before us. Thankfully, given there were no official surviving kin, Doc Kane could remain tight-lipped about Mrs. Craig's cause of death and we could just get on with things.

But the boys tore at their hair and collapsed in pitiful heaps when they learned the news. Never before had we witnessed such anguish take root in anyone. It was rumoured that, apart from the time Mrs. Craig slapped them both on the first day they met, she'd never allowed them to touch her while she was alive, not even once. Which meant that not until the old widow was dead did those two boys get to feel her skin, while lifting her into the ornate coffin they'd constructed themselves from some red oak they'd felled, which they carried out of her house and loaded onto their lumber wagon for transport into town. Watching those boys mourn a woman who never cared for them with any enthusiasm was a sorrowful sight for us all. What she was to them we'll never know: perhaps goddess, monster, mother, and guardian all forged into one impossible figure.

Given how she'd treated them, it came to our great surprise when a lawyer based in Kingston contacted us after the funeral. He'd drawn up a will by correspondence with Mrs. Craig, which named Everett and Harris Greenwood as her sole beneficiaries, providing they obey her one condition, outlined in a sealed envelope to be distributed to the boys. From the will we also learned that Mrs. Craig had indeed been siphoning off a small fraction of the stipend we'd provided for her care of the boys, to pay down a sizeable mortgage on the wooded property that her physician husband had incurred in secret, after thousands of losing hands of poker played with the loggers and labourers he treated.

Her final wishes further improved our opinion of Mrs. Craig, and the more tender-hearted among us imagined both of those boys living respectably on that property in perpetuity, running their modest business on the woodlot, every summer painting the old house a blinding white—a house that was of ample size for two sets of families, given they were familiar enough. We even dared to picture some little Greenwoods crawling over the roots of the trees they'd spared, with tire-swings hanging from their branches.

But the day after we delivered Mrs. Craig's envelope, we watched the Greenwood boys set about fulfilling her condition. They piled cords of their finest ash firewood up around the walls of the house that James Craig had constructed for his wife in the Land of the Trees. By day's end, the wall of wood stood as high as the second-floor windows.

They lit it at sundown. The fire burned for weeks.

RECRUITMENT

SOON AFTER THE churning embers of the Craig house died out, we saw a change in Harris Greenwood. He began to attend to his personal grooming: shaving his face diligently each morning and slicking his honey-coloured hair back with Brilliantine. He could be heard chastising his brother for failing to do the same, often marching him to the barber whenever he became too scruffy. It was during one of these visits that our town barber overheard Harris first propose his plan.

"Now that the woodlot's ours, Everett, we need to think bigger than thirty acres. Bigger than this township even," Harris said. "We're wasting good trees cutting them for firewood and you know it. It makes me sick to consider all the money we've put up the chimney already. So my plan is to bring in a crew from Kingston to cut down the entirety at once, then we'll have it milled for prime lumber and make a killing."

"Where will we live afterwards?" Everett said with genuine confusion, as though he'd never once considered dwelling anywhere other than among those trees. It was around that time Everett had started tapping the woodlot's sugar maples and selling his syrup by the roadside with their firewood.

"With the funds we generate, we'll buy another forested parcel," Harris replied. "A better one. With a proper house on it, not some crooked cabin. Then we'll do it all over again."

"We don't know anything about milling, Harris."

"You mean *you* don't know anything about milling."

"Why can't we just keep things as they are?" Everett asked. "We've got some good trees there. We could cut the pines, leave the maples, and make a good living selling syrup. We'll build a new house, a finer one, right on the ashes of Mrs. Craig's. We ought to be grateful for what she left us."

"Grateful?" Harris snorts. "For a rotten shack and a few buckets of food? We could lose this land any day and you know it. Some distant relative could come out of the woodwork and take it from us tomorrow."

Everett seemed to consider this as the barber snipped at his knotted mop. "You've always spoken for us, Harris. And you've done a better job of it than I ever could," he began. "But I still have as much a say in this as you. So you can log your half of the woodlot," he said, eyes locked with his brother's in the mirror, "you just leave mine the way it is."

"We need the whole parcel for the numbers to work," Harris said, shaking his head. "Otherwise, the transport fees will eat up our profits."

"Well, that's final," Everett said, shutting his eyes and crossing his arms beneath the barber's canvas smock.

"You've always been simple, Everett," Harris said, pulling on his coat before nearly bowling over another patron as he stormed out.

After that argument, Harris Greenwood was occasionally seen moping around the slapdash recruiting station that'd been set up in the old bank. Outside of school, it was the first time we'd sighted either of the brothers in town on their own.

By 1915, many of our eldest sons were already off fighting in the War, and few enough had been killed or maimed that there was still an enthusiasm for the effort. Eye-grabbing posters were pasted up in places young men frequented. Catchy wartime songs commanded the wireless. And even boys who for whatever reason weren't enlisted still sported military haircuts. Our meekest farmers and frailest clerks had been climbing over one another to board the transport ships for England, and from there to Belgium and France. Many viewed the War as the ideal proving ground for manly aspirations, and though he wasn't yet of age, Harris Greenwood may have heard a similar calling. Or perhaps, we can't avoid speculating now, those posters and jingles were the first occasion that anyone had ever wanted that poor orphan for anything, and the allure of it was impossible to resist.

When he finally accumulated the nerve to enter the recruiting station, he cut a convincing figure on first inspection—a well-built man who appeared years beyond his age. But it was his local infamy that worked against him that day. The induction officer recognized Harris immediately—he'd once lost a fight with Everett on the schoolyard, though the officer was three years his senior—and knew the Greenwood boys to be approximately sixteen.

So, as far as we were concerned, the matter of Harris's enlistment had been settled.

AN OATH

I, Harris Greenwood, do make Oath, that I will be faithful and bear true Allegiance to His Majesty King George the Fifth, His Heirs and Successors, and that I will as in duty bound honestly and faithfully defend His Majesty, His Heirs and Successors, in Person, Crown and Dignity, against all enemies, and will observe and obey all orders of His Majesty, His Heirs and Successors, and of all the Generals and Officers set over me. So help me God.

A FOUL SWING

IN THE END, Harris travelled in the Greenwood lumber wagon to nearby Kingston to enlist. In larger cities, the recruiters focused principally on weeding out underaged boys from the ranks of enlistees by using height and weight as indicators—measures in which the naturally tall and work-built Harris well exceeded his peers. We later read that the medical officer had described the recruit as follows in his enlistment papers: *A single man of no religious affiliation who labours in an unnamed township outside Kingston as a woodcutter, and with straight, blonde hair stands six-foot-one inches, and has a chest of 38-inch girth.*

Although they hadn't come to blows in years, after Harris returned home with the signed Articles of War clutched in his hand, there commenced a great fistfight inside the Greenwood cabin that lasted for hours and could be heard all the way from McLaren Road. Much of the crude furniture the boys had built together was put to splinters that night, and each of the structure's few windows needed re-glazing.

It came to our understanding that Everett had no desire to take up a rifle and preferred to remain on the woodlot forever; and though he could perhaps run the business himself, it would be a dreary proposition to do so alone. Seeing how those two had never been apart, it must've seemed to Everett that his entire world was about to collapse in on him.

Still, once the dust settled, a banged-up Harris Greenwood completed his basic training at Lethbridge, Alberta, over the following month. "He was studious, disciplined, and exact," one of our sons recounted after bunking with Harris at the camp. He excelled at mapmaking, gunnery, horsemanship, and artillery calculations, and at roll call his uniform was always painstakingly put together. We were surprised to hear that the formerly incorrigible Harris flourished within the military structure.

It was just a week after he returned from training to await his deployment in two months' time that Harris split his big toe clean in half with a foul swing from his axe. Initially, we chalked up the uncharacteristic misstep to the weight of his grief over Mrs. Craig, or to nerves attributable to the approaching combat or his inevitable separation from his brother.

That is, until a week later, when Harris drove their freight wagon into Ross Smith's plow, breaking the leg of the farmer's best mule—a debt that the boys would have to chop wood for three weeks to pay down.

Surreptitiously, Everett went to Doc Kane and informed him that his brother had been behaving peculiarly, walking into walls and eating up all the food on one side of his plate, leaving the other side untouched. A few of us who knew the boys accompanied Doc to their cabin, where, after Everett's not-so-gentle urging, Harris submitted to an examination. When it was established that his eyesight was degenerating—the boy spoke of it as a kind of black lace settling over him—some eyeglasses were duly fabricated. Yet they were expensive, and their effects would last only a few weeks before a pair of thicker gauge were required. Soon, instead of lace, Harris described a black aperture closing upon his vision—a porthole shrinking incrementally in diameter each day. With Harris's deployment soon approaching, a medical discharge was suggested by Doc Kane.

"They won't believe me," Harris was overheard sobbing outside the doc's office. "I wouldn't believe me either. Some sucker goes blind the week before he ships to Europe? Would you?"

And he was correct. We're sorry to admit today that we didn't believe him, not wholeheartedly. At the time there were plenty of stories circulating about men claiming all sorts of phantom ailments to avoid combat. One man in an adjacent county claimed to be Jesus Christ himself. And after conscription was instituted, this brand of cowardice became rampant.

Even Doc Kane himself confirmed that Harris's particular case of partial vision loss could indeed be a matter of malingering, especially since the boys had always been so blatantly obstinate with respect to authority. Either that or it could be a figment of mental exhaustion, brought on by all the tragedy those two had already endured. And according to the doc, since the blindness wasn't yet complete, there was no scientific means of testing for sure.

PRIVATE GREENWOOD

ON DECEMBER 18, 1915, the 116th Canadian Infantry Battalion embarked on the R.M.S. *Missanabie* from the Quebec City harbour. The majority of the battalion's soldiers were mere eighteen-year-olds fresh from Ontario's lumber camps and factory floors, all eager to test their mettle in the battlefields of Europe.

Among them was a private enlisted under the name Harris Greenwood, who would go on to serve under Lieutenant-Colonel Sam Sharpe, beneath whom he would win numerous honours and medals in his four years of combat service for bravery, mainly as a stretcher bearer. This starry performance was a surprise since, at first, many of his fellow soldiers wondered at Private Greenwood's apparent lack of knowledge related to military drills, procedure, or protocol. In addition to the sorry state in which he kept his uniform and equipment, it was commonly remarked among those in his regiment that it often seemed as though Private Greenwood had never been to basic training at all.

NO RETURN

THE DAY BEFORE his regiment's troopship was due to sail from Quebec City, Harris came staggering through the snow into town around noon, still in his bedclothes, his hands grasping blindly before him and hollering: "Where's Everett? Where's my brother?" He grabbed everyone he came across, tearing at their lapels, pulling them close so his dim eyes could gather an approximation of their faces.

When we informed Harris that the other boys in his regiment had departed by rail that morning, he let out a guttural cry and attacked the tavern with the dung shovel kept outside for the horses hitched there. After it took three grown men lying atop him in a snowbank to subdue the boy, Harris claimed that he'd woken that morning to find himself lashed to his own bedframe with a riding saddle. It was three hours before he managed to spin the heavy saddle around and work its buckles loose. When he did, he searched the cabin and found his uniform and service equipment gone. We have since all agreed that if Harris could've got his hands on his brother Everett that afternoon, he would have finally killed him.

We were reluctant to notify the Department of Militia and Defence of the switch, however, because even after all their missteps and delinquencies, we still felt some responsibility for those boys and didn't want to see either in a military prison. Besides, the Greenwood boys had taken an oath to provide the Dominion with a soldier, and they'd made good on that oath, and we saw no harm done.

After his brother went overseas in his stead, we seldom saw Harris Greenwood. Living alone with his vision failing, he was unable to cut more than a few cords for himself that winter, and to survive he was forced to sell off the stockpile they'd built up over the years. A few of us went out to his place that spring and found him almost fully blind, grubby, and half-starved. We took pity on him, passed the hat in church, and enrolled him in a newly established academy for the deaf and blind in Montreal. The headmaster there, a Mr. Gilles Thibault, had studied at Yale, and immediately took a liking to Harris's shrewd intellect, entrepreneurial ambitions, and uncanny strength. We've heard that Mr. Thibault installed Harris prominently on the school's rowing team, and that the boy's powerful arms and iron grip drove them deep into the national finals, trouncing many of Montreal's upper-crust schools by multiple boat lengths. Mr. Thibault arranged lessons for Harris in Latin, Greek, mathematics, and ancient history. By this point, Harris could only read with the aid of the thickest eyeglasses available, and only with the book held three inches from his face. Like an actor fighting to remain on stage as the curtains close and the lights are snuffed out, Harris feverishly gleaned all he could on every subject, especially forestry. In fact, it was with Mr. Thibault's recommendation that Harris applied to Yale's newly established forestry school, where a special oral entrance exam was devised which included questions on physiology, trigonometry, and botany. Harris trounced the exam and was the first Canadian to gain admittance to the esteemed program, and from all accounts he excelled there. He studied scientific log extraction and forest product management—activities he'd performed all his life, now on a much grander scale. Despite his disability, he was a popular fixture in the university's botanical laboratories and its legendary Peabody herbarium, where we've heard he passed his days opening each one of their thousands of specimen drawers, learning each tree by running its pressed leaves against his fingertips.

We can't claim this for certain, but many of us speculate that it must've been during his time there in Connecticut, probably all alone in his single dormitory room, when both of Harris Greenwood's retinas finally detached—like a pair of mussels that have lost their grip on a rock—and the world he'd known was gone for good.

COULD'VE GONE EITHER WAY

HARRIS RETURNED FROM Yale three years later, a new man. He'd
traded his logger's garb for a tweed suit and a well-formed hat. He
brought another man back with him, a short, sturdy fellow who drove
Harris's automobile and helped him get around. "Meet my second
in command, Mort Baumgartner," Harris proudly declared, shaking
each of our hands with his strong grip. What exactly he was in command of wasn't initially clear.

Still, we held a celebration at the community hall to mark our
native son's return. Harris claimed he'd written to his brother many
times over the years, but Everett could still neither read nor write, so
no replies were received. At the dinner, Harris toasted our generosity, and loudly proclaimed to have forgiven his brother for his trickery. He then expressed his intention to found a logging company
with him as a full partner, upon Everett's return. The coming post-
war boom was predicted to spike the price of commodities like metal,
chemicals, coal, as well as timber, and it was common knowledge that
lumber concerns worth any salt were poised to make a killing.

While they awaited the ceasefire, Harris and Baumgartner stayed
three months in the crooked log cabin, travelling extensively throughout the region, cruising for timber, making maps, hatching plans, and
tagging half of the Craig woodlot for logging. Then, just prior to
demobilization, we learned from a local boy who was serving overseas as a medical orderly that a Private Greenwood had been admitted to the No. 5 Canadian General Hospital at Liverpool.

"Was he hurt?" Harris asked when we informed him, his hands
clawing at the armchair he was sitting in.

We told him there was no mention of physical injury, and that he was awaiting transfer back to Canada. Harris then asked us to see to it that a letter he'd written for Everett be delivered immediately to the hospital, and that the orderly from our township read it to him personally and confirm that Private Greenwood had understood it. We did as instructed, though prior to sending the letter we steamed open the envelope—not out of nosiness, but rather to ensure it didn't contain some kind of murderous challenge or lingering grudge—and found an earnest proposition for the terms of their partnership, along with a stilted apology for Harris's stubbornness about cutting the entire woodlot, and a modified proposal to cut just half as Everett had suggested. It ended with a request for Everett to return home immediately following his discharge.

After Harris learned his brother had been read the letter and that he'd accepted the proposal and intended to return home, he borrowed funds from our local bank to finance a great feast to be held in Everett's honour. Harris and Baumgartner doubled their efforts in the weeks following, and managed to secure a preferred rate with the Canadian National Railway to have their timber transported to the mills in Kingston once it was cut.

It was another month of waiting before a wire finally came through from the Department of Militia and Defence that after four years of service, Private Greenwood had been discharged on June 3, 1919. His troopship was due to arrive in Halifax the subsequent day, so a feast was planned three days hence, allowing Everett ample time to travel home by rail.

Harris had the community hall adorned with paper lanterns and ribbons, and readied a great cask of lager he'd purchased. When the day arrived and Private Greenwood hadn't appeared on the morning train as expected, Harris was undeterred. At suppertime he went ahead and called for heaping plates of food to be set out, with the largest portion put on the plate his brother had preferred since they were boys. While we ate, Harris gave a long-winded speech, claiming that his brother "Can't even read a watch," and that his tardiness was further proof that Harris ought to hold the controlling share of their company. We laughed uneasily, while glancing at our own watches. When the last evening train had come and gone, and it became clear that his brother would not return, Harris took up the heavy plate of food he'd prepared and asked Baumgartner to lead him out to a nearby well, where he pitched it inside, the porcelain smashing to bits while it dropped to the water.

Harris wasn't seen for days afterward, until a lumber crew from Kingston arrived by rail and descended upon the Craig woodlot. From the road we could hear Harris loudly instructing them to leave no tree standing, even demanding that they take up the logs that formed the cabin and drag those off to the mill as well. When the job was done, Harris left on the same train that carried his logs, and we never saw him again—except in the pages of our newspapers and periodicals, of course.

His brother did return, eventually, though not for another five years, by which time Greenwood Timber had already established itself out West as one of the Dominion's leading lumber concerns. Though to claim that Everett had returned would be misleading. He was just as transformed as Harris had been, except in his case for the worse. Gone was the merry, easy-moving boy who'd made bows and arrows and hollered swears from the tops of the elm trees in the town square. His face had become all shadows and angles, his brow creased like old newspaper, and his once-happy eyes had hardened, as though they'd been screwed deeper into his head. It was clear from his general dishevelment that he'd become a drifter, the kind of malnourished man we often glimpsed on the margins of town, drinking out of rain barrels or carrying things off that no one was using.

Some of us speculated that he was too wounded in his mind by the butchery of war to dwell in regular civilization. The rest believed that his true nature had finally been revealed over there in Europe, and that he'd simply evolved into the sinister creature that he'd always been. Regardless, it was a pitiful sight to behold when we escorted him out to the decimated woodlot that his brother had sold off to a local land speculator. He walked among the stubble of stumps, each of them black with rot, his feet sinking into the old sawdust that still blanketed the ground like snow. He came to a rest on a stump near to where their log cabin had been and sat for about an hour, muttering to himself with a dulled, unfocused look, drinking from a flask he kept in his filthy coat, taking wild swings at insects whenever they dared to fly near him. To be honest, he appeared to be doomed, like the sort of man who'd already suffered more than his rightful share, and would only keep on suffering.

Still, we did what we could. We offered to billet him in our houses, just as we had when he and his brother were first orphaned. But Everett only balled his fists and snapped at us to leave him alone. Given that his combative streak seemed to be the only aspect of his character to survive the War, we didn't press the issue. Each morning, we brought a bucket of food out to the gutted woodlot, along with a pint jar of cheap spirits to replenish Everett's flask. We would set these on one of the stumps near to where he slept, upon the rectangular scar that the cabin had left in the grass. This was how it went for two weeks, until one morning Everett walked to the railway, hopped a boxcar, and disappeared for good.

Over time, at our teas, card games, and social events, talk would often turn to the Greenwood boys and what became of them. We'd imagine Everett living in prison all those years for what he'd done to that poor child, or off in some hobo jungle somewhere, among his fellow criminals, wandering on the fringes of civilized people. Next, we'd imagine Harris in his great timber mansion, the one way out in Vancouver we'd read about in our general-interest magazines, with its bowling alley, grand ballroom, and vast, manicured gardens. And we'd shake our heads at how it all turned out.

Despite the scandal and that shameful business with the Japanese, we always bought Greenwood lumber for our houses and to repair the church. And we'd boast to anyone who'd listen about where the great captain of industry had hailed from. But in the same breath, we were just as likely to whisper about his brother, the fugitive and felon who'd committed an unspeakable crime.

Yes, we saw the Greenwood family begin, which was a privileged thing to witness, if you consider it. And while the pettiest of us claim to have known that those two boys were cursed from the day we found them barefoot and cowering next to those burning rail cars, the rest of us know the truth. That just as easily, it could've been Everett who received the proper schooling and then lost his sight. And that just as easily, it could've been Harris sacrificing himself for his brother and turning out the ruined, wandering man. As far as those Greenwood boys were concerned, we know it could've gone either way.

1934

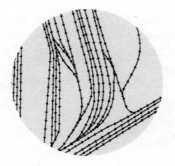

THE DUST

THAT MORNING A smothering duster envelops Temple Van Horne's farm, which sits five miles outside Estevan, Saskatchewan. So far this year these storms have scoured the lead paint from her barn, her house, and her library, leaving great swaths of raw pinewood white as a farmer's bared ass. The dust has felled her fence posts, drowned her auxiliary roadway, derailed the local trains, and sifted through the cracks and doorframes of even her tightest-built structures, leaving a thin film on carpets, bedspreads, and window dressings. Now, sipping her morning coffee in the kitchen, through the porch door she watches her Jerseys wander blindly, their heads bent low to vacuum up the blowing dust in hopes that some scrap of green lies beneath. Last week Temple slaughtered her best cow for meat after it gave brown milk, and she worries she'll eventually have to do the same with the others before they die languishing with mud bursting their bowels.

"How many times do I have to tell them that there isn't any grass down there?" Temple asks Gertie, who's preparing a vat of porridge for the farmhands, like she does every morning, always beating Temple to the kitchen even though she's pushing seventy.

"Cows are dim creatures," Gertie replies. "But if this drought keeps up the way it is, you'd be better off raising camels."

By mid-morning the rowdy wind falters and the dust settles, revealing a wide, prairie sky of almost lavender blue. Temple pulls on her work trousers and walks outside among the taupe, skin-smooth drifts of dust to survey the damage. She carries her second coffee in a tin cup back through the wheat fields, her palm clamped over the rim to keep the dust out, to where she discovers her seed crops entirely buried.

The drought has worn on for three years now, and these dusters are becoming ever more fierce and frequent. She's heard the local farmers grumble about the greedy Americans to the south who've plowed over their grassland with mechanized tractors. In their view, it's a plague from elsewhere: Texas, Oklahoma, Nebraska, Kansas. But the truth is that it's their dust too. If Temple thought anyone would listen, she'd point out that in a frenzy to harvest more wheat, they'd ripped up their buffalo grass with similar zeal. Ever since she was a girl, Temple has always consulted books when faced with a quandary, and in the drought's early days, she studied soil chemistry and scientific irrigation. She learned to rotate her crops and let the land lie fallow and regenerate, and at the agricultural hall in Estevan she'd warned the others to do the same. Yet their ways were set, and they weren't seeking advice from the local "Lady Farmer." Initially at least, Temple's techniques kept her soil black as slugs, moist as cake, except none of that matters now. The dust blew in anyway. Little did those old fools know: green things are all that keeps the land and sky from trading places.

With an index finger pressed to one nostril, Temple flings a tar-black ribbon onto the timber-and-wire fencing that marks the edge of her property near the rail line. Next, she hunkers low and scoops a fistful of dust, stands, then opens her fingers slow and watches the slight breeze chew it to nothing, while impossible budgetary figures likewise dissolve in her head. Even if a rain does come, the soil is baked to such a crust that the water will just run off. With her seed plants lost, she'll have to buy seed for next year, which will exhaust her reserve fund. She can't bear to hock the books in her library (some of the rarest volumes are worth good money) or to halt the free meals she provides to the vagrants she takes in, so her only option will be to sell some horses—that's if she can find a buyer who can still afford hay and oats.

She's heard people speak of farming as a peaceful endeavour, yet from the very outset Temple has warred with her land. She's plowed it up, cut it down, and beat it flat again. It's taught her things she'd never speak in polite conversation. Like the fact that Mother Nature's true aim is to convert us people back into the dust we came from, just as quick as possible.

Temple circles back past the library housed in the old church, then cuts over to the barn, where she finds a CN railroad detective conversing with a group of her men. Art McSorley is short, heavy-set and heavy-jawed, with pop-eyes like a strangled trout, a tin tie-clasp, oiled hair, and trousers hiked high over his solid belly, the resultant bulge bringing to mind the prow of a ship. He polices the entire continent-spanning CN line, and it's said he's more inclined to pitch you into the iron wheels of a running train and call it an accident than he is to book you for trespassing upon it. It's also claimed that McSorley reports a dozen such accidents yearly.

"What should I time you boys with? A stopwatch? Or a calendar?" Temple calls out, clapping to disperse her men, who make a show of jumping up, though they continue to linger nearby, aiming to catch the gist of the detective's visit and whether it concerns them personally.

"Some drunkards took a dip in the Estevan water tower over the weekend, Miss Van Horne," McSorley says disappointedly, his face like a fallen cake. "I was just checking if any of your boys here are still damp."

"I don't quite see how a water tower in little old Estevan is a concern of yours, Detective," Temple says when she reaches him.

"That tower serves the CN line, Miss. And any disturbance that happens within a mile of those tracks anywhere in this entire Dominion immediately becomes my business."

"Then maybe you can explain to me why it is that whenever anyone gets drunk in Estevan, you think they did so at my request?"

"Come on, Temple, people are saying they befouled it."

"Be*fouled* it? With their unclean souls?" she says breathlessly. "Goodness me, Detective!"

He leans in. "*Shat* in it, Miss," he says, fidgeting with his hat.

"And how are you so sure it was my men?" Temple asks, though she feels a twirl of worry in her stomach. Currently, she has thirty farmhands housed in the loft of her barn, eating her food, playing cards, twiddling their thumbs. Little wonder they're getting up to trouble. No place is more maddening than a wheat farm during a drought. "It could've been kids," Temple adds. "Or cows, for God's sake."

"Cows don't climb ladders," McSorley says. "And they were some of your transients, all right. The water has an oily film to it this morning."

Though her farm sits on the town's outskirts, the general populace of Estevan isn't particularly thrilled about Temple's meals for the poor or the library that she offers to those she takes in. *What interest do those bloodsuckers have in some old books anyhow?* she's heard them wonder aloud at town meetings.

"Some old bitty's earring goes missing some morning," Temple says, "and by ten o'clock you're convinced one of my men nabbed it."

"It's just the sort you attract," he says. "Most of them are career criminals. Fugitives. Parasites too lazy to scratch. The good folks of Estevan were pleased when you bought this place originally, Miss Temple, but nobody imagined you'd set up a soup kitchen."

"This isn't a soup kitchen, Detective. It's a farm. And like any farmer, I'll hire who I please. And I'll feed who I please, too." Temple is careful to avoid the motherly role with her men. They do their work during the week, and the weekends are theirs to squander, drink, and gamble away as they see fit. Normally, Gertie distributes their pay on Monday mornings—that way they have some days to get used to having money in their pockets before the temptation of a day off strikes. This past Friday, however, Temple paid them early while Gertie was up in Regina visiting her sister. She realizes now her mistake. Especially if this water tower story is true. She turns to scan the dusty faces of her men, who are performing odd jobs just within ear-shot. Once McSorley's gone she'll have each of them account for their whereabouts Saturday night, and anyone who returned with damp underclothing will be banned for a year. But the detective can't know this. Give him a little, and he's the type that'll push and push and keep pushing until she's off riding the rails herself.

"I'll look into it, Detective," she says.

"I thank you for that," he says, replacing his hat. "And Temple? I'd be even more inclined to ignore this disruption if you'd keep an eye out for me. A short while back, a vagrant got off a freight train in Ontario and beat a man in his own orchard, a senator's brother in fact. Now a beating is its own thing, but the unusual part here is that the tramp claimed to have an infant with him. And there's a power-ful man who has a keen interest in the identity of that infant, espe-cially if it's a little girl."

"I don't take in children, Detective. You know that. So no, he hasn't been here. And besides, we're a long way from Ontario."

"Well, the word is he's making his way west, seeking work, like the rest of these bums. And since you're about the only person hiring for a thousand miles, I thought I'd mention it. So if a man and a baby *do* turn up at your table, drop me a line. It'll go a long way toward repairing your good standing with both the CN Railway company and the fine citizenry of Estevan. Because if things get any worse," McSorley says, turning his eyes to the dust-choked wasteland that was once her field, "you're going to need somebody to come and dig you out."

TEMPLE

"YOU PICKED A dying world to show up into," Everett tells Pod, as dusty sails peel off the stricken prairie hardpan and fly up to scrape their eyes. Though they also have the dust to thank for their rescue: the express train they'd been trapped on for three days had halted this morning only after they'd passed into Saskatchewan and the locomotive boiler's air intake became clogged.

His thighs trembling from exhaustion and hunger, Everett stumbles some miles to the rust-red grain elevator at Pasqua, just as he'd been instructed by the group of tramps he'd met under a trestle after leaving the train. Noting the baby and seeing their ravenous condition, the tramps had spoken of a wheat farm owned by a woman offering free lodging and meals in exchange for a bit of fieldwork.

In the early afternoon, they hop a southbound freight on the third track from the road. It's a local, creeping slow under long, feathery clouds that bounce light like hammered copper. Everett chews up the dandelion greens that he pulled near the tracks and feeds the sludgy paste to Pod with his fingers, who accepts it, if unenthusiastically.

With the baby tied upright to his front, Everett jumps off at the Estevan water tower and veers south. Since he related to Pod the story of his boyhood back on the train, she's been babbling gibberish almost non-stop, and as he walks, she makes a series of long puffing sounds, almost like her own impersonation of a steam boiler.

The August sun gnaws his skin, and sweat slicks his neck as an exhausted darkness teases the edges of his vision. After a few hours of walking they come across an irrigation ditch, where a snapping wind kicks up more dust that pastes his mouth and cakes his eyeballs; Pod begins to cry and thrash her head to avoid it. While he'd like to tell her that things will get better, that soon they'll find her a decent home, or at very least a mouthful of water, he can't credibly bring the words to his lips. Then a figure wiring a fence to some timber posts materializes through the haze.

"That's far enough," the woman calls out when she sights him.

Everett stops. Pod pumps her legs impatiently for him to keep walking.

The woman pockets her pliers and saunters in his direction before pausing twenty feet away. Through sun-fired dust he makes out her work-built shoulders, her clothes pasted against her by the coursing wind. Her auburn hair is pinned up and she has a kerchief tied over nose and mouth.

"Came in on the ten o'clock?" she calls out, visoring her eyes with her hand. Given her directness and the rooted manner in which she stands upon the ground, Everett is certain she owns it. And anyone living this close to the line can probably set a watch by the whistles.

"That's right," he says.

"From the east? Before that?" She tugs down her kerchief. A rosebud of a mouth. A handsome nose. Eyes blue as fresh ink.

"I'm in need of a meal and some work. I was told I could find that here."

"And what's that you've got against you?" she asks.

He looks down at Pod against his chest, her chubby legs swinging in lazy circles as she squints into the amber shimmer. "An infant, ma'am," he admits.

"It wouldn't be a girl infant, would it?" she asks.

"It would," Everett says, impressed that the woman can gauge such a thing at a distance.

Now her hands go to her hips and she turns her head and rests her chin on her shoulder for a long moment. Over the wind's moan, Everett hears a curse escape her. She's a hair taller than him, wearing a man's box-toe boots, a broadcloth shirt, and canvas trousers.

He lowers his gaze. He doesn't know if it's thirst or hunger, but already he's drunk in the sight of her to the precipice of wooziness.

"Unfortunately, I've already got more farmhands than I got farm," she says. "As you can see, it isn't exactly a boom year. Besides, it's not my regular practice to take in infants."

"I understand that," he says, too exhausted to argue. The thought of trudging back to the tracks nearly shatters him right there. "We're sorry to bother you." He turns and prepares to plunge back into the cloud.

"The rails are that way," she calls out, pointing in the other direction.

"Thank you," he says, turning his feet to correct his bearing.

"The dust may get worse as the day wears on and the wind really finds its legs," she says as he's again about to start off. "You'd best keep the sun to your right. And go quickly before it shifts on you."

"I appreciate it," he says.

"And keep a rag over her face or she'll develop a cough," she adds after he's taken his first step.

Her interest in the child's welfare is cause for some optimism, so Everett decides to risk a proposition. "Forgive me for mentioning it," he says. "But it seems to me that your field could do with some trees for a windbreak. Maples are best. Five-foot spacing. Maybe a hundred trees. They'll come up quick. And in just a few years they'll do you some real good. I'd be happy to put them in for you along the lot line, if you're interested. I know trees as well as anyone."

She nods. Holds his eyes. In the time she's been standing there, the drifting dust has nearly buried both her boots.

"You two are thirsty and hungry, I suppose?" she says.

"We've missed some meals," he says. At the mention of food his knees nearly buckle.

She mutters under her breath again and glances around, almost as though she's ensuring no one is observing them, then looks back at him. Her brow furrows, deep-creased like tilled soil—a field herself. "Just until we get some trees in," she says, waving them onward, yet still walking twenty feet ahead. "Then you're on your way."

After following her for a while, he sees a farm appear as if conjured from the dust. "Half of the men up there are either sick or consumptive," the woman calls back while gesturing to the barn's loft. "So you and your baby can take the spare room in the house. I don't want your little one catching anything."

She escorts them into the house, where cloth is tied over all the doorknobs to prevent static shocks from the arid air. The large, linoleum-floored kitchen reminds Everett of the army: everything oversized, a colossus of a wood-fired range with six cookplates, a set of huge skillets, and great enamelled pans and roasters—all capable of tremendous output.

She introduces him to the cook, an elderly woman named Gertie with a pinched mouth and a kind yet terse demeanour, who shows them to the spare bedroom. While Everett is unbinding Pod from his chest, Gertie fetches water from the cistern in the cellar and fills the basin. The water is unexpectedly sweet and clear, and before bathing Pod, Everett lets her drink, then gorges himself until his gut pouts over his buckle. While he floats Pod in the basin—her green eyes bright, her lashes jewelled with drops—Gertie returns and begins pinning bedsheets up over the windows.

"There's no need for all that," Everett says. "She can sleep in broad daylight if need be."

"Miss Temple insisted," Gertie says through the pins in her mouth. "It's for the dust. You should wet the sheets before putting her down. Dr. Stone said some youngsters in Estevan have caught the dust cough so bad they're snapping their own ribs. Normally, we don't accept little ones here. But Miss Temple is making an exception in your case."

"We won't be staying long," he says.

"You're putting in some trees. That right?"

"Yes," he says, swirling Pod in the wash water, which has already gone a turbid grey with her grime.

"And then you'll move along," she adds while she pins the last sheet, more as a statement than a question.

"That's right," Everett says.

"Good," she says while briskly making her way to the kitchen. "The other men will get jealous with you bunking here in the house and not out in the barn. And a jealous man is a stupid man, in my experience."

After Pod's bath, they're called out onto the large porch that sits beside a wide-spreading willow, where a communal table is already seated with thirty or so men. Everett scans the table for the woman, Miss Temple, and can't locate her. Gertie appears from the house with a large roasting pan of toasted cheese sandwiches and a kettle of creamed chicken stew. When the bell is rung, Everett goes to sit, and as he approaches the only available space on the bench, a large man puts up a muddy boot and blocks him.

"Pardon me," Everett says, yet the man begins to speak loudly and obliviously with his tablemates. Famished and eager not to invite trouble, Everett ignores the slight and sits on a nearby apple crate with Pod in his lap. He blows the stew cool before spoon-feeding it to her. After just a few mouthfuls, she spits up into the dust.

"I don't mean to be fussy," Everett says to Gertie at the table. "But is there any goat's milk around? This child can't stomach cream or cheese."

Gertie puts down her spoon and purses her lips. "Our last goat died last month," she says. "But we'll see what we can drum up."

"I heard of choosy beggars," the roughened man who took his seat grumbles into his cup. "But I ain't never heard of no choosy beggar baby." Everett keeps his eyes down while the others within earshot chortle.

"This is the softest meal we have," Gertie says when she returns, covertly handing Everett a small bowl of smooth porridge, aiming to conceal the special treatment that they're receiving from the others.

Everett sits at the crate again, this time facing away from the table, and watches Pod gleefully work the beige paste between the ridges of her gums like a ruminant. Though she seems to like it well enough, he still worries she ought to eat more than she does.

THE GREAT LIBRARY
OF ESTEVAN, SASKATCHEWAN

ONE COULD CLAIM that it began the way all libraries must: with a single book. But in truth the idea passed to Temple Van Horne from her father, a Calvinist minister who was lured from the Netherlands to the Canadian prairie by a government parcel of land, a man who always kept a table on his porch. Each night after the fieldwork was done, Temple and her father would lay out four place settings—four starched napkins, four forks, four spoons, four plates, four glasses of water—then dish out four helpings of the same meal they were about to enjoy inside. "When you live near the railroad," he'd say, "it's a matter of decency. Nourishment—God distinguishes not the spiritual from the intellectual from the physical. We don't either."

Temple's Austrian mother resented the charitable practice, called it "spraying perfume on manure," and made off with an itinerant water dowser the summer Temple turned ten. That Christmas, her mother wrote a series of letters begging to return home, but her father burned them all.

While strict, her father brimmed with ideas and inventions, and always seemed to be reading every book other than the Bible. At heart he was more farmer than preacher, and spoke blunt and plain to Temple on sexual matters—at the dinner table it was all bull semen and goat rutting and chicken sexing. Nakedness went unremarked in their household, both hers and his. And when she turned sixteen, he looked upon the nervous parade of young suitors—bloodless beanstalks droning lengthily on the subjects of wheat varieties and well-prepared picnics—more with the amusement of a livestock auctioneer than anything like protectiveness.

Then, when Temple was eighteen, her father died of a stroke in their claw-foot tub, a mechanical engineering manual swollen to double its normal size floating barge-like over him. After that, Temple completed her training as a schoolteacher and spent the next three years in a one-room schoolhouse. Though she enjoyed the company of children, she disliked instructing them in anything but literacy. For the younger grades especially, it was mostly giving orders to sit and stand—*up, down, up, down*. She felt a perpetual sadness for them, showing up in the same rags each day, coughing and quarrelling and skinning their knees, destined to forget her lessons the second they quit school to go plow the same exhausted fields their parents had.

Still, she persisted, and at twenty-one, Temple met a man named Jurgen Kohler, who was himself a wheat farmer as well as a part-time inventor. Humming with schemes and ideas, he was the first man she'd ever met who reminded her of her father. After a brief courtship, they married and moved into the house Temple had inherited. At first things were amiable, until a year passed and Jurgen began applying for patents related to a water pump he'd invented. After repeated denials, he took the habit of belittling Temple, under his breath at first, usually before bed or while preparing for the day's farming—a vocation he'd come to believe was beneath him. He'd bemoan what he called her "schoolteacher's view of the world," as well as her penchant for reading fiction, calling it "soft-headed." At twenty-five, Temple lost a child and her ovaries after an ectopic pregnancy ruptured her Fallopian tubes and nearly killed her. She returned from the hospital in Regina to find her husband had made off for the United States to seek his fortune as an inventor, without even taking the trouble to divorce her.

Instead of leaving her devastated, the demise of her marriage taught her the folly of hitching her entire being to the horse of one man. She quit teaching, sold her father's house, and purchased a two-hundred acre farm a hundred miles to the south, near the rail junction of Estevan. The house was well built and boasted good-sized rooms with sturdy timber bones, a bomb-proof cookstove, numerous outbuildings including a barn and a long-abandoned woodframe church, and a sweet, windmill-pumped well that to that day had never failed, even when most of the wells in the vicinity had come up dry during the drought.

The day she took possession, Temple set her own table on the porch: turkey, potatoes, and dinner rolls, two heaped plates, with silverware and glasses of lemonade and napkins appliquéd by her grandmother, all perfectly arranged. The next morning, she found the food untouched—if you discounted the flies swarming the turkey and the wood-bugs mountaineering on the potatoes. Undeterred, the next night she fixed roast beef and lima beans and sat inside with the lights out, eating and reading by a match struck every now and then, so as not to spook them with a lamp. After weeks of wasting good food, one evening around nine she heard some shuffling outside. Then cutlery scraping. Then a few low voices. In the morning, she found the plates neatly stacked, each bone-white, licked clean.

She set a table for four the next evening, and this time they came earlier, four bedraggled figures climbing the stairs that faced the direction of the railroad. She wanted to call out, "You can quit all your creeping around!" but knew she'd shame them if she spoke. When word got around, she heard some arguments out near the runoff ditch, though these soon settled themselves. After that, never did the same visitors come on consecutive nights, and she figured they'd established some code of conduct, a kind of schedule, and admired them for it. The men conversed quietly over the meals, and always removed their hats. There was only the occasional woman—a fact that troubled Temple, because in her experience women hungered just as regularly as men. One of the first who ever came was Gertie, who'd fallen destitute after losing her husband and three adult sons to the flu, and whom Temple hired immediately after she knocked at the door following her meal to help with washing up.

When the Crash hit five years back, Temple had carpenters construct an even larger covered porch, extending out near the willow tree, and set a big table beneath it. Though No. 1 Northern wheat had dropped from $1.43 to sixty cents a bushel as the drought dragged on—two years, then three—her well held, and the farm remained profitable. Though Gertie thought it a bad idea, Temple began to allow guests to sleep in the hayloft in return for a morning's labour in the field, and was pleased to see that the work did them almost as much good as the food. Even as a girl, she'd had a mind for the repair of broken things—including birds crushed against a window and prairie dogs maimed by her father's horse-drawn thresher. She was an expert maker of splints and patches, poultices and bandages, which her father encouraged. And today, in her better moments, she feels she's honouring his memory with this great unprofitable enterprise.

Three years ago, while recalling her father's words on nourishment, a vision seized her. That evening she lined the old church on her property with some makeshift plank shelves, but it took a full calendar year to collect enough books to fill the first one. Then she had the idea that those seeking a meal and shelter might bring one as payment—any book as good as any other. Thus it came to be that in an old church just outside Estevan, Saskatchewan, is housed one of the world's great libraries. Its books were not bestowed or bequeathed—in fact, few were purchased. Most were stolen, found, begged for, borrowed, or brought from the world's farthest corners by the world's lowest people. Gathered by vagrants and vandals, convicts and parolees. Tramps, prostitutes, and husband-killers. Larcenists, bank robbers, and check-kiters, as well as decent men and women just down on their luck. Her collection is not catalogued. Its titles sit on shelves of rough-hewn lumber and stacked brick, balanced as precariously as the lives of those who acquired them. To make a withdrawal, a patron must simply bring another book in exchange, no questions asked. Books come to Temple with banknotes tucked inside, or locks of hair, bloodstains, theatre tickets, love notes, or hastily scrawled threats—all discoveries that flush her with a kind of archeological delight. Once a man brought a two-volume illustrated Dante's *Inferno*, with a different wildflower pressed between every second page.

As far as circulation goes, the Russians are popular (her patrons are well versed in the dialects of depravity, betrayal, madness). As is Homer, the bard of ill-fated homeward journeys. Books on canning and food preservation are equally popular. As are how-to manuals. Anything that allows for more to be done with less.

Still, Temple has no illusions concerning her library's impact. Her books won't lift anyone from their low station. They won't right wrongs or save wandering souls from perdition or fill grumbling stomachs. But they might let a few scraps of sunlight fall into some lean, desolate lives, and that's something.

Over the years, however, any babies she's allowed on the farm have always brought trouble. People come looking for babies, usually dragging a whole mess along behind them. She was all set to turn the tramp and his infant away at the fence line, which perhaps would've been doing them a favour, given McSorley's habit of appearing on her farm every month or so to see what fugitives she's harbouring. But the man's understated "We've missed some meals" made her reconsider. From her dealings with the needy, she knows it's the ones who don't complain who are the greatest cause for worry. It's the quiet ones you find tucked away in a corner somewhere, eyes glazed over, starved, too proud to ask.

If McSorley *does* catch them here, bunking in the house no less, at best he'll see her run out of Estevan for good; she doesn't want to consider his worst. So her plan is to keep them just until the windbreak is in: a week, two at most. She's had Gertie put some sheets up over their windows to discourage prying eyes. And besides, this Everett doesn't appear to pose any imminent threat to the girl. Though if he does anything strange, she'll be the first to call in

McSorley herself. And if all goes well, once the pair is restored they'll
be on their way. If Temple's father taught her anything, it's that no
one deserves to be hungry. Not even kidnappers. She's hosted worse
on her farm before. And there are likely even worse to come.

FULL TITLE

HARRIS GREENWOOD HAS never liked his mansion. Even though it's built from some of the grandest trees that ever lifted from the soil, criss-crossed with beams hewn from Douglas fir, sequoia, and red cedar—trees already head-high when Napoleon drew his final breath. Built in Queen Anne style, with thirty-five rooms, including four parapets, parquet floors, two tiers of balconies, a private bowling alley, rosettes and mouldings of walnut, cherry, oak, and maple, all crafted by the finest Scottish woodcarvers, it's expensive to maintain, overlarge for his needs, and easy to get lost in. Yet for the first time since its construction, Harris is grateful for its enormity. Because such a large domestic staff is required to run it, no one views it as odd for his describer to take up residence there following their homecoming from Asia.

But Harris finds his return to his usual office routine strangely agonizing. Perhaps he's depleted from the journey, or perhaps he caught some exotic bug on the steamer, but the morning hours inch by as he shifts in his seat and his mind wanders like an abandoned dog. His desk, once a sturdy lifeboat in the waters of his daily routine, now sits before him as inert and dispiriting as a gravestone.

By the afternoon, Harris can barely follow Milner's supply chain reports or Baumgartner's briefs on the Chemainus mill dispute he brutally halted by hiring local thugs to disperse the complaining workers. And by suppertime, his desk is cluttered with unanswered correspondence and unread land leases and documents in want of signature.

The truth is that he'd much rather be reclining on the divan in his room, as Feeney recites Keats in his cello-like voice, before they dine together on the veranda and discuss some bit of esoteric news they've alighted upon in the papers. To prevent suspicion, Harris has ordered Feeney to resist visiting his room after hours, the way he had so freely on the ship, and has decided to limit his presence in the Greenwood Timber Company offices unless it's deemed necessary.

To ease the drudgery, Harris arranges a visit to one of his remote mills—along with his describer, naturally. Baumgartner would normally accompany Harris on such a trip, but Harris makes a calculated risk in requesting that he remain in Vancouver to assess their inventory for the big Japanese order personally. Thankfully, with no burr of suspicion in his voice, Baumgartner agrees.

Harris and Feeney sail the schooner to Victoria, then unload the Bentley and drive north. After a numbing ride over miles of corduroy logging roads, they arrive at the first mill near sundown. Harris is thrilled to be back among the frenzied activity of a logging outpost in late summer, with its sawdust and sap and *chock-chock* of bucker's axes. He delights in the shrieks of whistles, the rattles of hooked boom chains dragging his logs from the water, the floorboards torn to splinters by his fallers' spikes, and the ringing gang saws he can feel in the roots of his teeth. They make camp in a nearby valley, and with no prying eyes about, Feeney visits Harris's tent, though he's always careful to leave before first light.

The bucolic spirit of the tour comes to an end, however, when a ten-foot circular blade is thrown from a gang saw, leaving a man riven in half from forehead to vitals. It's such a grisly scene that Feeney refuses to describe it, though a millwright later informs Harris that after completing the cut, the bloodied blade ran like a banshee into the forest and lodged itself in a tree a mile distant. Men in Harris's employ die with some regularity—he signs their notices and pays a paltry severance to the family, which there usually isn't.

Yet to be so near this particular death disquiets him. With Feeney now at his side, Harris is newly alert to the brutality of logging and the general frailty of life. And after a ramshackle service held near the log skids, Harris cancels a final excursion to hunt rare woodland birds for his collection and hastens their return to Vancouver the following day.

When they arrive at the Greenwood mansion, Milner and Baumgartner immediately request an emergency meeting.

"We've taken stock while you've been on your little gallivant, sir," Baumgartner says. "And things don't look good for the Japan deal."

"Oh, we'll find the trees, we always do," Harris says confidently.

"I doubt you've forgotten, Mr. Greenwood, but we're contractually obliged to provide the Japanese High Command with *seventy million* feet of Douglas fir railway sleepers, all slathered in creosote," Milner says in his schoolmarmish tone. "And with many of our land leases expiring imminently, even if we use up all of our existing overstock, we don't have the trees to cut them."

Harris now realizes that his trip had been imprudent, and perhaps even reckless. He can't help noticing a shift in tone among his senior employees, a heightened air of secrecy and wariness, as though they're managing him more than obeying. Again, the memory of those dead swampers pops into his mind.

I'm the one signing the cheques here, Harris reminds himself. And if either Milner or Baumgartner dares to challenge him, he'll run them out of the province, not to mention his company. That said, they know his affairs better than anyone, and if this Japanese deal falls through, he'll be finished. And, perhaps most importantly of all, so will his arrangement with Feeney.

So Harris needs trees. It's not like he's never faced this predicament before. The eastern Canadian stock is long exhausted—which is why he broke West in the first place—so his only hope is local timber. When he inquires about some parcels of MacMillan's that could suit their needs, Milner reminds him that ever since Harris undercut MacMillan for a lucrative railway trestle contract in central B.C., their rival will neither sell nor lease them a single acre, and neither will any member of his syndicate.

"Why not buy full title on the Port Alberni parcel from Rockefeller?" Feeney interjects from the office's margins after the discussion has stalled.

"Mr. Greenwood hired you to be his eyes, chum, not his mouth," Baumgartner snaps.

"That's enough, the both of you," Harris says, leery of appearing overprotective.

Perhaps Liam has a point, Harris thinks. Traditionally, Greenwood Timber never seeks full title. Instead, he's always preferred to lease cutting rights from the Crown or private landholders. That way, after he logs the land to his heart's content, ownership of the ugly slash and stumpage reverts to them. Yet with the stock of accessible old-growth shrinking, firms are holding tight to what they've got and electing not to lease cutting rights at all. With MacMillan's syndicate united against him, a tract the size Harris needs could only be had from a foreign concern—John D. Rockefeller's Port Alberni parcel being the best bet. In addition, Harris realizes, the parcel could include that little secluded island he'd half-burned, a place he's been daydreaming about bringing Feeney someday, where they could perhaps build a little cabin retreat if it all works out.

So what if he bought it outright? After all, Harris began his company by clear-cutting the Craig woodlot that he and Everett inherited, then selling off the land at a tidy profit. When Greenwood Timber was in its infancy, Harris often acted as his own purchasing agent, talking the crustiest of landholders out of their family plots. Except he can't propose a sale of this magnitude by telegram. Not to a man like Rockefeller. And he can't possibly travel to New York—a frail, blind Canadian cuts a pitiful figure in that world. Besides, Harris can neither shoot pheasant nor play bridge nor gossip about New York society. He wouldn't even get a meeting.

"We're finished if we can't get our hands on more trees," Harris says exhaustedly into Feeney's neck later that evening, after his describer has brazenly broken their rule against nocturnal visitation and snuck into his bed for the first time.

"I have an idea," Feeney replies. "But you're sure to dislike it."

"Well, come on," Harris says, kissing his neck, "out with it."

"Remind me again how you feel about parties?"

SAPLINGS

THE MORNING FOLLOWING Everett and the baby's arrival, Temple asks one of her men to take the tractor and fetch a hundred maple saplings from Fritz Schelling, whose hog farm borders some of the last glades in the area that haven't been razed for cropland. She'd prefer to select out the saplings herself, but a few years back Schelling had proposed marriage without so much as speaking three words to her previously, and since her refusal he turns the colour of ripe rhubarb whenever he's in her vicinity.

Normally, her men jump at an errand that alters the day's predictability, but each man she asks drags his feet and claims he can't drive the tractor. Word of McSorley's interest in the baby has surely spread, and Temple knows that her men certainly don't want anything around here that will intensify his scrutiny. And Gertie has reminded her of how much they disapprove of anyone enjoying preferred treatment, like staying in the house or having special meals prepared. So it seems a pact has been made among them to complicate matters for the new man until he moves on.

It isn't until after Temple threatens to cut dessert for a week that the youngest farmhand agrees and returns with the saplings by noon. Temple offers to have Gertie mind the baby while they work, but Everett declines. "Pod's used to watching me lug things around," he says. "And she might learn something."

They take Temple's pickup, slung low with seven jute-wrapped maples, out toward the lot line, where a dusty wind blares from the south. They drive with the windows cranked tight, the child propped in Everett's lap as he calls out the few landmarks visible in the haze. Whenever she starts to fuss, he bangs her tiny feet together like little cymbals.

"I tried a caragana shelterbelt out here years back," Temple says, aware that it makes no difference to him what she tried. "Wasted some good saplings. I still don't know why they didn't take."

"There's no surefire way to know if one will," he says. "You can put a tree in the ground with all the care in the world, and still some switch gets flipped and it dies on you. In my opinion, the tree decides whether it's worth the effort of going on living or not, and there's no way you can convince it otherwise. They're finicky things. But we'll do our best with yours."

When they park, he exits the truck and lays the baby atop his shirt on the vehicle's leeward side, near the front tire. Temple goes and drops the tailgate. "The sun's the proper angle here," he says, while together they lift the first jute-wrapped sapling from the bed, gripping its heavy root ball from underneath. He scans the terrain, kicks at the dirt in a few places, and selects a spot. "Soil's right. And they'll cut the wind here just fine." When the baked hardpan refuses a few stabs with the spade, they take turns swinging a pick to loosen it. While they're both shovelling out the hole, a nearly imperceptible wail causes Everett to bolt back behind the truck. Temple follows and watches him flick away the spur-throated hopper clinging to the child's cheek. "You little bastard," he says, stepping on the bug. "Not you, Pod," he adds, taking her up for a moment to soothe her whimpering.

When the hole is knee-deep, they shovel in some blood meal then lower the tree, which he rotates to face north, claiming he can tell how it was oriented before it was dug up; Temple can do the same with a wheat sheaf, but trees are a language prairie dwellers don't speak. When the time comes to refill the hole, his face reddens. "I usually relieve myself in there, before closing the dirt over," he says bashfully. "It tricks them."

"Tricks them how?" Temple asks, straining to take his primness seriously.

"It may be a superstition, but I've heard it convinces them that the soil's better than it is. So they try their best from the outset," he says.

"Have at it then," she says, turning around and crossing her arms.

When he finishes, they cover the root ball over with dirt, tamping it with the backs of their spades. Over the course of the afternoon they manage to drop six more maples into the ground, placed at five-foot intervals. They sit mute during the ride back, neither of them able to lift their arms over their head, the child asleep in Everett's lap like a cat.

"Only ninety-three more to go," Temple says exhaustedly when they reach the barn. At this rate of planting, Everett will be here two weeks. Even so, she's not worried, given that McSorley's visits land every month, give or take, a stopover he makes while cutting across the prairie by rail. Everett and the baby will be long gone by then.

"I keep some books in that old church over there," Temple says after they've unloaded the tools. "You're welcome to any volume you'd like. Just bring one back someday to replace it."

"I'm ashamed to admit that I can't read," Everett says. "But it's good what you're doing here. People speak highly of this place all down the line."

Back at the house, Temple parts the leafy skirt of the willow that hangs all the way to the ground. "I've got some water in here if you're thirsty," she says, leading him into the canopy. Inside, the ground is cool and moist, the high dome forming a green, leafy room. Everett lays the sleeping infant down on his shirt, and he and Temple sit with their backs to the trunk. She fills two pewter cups with a wooden dipper from a bucket as the willow's switches sway, allowing cuttings of light between them.

"I prefer it in here to those dusty fields of yours," Everett says. "I'm not used to seeing that far. Too much distance makes me dizzy."

"This farm's previous owner was English," Temple says. "And when he first settled here he encircled the house with willows and Garry oaks, except they all came up dwarfed and stumpy from lack of moisture. But somehow this one willow thrived. Must be an underground spring feeding it, the same one that feeds my well, I expect. Where it runs to or from I have no idea."

After they've replenished themselves, they both sit quiet for a while and listen to the sighs of the leaves.

"So how does a child get a name like Pod?" she asks. He'd used it when he shooed the hopper from her face, and for a moment he looks stunned, as though he's never heard the name spoken aloud before.

"Oh, it's more a nickname," he says dismissively. "Like 'seedpod.' Those little whirlers that maples send out—she reminds me of one. She'll have a different name someday. A proper one."

"When's that?"

His eyes go vacant and seem to look inward. "When I get her where she needs to go."

"She yours?" she asks, as lightly as she can.

"I'm her uncle," he says. "We're headed out West. Her family lives there."

"You know, nobody ever accused me of nosiness," she says. "I don't pester those who turn up here with questions about their past. I figure if you're here, you need to be. But there's something I have to say. A short while back a railroad detective came around, a man named McSorley. He said he's hunting a tramp who beat a man and has taken to the rails with a kidnapped infant."

"I'm her uncle," Everett repeats tensely, though he reddens at the ears.

She exhales. "That child doesn't look a thing like you, Everett."

He turns from her gaze and pours himself another cup of water, then holds up the cup but doesn't drink, using it to conceal his mouth while he speaks. "Think what you like. I didn't kidnap anyone."

"You're an awful liar," she says, patting his head as if he's a boy. "But no kidnapper ever fussed over a child the way you do that one. So I'm going to act like I believe you. Still, you'd best not linger here. Once we've got those trees in and you two are back to full strength,

I'll pay you for your work and you can be on your way. McSorley is about the only person in the world my men are afraid of. But they value this place even more, so I expect they'll keep your presence here to themselves. In the short term, anyway."

"You're kind," he says, taking another sip of water. "We'll get those trees in. Then we're gone. You have my word."

THE HISTORY OF SEED CRUSHING
IN GREAT BRITAIN

THE NEXT EVENING, after the tree planting is done and Everett and Pod have eaten dinner on the porch with the others—who have allowed them a place at the table, but still greet their presence with disdain—Everett sits at a pew in the ramshackle library, where beleaguered books climb the walls in toppling towers. By lamplight he wills his eyes to read Pod's journal, hoping that the great surplus of words collected on the shelves will somehow rub off on him, just from his sitting close by. Though the jam smears are permanent, as is the coal dust blackening its pages, he hopes to someday repair the journal's cracked cover and preserve it for Pod as a gift. She may care to read it someday, once he finds her a good home and someone to teach her how. It will be a comfort in a life lived without kinfolk. If Everett had something like that when he was a boy, something written by his true mother, whoever she was, maybe he would've turned out better.

He hears the door come open, and swiftly he snatches a book from the nearest shelf and stuffs the journal into the gap it left behind. He splits the new book before him and leans in close, feigning intense concentration.

"Where's the little one?" Temple says beside him, her hand alighting birdlike on his shoulder, a gesture that steals his breath whenever she does it.

Everett points to the sleeping baby packaged in blankets beneath the table.

"I thought you couldn't read," Temple says, easing into the opposite pew.

"Not properly. My brother Harris was the one who got his reading and numbers while I cut wood to feed us."

"Is that who you're taking the baby to?"

Everett silently curses himself for letting the name slip. "Yes," he says.

Mercifully, she lets the subject drop and reaches out to examine the spine of the book before him: "*The History of Seed Crushing in Great Britain*," she says. "I read this when I first bought this old place. Boring as a ten-hour sermon. You have an interest in seed storage?"

"Sure," he says, eager to change the subject. "You read all these books?"

"Oh, no, no," she says, glancing around. "There are more books here than anyone could ever hope to get through in a lifetime, which is sad if you really consider it."

"You've read some, though?"

"Sure."

"How many?"

"A fair number, I suppose."

"You should be proud of that," he says, eyeing the crowded shelves.

"Well, I guess I am," she says, as though she's surprised herself.

"What kind of books do people like me usually fancy?"

"People like you?"

"Tramps," he says. "Hermits. Lowlifes."

"*The Count of Monte Cristo* is popular with the lowlife set," she says slyly. "Not sure why that is. Revenge, I suppose. Sometimes when people lose everything, all that's left are their grudges. Also Dickens. Dostoevsky. Pulp novels. Detective stories. Not much interest in romances, unfortunately."

His face burns at her mention of this last subject. "And what kind of books does your type fancy?" he manages to get out.

"Who, us farm-bound spinsters?" she says. "We tend toward tales of escape. Adventure. Exotic locales. Egypt. Siam. I've read about Paris so much I no longer feel the need to go there."

"I was in northern France during the War. But I never saw Paris."

"Many of the folks here were once soldiers. What did you do there?"

"I wasn't much of an infantryman, so I did carpentry, mostly. Tables for the radios and planks to keep the soldiers up out of the mud. Otherwise, I carried stretchers. I probably carried a thousand men, most of them halfway between living and dying."

Her lips tighten over her teeth. "That must have been painful," she says. "To see all those people torn up like that." And her statement's naked simplicity unlocks something in Everett's chest. How easily she's linked what he witnessed in the War with the disquiet that afflicted him afterwards, like a blade that'd entered him through his eyes and broken off inside his head. Sights that, in the last days of the War, rendered him unable to speak or sleep for more than a few hours at a time, which landed him in a special hospital for soldiers suffering the same condition. It was what prevented him, after he was sent home, from joining Harris on their woodlot like he promised, and kept him drinking and roaming all those years afterward. But Everett can't express any of this now, so he directs his attention again to the incomprehensible book before him.

Pod starts whimpering beneath the table, opening and closing her tiny hands like a crab, and Temple stoops to take her up. Everett likes how she holds her, bouncing easefully on the balls of her feet.

"You know, I could help you," Temple says. "With your reading, I mean. Maybe not this one." She points at *The History of Seed Crushing in Great Britain*. "But I was a schoolteacher before I bought this place, and teaching people to read was the only part of the job I didn't mind."

"Oh, there isn't much hope for me," he says.

"I've instructed greater fools than thee," she says in a haughty voice, and carries Pod over to the shelves, right near to where he stuffed the journal. His stomach drops, though thankfully, she selects a different book. "Here," she says, sitting beside him, and suddenly he's shamefully aware that his ratty clothes haven't been washed in weeks.

"Try this," she says, pointing to the first line, a crescent of soil lodged permanently under the nail of her index finger. "It's called the *Odyssey*."

He has no choice but to try, and while the black type is easier to identify than the unruly handwriting of the journal, the words themselves are convoluted and meaning refuses him. Letters scatter from his eyes like roaches from a lamp. He trips and stumbles with his tongue for a while until he gets too embarrassed and says he's all worn out, and they walk back together to the house before turning in for the night.

In bed that evening, Everett decides against returning to the library for the journal. If this railway detective turns up, Everett will have better luck claiming that Pod is lawfully his without the journal there to connect her to R.J. Holt. While Everett hates being separated from the book, he doubts any tramp will unwittingly pull it from the shelves, especially since it's such a slight volume with nothing written on the spine.

On account of the iron-hard, sunbaked soil, the tree planting progresses more slowly than planned over the following week, and they average just six or seven trees daily. Each evening, Temple meets him in the library for his reading and writing lessons, though after swinging the pick all day it pains him to clutch a pencil. She sits close while he forms crude letters, and listens patiently to him crawling through the *Odyssey*. Luckily, literacy isn't quite as difficult as he recalled. Mostly, it all hinges on learning the pranks that letters play—the way *c*'s can act like *s*'s, the way *e*'s can be there or not—and gradually he improves, if only slightly. And there are moments when what he reads nearly pleases him.

After two weeks the windbreak is nearly finished, and Temple asks him to keep out of sight during the days, in case McSorley comes around. They continue to meet in the library after the sun sets, sitting incrementally closer together on the pew. He talks more about the War, and she talks about the books she's read and how she wishes her father were alive to help catalogue her library. When the day comes for them to drop the hundredth tree into the ground, they drive back to the house in a shared silence, as though from a funeral. That night, she invites him into her bed.

VANCOUVER

SOMEWHERE UPON THE limitless Canadian prairie, Harvey Lomax's first-class dining car rides into a crenellated tower of coal-black dust, thousands of feet high. The dust cloaks the train and the dining car goes dark. Though it's lunch, the waiter brings candles so they can see their food, and Lomax dampens his handkerchief and wipes his face while a fuzzy film of dust collects on the surface of his soup. The well-heeled gentleman adjacent to him abandons his bowl. Lomax, however, stirs the dust in and spoons it up.

Arriving days later in Vancouver, a place he's never been, he's awed by its forested mountains and gleaming ocean surrounds. With the two hundred dollars he earned with that swindle back at the hotel in Toronto nearly spent on his ticket, meals, and enough opium for the journey, he stops at a bank near the rail station and attempts to draw funds from his general account, which the clerk informs him is empty. Given his lean predicament, he takes accommodations with the loggers in a squalid hotel on skid row, and vows to further limit his opium intake (unlike his father, his self-control remains resolute), striding bravely past the city's numerous opium dens. To keep his back from slowing him down, he smokes a conservative, maintenance amount, three times daily, and never more.

He rides the streetcar south to the Greenwood Timber offices, which are housed in Harris Greenwood's mansion. At the door he announces himself as an agent of R.J. Holt of New Brunswick, and asks a secretary named Milner to arrange a meeting with his boss.

"I'm afraid Mr. Greenwood is too busy planning his soirée," Mr. Milner says. "Is this in reference to Mr. Holt's attendance?

Many captains of industry will be there. I hope Mr. Holt still plans to attend?"

"He certainly does," Lomax says. "And I'll be there as his assistant," he adds, and is soon leaving the mansion with an embossed invitation.

Back at his squalid hotel, Lomax assesses his wardrobe, which has become degraded over his journey: his suit coat is rumpled and pitted with cigarette burns, his shirt collars are yellowed, his hat crushed. He cables Lavern, both to alert her to his location and to assure her that he's closer than ever to completing his mission. He also asks her to liquidate an old account they'd set aside for Harvey Jr.'s education, just some money her father left her when he died. Her reply comes over the wire within a half hour:

CABLING MONEY YOU REQSTD STOP BALIF CAME TO
HOUSE YESTDAY STOP HOLT EVICTNG US HRVEY STOP
STAY WITH MY MOTHER NOW STOP COME HOME PLSE
STOP LAVRN

Lomax clenches his teeth until they squeak. Holt had threatened "further discipline" if he didn't return, yet some secret part of Lomax never believed he'd actually follow through with it, not after all the loyal years he'd pledged and all the debts he'd collected on Holt's behalf—and especially given what Lomax knows about his sordid affairs. Now it appears that Mr. Holt has discarded him with as much thought as he'd give to one of his girls. Which means there's nothing left for Lomax to do but find the child and the journal before McSorley does, then use them as bargaining chips to save his house.

With the money from Lavern in hand, Lomax locates a tailor. During his tuxedo fitting, the tailor convinces Lomax to buy a jacket two sizes smaller than he normally would. Perhaps there's a different sizing scheme on the West Coast, or perhaps he's lost some weight after these months on the road without Lavern's home-cooked meals.

That Friday evening Lomax arrives at the Hotel Vancouver, where rabble-rousers have assembled out front, hollering about the Crash and the inhumane conditions in Greenwood Timber's lumber camps as though the rich people stepping from their shining cars could possibly care. Brandishing his invitation, Lomax pushes through the fray and enters an opulent ballroom, where jewels glimmer against women's clavicles and sails of mauve silk flow across the high ceiling. After spotting a man he's certain is Harris Greenwood, Lomax drinks tonic water at the room's periphery, waiting for the chance to approach his table. When his assistant makes off, the seat beside Harris becomes vacant. Though the tycoon appears to be in a foul mood, muttering bitterly at the plate of clams set before him, he doubts he'll be presented with a better opportunity.

"Sorry to disturb you during your meal, Mr. Greenwood," Lomax says, leaning down to speak into the man's ear. "I'm here concerning a matter related to your brother."

"How dare you ambush me with this nonsense while I'm eating," Harris says drunkenly, rearing back and casting his vacant eyes in Lomax's direction. "My brother is deceased, sir."

"I suspect this may come as a surprise, but I'm happy to report that you're mistaken."

"Oh, really! Then where is he?" the tycoon barks, swinging his head around for effect. "Is he here? Sitting right across from me at this table, perhaps?"

"No, sir," Lomax says, trying to calm him down. "I'm unsure of his current whereabouts. Though I have a fairly good idea that he's headed—"

Harris Greenwood interrupts to suggest that Lomax is running some kind of confidence scam, and then threatens to have him ousted from the party, so Lomax takes his leave. After nearly two decades in R.J. Holt's employ, he should have known better than to approach a half-pissed industrialist at full froth. Now he's gone and squandered the best card that he'd held in his already abysmal hand.

As he makes his way through the crowd, Lomax spots Mr. Holt himself, dressed to the nines, having already attached himself to a waitress half his age. The nearer Lomax gets to him, the more a maelstrom brews in his gut and flows upward, filling his mouth with a taste like dirty pennies. Lomax pictures his seven children clambering over one another in Lavern's mother's tiny apartment—he is just a few feet from Holt's back now—then those bruises he saw on Euphemia's wrists and neck and never said anything about—and the jagged urge to pulverize this man beyond recognition becomes nearly irresistible. But this isn't some lowlife who Lomax is tasked with collecting on. He can't just pummel him until he signs back over the deed to Lomax's house. Like the other tycoons here, Holt owns stores and apartments and banks and coal mines and steel mills and factories and forests and lakes, and that gives him power. And if Lomax is ever going to have a chance of protecting himself from that power, he's going to need that journal.

Lomax drags himself to the restroom and locks himself in a stall. To dispel the foul taste in his mouth, he burns some opium in a soup spoon he snatched from a table, drawing deep from a pirouette of lifting smoke. This method's output is more unpredictable than when taken via cigarette, and he bobs down into the sea of himself for a while—how long he doesn't know.

When slowly he surfaces from his inner ocean, Lomax becomes aware of a pair of voices in the adjacent stall. Male registers, employing soft tones normally reserved for women or children. Lomax has encountered his share of such men in his time doing debt collection. Once, he collected money from a father who'd abandoned his five toddlers and beauty-queen wife to go dress up in her underwear and cavort with another man. Usually Lomax pegs them early: the light-footed way they stand, the hungry way they seek out the eyes of others, how their gaze always seems to linger too long. Yet any fool could decipher the soft sighs that emanate from the next stall over.

When the men finish their seamy business, they exit their stall and stop at the sink to wash up. It's then Lomax goes on tiptoe to peer over the top of his own stall, which allows him as much of an eyeful of the pair as he's going to need.

THE SOIRÉE

IN SHIRTSLEEVES, SILK top hat, mother-of-pearl cufflinks, and bone-white spats, Harris Greenwood waits nervously upon a plush lounge chair in the Lieutenant Governor's suite of the Hotel Vancouver, nipping at a tumbler of sake, alert to the fading din of voices from West Georgia Street below. There'd been demonstrators outside, some former employees who'd since degenerated into un-grateful riff-raff, shouting at his guests' Packard limousines as they pulled to the curb. But the police quickly got a handle on things—he heard the clunks of their truncheons and the animal growls of the men as the disturbance was quashed.

"How do I look, Liam?" Harris asks pre-emptively, after catching Feeney's sea-spray scent nearby.

"Like sawdust royalty," Feeney says a few feet to his right, before guiding Harris by the arm to the elevator. They descend in silence, and the doors open to the fray of the ballroom, where the band's sonic fer-vour and the warm crush of guests swallow him whole. Harris can feel the shuffle-step vibrations of dancers through the floor. Usually, he finds jazz intolerable—most music, actually. It intrudes on his mind and directs his thoughts in ways he expects it doesn't for those with sight. And yet, perhaps because Feeney is at his side, he finds some amusement in the intricately thumping rhythms, the brightness of the horns, the drowsy wandering of the clarinet, and nearly forgets the fact that it's all costing him a tidy fortune.

The soirée had been Feeney's idea. There'd been a recent trade exposition in San Francisco, and the captains of industry in atten-dance were quite glad to be diverted to the backwater outpost of

Vancouver for a spree of on-the-house revelry. The newly constructed Hotel Vancouver's financers had gone belly up during the Crash, leaving the building unfinished, so Harris paid a hefty special consideration fee to host it here. But such a party would have been unthinkable without Feeney: Harris couldn't possibly face its social demands without his trusted describer at his side.

Feeney leads him to the bar, where they sit on high stools and listen to gravel-throated men guffaw in unison. Feeney hands him a fresh sake, of which Harris has ordered a case from Osaka and has already burned through half. He knows he shouldn't have more, as he's already beginning to experience something of a "little hell," but he brings it to his lips anyway.

"Go ahead, describe my party to me," Harris says, spinning around before leaning back against the bar, his tongue limber with drink.

"Diamond-drenched women in close-cut silk saunter past," Feeney says, hamming it up. "Clasped to the arms of ugly old industrialists richer than Olympus. Already your guests seem to have aligned themselves according to what feature of Mother Earth they've committed themselves to destroying. Gold men in the corner. Oil near the exits. Railway executives and coal magnates colluding near the bar. I see Sir James Dunn of Algoma Steel. William H. Wright of Lakeshore Gold is positively maroon-faced. The king of the grain elevators, C.D. Howe, is sucking down a canapé as though it caused him harm. And the lecherous R.J. Holt of Holt Industries looks like he could fuck an ottoman."

"Any sign of Rockefeller?"

"Not yet. The word is he was an accomplished rower in his day, and is still quite handsome. If rich industrialists are your fancy," Feeney remarks, digging a covert elbow between Harris's ribs.

"How about conversation?" Harris asks. "I can't make anything out in all this racket. What's in the air?"

"Well," Feeney exhales. "Mostly the talk is of Roosevelt. The creeping rot of socialism. Japan's sabre-rattling. The worries in

Europe. Balloons moored to buildings. Chesty movie starlets. Oh, and I heard a rousing speech endorsing those draconian work camps that Prime Minister Bennett has enacted as an antidote to the Crash."

"I should be giving the speeches," Harris grumbles. "I'm the one paying for all this hot air."

Since the Crash, the skittish Canadian banks have been reluctant to lend venture capital, especially not to financially imperilled lumbermen, so Harris was forced to secure purchase financing for John Rockefeller's Port Alberni parcel from a London firm. Now all he needs to do is convince the American to sell—a gambit that he and Feeney have planned for later.

When the dinner bell is rung the pair take their seats to the chime of crystal glasses and the slurp of consommé. Harris has tucked himself and Feeney away from the powerful tables, mostly because Harris disdains dinner conversation at formal affairs, the smear of unrecognizable voices coming pell-mell as he is invariably trapped beside some self-interested boor.

"I'm off to hunt the elusive Rockefeller," Feeney says after their salads. And before Harris can protest, he's gone.

"Clams for *monsieur*," a waiter says from somewhere to his left, and Harris proceeds to chase the little flaccid lumps around the buttery skating rink of his plate, while everywhere glasses clash and laughter brays, a kind of auditory miasma that only amplifies his unease. He hadn't planned to spend even a portion of the evening alone, and in Feeney's absence, his tie feels as though it's been tightened. Harris keeps his eyes low to avoid projecting the impression to those at his table that he'd care to converse.

Then the deep voice of a man materializes through the din. "Sorry to disturb you during your meal, Mr. Greenwood," a stranger says from where Feeney had just been sitting. The man goes on to suggest that Everett is somehow miraculously alive. But Harris has dealt with such fraudsters before. Once, a woman claiming to be his daughter turned up at his mansion and demanded that Harris buy her a new washing machine.

"And let me guess, all you need is a tidy sum of money and you'll deliver him to me, is that correct?" Harris booms out. "I can assure you that I'm not some gullible War widow easily duped by promises of resurrection." Now he begins to yell: "So beat it before I have my assistants throw you out, face-first!"

"My apologies, Mr. Greenwood," the deep-voiced man says with perplexing calm in the face of such a threat. "Perhaps another time."

When he's sure the man is gone, Harris is left huffing, and reaches for his sake to allay his rage—only to discover it replaced by a flute of champagne, which he doesn't care for but gulps anyway. If only that deplorable grifter were right! If only Everett had joined him after the War, as he'd promised, and hadn't gone off wandering. What they could've accomplished! If his brother were here now, together they'd turn out the lot of these vampires and leeches, because that's what they are, here to suck the blood of all he's built.

As the waiters have been silently refilling his champagne, Harris has lost count of his drinks. His face is clammy, his armpits damp, and there is a numbness to his cheeks that provokes him to rub them with his palms. He hears scattered laughter, and without Feeney, there's no way of knowing if it's at his own expense. And where *is* Liam? How long has it been? No doubt he's chatting up John D. Rockefeller—what a noble sacrifice!

When the band breaks, the voice of a woman is revealed some seats to his right, prattling on about a newly proposed Dominion Forest Service. Harris encountered the term *ecology* at Yale and liked the idea—the conservation of exceptional forests for the purposes of science and recreation. Still, he wonders how it could be implemented without strangling industry. The current fashion is to create reserves, preserves, national parks, like Roosevelt has done in the U.S. It's as if the man won't rest until the world is one big sandbox for mankind to play in. *No, better to cut them now,* Harris thinks. *Get some use out of them. Start the regrow sooner than later.*

"Yes, yes, trees are lovely," Harris hears himself mutter.

"Pardon me, sir?" a woman says. "I didn't catch that. Can you speak up?"

"You think trees are sacred," he says. "That they love you. That they grow for your enjoyment. But those who really know trees know they're also ruthless. They've been fighting a war for sunlight and sustenance since before we existed. And they'd gladly crush or poison every single one of us if it gave them any advantage."

"I daresay that's a rather bleak view of the world," a woman says, whether it's the same woman as before he's not sure.

"Madam, I have no *view* of the world," Harris pronounces, re-using Feeney's line of indignity while hoisting a fresh glass of champagne, the taste for which he's now fully acquired—like the crabapples he and Everett once hurled at each other on their wood-lot. "And what can be more bleak than nothing?" he says.

The woman wonders aloud who invited him as a hand brushes his lapel.

"Everything all right?" Feeney says.

"Where were you?" Harris replies, his voice ragged, not his own. "You know I hate dining alone. A vile con man approached me and I had to send him packing."

"Poor baby," Feeney says. "But I found our Rockefeller. In a cloud of cigar smoke on the balcony."

"What took you so long?"

"I was arranging a chat between you two later this evening. Following the entertainment."

"Oh, I'm sure you enjoyed that," Harris says. "And get me some more of this champagne, will you? I've acquired a taste for it."

"I doubt that's a good idea," Feeney says, pressing a glass into Harris's hand, in which he's disappointed to discover seltzer.

"Then escort me to the men's room," Harris says amid a sudden wave of nausea brought on by the lingering taste of clams. "That's an order." Harris rises from his chair, dragging Feeney behind him, roughly bumping guests as they go. In the stall of the water closet, the nausea dissipates and Harris finds that alcohol has dampened his anxieties concerning their discovery, so he seeks out his describer's lips and presses them to his own. Feeney tastes of cucumber and tea and cedar shavings.

"I won't be in any shape to meet Rockefeller later," Harris declares while washing up at the basin following their intimacies. "So I'm going to proposition him now."

"Harris, you need to quit this idiocy. Or you and your childish behaviour will derail everything."

"That wasn't a request, Liam. And I can still manage quite capably without you," Harris says, fumbling around until he exits the lavatory, brushing his open hand along the hotel's velvet walls for both direction and balance. He can hear Feeney trailing at his heels, quietly urging him to reconsider. In the dining area, Harris commands a waiter to escort him to the balcony.

"Mr. Rockefeller," Harris bellows affably when the cool, cigar-tinged night air touches his face.

"Mr. Greenwood! There you are," says a warm and resonant voice with an East Coast accent that reminds Harris of his years at Yale. They shake hands, and while Rockefeller's hand is soft and uncallused, he counters Harris's strong squeeze with an equally strong one of his own.

"We were just discussing the deal you've cut with those yellow howler monkeys," Rockefeller says, with the slight slur of a man standing on the doorstep of inebriation but yet to step inside. As he speaks, Rockefeller pats Harris on the back of his jacket.

"I sell wood to anyone," Harris declares with a grin. "Regardless of their zoological heritage."

"Well said, well said." Rockefeller pats him again, this time on the neck, as if he were a trusted retriever, and Harris nearly bats the hand away. "But respectfully, Mr. Greenwood, we're of the opinion that we ought not be aiding these Japs. They've invaded Manchuria. And rumours are circulating back at the Capitol that the United States is next."

"You've ceased all your Japanese oil shipments, then, I presume?" Harris says, pausing to let the barb sink deeper, then smiling to mitigate it. "They need a railroad, Mr. Rockefeller. And I'm providing them the lumber to construct one. What they do with it isn't my concern. I've already cut half of the sleepers, and all I need is a bit more acreage to supply the remainder."

"I already know this, Mr. Greenwood. And as I informed your agent, I will *lease* you cutting rights, nothing more. Though this time around it seems like there could be some competition from your colleague, Mr. MacMillan. Of course, I will gladly accept bids from you both."

"That won't do," Harris says. "I'm seeking full title."

"Mr. Greenwood, it seems to me that this charming nation of yours is just one gigantic set of woods. So why don't you muster up some initiative and go and purchase some *other* portion of it?"

Ever since his boyhood days of haggling over the price of firewood by the side of McLaren Road, Harris has felt most himself during a negotiation. So he drains his glass and directs his eyes to where he suspects Rockefeller's are. "Sir, I've paid you a tidy sum in leases over the years, and I've been happy to do it. But this time, I need to purchase your Port Alberni escarpment, including its attached islands. Full title."

"And as I said, that land is not something I'd care to sell, Mr. Greenwood. These aren't the old days. They aren't manufacturing any more islands any time soon, the last I checked."

"This is a mere morsel to a man of your holdings, Mr. Rockefeller. You won't miss it for a second."

"It's a fine party, Mr. Greenwood," Rockefeller says. "But I've been subject to your sales pitch for long enough. Good evening."

Harris turns and braces himself at the balcony railing as the men snicker at his expense, just as they had at Yale. How they shook his hand publicly and spurned him privately, more for being a backwater Canadian than for his blindness. To men like Rockefeller, this country—the greatest storehouse of natural materials the world has ever known, first stolen from the Natives, then sold off bit by bit to foreign interests like him—has always been just a place for them to tear things out of. And for a dizzy, drunken moment, Harris pities the trees. Especially for the trusting way they declare themselves to the world with their grand upward reach. At least gold and oil have the common sense to hide.

Still, without more trees to cut, Greenwood Timber will fail, and Harris and Feeney will be left as unprotected as those two swampers found embracing at his lumber camp. A sudden and renewed ferocity circulates through him, and with it a memory of Feeney mentioning that Rockefeller had been a competitive rower in college.

"Sir, these are trees you've never seen," Harris calls out in the direction of the cigar smoke. "Growing in a part of the world you'll never visit."

"Greenwood, are you deaf in addition to blind?" Rockefeller asks. "Or simply dim-witted enough to think that just because you've thrown a party, you'll set the terms here?"

Harris ignores the insult and closes the gap between them, cuffing the solid bicep beneath Rockefeller's silk jacket. "Oh, come on, John!" Harris says with tense joviality. "Even though I cut the wood that made the railway you rode here on, and the mansion you live in, and the books your nannies read to your children, and the stocks of the guns that won your wars, and every stick of furniture you ever sat upon, I'll still never be your equal, will I? So how about you arm wrestle this helpless, backwoods invalid, and prove your superiority right here in front of everyone? If I win, you sell me that Port Alberni parcel, with its attached islands, at reasonable terms. And if you do, I'll cancel my deal with the dreaded Japs and you and your nation will be safe once more. What do you say, sport?"

HER BEDROOM

TWO BLUE EYES, another nose, another mouth, an array of pearly teeth, all hovering there above him, inches from his own. "It's been years since I've been watched up close like this," Everett whispers.

Temple laughs and he worries for a moment she's pegged him as simple. "Well, it's about time someone got near you," she whispers back, lowering herself down against him, her breath electric against his neck. "You've been on your own too long."

During those first years after he settled on his sugarbush, hand-some women would visit Everett's dreams—always more frequently in spring—their hair plastered with river water, their skin moonlit platinum. While these visions eventually subsided, already he knows that this time spent with Temple has left any return to a former state of dormancy unthinkable. Still, he can't shake the nagging suspicion that it's all some practical joke—the cruel sort he and Harris sprang upon each other as boys.

"Lucky for me," Temple adds with a crooked smirk, "you're the illiterate hermit I've been waiting for."

"I suppose that makes you the helpless, farm-bound spinster of my dreams," he says with mock sincerity, flipping her over to rise on his arms above her. But immediately she knocks out the joints of his elbows and he topples against her, clonking heads, and then they wrestle awhile, bumping an unlit hurricane lamp to the floor. Pod stirs at the ruckus, huffing in the improvised crib they've made of the galvanized woodbin nearby, the child nestled in amongst the clothes they shucked off hours previously.

"You never had any babies yourself?" he asks after they've

collapsed, realizing too late that although he intended to rekindle their earlier banter, the levity of the moment is now lost.

"No, never," she says sombrely. "I conceived one, but there was some trouble with it and I lost the ability. My husband ran off after that—he'd always rattled on about the truckload of precocious children we'd have, so I half expected it. But I'm happy he left. Family life was never for me. I'm more useful running this place than I am worrying over some snotty noses."

They lay in silence for some minutes, Everett eager to apologize for the flippancy of his remark, yet unable to broach it without sounding like a sniveller.

"Everett, how did that child really come to you?" she asks, pushing her fingers through his hair.

As he prepares to reassert his story about being Pod's uncle, her eyes latch upon his and a soft, lush feeling engulfs him. "I found her," he says. "Hung to die on a tree." After this initial tug, the story of his life on the woodlot unspools from him, in the same easy way the story of his upbringing had for Pod back on the freight train. He tells Temple about finding the maple forest after drifting for years, about how he quit drinking and constructed his shack.

"At first I saw the child as a hex put on me," he goes on. "Except now my only concern is that she doesn't come to harm. And that includes from me."

"Was it you who beat that senator's brother in Ontario?"

He nods. "Pod would be dead if I hadn't. And that's exactly why I need to pay someone decent to raise her. Trouble finds me wherever I go. Always has. I never had a good home, so what do I know about making one for her? She deserves a better start than I'd ever give her."

"And how exactly will you finance this better start? With syrup? During the worst times anybody has ever seen?"

"That brother I mentioned?" he whispers. He knows he shouldn't tell her, but he needs her to know that he's not some illiterate dunce with foolish plans. "Is Harris Greenwood."

Ashamed of his boast, he buries his face in the pillow.

She squints. "That barn over there was built with Greenwood lumber," she says skeptically. "You aren't pulling my leg, are you?"

He shakes his head.

"You're planning to ask him for help. Why haven't you already?"

He tells her that he hasn't set eyes on his brother for eighteen years, and that while they aren't brothers by blood, they are in every other way. "The woman who cared for us never let us in her house. Just kept us outside like a couple of dogs. She hated us, deep down."

"You can't say that, Everett. I'm sure she had her reasons. You can never be certain why people behave the way they do."

"Still, she willed us that woodlot jointly when she died. Harris wanted to log it completely, but I refused. Then after the War he wrote and asked if I wanted to start a lumber company with him, beginning with his half of the woodlot, and I said yes. But I had trouble making it home and got caught up wandering. I did make it back, eventually, though not before he cut all the trees and sold off the property. I hated him for years for what he'd done. Except now, with Pod in the picture, my plan is to ask for my stake and use it to find her a good home."

"Sounds like a fair proposition to me."

"I doubt he'll receive me kindly, though. He always had a temper. But now that your windbreak is in, Pod and I should start heading west in the morning, so I guess we'll soon find out."

"I'd like to say I need some more trees planted. Or that you ought to finish your lessons in the library. But yesterday I heard the mailman claim that McSorley is in Manitoba, chasing some Yankee wife-killer up from New York. He'll come to Estevan next. But today is Friday, and he can't possibly make it here until Monday at the earliest." Temple takes his hand in hers. "So stay. One more day."

After Everett agrees, Pod wakes, mewling and grunting. When he stands naked by the bed to re-swaddle her, he leaves his own image silhouetted on the sheet in tan-coloured dust, as though Temple has been lying with his ghost, and the sight of it spooks him.

Temple is asleep by the time he returns, making quick, unintelligible sounds, a series of *hmmph*s. He wishes he could wake her and ask what she's *hmmph*-ing about, whether it's related to all the books she's read and all the unique thoughts she has that he can't stand not knowing about. He rocks Pod while Temple fusses and kicks at the sheets in her sleep, a nocturnal restlessness he'd like to read as evidence of a greater one. A desire for something else, perhaps even somewhere else.

At daybreak Everett watches Temple rise and begin pinning up her hair at the mirror. He admires the way stray hairs slip from her hairpins no matter how tightly she gathers them. The way her shoulder blades draw together and nearly touch. All a great glory that she doesn't seem to register.

"What were you dreaming of last night?" Everett asks.

"Oh, it's the same every night since the drought: roaring rivers; clear streams; lakes as still as oil."

"I dream of trees, mostly," he says. "Trees I once knew. Trees I don't know yet. Sometimes they're aiding me, and sometimes they're falling on me. Sometimes I'm planting them, and sometimes I'm cutting them down. But they're always there. I think if you ever cut my head open, it'd be one big root ball in there, all tangled and grown together."

After her hair is pinned, Temple pulls on some dusty trousers and a work shirt while Everett gives Pod her morning feed of goat's milk, which Gertie has managed to get from the adjacent farm. When Pod is finished, he burps her over his shoulder and she gives a gummy smile.

"You run back to your room now before Gertie shows up to cook breakfast," Temple says to Everett, returning Pod's smile. "I'll have her go to the lockbox and get your pay before the men are up. The last thing we need is them seeing you two getting more special treatment."

A TELEGRAM

HARRIS OLD BOY STOP HAD ROARING TIME IN
CANADAS WILD STOP EVEN ENJOYED OUR CONTEST
TO CONCLUDE EVE STOP YOU CRAZY CANUCKS
STRONGER THAN YOU LOOK STOP AS PER OUR WAGER
WILLING TO VEND PARCEL AT PRICE DISCUSSED STOP
CONTACT SECRETARY TO FIX PAPERS STOP YRS
JD ROCKEFELLER

KEEP HER

"TEMPLE?"

"Yes?" she replies, her voice half-there beside him.

"Do you think—?"

A long pause.

"Yes, Everett?"

He coughs, unable to say it. It's Saturday, their last night together. He spent the afternoon lying low in the library, examining the journal, though he still can't read it properly, and mulling over an idea. He hears the wind slur through the willow outside Temple's bedroom and it's an encouraging sound.

"Do you think a baby can love a person?" he says finally. "Even if they don't have the word for it yet?"

Temple flips onto her side in the bed to regard him, their legs braided together. "Of course that little girl loves you, Everett."

"Aw, if I left her tomorrow she'd forget me in a week," he says, a burning sensation flaring upon his neck. "Two at the most."

"I doubt that. Some part of her would remember you."

"Then how's a person supposed to know for certain, when a child can't say it herself?"

"Because it's plain as day. That's how."

"I never had a knack for living before she came to me. It was more like I was killing time until I was gone."

"She didn't come to you, Everett. You rescued her! Why didn't you just leave her in the forest?"

"I nearly did," he admits, though the words nauseate him. "And there were times afterwards . . . when I considered worse than that."

"Well, so what?" she says with a dismissive squint. "I entertain all kinds of notions that don't matter, not like actions do. And why would you get the law turned on you and forfeit your home, all to just give her away?"

Silence.

"You're going to keep her, aren't you?"

Silence again.

"It's possible I might," Everett says, nearly inaudibly.

"Might what?"

Everett takes a deep breath then swallows. "Keep her."

"Well, good."

"But we'd need somewhere quiet," he says. "A wooded place where trouble can't find me the way it does when I'm in cities. With the money Gertie paid me today, and a bit more from my brother, we could get a fair start. I'd ask you along if I thought you'd ever leave this place."

"There isn't much chance of that, Everett," she says.

"You already know this, but your farm is withering away. You shouldn't have to worry about it anymore. We could find some land nobody's using. A piece they forgot they owned. I'll show you how to sugar trees. We'll swim in rivers. Raise Pod as our own. You could keep a little library. We could even marry if we wanted to."

Temple lets out a long sigh. "Oh, that sounds fine, Everett. Truly. Except I tried that once, and matrimony is a grave I won't be buried in again. Besides, this farm isn't dead quite yet, and these dunces will run it into the ground without me. It's a sturdy house," she says. "I expect to be carried out of it."

"Then I'll come back," he says. "After things cool down."

"And what about McSorley?"

"He'll lose interest eventually. With the Crash, there's no short-age of fugitives for him to hunt. We could claim the baby is ours."

Her face hardens. "I'm not looking for a child, Everett." This she says in a tone normally reserved for loafing farmhands. "There are women who are mothers and there are those who aren't."

"You wouldn't need to lift a finger in her direction," he says, almost pleading. "I'm practised at caring for her now. Someday she could be climbing those maple trees we planted out there on the lot line."

"This is no place for a child and that's final," Temple snaps, and Everett shuts his mouth.

They lie for a while. Dust scrapes the window. Everett starts to speak a few times and fails. He scrubs his rough hand over his face.

"Temple," he says.

"Umhmm," she says, half asleep.

"If you can't go with us, and you can't have us here, it looks like there isn't much future between us."

"If you cut it that way, Everett, then I suppose not."

"Then how about I come back here and bother you. I mean, once I've raised her and all this is over. With no expectations or anything. Just to come and visit you. Maybe I'll take you to a moving picture in town."

"I'd like that, Everett. I'll be here, I imagine. Still setting the table out on that porch. Still shovelling out my damn house." Then she gets a sad expression. "Except people don't come back to a place like this if they don't need to. And you don't strike me as the type who'll need to."

"Well, I will. I swear it."

She taps the pad of her index finger twice on his forehead. "It's sweet of you to say. You won't. But it's real nice to hear it."

FLYING OFF ON YOU

AT BREAKFAST ON Sunday morning, they roar up the access road, dragging corkscrews of dust behind them, fine as confectioner's sugar. Temple is out back, beating the laundry with a broom handle before she takes it in, when she sights the three squad cars—and several private automobiles, owned by men from Estevan who've ridden along more to gawk than assist.

They pull up to the barn and Detective McSorley bursts from the car, ordering his men to surround the structure and padlock its doors. The detective is nearly rabid when Temple reaches him, his tie flying horizontally in the stiff gusts, and there's a gerbilish, insomniac cast to his eyes. "I've got it from a good source that a vagrant is keeping a baby here, Temple," he says, pointing a thick finger at her face.

"Oh horseshit, Detective. What source?" she says indignantly. "Looks to me like the Estevan rumour mill has kicked into full gear now that it's nearly harvest time and there's nothing to harvest but gossip." She casts a quick glance back to the house to confirm that Everett isn't visible.

"I've had enough of your mouth," McSorley snaps. "Some of your resident drunks took another dip in the water tower last night. But this time I had a man posted there. And when they were caught, to save their skins they swore that there's a baby girl staying here, and has been for nearly three weeks. Living in the care of a tramp who goes by the name Everett."

She has to fight against taking a quick, gulping breath. How could this be? She hadn't made the mistake again of paying her men on a Friday, and she doubts any of them have money left over from the previous payday. She glares at the filthy faces that peer down from the hayloft's high outswing doors—but she'll have to deal with them later. Right now, Everett and Pod need a head start.

"Well, you heard wrong," she barks. She's always masked her deceits with outrage—it's a trick her father taught her. "The only infant currently on these premises is standing right in front of me. And I'd appreciate it if you didn't harass my workers and spook my animals just because some old drunks thought they saw a baby. I'll be lucky if my hens lay again after all this commotion."

McSorley brings his burning pop-eyes up close to hers. Humid, eggy breath. Spittle scumming his mouth's corners. And in an instant, the reports of him throwing hobos under the wheels of running trains seem dead accurate. "Temple, you know I'm the only reason you're still operating here? I took pity on you, living with no husband in this godforsaken place. But today I'm afraid my desire to shield you from the more judgmental citizens of Estevan has expired."

"I've got it," she says, softening her tone, trying a bit of charm, anything to buy time. "The child those idiots saw was probably my sister's. I'm caring for her daughter while she's off looking for work."

His face relaxes, if only slightly. "That so. Well, I'll still need to see her."

"You can't."

"And why's that?"

"She's at the doctor's in Estevan. She's got a cough. It's the dust."

They lock eyes.

"But you're welcome to drop by and see her in a few days," she adds warmly. "I'm sure she'll have recovered by then. I could even get Gertie to fix a picnic basket for us."

McSorley's cheeks flush with blood. "I would enjoy that picnic, Miss Temple," he says, examining her skeptically. Then he removes his hat so that his oily hair whips about in a dozen black tentacles. He directs his gaze to the horizon, where a bank of cast-iron clouds tumble in the far distance. "But you'd be smart to get that baby home and keep her down in your storm cellar for the next while. Cyclones were reported in the Dakotas just over the border yesterday. Should be here by tomorrow. And your sister will never forgive you if you let that poor child of hers go flying off on you."

"I'll do that, Detective," Temple says, taking his elbow to ease him in the direction of his automobile. "Straight away."

But McSorley slips himself free of her grip and turns back to his men. "You know what?" he says, replacing his hat with a grimace. "I think we'd better do charitable Miss Temple here a favour and make sure that little baby girl of her sister's wasn't misplaced somewhere here on the farm. Search the house first. Then the barn. Then that goddamned library."

INTO THE MOUNTAINS

"I KNEW THIS was a poor idea," Gertie says at the kitchen window, as she and Everett watch the cars slide to a halt at the barn. Everett gathers Pod up from her high chair without even wiping the porridge from her face. Outside, he sees Temple hurry over to approach a stocky policeman. "There," Gertie says, "Miss Temple will handle Detective McSorley. Now you two cut around back and hide in the old storm cellar beneath the library."

Everett has just tied his boots when McSorley shakes loose from Temple's grip and shouts some orders at his men, who start toward the house. Without stopping to grab his things or even his envelope of pay from the spare room, Everett bolts with Pod through the back door, dashing out into the dust-swirled field behind the house. He sprints in the direction of the railway until the farm disappears. Then he sets Pod down in a drainage ditch and crawls snake-wise back to the library near the property's perimeter. The men are searching the barn now, so Everett rushes inside the library and finds the journal among the teetering shelves of books. He sets it on the table and takes up a blunt pencil. Inside the front cover, facing the first page, he frantically scrawls *PROPERTY OF*—the spelling of which he only guesses at. With that part done, he writes a name, first then last, as legibly as his unpractised hand can muster. It's a name he invents during the very act of setting it down, a name he hasn't a clue how to spell, though he writes it anyway. It's the name he'll give Pod after their circumstances become decent and permanent. A name, he imagines, befitting the fine woman she'll someday become.

When he's finished he shoves the book back onto the shelf, memorizing its location for the day he returns. For a moment he considers scribbling a farewell message for Temple, but it could give them away. So instead he finds the *Odyssey*, the entirety of which they'd read together during those nights after tree planting, and opens it to the first page, leaving it there on the table, hoping it will be enough.

"There you are," Everett says when he returns to the drainage ditch, stepping on the head of a hoop snake that's just two feet away from where Pod lies. He takes her up and gallops, lungs wheezing, to the rail junction at Estevan, then hops the first northbound train he sees, a passenger rig of about twenty coaches. With the crew lurking about, Everett ties Pod to his chest with his bootlaces, then climbs a ladder onto the car's slick roof, where he lashes his belt to the service handles in case he nods off or the train banks sharply.

They ride all day into Alberta, watching the treeless prairie submit to plateaus of grassland. To the right of the tracks bison stand flicking their tails, a hundred monoliths against the drought-yellowed grass.

Though they're hungry, the ride in open country hypnotizes Pod and keeps her from complaint. Falcons dogfight and turn high circles as the train passes over deep gorges upon steel trestles, and the cars arc before them, each one the nodule of a spine, a great iron dragon flying low over the land.

They abandon the passenger train at Calgary, because even in late summer they'll freeze in the Rockies riding topside. Everett traversed the mountains frequently in his hoboing days, and though he was mostly drunk, he recalls a slow climb between icy crags and granite faces, where big-horned sheep picked their way across blue glaciers. He finds some tin cans and fills them at a rain barrel, stuffs his pockets with some wild turnip he digs up near the tracks, then hops the second-to-last caboose of a long freight. The door is padlocked, so he crawls down through its cupola. Inside, he and Pod conceal themselves beneath the little table where the crew eats their meals.

He feeds her raw, chewed-up turnip as the train wends up among the shoulders of cloud-draped mountains, its wheels shrieking on the frosty tracks. Darkness falls and stars blaze into the caboose's windows. Everett gives Pod a piece of cedar kindling to chew when her gums start troubling her, as they've been doing more and more lately.

In the high mountains the sky appears closer, though he knows it must be a trick of the mind. Five hours into the ride, the windows blacken with a wash of snowflakes. The temperature plummets and the train grows louder in the cold. From a footlocker Everett fishes out a coat, which he drapes over them, and a watch cap, which he pulls down over Pod's head. He ignores the coal stove in the corner, which would invite detection.

They ride for hours in the clawing cold, his body sore from shivers. Pod grows listless, her nose scarlet even after he blows on it, recalling the same catatonia in which he'd first found her. When her lips turn blue he gives in and lights the stove. After it catches, he adds three small lumps of coal and props Pod before the growing flicker. In a few minutes she perks up, just as a bang comes at the door.

A PICNIC

AS HE DOES every Friday when the weather is fair, Harris escapes his office at noon and has Feeney drive him to a greengrocer, where they purchase fruit along with some French cheese and bread. Next, they drive to a secluded beach that overlooks the inlet, where they lay out on a blanket for the afternoon. These recreations are much needed. After Harris trounced John D. Rockefeller in their arm wrestling contest (a life spent chopping wood had never proven a more valuable asset), they finalized the purchase agreement for the Port Alberni parcel. At Harris's insistence, the deal included the small, nameless island that he'd set on fire after discovering log poachers there, and even before he officially secured the title, Harris ordered the construction of a cabin retreat on the island, as a surprise for Feeney.

In a rush to fulfill the Japanese order, Greenwood Timber's crews have been cutting in triple shifts, and though the autumn rains have begun, Harris has ordered them to fell trees seven days a week, in blowing winds and storms. Two of his experienced high-lead fallers have already perished, one by lightning, the other hung in his rigging. Despite these tragedies—or, more accurately, *because* of them—thousands of eighteen-foot spars bearing the *G* of Greenwood Timber's imprint are being tugboated daily down to his Vancouver booming grounds, where they're gang-sawed into sleepers, creosoted, and stickered to await shipment across the Pacific.

The ten per cent fronted by the Imperial Railway Purchasing Group and the London firm's financing are long spent, so to pay for the labour overages Harris has liquidated his margin accounts and major holdings, including his stocks: Home Oil, Okalta, and even General Electric, which had only just recovered after dumping 500 points in the Crash. But Rockefeller's timber is fine and easily accessed, and given their currently roaring output, Harris is on track to fill the Japanese order on schedule.

There on the beach Feeney reads Harris an entire gazette in his lilting, musical voice. When a cool wind rises off the water, it provides them a good excuse for a blanket draped over their bodies—one can't be too careful—allowing them some discreet contact. After a while they arrange their lunch upon a giant fir stump, rumoured to have been felled by Captain Cook himself to replace the snapped mast of one of his ships. While they eat, Harris drags his fingers along the stump's ridges, and over the course of their meal, he assesses the tree's age to be 748 years, a span of time that included ten distinct periods of drought—indicated by thinner, denser rings—and he realizes with delight that he's read the tree's history as one would Braille. It may be the tender-heartedness that often afflicts him in Feeney's company, but he almost finds himself pitying the tree, as one might a human being whose life was cut unnecessarily short. But he shakes his head and drives the silly notion from his mind.

Following lunch, he and Feeney indulge in a nap beside the stump, until a deep voice wakes him: "My apologies for troubling you again during your recreations, Mr. Greenwood."

Harris feels Feeney tense beside him, while he inventories his body to ensure that none of his limbs were improperly draped over his companion.

"You *have* disturbed Mr. Greenwood, sir," Feeney says protectively. "And if you'd like to make a proper appointment, I suggest you speak with his secretary."

"I went by your offices this afternoon," the man says politely, and now Harris places the voice: the con man who approached him at the soirée. "And your associate, Mr. Baumgartner, indicated I could find you here."

So he's finally betrayed me, Harris thinks. Everyone he's ever trusted has, eventually. Mort just took a bit longer than the rest.

"It won't take a minute, sir," the man persists. "I've got your military discharge photograph here, Mr. Greenwood." Harris feels a piece of thick paper pressed into his hand.

"You'll forgive me if I can't confirm this as fact," he says coolly, standing up to face the voice.

The big man chuckles. "You'll have to take my word for it. But I regret to inform you that the dark-haired infantryman pictured here looks nothing like you."

"If you're here to show me an unbecoming photograph, sir, I'm afraid that you've wasted your gasoline."

"What did you do during the War, Mr. Greenwood?"

Harris has yet to correct Feeney's false belief in the popular rumour that he was blinded while serving overseas, and since this huckster seems harmless enough, Harris can stomach a few uncomfortable moments alone with him if it means saving himself the embarrassment.

"Why don't you go fetch some water from the automobile, Mr. Feeney?" Harris says.

"Are you sure, Mr. Greenwood?" Feeney replies hesitantly.

Harris nods, then listens to the crunch of pebbles as Feeney works his way down the beach to the parking lot. "Is he gone?" Harris says.

"He is," the man replies.

"Actually, I didn't serve in the War, Mr. . . . ?"

"Lomax, sir. Harvey Lomax."

"It was a common misunderstanding during those frantic times," Harris says. "I was blind as a bat when my brother enlisted, and he was errantly entered under my name."

"Well, sir, I'm pleased to tell you that I stood before your brother, the man pictured in this photograph, four months ago in a rooming house in Toronto."

"That may be so, Mr. Lomax," Harris says, struggling to perform neutrality, though his heart kicks against his breastbone. "But he and I went our separate ways long ago. And you'll understand that I'm not exactly the sentimental sort. So this miraculous resurrection holds no interest for me. Good day to you, Mr. Lomax."

"You know," Lomax persists, as though he hasn't heard a thing Harris has said, "I intended to speak with you further at your party. Unfortunately, you and your assistant were off in the bathroom for much of the festivities."

There's a long, searing silence, during which Harris has trouble breathing. It's as though he's sucked in an entire lungful of sawdust, and now lacks the air to expel it. "I wasn't feeling well," he says after forcing his lungs into motion. "I ate a bad clam." He gropes for the stump and sits himself down upon it as casually as he can manage.

"Of course, of course," Lomax says. "But what happened in the lavatory at your soirée doesn't concern me nearly as much as your brother's whereabouts, Mr. Greenwood, I can assure you of that. Has he contacted you recently?" Lomax sits on the stump beside him, and up close he has an odd, exotic smell, and a deep, resonant voice that seems to be angling down from a great height, even while sitting.

"No, he has not," Harris says. "And I don't expect he will."

"The thing is, sir," Lomax says, "I've secured records confirming that you've accepted medals and a pension for your distinguished military service with the 116th Battalion of the Canadian infantry."

"I've accepted nothing, Mr. Lomax. They sent me my brother's medals and pension in error, both of which I've held for him in trust."

"So he could come to claim them?"

You idiot, Harris thinks. "Yes, well, I suppose it's possible."

"Sir, I'm here only because I believe that we can be of mutual benefit to one another. My employer, R.J. Holt of New Brunswick, has an interest in locating your brother, who's taken something of his. And we'd like your help in finding him."

"I'm listening."

"We suspect your brother is making his way west, possibly to you. So all I need is for you to let me know if, and from where, he contacts you. You do that, and your lavatory habits will remain forever unremarked."

"Alive or dead, I highly doubt my brother wants anything to do with me, Mr. Lomax. But if you hold to your word, regardless of whether I hear from him or not, you have yourself a deal."

"That settles it," Lomax says, rising to his feet and shaking Harris's hand. "I'll drop by your offices next week."

"For what purpose will you drop by my offices, Mr. Lomax?" Harris asks. "We've reached an understanding. You provide me with your details and I'll alert you if my brother contacts me."

"Oh, sure," Lomax says. "Still, I'll nip by your offices next week, just to see how things are progressing. Good afternoon, Mr. Greenwood."

After he's gone, Harris remains seated on the wide stump for some time, his eyes stinging in the pungent sea breeze. It will be hours before he can draw an easy breath.

STORM CELLAR

THE DAY AFTER Detective McSorley and his men search her farm and scare Everett and his child off, Temple wakes early. Normally a fountain of idle chatter, Gertie is silent while she prepares the percolator as though it's a holy sacrament. Yesterday Gertie tearfully confessed that one of the men had spotted her fetching Everett's envelope of pay from the lockbox before handing it to him. Gertie hadn't thought much of it at the time, but after McSorley left, she discovered the lockbox had been jimmied open. The group of men who did it took no more than what was owed them on payday, but they did it because they resented Everett receiving his money early. They then walked into Estevan to drink cheap whiskey and swim in the water tower. But the damage was done, and while the money was lawfully theirs and they were right to expect equal treatment, Temple still banned them for life for disobeying her.

After McSorley unsuccessfully searched the farm, he begrudgingly accepted that the child reported on her farm was in fact her sister's. The detective was, however, correct about one thing: the coming weather. Over breakfast the sun only manages the faintest bruise of orange behind the tide of dust gathering in the south. By ten o'clock, the butterflies and grasshoppers are fidgety, clacking suicidally against the windowpanes of the house as if trying to shatter the glass to seek refuge inside. By noon, the oddly chilly wind is forceful enough to flutter Temple's eyelids against her eyeballs. It seems to blow from every point on the compass—not in gusts, but steadily, as though from a fan. The sky purples throughout the afternoon, and by the time her farmhands are on the porch for supper, a lacerating dust is throwing buckets and feed sacks against the siding of the house, while out in the distance an inverted mountain, black as coal, races directly at them like a highballing train.

The temperature plummets and an eerie, greenish light falls as Temple and her men leave their plates where they are and rush to unhitch the livestock so they don't strangle. With that done, Temple and any men who haven't already run off make for the storm cellar beneath the library. She watches the windmill pump detach from its housing above her well near the willow and take to the sky as though lifted by invisible wires. As they pull closed the storm doors, she's wracked by the sudden fear that she's locking Everett and Pod out, even though she knows they've already escaped west. If only she could rescue at least some of her library's most valuable books—those handsome volumes of Dante with the wildflowers pressed between every second page, or that copy of the *Odyssey* that Everett had risked leaving out for her to find in the library—but there's too little time.

Shut in the storm cellar, Temple feels the very atmosphere convulse. She'll learn later that by the time the cyclone reaches Estevan proper it measures a full country mile wide, dragging its helical blade like a plow over a fifty-mile stretch of earth before it will finally dissipate. The devouring wind takes grackles, chickens, prairie dogs, cows, crows, and jackrabbits—creatures domestic or wild, it doesn't matter—into the air, and batters them against the other things wheeling there. Telegraph lines snap, automobiles roll and crumple, rail cars rise from their tracks and twirl lazy circles like wingless airplanes. Granaries become dervishes of boards and nails, and most of the area's trees are yanked from the ground as easily as one pulls a ripe carrot.

She hears her house go first: a crackling bedlam of shattered timber and glass thrown in a hundred-foot radius. When the vortex approaches the church, she feels the air pressure drop and hears the glass explode inward above her, a million shards of shrapnel thrown across the library's dusty floor. When the roaring cone touches down on the library, she hears the roof removed with a tremendous screech of pulled nails and an almighty sucking *whoosh*. Then comes the uncanny sound that Temple Van Horne will surely never forget, not in all of her life: ten thousand books drawn up into the sky, all at once.

A RETREAT

BEFORE WAKING HIM, Harris gently blindfolds Feeney with a silk necktie. He then spends nearly an hour clumsily aiding his describer with his dressing, and after that they're driven to the harbour where they board Harris's schooner, crewed by men he's hired just for the day, men of no association with Greenwood Timber whatsoever.

As per Harris's instructions, the ship cuts across the inlet, passes Port Browning, then bears north. Gulls squawk and salt spray dampens their faces. "Tell me what I'm looking at," Feeney says midway through the voyage in a pitch-perfect imitation of Harris. And Harris proceeds to conjure the picturesque seascape of his imagination in his best Irish lilt.

After some hours they drop anchor and are rowed to the small jetty in a sheltered bay, which Harris knows is invisible from the inlet.

"What do you see?" Harris says, removing Feeney's silk blindfold when they step from the rowboat.

"A forested island. Green and lush as any I've laid eyes on. Where Douglas firs poke their delicately needled fingers into the clouds."

"Rockefeller hadn't even bothered to name this place before he sold it to us," Harris says as they leave the jetty with their bags and supplies while the rowboat departs. "Before the English conquered it, the local Heiltsuk called it Qanekelak, which I'm told means "shapeshifter" in their language. I considered naming it after you, though that would draw undue attention. So I've gone with my second choice: Greenwood Island."

"Inventive," Feeney says, before they set out upon a deer path no wider than their shoulders.

"Well, look at this," Feeney says, after he's led for a half hour.

"Describe it to me, Liam," Harris replies.

"Amid a glade of fir, cypress, and cedar, upon a low rise," Feeney narrates as they come to a stop, "sits a cabin, overlooking the sea, its rough-milled siding still pink and unsilvered by the sun."

"Built by the finest carpenters on the coast," Harris adds, "using the timber they brought down to clear the site." His original plan had been to have the cabin ready by year's end, but after Lomax's ambush on the beach, he paid through the teeth to spur the construction along. He requested a modest yet elegant structure of an unadorned, rugged design—the diametrical opposite of his mansion—one intended to merge with the forest rather than to dominate it.

"It's ours. A place we can live as ourselves," Harris says, coaxing Feeney inside. "While the ocean is visible from the upper floor, the cabin is entirely hidden from the sea. So we won't be troubled here. By anyone."

Returning to his office after Lomax confronted him, Harris had immediately fired Baumgartner with no severance for sending him their way—in what was no doubt a malicious ploy to undermine his and Feeney's relationship. Harris has since related to Feeney the details of the encounter, including the report that Everett lives, which Harris's skeptical nature still won't let him fully believe. He's also assured Feeney that even if his brother is indeed alive, the great unlikelihood of him contacting Harris after so long seems a reasonable risk to take in order to secure their safety.

But for the past month, Lomax has appeared each morning at the Greenwood Timber offices, not to request a meeting or threaten Harris in any way, but to sit in the waiting room for hours reading gazettes, taking breaks to smoke his odd-smelling cigarettes in the yard, though the waiting room is outfitted with ashtrays. Still, Harris only needs to put up with this man a little while longer—just until the sleepers are all cut and the creosoting is complete and the Japanese deal is done.

As the pair steps into the cabin for the first time, Harris again asks Feeney to narrate. To his delight, Feeney exhibits a particular admiration for the custom-built, literature-filled shelves that line the high walls, and that night, after a dinner of salmon fillets that Feeney roasts on fragrant cedar planks, he reads for hours to Harris, who drinks in his voice like milk.

Later, in bed, with any possibility of being discovered as remote as it's ever been, their solitude so complete that Harris nearly weeps with relief, they lie listening to the soft creaks and pops of the fresh-cut timber beams as they cure in the heat of the stove. "Most people believe that wood dies when it's cut," Harris says. "But it doesn't. A wooden house is a living thing. Moving moisture through its capillaries. Breathing and twisting, expanding and contracting. Like a body."

"Well, I'd appreciate it if this body of yours would knock it off and let us get some sleep," Feeney says, his head buried beneath his pillow. "Because the quiet of this place is what I love most."

The following morning they hike through the burned section to where Harris knows the tallest trees on the island congregate. Feeney halts at the foot of the grandest one, a titanic Douglas fir, over two hundred feet tall and wrapped with foot-thick bark, and they hold hands in silence as they examine it for some minutes, their necks canted.

"It's magnificent," Feeney says after a while. "I know of no better way to describe it."

"I tried to burn this forest down once," Harris says. "It was stupid of me. But it survived. And I'm happy it did."

"Good thing you're so ineffectual," Feeney quips.

"It's strange, isn't it, Liam," he says as they continue to gaze upward, Harris doing his best to imagine the latticework of high branches, "how one only needs to purchase the land on which such a thing is rooted, before one is permitted to destroy it forever? And, strangest of all, there exists no power to stop you."

Feeney scoffs. "Where I'm from, ancient trees are considered apartment buildings for spirits," he says. "So I expect there may indeed be a power to stop you, Harris. It just isn't awake yet."

Harris turns and holds Feeney's elbows. "Once we ship the sleepers and this business with Japan pays out, I'm going to sell the company. I'm weary of men dying in my employ. And I've lost the stomach for cutting trees like this one. After I sell, we could reside here full time. It would be our place to begin anew. To be free from men like Lomax. Would that suit you?"

"For the record, I detest this idea of you giving up your brother," Feeney says reluctantly, though Harris can tell the idea of living here together has charmed him. "So why not tell Lomax to piss off right now?"

Harris shakes his head. "If he exposed us, we'd be arrested for indecency. Greenwood Timber's stock would be worthless overnight. There'd be nothing left for me to sell. What would we do then? Chop firewood? Do you know what becomes of men like us without the armour of wealth, Liam?"

"I'm not afraid of being broke. As a poet it's my natural state. And living here, we wouldn't need much."

"No, we must see this Japanese business through. I'll sail the remaining lumber over there myself if I must."

"Fine, fine. But I admit it, I do like it here," Feeney says. "Besides, I've always dreamed of being hidden away like some priceless treasure."

"Good, then it's settled," Harris says.

"There's just one thing that bothers me about the cabin," Feeney says forebodingly as they start the hike back.

Harris's stomach plummets. He's thought of everything, hasn't he?

"It only has the one door," he says. "And great treasures like myself always need more than one exit. No matter how protected we are."

So that afternoon Feeney uses the tools left behind by the carpenters to cut a small, second door at the rear of the cabin, right next to the kitchen. He isn't much of a craftsman—this Harris surmises by running his hands over the crooked and splintered opening he's hacked into the wall—but Harris leaves this unmentioned. It's nearly midnight when Feeney finally gets the door to hang without sticking in the jamb, and Harris pops a bottle of sake to celebrate. While they drink, an eagle swoops so close to the cabin's window they can hear it rend the air like fabric.

FIRVALE

WITH SHACKLED WRISTS, Everett is ushered from his holding cell into a closet-sized courtroom, where an ancient judge presides. He shuffles documents and raises his bloodhound face, seeming to regard Everett not so much as a man, but as some unfortunate aspect of the decor. A Mountie tells of Everett's capture, how after he was thrown off a train in the high mountains, he broke into a prominent Firvale house, looted it, and burned up most of its furniture.

"Is this account accurate, Mr. Bowater?" the judge asks.

When the constables pulled him and Pod from the house this morning and carted them down the mountain to this gold-rush town set in the crotch of two rivers, Everett claimed he was an itinerant farm labourer named Saul Bowater from Calgary. When fabricating a name, Everett knows to bend toward the eccentric—less chance that some other tramp's used it previously.

"We were half-frozen, sir," Everett says. "It wasn't stealing. I needed a fire to warm my child."

"Oh, burning up good furnishings is by all means theft," the judge says smugly. "Wouldn't you agree, sir? In that it unlawfully restricts the owner's proper right of use in perpetuity?"

While Everett believes there's a distinction to be made, he knows better than to argue with a jerkwater magistrate with points to prove. "I wasn't exactly seeing it that way, sir."

"But would it be correct to submit that you had a good and understandable reason to be burning this furniture, in that that you lack the funds for proper accommodation?" the judge says now, with what seems to be genuine kindness.

"I suppose that's true, sir."

"Let the record show that the accused admits to vagrancy," the judge proclaims.

"Now hold on," Everett says. "I'm no vagrant. I'm just hard up." There was a time when he was practised at this chess game of details, this weaving of the right words, but he's too weary for it, and his mind keeps straying to Pod, who they've taken from him—to where, he doesn't know.

"Bah," the judge says. "You've never done an honest day's work in your life. Guilty of theft, trespassing, *and* vagrancy." He raises his gavel.

"What will become of my daughter, sir?"

"Have you any family to care for her while you're incarcerated?" replies the judge, setting down his gavel to rub his flesh-hooded eyes.

Everett's mind flashes to Harris. Back in the logging camp where Everett was arrested, the surrounding slopes were entirely stripped, leaving only a black peppering of stumps arranged like seats in a coliseum. Upon some stray logs Everett saw the stencil of the Greenwood Timber Company, which had built both the sawmill and the house he was arrested in. And for a despairing moment, he considers invoking his brother's name to the judge. It's certainly not how he'd imagined approaching Harris after so long—with a plea from jail—and Everett knows it would be a mistake.

"I've no family, sir," he says.

"Then she'll remain in Crown custody while you serve out your sentence, and you can properly demonstrate your parentage at the time of your release," the judge says with naked disgust. He waves his gavel and the bailiff yanks Everett from his seat. He's pulled down a dank hallway into a tiny cell, fetid with the odours of caged human. A tar floor, an iron cot, a tin bucket for his waste. He sits for three days, pinching bedbugs between finger and thumb, soaking the hard-tack they give him to get it down, worrying about whether they'll connect him to that man he left beaten back in Ontario.

In Pod's absence, Everett is but a shadow thrown upon the wall. To be deprived of her for even an hour is like a sickness, but for days? It's a plague. He inquires after her whereabouts a hundred times daily.

"You aren't feeding her cow's milk, are you?" he calls out when he thinks he hears her crying over the drunken slurs of the other prisoners.

"Shut your yap!" the guards bark, kicking the bars with iron-toed boots.

"She can't stand cow's milk. It makes her sick. She needs goat's milk."

Soon, whenever he mentions the child the guards begin striking him with a long hickory pole that reaches deep into his cell, which drives his questions inward, but doesn't halt them. *Is she frightened? Does she look for me when she wakes and I'm not there? Is she sitting in her own waste? Bawling herself to sleep?* Over the years on his sugarbush, Everett had grown accustomed to the taste of loneliness. He'd even come to prefer it, the way a taste for strong liquor can be acquired. Yet it's one he can no longer stomach. After days with no mention of her whereabouts, Everett turns desperate and begs one of the ragged boys who wash the jail's stone floor to bring a message to the judge.

"You think he listens to me?" the freckled boy says, glancing sideways at the guards who'll cuff him if he's caught conspiring with prisoners.

"Tell him to contact my brother," Everett says. "He's a prominent man: Harris Greenwood. The very same one who built Firvale. If the judge could get word to him, he could sort all this out."

Everett watches the boy's eyes widen at the mere mention of such a mighty name. And for perhaps the first time in his entire life, the name Greenwood finally works in Everett's favour.

ONE OF THE MOST DANGEROUS
THINGS THERE IS

"AND HE HAS him incarcerated there?"

"Cabled this morning," Milner says.

"And we trust him? This judge?" Harris asks while pacing his office, weaving expertly among his screeching birdcages. "He's our man? He doesn't harbour some grudge against us, does he? I can't recall the particulars of the contract. Where was it, you said—Firvale?"

Milner pulls the file and reads aloud for Harris's benefit. An escarpment near the Rockies they'd leased for a song from the local municipality five years back. A two-year cut job. They'd built rough bunkhouses for workers and several proper homes for visiting mill managers and governmental dignitaries, along with some wells and roads. It was clear-cut logging, the sticks dragged down the valley and humped back to Vancouver by rail.

"Turned a tidy profit on it," Milner says. But they've done so many cut-and-run jobs of this sort, Harris still can't place it.

"And the judge indicated that my brother *explicitly* requested my help?" Harris says. In his deal with Lomax, Harris agreed to sound the alarm only if his brother *tried* to contact him, not merely if he learned of his whereabouts.

"Yes, the judge indicated that the prisoner asked for your assistance specifically. But any criminal can claim what they like, Mr. Greenwood," Milner says tersely.

"It's him," Feeney says from the back of the room. "I know it. Why the hell else would he name you?"

"Thank you, Milner," Harris says. "That will be all."

Over a solitary lunch eaten at his desk, Harris's mind slips back to the day of the feast he'd prepared to celebrate Everett's return from Europe, and the plate he heaped high and set aside, the same one he dumped down a well when his brother didn't come home. Harris had forgiven Everett for going to war in his stead, and was willing to view his actions as merely another episode of their great brotherly competition. He'd envisioned for them a great future—his education and entrepreneurial know-how combined with Everett's felling experience and intuitive understanding of forests—Greenwood Timber would have made its first million in half the time it had taken Harris on his own. And yet Everett chose to stay away. So why would he turn to Harris now, after all this time?

Harris pushes back his plate and shakes his head. While once he would have gladly offered up his own life to save his brother's, with Feeney in the picture and this snake Lomax hovering and ready to strike, he has more than Everett to protect now. After the maid removes his tray, Harris picks up the phone and summons Feeney to his office. "I need you to fetch Mr. Lomax," he says, "who I'm sure is out smoking in the garden."

"You aren't really going to offer up your only brother to that ghoul?" Feeney says.

"This isn't offering him up, Liam. It's a simple matter of putting two parties in contact. R.J. Holt wants something of his returned, and Mr. Lomax has assured me that Everett won't be prosecuted as long as he complies."

"And you believe him?" Feeney asks.

"Not completely. But I can't afford to shirk my end of our bargain, not now. And may I remind you that Everett and I aren't brothers by blood. It was an agreement, made by equally desperate parties."

"But it worked," Feeney says. "Your agreement. You survived."

"Liam, Mr. Lomax will either make things very easy for us, or very difficult. But be certain: he's going to do one or the other. If he learns Everett contacted me and I failed to inform him, we're finished. What's coming to my brother is already on its way; I'm only spurring it along."

Feeney says nothing, and Harris knows him well enough to register his silence as disapproval. Just then a sudden sense of intrusion comes over Harris, and for the first time he regrets ever mentioning his brother to Feeney at all. He's been reckless with his personal history and has made too many of his most private thoughts known to his describer; he's allowed Feeney too deep inside the high walls that have for so long guarded him against those who would ruin him. Harris decides he'll be less liberal in the future.

"I understand your position, Harris," Feeney says, breaking his silence and putting a warm hand on his back. "But this Lomax reminds me of a tree that's been sawn right through and still won't fall. And while I'm more a sailor than a lumberman, I did my time in your camps, and one thing I learned there is that a tree that's been cut through and still won't drop is one of the most dangerous things there is."

GET YOUR THINGS

THE NEXT DAY a pop-eyed man enters Everett's cell and stands beside his cot. He's thick, short, like a wolverine trained to rear upward and walk. McSorley, he calls himself—the railroad detective whom Temple had been so worried about.

"You've come a long way, Greenwood," he says. "But I knew you'd get pinched for something eventually."

"I don't know who you think I am, sir. But I'm no vagrant."

"You're right," he sneers. "You're worse than that."

"Me and my little girl are making our way west, not troubling anyone."

McSorley huffs though his broad nose. "Now she's yours, is she?"

The two men lock eyes. Everett says: "You heard me."

"I'm no expert," the detective says, "but as far as I know the male species can't conjure up one of those little bundles of joy on their own. So where's her mother?"

"Her mother's deceased."

"You seem real broken up about it."

"Remind me how it's your business?"

"Now listen to me, you bum," the detective hisses while baring his teeth, which are disturbingly identical to one another, as though they've all been cast from the same mould. "That child is yours as much as it's mine. The judge said you don't have papers for her, that right?"

"Lost in a fire," Everett says flatly.

"Then you just tell me what hospital she was born in and we'll have them do you up some new ones."

"I look like I can hire a doctor? She was born in our little shack, beside the woodstove, same as I was. Her mother didn't survive the night."

The detective takes a furious stroll around the cell, readying another tack. "You recall that man you beat in an orchard back in Ontario? Near the tracks? Sure you do. Well, he's the brother of a senator."

"We didn't get off in Ontario," Everett says with as much composure as he can manage. "We caught express freights clean through."

"Funny, because you were identified by a flophouse manager in Toronto, and we found a baby's flannels and sleeper in the creek in that orchard, all of which doesn't matter much. That man you beat will put the finger square on you when I bring you back east. Beard or no beard."

Everett says nothing. What he did to the man was unavoidable, though silently he curses the world for requiring him to harm one person to save another.

"And when you go away for what you did, that little girl becomes a permanent ward of the state. When she does, she'll be swiftly adopted by her father, R.J. Holt."

"I'm her father," Everett says, crossing his arms. "And nothing you say changes it."

McSorley yanks his hat down over his meaty brow. "We'll see about that, Greenwood. We leave tomorrow."

Everett stays up late, rehearsing his story, practising the expression of shock he'll assume when the man from the orchard identifies him. But if it all falls apart and Everett loses Pod to R.J. Holt and faces more penitentiary time, he plans to dash his own head against the stone wall of his cell and put an end to it. Because after living free for so long, he won't survive being imprisoned again.

McSorley returns early the next morning, except this time he's tight-lipped, almost chastened. With him is another man: enormous yet sickly, with sweat rimming the deep caverns of his eyes. Though Lomax is emaciated, and has an even more sinister and demonic air about him than when Everett first laid eyes on him at the rooming house in Toronto, he has Pod in his arms, wrapped in a soft blanket, and all other details drop away. Everett's whole body sings at the sight of her.

"Thank you for your time, Detective," Lomax says, shaking McSorley's hand, his voice croaky and underpowered. Given the detective's evident disappointment, it's clear to Everett that these two men have opposing aims, and that McSorley has been somehow bested—how, Everett cannot say.

"Get your things," Lomax says in a voice like ashes.

Monster, apparition, rescuer, executioner—to Everett it doesn't matter what this man is, because he has Pod in his arms and all the iron doors are swinging open.

SENSIBLE

AT THE SMALL train station near the jail, a private coach awaits. Its gleaming wooden shell, filigreed with gold leaf, clashes absurdly with the hardscrabble mountain surroundings. To dissuade Everett from running, Lomax insists on carrying the child aboard himself, though she writhes against him and her very presence unnerves him—the neat contours of her face uncomfortably reminiscent of Euphemia's. Besides, Lomax has already handled his fair share of babies in his life, and he would rather not be put in mind of his own brood back home, now homeless and shacked up with Lavern's mother. Though with both Everett and the baby in his custody, the Lomax family's prospects are looking much improved.

Once they find their seats, Lomax passes the child to Everett, who clutches her against him, murmuring in her ear.

"Old R.J. has a fine coach here," Everett says, after the baby has dropped to sleep but the train has yet to move. "Where's it headed?"

"It isn't Mr. Holt's," Lomax says.

"Whose is it, then? Yours?"

"This is your brother's personal coach. Cut from a single redwood. One tree, hollowed out like an Indian canoe. Impressive, isn't it?"

"Huh," Everett says tonelessly. "Back in Toronto you claimed you were Holt's man."

"I am. But Harris Greenwood and I currently share interests. Unlike you, your brother is sensible."

"And he told you where you could find me?"

"After he learned of your imprisonment, and out of his great concern."

"Some brother."

"He has your well-being in mind, Everett. As do I. Remember, I'm the one who just told Detective McSorley that the child is rightly yours and that we were together in Toronto on the day that senator's brother was beaten."

Everett shakes his head. "I figured you would've quit long ago," he says.

"I'm about as stubborn as you are, it seems. But we just need to settle one more matter before we can all go home—those of us who still have homes, at least. I'm talking about the journal."

"You and me aren't settling anything."

Lomax exhales loudly. "Well, that'd be the kind of stance that allows me no choice other than to inform McSorley about my mixed-up dates, leaving you unaccounted for on the day that man was hurt."

Everett throws his eyes to the window, as though he's calculating how much force it will take for him to break it. Lomax regrets giving him the baby, but if he rises, this time Lomax is sitting close enough in the small compartment to grab him.

"You know what I can't figure?" Lomax says after a while. "You did everything you could to try to rid yourself of her. And then you did everything you could to keep her. It doesn't make sense."

"People never make sense." Everett says. "You just learned that?"

"Look, the police said you weren't found with any journal," Lomax says, knocking a Parliament from its package, then reaching across the rail car to offer it to Everett. "But if you hand it over, along with the child, of course, I won't turn you back in to McSorley. There might even still be the possibility of a reward. So where is it?"

"Oh, that's right, I remember now," Everett says brightly, ignoring the cigarette. "I sent it to the editors of the *Globe*."

A crimson rage geysers through Lomax as he drops the Parliament and lunges forward to clamp one of his immense hands around Everett's windpipe, squeezing its rubbery cartilage with a firm yet even pressure, as though he's juicing a lemon. Everett chokes and his molars clatter together, and his eyes bulge and burn like comets. Lomax can feel the clockwork surge of Everett's pulse, and knows that if he squeezed just a little harder, he could bring the tips of his fingers together around Everett's neck. "Mailed it to my brother from Toronto . . ." Everett manages to say with a metallic rasp, and Lomax lets up a little to reward him for telling the truth. "But I'll get it for you if you take me to him."

Lomax takes one final squeeze before releasing Everett's throat. "There, now that's the first sensible thing you've said all day," he says while straightening his rumpled jacket. "And I guess you've just answered your own question about where we're headed," he adds, as Everett coughs and retches with the child still asleep in his lap. "We're going to visit your brother."

THE ECONOMY OF NATURE

BY THE RHYTHMS of the axe-work, Everett recognizes him long before setting eyes on his face. Out behind the grand mansion, with its spreading east and west wings, its manicured gardens, and its spouting stone dryads and nymphs, Everett watches in amazement as the blind man grasps another round of fir without groping for it, then heaves it up onto the cutting stump. Next, he draws a calculated step back—the maul poised over his shoulder—and strikes the round, dead centre on the heartwood, sending two near-equal pieces jumping left and right. Harris was always good with an axe, and it cheers Everett to know that wealth hasn't spoiled the talent, despite the fact that he's cutting firewood next to a rose garden.

Everett would rather not approach Harris while he's holding an implement that could cleave Everett's head in two, but Lomax is keeping Pod in a bedroom on the second floor of the mansion, and though the longing to clutch her against him and bury his nose in her neck nearly kills him, Everett's done his best to appear unbothered. He knows his position will weaken if Lomax gathers the true depth of his feelings. But Lomax has given him until tomorrow to produce the journal, and he needs his fair stake of their inheritance if he and Pod are to have any hope of escape. Everett tucks his shirt into his filthy trousers, combs his fingers through his hair, and walks closer, halting just out of Harris's swing range.

"I thought rich tycoons were supposed to be fat," Everett says from behind him.

Harris freezes mid-swing, then lowers the maul to rest upon his shoulder. Though his ropy body is still strong, Everett senses a subtle failing of his balance, a slight seismic tremor, as though the garden were a ship that had just come into its berth.

"You know, after all this time, no one's told me where they keep the damn food in this place," Harris says, turning to reveal wide, vacant eyes, with the lower half of his face wavering somewhere between mirth and rage.

Despite his brother's sightless condition, Everett suddenly wishes that he were presenting himself in finer clothing and under less self-interested circumstances. "Don't you have anyone to do your chopping for you?" Everett says, nosing some of the neatly quartered wood closer to Harris's pile with the toe of his boot.

"There are about forty thousand jobless men in this province alone, brother, all eager to do my chopping for me. That doesn't mean I don't care to do some myself."

Though he's still an inch taller than Everett, and still has that shrewd, appraising cast to his face, there's a new aristocratic airiness about his voice. Faintly English. The residue of good schooling, Everett guesses, and he's proud of Harris for bettering himself. There have been moments over the years when Everett has missed him so acutely he's thought he would suffocate of it. While he's envisioned their reunion thousands of times, it's usually involved fisticuffs and the gnashing of teeth. Never once has it gone like this, with a return to their old banter, a slip back into the deep groove of their ways.

Harris turns back to his work and drops the maul, neatly cleaving another round. "I'd say you haven't changed," he says. "But you probably have, given how you've treated yourself. Your voice is slower. Rustier. There's more earth to it."

"Is that why you sent your big retriever to fetch me? You wanted to hear my voice but were too busy playing logger to come find me yourself?"

"Let's be clear, brother: I asked Mr. Lomax to collect you after *you* requested *my* help," Harris says sternly. "And after speaking with him, it became evident that he might be the only person who could fish you out. Providing you're reasonable, which, knowing you, I hardly expect to be the case."

Everett bristles at his brother's parental tone, that old self-appointed authority, always speaking for them both, always deciding which trees they'd cut, always the first to call for lights out in their cabin. "You know me best, Harris," he says. "I'm everything but reasonable."

Harris stacks the wood he's cut, hangs the maul, and asks Everett if he's hungry. Everett nods, then realizes his mistake and confirms the fact aloud. They pass through a tall garden door into a grand room beneath a chandelier of a thousand shards of suspended crystal. Everett has never seen such opulence: walls of bookcases fronted with cut glass; a floor of green marble, smooth and lustrous as silk; the room's trim and banisters all hewn from the finest and tightest-grained redwood. Everett is further astounded by Harris's uncanny ability to avoid all of the furniture by memory, without the use of a cane or a guide.

"Quite a spread you've put together," Everett says. "Your mansion appears to be a fair deal straighter than that old log cabin we put up."

"I knew that if I built it modestly," Harris says, "they'd call me a miser. And if I built it lavishly, they'd accuse me of showing off. So I chose the latter."

Amid the smell of old wood and leather, they sit in wing chairs near a fireplace full of embers that pulse orange behind a steel grille. The westerly windows overlook the property's private wood of oak and beech—the few trees that Greenwood Timber has yet to cut down, it seems. Surely, Everett thinks, Harris will fell those closest to his house last.

Servants present tea along with multi-tiered platters of cakes and dainties.

"So, how've you been, brother?" Everett says, smiling under the preposterous weight of all that isn't contained in his question, and the idea of summing up an eighteen-year absence from the one person you know foremost in life with a word such as *fine*.

"Quite well," Harris says, his jaw half-clenched at Everett's old habit of making light of serious matters. "Considering. You?"

"I haven't managed to quit living quite yet, despite my better efforts," Everett says. "I did eventually return to our old cabin, though a little later than promised, I admit. But it was gone. The woods, too. Any idea where they went?"

"Oh, you did come! How kind of you! And here I thought that you'd chosen a life spent in the gutter over working alongside your invalid brother. Silly me," Harris says tensely, taking a sip of the tea that a servant has placed in his hand.

"I cursed you for years for what you did," Everett says, struggling to retain his composure for the sake of Pod's future.

"And you don't curse me anymore?"

"No, I let all that go. I've got other things to worry about now."

"Well, you should be worried. This Lomax fellow has it in for you."

"I could give him the slip for good anytime I wanted. Except this child needs some stable and decent circumstances to grow up in— not like how we did. So I'm here to ask for my fair stake of what Mrs. Craig left us."

Harris rises from his chair and slowly paces the room with his teacup tinkling against its saucer. "You know, after the Armistice," he begins, "I contacted the Department of Defence, pretending to be you. They informed me that I had indeed stepped off a ship in Halifax, but that was the last anyone had heard of me. Over the years, I often imagined you out there wandering, and then, after I'd given up hope, I imagined your bones lying somewhere nobody ever looks."

"I had some difficulties, Harris. The War wasn't good to me. I was all mixed up in my head. I can see that now. It took me years to find a place to settle, and even then I knew it was better for me to keep away from people."

"Yes, Lomax informed me about your little syrup operation. A shame that you didn't have the foresight to purchase the land first.

Odd, isn't it? How we both ended up relying on trees—in different capacities, mind you. But of course, Everett, you're entitled to half of the Craig woodlot proceeds. I'll have a cheque prepared immediately. I'll also include the military pension they sent me over the years as well. It will be a tidy sum."

Everett is stunned by his brother's frictionless generosity. He'd expected more fireworks, a return to their squabbling ways, more gristle, less meat. "All right, then. I suppose that settles it," Everett says, slapping his thighs and rising from his seat. "We'll be out of your hair before you know—"

It's then that Harris turns, cocks his arm, and hurls both his teacup and saucer twenty feet across the room and into a glass-lined bookcase, a hail of splinters pattering the floor. "'Competition is most severe between allied forms which fill nearly the same space in the economy of nature,'" Harris says calmly, as though nothing had transpired, his barren eyes swung as wide as they'll go. "That's Darwin."

"Never met him," Everett says, closing his fists, thinking that it's just like his brother to wield his book-learning as a weapon. He feels that old magma of anger in his chest, the fighting spirit that bound them together for so long.

"I don't expect you would have," Harris says. "They had a Braille edition of *On the Origin of Species* at Yale, a very rare book. And when I read that passage I thought it encapsulated our dealings quite well."

"I was trying to help you," Everett says.

"*Retinitis pigmentosa*," Harris replies. "That's the term for it, brother. Awful-sounding, isn't it? A degenerative disorder. And though the doctors can name it, the cure still evades them."

"We didn't need a name to tell us something was wrong."

"Well, I didn't ask for your help," Harris says, his temples pulsing visibly, the way they always have whenever he believes he's been wronged.

"I never said you did. But you needed it just the same."

"When you left for France, I was alone. Ashamed. Fumbling about in our little cabin, with the darkness closing in. I became the object of their pity."

"You deserved some of that pity. You'd have been helpless in those trenches, Harris. The Kaiser would've walked over and shot you himself."

"Look around you, brother!" Harris announces loudly. "See everything I've accomplished and tell me how *helpless* I am now. Do I still deserve your pity?"

"A big house made of trees that other people cut down for you is nothing to me, Harris." Everett is yelling himself now, and it feels good in his lungs. "Me and my girl took refuge in a town you built then abandoned up in the mountains—Firvale? It looked more like a place the devil takes a holiday than what you'd call an accomplishment!"

"Is everything all right, sir?" says an Irishman who enters the room, fixing a fierce stare on Everett. "I heard a crash."

"Oh, I'm fine, fine!" Harris yells. "Just catching up with my brother!" The Irishman's presence seems to settle Harris, however, and he sits back down with a sham of a smile pasted to his face. "So what battlefield heroisms did I perform? A great many, it seems. They mailed me a bucket of medals."

"You weren't brave," Everett says. "You nearly shit yourself during the tiniest skirmish. You mostly carried stretchers and built things out of wood. When you came back, you couldn't look at a human face without seeing the skull beneath it smashed. For years after you didn't sleep more than a few hours at a time, and not at all without a bottle in you. That sugarbush was the only thing that kept you from sticking a cocked revolver in your ear and pulling the trigger."

"Yet now with this child in your arms," Harris says, "things have changed . . ."

"That's right," Everett says. "A person seldom knows they're starved for something until they get a taste of it."

"Mr. Lomax claims that the baby is in fact R.J. Holt's, born to his mistress is my guess, which is why they've so far neglected to involve the authorities. The word *kidnapping* wasn't used, but the insinuation was there."

"That's a lie. I found her left to die in the trees. Just like we were," Everett says. "But at least we had each other," he adds. "This child doesn't have anyone except me. So Harris, you just cut me that cheque and I'll make for—"

"It's not quite that simple, Everett," Harris says. "Because if I just let you run off, Mr. Lomax will make things difficult for me."

"That's why you sent for me, isn't it?" Everett says. "Not because I asked for your help. He's got your ass in the ringer, too."

"May I interrupt this charming reunion to make a humble suggestion?" says the Irishman, who appears to be some kind of assistant, though Everett is astounded that a subordinate would employ such sarcasm with his employer.

"We'll discuss this later, Mr. Feeney," Harris says.

"Given Mr. Lomax's faltering loyalty to R.J. Holt and his own downtrodden state, what if you offered him a good sum of money for the child?" Feeney asks Everett, ignoring Harris completely. "To my eye, that man seems ground-down enough to take it."

"You think my pension and my inheritance together would be enough?" Everett asks.

"You've both forgotten this book he's after," Harris says impatiently. "He seems to want it even more than he does the child."

"That's the problem," replies Everett. "I left the journal somewhere safe. But I told him I mailed it here. And even if I *did* have it, he's not getting it. I believe the child's mother wrote it, and it's all the girl has left to tell her where she comes from."

"You've read this journal?" the Irishman persists.

"As much as I was able," Everett replies. "But I had it for some time."

"And has Lomax laid eyes on it?"

"I can't really say. I don't expect so, seeing how it was the mother's private diary and was bundled up with the child."

"Then why don't we fabricate one ourselves?" the Irishman says. "You could describe to me what it looked like."

"Mr. Feeney is something of a writer," Harris interjects. "But he won't be involving himself in any of this. Now Everett, I really think—"

"You'll need to point out the proper journal," the Irishman interrupts. "Do you remember it?"

"Sure, I could give you a general sense," Everett replies. "It was fine penmanship, though. With writing on every page. And Lomax needs it by tomorrow. You figure you could fill a whole journal in a night?"

The Irishman shrugs. "It won't be my finest literary achievement," he says. "But I'll see what I can manage."

SHOEBOXES

AFTER THE CYCLONE has done its worst and moved on, the storm doors are left immobilized by the rubble that was hurled against them. It takes Temple, Gertie, and the dozen remaining farmhands the entire afternoon to chip their way up through the library's thick floor planks with a dull hatchet and a ballpeen hammer. When they emerge from the cellar into the haze of a dim, dusky sun, it's as if the whole prairie has been tucked under an old brown quilt. As far as Temple can see, the dust has drifted into long, smooth hummocks that swallow all sound, the way snow does. She nearly screams, just to test if she could hear herself at all.

"Oh, I'm so sorry, honey," Gertie says as they tour the ruins of Temple's barn and house, including her fences and pens, which are all splintered and strewn across the torn-up land like a child's discarded toys. Farm tools and the carcasses of wind-bludgeoned birds have been flung everywhere. A tree she doesn't recognize pokes up through the windshield of her truck, its roots turned upward in the breeze like a demonic bush. And the library itself is decimated, now resembling a bare, wooden barge foundering in a great ocean of dust. The only landmark that remains upright is the willow near the house. Although a large bough has cracked off and most of its leaves were stripped, the trunk appears intact.

"I'm not sure this world wants us anymore," Gertie says as they pick through the rubble for the few personal items they'll bring on their long, dusty trek into Estevan. After they set out, they soon pass the shelterbelt of maple saplings that Temple and Everett planted together. Still too small for the wind to have gotten a proper hold of, they look likely to survive, which is a consolation, even if Everett will never return to see them.

Over the ensuing weeks, Temple and Gertie sleep in the basement of the Knox Presbyterian Church. Temple spends her days haggling in the offices of insurance companies—a battle she'll eventually lose, when the most senior adjuster finally concludes: "We covered you for a farm, not a halfway house, Miss Van Horne."

With no money to rebuild and nowhere to go, Temple falls into despair, and momentarily considers selling her land and taking a vacant position as a schoolteacher in Estevan. But when word gets out on the railway lines and among the hobo jungles that her farm was destroyed and she's been left destitute, bedraggled men and women set out in the dark from all across the continent. Convicts, criminals, the unemployed: they come nightly from the direction of the tracks, and each leaves a shoebox on the back steps of the Knox Presbyterian Church. Every morning, Temple carries the shoeboxes into the basement and finds them stuffed with stolen watches, or silver cutlery, or old gold jewellery, or bloodstained bills, or mere handfuls of filthy nickels. Upon these shoeboxes is always scrawled the same words:

FOR THE LADY WITH THE TABLE ON HER PORCH

THE SECRET & PRIVATE
THINKINGS & DOINGS OF
EUPHEMIA BAXTER

AS LOMAX TURNS the journal in his hands, it's as though the planets have been marshalled back into their rightful orbits, as though he's smoked the purest opium ever to be extracted from a poppy by humankind, as though the lightning in his long-tortured spine has been cured and the Crash has ended and his family is back home in their little bungalow and the fog of sadness that's trailed him since he was a boy has at long last been dispelled.

Let the Greenwoods have the damned thing, Lomax had thought the second Everett offered him that big wad of cash along with Euphemia's journal in exchange for the child. Harris has the means to support it. And Everett obviously cares for the baby more than Mr. Holt ever would. All he ever wanted it for was to serve as a trophy in the display cabinet of his legacy. So when Lomax returns to Saint John, he'll simply tell Mr. Holt that Everett Greenwood wasn't the right man after all, and that the baby was sickly and had died while in the custody of a different drifter who'd found it. *But through my own cunning, sir*, Lomax imagines himself saying, *I still managed to recover Euphemia's journal, which I've got right here . . .*

Of course, Mr. Holt will again grieve the loss of his child. But he said it himself: *If at any point you are faced with the choice of which to recover, the child or the book, choose the book.* And returning the journal to Mr. Holt will go a long way toward setting things right with his former employer, which Lomax needs to do if he ever expects to reside anywhere on the Eastern seaboard in peace.

And the Greenwoods' money will be more than enough for him to reclaim his house from the bank. No more mortgage. No more

debt collection. And rather than wasting his energies shaking down
deadbeats and tending Mr. Holt's stable of girls, Lomax plans to seek
training in a useful job, something productive, perhaps as a builder
or tradesman.

After striking his lucrative deal with the Greenwoods, Lomax
left skid row for a fine suite with a view of the snow-topped mountains and Vancouver's dazzling harbour, and now sits leafing the journal's pages, which teem with Euphemia's graceful penmanship. He
flips to the back of the book, to what must be her final entry, likely
written the day he last saw her, after he returned to the estate to
check on her condition, just hours before she fled into the woods
with her child. Yet surprisingly, he finds nothing but poetic observations about the weather and how stunning the leaves of the oak tree
are. To his relief, and despite what that liar Blank had told him,
Lomax finds no mention of either himself or Mr. Holt whatsoever.
In fact, if he weren't so pleased to have secured the book and solved
all his financial woes in one brilliant stroke, Lomax would almost be
disappointed that Euphemia never thought to write about him at all.

His suite has grown damp, so Lomax proceeds to light a fire. And
since he already has the matches out, he allows himself a celebratory
ball of opium, his last—this he decides resolutely. Now that he won't
be stuffing himself into cramped train berths or pounding the pavement all day, he'll have no more need for opium's pain-dampening
effects. The rich smoke sends him into a gorgeous stupor, and he
slides through a series of blissful states, almost like rooms, each fur-
nished with a new and singular pleasure.

By the time he returns to himself, the fire is spent and the room
is too warm. He dresses in the new worsted suit, wingtips, and pork-
pie hat he'd purchased earlier for his journey home. With the
Greenwoods' cash in his pocket, he saunters down to the street,
intending to find a meal, perhaps a bit of beef Wellington to restore
his strength, and spots a suitably appealing restaurant. But before
taking a table he detours to the rail station and purchases a first-class

ticket to Saint John, scheduled for tomorrow morning. He then cables Lavern, informing her that his job has concluded successfully, and that he'll be returning in three days with the means to change their lives forever. His throat thickens when he signs the salutation: *Undying Love, HBL.*

That bit done, he starts back toward the restaurant he's selected. To save himself some time, he takes a shortcut through a narrow alley that edges Chinatown, which, it turns out, leads him past an opium den housed in a run-down hotel called the New Sun Wah. With his train ticket tucked snugly against his breast, his jacket pockets stuffed with cash, and his triumphant journey home to Saint John assured, he allows himself just a peek inside the door.

GREENWOOD ISLAND

HERE FOLLOW THE sweetest months of Everett's trouble-plagued life. Which isn't saying a great deal, but that doesn't alter the fact that during the coming decades of his penitentiary sentence, Everett will often revisit the splendours of his winter spent with Pod on his brother's small, forested island. And he'll be able to wring just enough joy from these recollections to face the treeless isolation of incarceration without submitting to despair.

"Now that you're broke again, you can't go setting up a syrup operation in the dead of winter," Harris said the day after Lomax, in exchange for Everett's inheritance and the bogus journal, agreed to lay the matter of the child to rest, providing Everett kept Pod as his own in some secluded place and didn't stir up trouble. "I'm not using my retreat quite yet," Harris added, "so you're welcome to hide out there until spring."

"And if Lomax isn't convinced by our little scam and *does* come sniffing around again," the Irishman added, "then fat chance of him finding you there."

The truth is that Everett is tired of running. And he knows Pod could use some time spent in one place, especially now that she's not so little a baby anymore. When the Irishman delivers them to the island the next day, Everett is pleased to discover the cabin is nothing like Harris's mansion. Though finely built, with neat, tight-fitting post-and-beam joinery, there is little ornament to it. Well concealed from the water, yet still boasting a view of the bay, Everett's guess is that Harris uses it to hide away with the Irishman, which explains why they speak so freely with each other. But none of that is Everett's business. He saw it in the War, men becoming sweethearts, and it never bothered him a whit.

Each Tuesday, the Irishman—who, before becoming his brother's describer, was a tug pilot who hauled booms for Greenwood Timber—brings the week's supplies in a nimble wood-hulled skiff. Everett places Pod in crude crib he's built her so she doesn't crawl to the woodstove and scald herself, then hikes to the small jetty to collect the supplies from inside the insulated box where Feeney leaves them. Fuel for the lanterns, tins of matches, coffee, cheese, apples, canned corn and peas, sacks of cabbage and potato, sides of ham, butter, maple syrup, flour, Mother Bailey's Quieting Syrup for Pod's teething, and a huge jug of goat's milk. Everett has never seen such a bounty assembled in one place, and keeps a rough tally so he can reimburse his brother someday, after his time here is finished.

As winter rains wreath the island, wet plumes of fern and softly needled hemlock stroking the cabin's walls, Everett and Pod sleep together in the same bed beneath the upper floor's tall windows. Pod has grown burlier, and now kicks him like a mule in her sleep. Still, Everett wakes rested in a way previously unknown to him. Here on the island, there's no chance of being beaten by railway detectives; of tramps rifling his things or stealing his boots; of Mounties finding and razing his shack; of artillery shells screaming down upon his bed or chlorine gas seeping under the door.

Each morning he wakes to Pod's babbling and carries her downstairs to fix breakfast: wheat porridge splashed with goat's milk or flapjacks drowned in a maple syrup so inferior to his own that it's a different thing entirely. After strapping Pod into a chair with his belt, he sits with an enamelled coffee pot all to himself, watching her miss her mouth with her spoon, and often finds himself smiling for no reason at all.

By February, she's pulling herself to standing at the coffee table. Everett sets anything valuable up high so she can't topple it over, and crudely sews canvas patches on the knees of her creepers after her

scooting around wears them through. She fears the roar of the gasoline washing machine, so he sets their clothes out in the rain to wash,
and when he folds their clean laundry into the closet, the sight of
her flannels and creepers stacked up all fresh and orderly fills him
with an almost impossible serenity.

At supper one evening, they hear the breach of killer whales in
the pass and hurriedly wash up before hiking to the shoreline. There
they stand among the flesh-like madrones that lean over the sea. And
when the black fins pass, twelve or so of them, their calves dawdling
behind, it is close enough for Everett to smell the fermented pun-
gency of their spume. He clutches Pod tight as she strains against
him, eager to join the whales in the grey water.

Behind the cabin is a small shed, stocked with well-oiled tools
and a stack of stickered fir planks that went unused during the construction. He goes about building a proper woodshed, setting its
posts on flat stones he hauls from the beach. He works with Pod in
her crib nearby, where she covers her ears at the harsh growl of the
crosscut saw. After the day's carpentry, he takes her for long walks
in the misting rain before supper, and it's then Everett discovers that
while half the island is towering old-growth, the remaining half is
newly burned, with shoots of bright green fireweed and thistle
threading up between the charred stumps and limbs.

As spring approaches and the days lengthen, they pick over the
island's sandstone bays and watch the tide climb the rocks near the
jetty. Blue herons step carefully in the shallows, their rapier beaks
stabbing the water. From among the driftwood and afghans of sea-
weed, Everett chips off oysters for his supper. Pod jams their pearly
shells in her mouth, rubbing them over her newest shard of tooth,
another shell itself.

Often Everett is struck with the desire to communicate with his
brother. Yet because he still cannot write with any fluency, he has the
Irishman instruct him on the use of the shortwave radio that Harris
installed in the cabin's second bedroom so he could keep abreast with

his affairs back in Vancouver. Each night at exactly nine, after Pod is asleep, Everett puts his lips to the set's microphone, presses the black button, and begins to relate the details of his day: the grey ocean and the impossibly tall trees, the way Pod is afraid of her own reflection in the mirror, or the pungent breath of a killer whale. At first Harris makes no reply, and at times Everett just sits listening to the static hiss, imagining this is in fact his brother breathing.

Then, just as he's describing at length the largest tree he'd found on the island so far, a mammoth Douglas fir so tall and thick it denies comprehension, Harris interrupts him to recite a poem. During the stiff but amiable conversation that follows, Pod wakes to the voice and crawls over to the fizzing radio, her eyes split quizzically wide at the sudden appearance of this stranger in the room. When the brothers sign off, she crawls around to the other side of the radio's walnut enclosure to search out the source of the voice. She shrieks with delight when no one is there.

THE NEW SUN WAH

LOMAX SPENDS WEEKS in his curtained bunk, one of many that line the walls of the large room, a colossal roaring stove at its centre.

Hourly, a tall boy with thick glasses presents Lomax with a bamboo pipe, and after he smokes, the boy rubs his back muscles with smelly liniments, while Lomax curls into himself like a baby. When the boy brings meals Lomax waves them away. He takes only nips of liqueur, lychee nuts, ginger candies, and fragrant teas steeped with opium seedpods. For entertainment, he watches ghosts flit on the walls, and has become convinced that all he requires in this world can be provided by this miraculous boy with thick glasses. He knows exactly how Lomax wants his pipe layout arranged. Knows never to put milk in Lomax's tea—which he hasn't been able to stomach since his days of collecting on milk accounts. And most importantly: he knows just how tightly to pack the next bowl and exactly when to light the next match. He's a priest. A brother. A father. And if there's any relief to be found after Lomax's long life of suffering and drudgery, it's to be found here, in this boy's ministrations.

When Lomax develops a nagging cough that worsens to the point of retching, the boy presents him with a gift: "Upon the house." An eyedropper attached to a hypodermic needle with blue sealing wax. Lomax watches the boy cook the laudanum powder in a tin spoon over a coal oil lamp, caressing it with flame. When the boy sets the spike, Lomax watches his own blood bloom in the glass chamber like an orchid. The boy's first squeeze of the dropper sends him swimming out from the filthy, tepid bath of normal experience and into the clean, invigorating ocean of infinity. And in this singular and breathtaking moment, Harvey Lomax knows he will never smoke opium again in his life.

The boy keeps Lomax's wad of money in the house safe, and his laudanum locked in a tin box next to his bunk, away from the conniving of the withered wraiths that recline in the room's other bunks. The boy changes Lomax's sheets and holds the bedpan beneath him to save him the tedious trip to the lavatory. The boy was even kind enough to call Lomax's previous hotel to ask them to pack up his effects, which included the slipcase and the journal. They'll hold them until he needs them, which will be any day now, Lomax assures himself. Though his rail ticket to Saint John is long expired, he still has plenty of money and will buy another as soon as he's restored. Never once has he wavered in his ultimate intention to return home. Often he imagines how his seven children will scramble and clamour for his attentions when he does. Perhaps his absence will make them all the more appreciative of his affections in the long term. While it's painful to admit, his own father's disappearance had taught him that he must make his own way in the world, rather than wait around for a path to be cut for him.

To spite his father, Lomax had lived his entire life putting the needs of others before his own. He'd supported his mother with milk collection, and then Lavern and his children with debt collection, and he realizes now that he's held himself to an impossible standard. And these few lazy weeks of respite at the New Sun Wah are the least he deserves after a lifetime of stalwart dependability.

Often he wonders: At which point did my own father decide that he'd never go home? Lomax had hated him for so long that the hate had hardened, fossilized, and become the very structure of his self, like the steel that girders a tall building. But during his long search for the journal and the child, Lomax has gained a fuller understanding of his father's decision to abandon his family. Maybe it's a child's notion that such decisions are consciously made at all, when in truth, we live at the mercy of the world. Financial crashes and train crashes.

Earthquakes. Wildfires. Hurricanes and cyclones. Diseases and droughts. Gears turn. Levers lift. A boy squeezes the bulb of an eye-dropper and releases a rubber strap with a *whoosh*, and everything changes forever.

TRAPS

AS CONTENT AS Everett is on Greenwood Island, not a day passes without a haunting from Temple. The topmost button of her calico dress that she keeps undone. The languid yet purposeful saunter that carries her about her farm. The efficiency with which she can dig a hole and drop in a tree. The way she drinks coffee, like it isn't only saving her life but also her mortal soul. The way she hooked her hair around her ears when they made love, as if to better hear him pant. And it seems the gravest injustice that there could be so many beds in the world, yet still he and Temple can't manage to share any one of them. Often he finds himself describing her to Pod as though they'd never met, as though Temple herself hadn't held Pod during his lessons in her library while Everett bumbled his way through the *Odyssey*.

With spring around the corner, Everett has decided that he's finished with sugaring and would prefer to live on the island indefinitely. During their regular radio conversation the previous evening, he put the idea to Harris, who agreed to give him a plot of land adjacent to the existing cabin. This summer, Everett intends to build his own cabin, similarly crafted, and when it's done he'll ask the Irishman to write a letter to Temple for him, inviting her to join him here. When she refuses, which of course she will, he and Pod will travel back to her farm, and when Temple refuses him still, Everett will reclaim the journal from her library and return here.

To earn money, Everett will do carpentry work with the tools he's found, constructing simple furniture to sell in Vancouver. By the time

Pod reaches school age, he'll have the money to bring in tutors to educate her. Greenwood Island will be a fine place to raise her, and Harris and the Irishman will provide her with some companionship outside of his own. Besides, the burden of Pod's care will only lighten as she develops. In fact, just that afternoon she stood under her own power without clutching at a chair for balance, and even took a few bowlegged staggers, her thighs so wide-set her rear end nearly dipped to the floor.

To celebrate her triumph he cooks flapjacks for supper, though the merriment of the occasion is spoiled when he goes to the wood-shed to fetch some firewood and discovers the steaming carcass of a three-point buck: its windpipe torn out, tongue eaten, bowels pierced and stinking, blood only barely crusting the rims of its wounds. Everett burns the carcass, saving only the tenderloin, which he fries the next day with wild onions and nettle for Pod's supper. With great gusto she eats the meat that he chews up for her, pink juice flowing in broad rivulets down her chin.

Aware that no eagle or bear is capable of such a surgical kill, Everett tells his brother about the incident that evening. Harris says it's rumoured that cougars catch rides on stray log booms and strand themselves on islands like these, where they promptly eradicate the deer population, effectively starving themselves to death. Everett aims to acquire some goats this spring, to provide milk for Pod and keep her company as she grows, but a cougar would take them one by one. And with such a terror stalking about, he can't leave Pod alone in the yard for a second—or even in the house with a window open, for that matter.

It's then he remembers noticing a battery of leg traps in the woodshop's rafters. They're massive, built for grizzlies most likely, with snapping jaws wide enough for a grown man's boot. He takes them down and sets them in a perimeter around the cabin, and on the second night he catches a mink, which the overpowered trap cleaves neatly in half. Though he's loath to maim or kill a creature of a cougar's magnificence, it's only once the traps are set, and the Browning rifle he'd requested from the Irishman is hung high on brackets next to his bed where Pod can't reach it, that he's again able to rest easy.

SHORTWAVE

"WHY DIDN'T YOU give yourself more initials over the years?" his brother's voice says, distant and tinny with radio crackle. "You fat cats love yourself some initials. How about 'H.P. Greenwood'? Or 'H.T. Greenwood'? That last one sounds extra-impressive."

Harris laughs. "That may have helped, brother. A man in my position needs all the gravity he can get. Though I suspect it's too late for more initials now."

"Then maybe I'll bequeath some to this little girl I've got here. To help her along a little. She deserves some respect after all this."

"Have you decided on a proper name for her yet? You can't go on calling her Pod forever."

"I have one in mind, but I'm not quite settled on it. You'll be the first to know when I am."

Since they've begun conversing each evening, Harris has incorporated the ritual into his daily routine. His first shipment of sleepers has finally reached Japan, and now that he's received payment, Greenwood Timber is once again in the black. And after a long day at his desk, restoring his credit with the London firm, or ensuring that his cargo arrives on schedule, he's grown to appreciate his brother's voice nearly as much as Feeney's.

It was arduous at first. But the words came eventually, each brother taking his turn like children with a new toy. Often Harris marvels at the uncanny familiarity of Everett's voice—at times it's as though it originates from inside his own mind rather than from the radio's speaker. Mostly, they stick to pedestrian subjects and occasional reminiscences about their woodlot and its notable trees, their greatest fights and greatest meals.

"Remember how we used to climb those elm trees at the centre of town and swear our heads off?" Everett says.

"Or when you shot that terrier by accident with one of your arrows," Harris adds. "So we skinned it to hide the evidence? But they caught us anyway?"

When talk inevitably turns to the beguiling Mrs. Craig and what her grand house looked like the night it burned, the brothers grow sombre, and there are long, empty gaps of static.

"Just promise you'll take care of Pod if something happens to me," Everett says to conclude one of those silences, on the last night the brothers will speak. "I don't want her left all alone in the woods somewhere like we were."

Harris has come to realize that the reason his brother didn't join him after the War wasn't because he preferred living without an invalid to attend to; it was because of his own suffering. Feeney has told Harris about "war shock," the wound of the mind that soldiers can receive in battle, and Harris pities Everett for what his had cost him.

"She'll never be alone like we were," Harris says. "You have my word."

Originally, it was Feeney's suggestion to let Everett and the baby hide out at their retreat, but after some convincing, Harris has warmed to the idea. He's even agreed to give Everett his own plot of land on the island. And once this Japanese business is concluded and Harris liquidates his company, he looks forward to living together as neighbours.

Yet, despite this restoration of their brotherly bond, a deep and frightful suspicion still clings to Harris: that nothing good can possibly endure. Not ever. And that the gruesome power that brought those two trains together, stole away his sight, scrambled his brother's mind, and left Pod abandoned to die in the woods, isn't quite finished with them yet.

THE VALISE

THE NEW SUN Wah is raided by Mountie constables early on a Saturday morning, when its withered guests are at their most somnolent. After the spike is roughly yanked from Lomax's arm and he's hoisted from his bunk and thrown to his feet—his first instance of uprightness in he can't remember how long—he's struck immediately in the mouth by an overzealous constable, a man more accustomed to drunken loggers and wild-eyed gold-rush casualties than docile dope fiends. Blood gouts onto his silk pajamas and two bottom teeth that were previously loose now roll about freely in his mouth like a pair of unlucky dice. The police collect the paraphernalia from beside the bunks, including Lomax's hypodermic kit and tin of laudanum powder, and haul him and a few other emaciated men out into the drizzly alley.

When they arrive at the stationhouse, through broken teeth Lomax manages to identify himself and explain the vital errand he's performing here in Vancouver: running down a debt for Mr. R.J. Holt of New Brunswick. When he informs them that he was only frequenting such an establishment to find the fugitive, and that he'd like his money returned to him immediately, the constables laugh in his face.

As they're marching him to the train station to stick him on the first coach back to Saint John, Lomax notices that they're passing his former hotel, and hurls himself to the wet pavement. If he must return home, penniless and defeated, to prostrate himself before Mr. Holt and beg for his life back, the journal is the one thing that could convince his employer that this whole botched expedition was ultimately in his best interests.

As the constables begin striking Lomax to coax him to his feet, he makes a tearful plea that he won't survive the transcontinental journey without his medicine, which the hotel is holding for him. After a short conversation, the police begrudgingly drag him inside. To his relief, the baggage desk produces his valise, and Lomax rummages to find both the journal and the slipcase buckled into the side pocket. To make room for his personal effects, Lomax takes the slipcase and journal and pushes them together. But when the two merge, the journal is left rattling around inside the larger slipcase, and by his estimation the book is a full inch narrower—a relatively tiny measurement, though it's more than enough to throw Harvey Lomax into an inchoate fury. He curses Everett Greenwood's everlasting soul and hurls what remains of his girth against the surrounding Mounties, who fight viciously to restrain him. He's struck in the mouth again and a ribbon of blood unspools onto the hotel's marble floor. Lomax grunts and bellows and strains to escape, until they drive a nightstick into his throat and five men ride him to the ground.

That illiterate bum and that blind, snivelling fairy must have been scheming all along to keep the authentic journal for themselves, all so they could use it against Mr. Holt someday. Why else would they risk passing off a forgery?

Lomax can't possibly return to Saint John now, not empty-handed like this—and just then a word fits into his broken mouth like a key into a lock.

"Kidnapped," he says, spitting it through the gaps in his teeth.

"What did you say?" the Sergeant barks.

The men let off a little and Lomax sucks cold air over his bloody gums to numb them. "R.J. Holt's infant daughter. Kidnapped."

After he's uttered his magic word a second time, the constables seize his lapels and hoist him from the ground and bombard him with questions. Harvey Lomax informs them that while he doesn't know where the cold-blooded fugitive Everett Greenwood has taken Mr. Holt's precious little girl, he knows someone who does.

AT THE TREELINE

EVERETT FIRST SUSPECTED something was amiss when, earlier that evening, Harris's voice didn't crackle through the shortwave at the usual nine o'clock. At first, he told himself his brother had fallen asleep, or was occupied by the lumber shipments to Japan he'd been so worried about. But now, near midnight, sitting up sleepless in bed, hearing the faint chuff of a steamer's boiler throb through the mist like the heartbeat of a whale, he's certain that something is wrong.

Fishing boats and logging tugs sometimes pass near Greenwood Island, but never this close. Luckily, the steamer's crew mustn't be able to locate the jetty where Feeney leaves their supplies, so Everett expects they'll anchor in the bay and row to the pebbly beach east of the cabin. After a while, he spots armed men come stalking through the brush in the spectral glow of the full moon, at a slow pace that suggests the expectation—or worse, the intent—of trouble.

Eight Mounties in crimson tunics, stetson hats, and blue breeches with yellow piping take up positions at the treeline, along with two more men in street clothes. They form a half-circle that sweeps around behind the woodshed that Everett built during his first days here. They squat low on their hams, level their carbine rifles at the cabin's front door, and wait.

Delicately, Everett nudges up his bedroom window, propping it open with the edge of a slim book he'd been trying to read to Pod, and pokes the barrel of his Browning through the crack. After observing them for a half hour, he picks out McSorley's stocky silhouette approaching another man behind a tree, who Everett would bet his life is Lomax, though he looks even more gaunt and feeble than ever. Everett had watched the Irishman write furiously through the night to fabricate a suitably convincing journal, wearing through two pen nibs in the process, but it seems Lomax has detected their deceit in the end. Or maybe the book alone wasn't enough to satisfy him. Maybe it never was.

But the longer he sits, the more Everett becomes aware that the Mounties are all mere boys—with protruding ears and thin wrists, skittishly twisting their necks to check their flanks every few seconds—recalling to Everett the young faces he'd fired at across the trenches in Europe. He realizes that no matter what these boys intend, shooting them would not only endanger Pod, but would be no different than turning his gun on the flea-bitten children he saw in that orphanage back in Toronto. So he removes the Browning from the gap, rehangs it on the wall, and returns to check on Pod in bed. She is sleeping with her rear stuck in the air, working her tongue against some dreamy pabulum.

He leaves her and creeps down the stairs, avoiding the windows, to fetch his boots, mackinaw, and a bottle of goat's milk from the kitchen, into which he shakes a good dose of Quieting Syrup. When he returns upstairs, he goes to the second bedroom where the short-wave is kept. Softly, he depresses the microphone's black button, and into the perforated metal receiver he whispers Pod's true name, the same one he'd pencilled in the journal back in Temple's library, the same one he was planning on giving her only after their cabin was built and her mother's journal was recovered and their lives had begun anew. Except now that things aren't about to work out the way Everett planned, she needs her true name more than ever. Drawn from that strange, unkillable tree under which he and Temple first rested and drank water together, the tree that wouldn't die no matter how long the drought wore on. And even if Harris isn't present in the radio static to hear Everett speak it, her road name has been left behind, and she is Pod no longer.

HIS VOICE

AN HOUR AFTER the constables leave his office, Harris remains at his desk, swirling a crystal tumbler of sake with a trembling hand. On the floorboards he hears the soft patter of the Italian loafers he bought as a birthday gift for Feeney, who's always known how to make the right amount of noise to avoid startling him.

"I gather it was Lomax who brought them?" Feeney asks.

Harris dips his chin. A slow nod.

"He ferreted out our little forgery, I take it?"

Another nod.

"Took him long enough. I was beginning to suspect he was more brainless than we originally thought. But the police can search all they want. They'll never find them." Harris hears the creak of Feeney easing into the leather armchair.

"Lomax told the police that my brother kidnapped R.J. Holt's baby, and that he is now holding her for ransom," Harris says.

"So what did they say after you told them the truth?"

Harris exhales. "I confirmed that my brother has a child. And that the child indeed isn't his. Everything else is speculation."

"What does it matter if she isn't? She was left for dead."

A pause.

"Harris."

He takes a long drink.

"You told them more than that."

Harris sets down his glass. "Liam, when Lomax first arrived at the house, he took me aside and threatened to tell the police about us right then and there."

Feeney scoffs. "Well, we know a little about him! I can spot a dope-head when I see one! That ghoul's pupils are no bigger than periods on a page. And he's got a right sluggardly walk. We'll have him searched. We'll crucify the fucker."

Harris smiles weakly. "Dope-head or not, he can still ruin us."

Feeney takes a slow breath. "So what did you say?"

Harris resists a spiky urge to throw his tumbler of sake at the wall. "Harris?"

"They'd charge us with indecency first. Then they'd seize the company. We'd never see each other again. Wealth is our only protection, Liam. Without my signature on their paycheques, they'll eat us alive."

"What did you tell them?"

"Legally speaking, my brother stole that infant," Harris says. "And he's unhinged to think that it's his to keep. Perhaps more jail time will do him some good."

"You poor, fearful man," Feeney says, and Harris can tell from the muffle of his voice that he's brought his hands to his face. "And what about these conversations you two have been having on that wireless over there?"

Just after Harris had given Lomax the exact location of his cabin on Greenwood Island and they'd raced off to apprehend Everett, his brother's nightly salutation had come over the radio. Almost to punish himself, he left the set on, though he found himself unable to answer. Instead, he'd sat listening to Everett repeat: "Come in, Harris. Harris, come in."

"He made his own decisions, Liam," Harris says. "He and I can't go on rescuing each other forever."

"And your promise to let them live on the island?"

When Harris had first agreed to that idea, Everett had whooped so loud that the radio crackled like a bomb had gone off.

"Plans change," Harris says, taking a belt of sake. "Everett knows that better than anyone."

"But there's still time to fix this!" Feeney yells. "We must go to him. Straight away. Lomax didn't leave that long ago. If we take the skiff, we can beat them there."

How, Harris wonders, could a poet possibly understand that to survive in a world as vicious as this one, you must be like a faller's axe: sharp, brutal, purposeful, and relentless. Just as he told Feeney when they first met, Harris is a lumberman, through and through. And a lumberman is always capable of doing what needs to be done. Even if it means cutting off a diseased limb to save a tree. Even if it means letting go of one treasure in order to hold on to another.

Harris rises to his feet, hoping to appear impassioned, loving, worthy of the great sacrifice he's just made; instead, he feels his face twist into a sneer as he speaks: "I'd turn every tree on this Earth into matchwood if it would keep you from harm, Liam. And the same goes for people."

He hears Feeney clap his hands. "Fine. If you won't go to him, I will."

"As your employer, Mr. Feeney, I forbid you to pilot any of my skiffs."

Feeney lets out a long breath. At last he says, "Then I believe I won't be able to provide my descriptive services to you any longer, Mr. Greenwood."

Though Harris's weakest self has always feared that these words of betrayal were coming—because nothing good can endure, not for him, not for Everett either—he can scarcely believe his ears. More than the words, it's the curt, professional tone that Liam's normally warm voice has assumed that wounds him most.

"You said you'd never betray me," he says quietly.

"I haven't," Feeney replies. "But you beat me to it."

"Fine, then you're fired," Harris says, with equally professional chilliness, trying to get a rise out of him. "I'm afraid you've lost your knack for the accurate description of the world anyway."

Harris waits, expecting Feeney to retort with his most lacerating remark yet. Something spectacularly irreverent and clever. He allows him a few moments more, ample time to work up a proper response.

At this moment Harris will gladly suffer any insult, as long as it will rekindle their exchange and inch them closer to reconciliation. But he hears only his birds, rustling in their cages.

"Well, what do you have to say for yourself, then?" he says fiercely after an entire minute has passed. "Liam?"

Harris feels his way around his desk, knocking some supply briefs, along with the crystal tumbler of sake, to the floor.

"Are you still there?"

He hadn't heard him rise from the leather chair, nor had he heard footsteps on the floorboards, nor the clatter of the door's hardware. He goes to the chair and feels the warmth he left in the leather seatback.

"Oh, quit playing games, Liam. You know how I hate to be surprised."

Harris directs the concentrated power of his remaining senses out into the room, feeling its textures and hollows, its planes and curves. He hears many sounds—the hiss of the shortwave that he left on in the corner, the flitter of birds—but his describer is not among them.

What he needs now, above all else, is his voice. Ever since he first heard Feeney read that unusual bit of Tennyson here in this very office, his voice has forever altered Harris's very composition, reshaping him into a new being altogether, a new set of cells with a new animating force strung between them. But he may never hear that voice again. The thought opens a canyon in Harris's stomach, and he cries out and overturns the armchair where Feeney was just sitting, staggering himself backwards in the process. He kicks to free himself from a cord that's become entangled in his legs, while the electric lamp to which it is attached topples to the floor. When the bulbs smash, Harris Greenwood swears he can feel the light leave his skin.

RIFLES

LOMAX CAN'T PROPERLY reckon how long the crossing takes. It's an unending churn on the strait's black, head-high swells, and he sways nauseously with the boat's every lurch.

"The book *and* the child, Mr. Lomax," Mr. Holt had said when they spoke over the telephone back at the stationhouse in Vancouver. "Bring them to me, and you have my word: all will be forgiven." Mr. Holt had then contacted Detective McSorley and insisted that he and Lomax join forces. So they've struck a deal: if their raid succeeds, Lomax will return the baby and the journal to Mr. Holt, while McSorley will become the hero who captured the dangerous kidnapper and fugitive Everett Greenwood.

The remote island where Everett has been hiding out for the past several months is beyond local police jurisdiction, so McSorley has enlisted some recently recruited Mounties to join them. Two of the Mounties grew up trapping prawn and crab in these treacherous waters and know well its channels and currents, even in the dark. Seafaring experience aside, the boys look like they've come directly from their high school graduation. But everyone in the West is too young, it seems to Lomax, a bunch of babies tussling over land that isn't properly divvied up yet.

When they reach the island there's no wharf, so they anchor out in the bay and row in from there. Whitecaps ruffle in the dark as they make landfall and creep westward through thick brush of salal and blackberry bramble, under a moonlit sky that's nearly erased by the island's enormous, malevolent trees, an unholy chorus of wind singing in their branches. Lomax has never seen trees so large. And for a moment he's walking through the ruins of an ancient city, amid its towers and monuments, its statues and cathedrals. With a shudder, he averts his eyes to his feet.

Soon the cabin resolves in the moonlight, and McSorley directs the men into a loose perimeter. The father of one of the local boys was the lead carpenter of the crew that erected the cabin for Harris Greenwood, so they know that the structure has only one door, in the front, facing the direction of the sea.

"What if he panics and hurts the kid?" McSorley asks Lomax, as they crouch behind one of the massive trunks.

"Once he knows he's cornered," Lomax says, "he'll likely turn himself in. And no harm will befall the girl."

"So why don't we take him straight away?" McSorley says.

"He was a soldier. And he's a damaged man. He could react aggressively if we startle him. Best to wait out the night and reason with him in the morning. It's an island. They're not going anywhere."

As the men spread out and assume sentry positions, Lomax rests against a woodpile, squeezing the heavy rifle in his hands. It's been six hours since his last spike of laudanum, and already he's contracted a chill, his veins itching like they've been buffed with poison oak from the inside. Luckily, Lomax kept a small vial of powdered laudanum in the pocket of his pajamas, which he plans to take through his nose if his condition worsens.

And sure enough, as the night's hours grind past, he begins to sweat profusely and a thick film coats his eyeballs. Soon he feels as though an electrified knife has been plunged into the centre of his back, and spectral voices begin calling out softly from the shadows.

"What's that?" one of the local boys posted nearby asks him.

"What was what?" Lomax says.

"You were saying something," the boy replies.

"No, I wasn't."

"Yes, you were," the boy says. "You were talking about a woman and her baby."

"Shut up," Lomax says and tugs his hat down over his sopping brow. Hungering for peace from the voices and respite from his burgeoning agony, Lomax dips a pinky into the laudanum and snorts just a dash of the ochre-coloured powder. A silver shiver pours through his sinuses and pools in his brainstem, and his insides become gentle with clarity and comfort. The stars, which before seemed faint and inconsequential, just barely visible through the towering canopy, now blaze like embers. A while later he vomits discreetly into a shrub, though the act is cleansing, beautiful.

Somewhere around four in the morning, one of the local boys nudges Lomax and asks him to mind his post while he urinates. Lomax nods, then watches the boy buttonhook behind the woodshed. Suddenly, a loud metallic crack sounds from that direction and the boy screams out as though shot. At the commotion, the young Mountie ten feet away from Lomax starts to breathe heavily and swing his rifle around in a panic, his eyes as wild as a storm. When the injured boy begins to plead for his life in an anguished cry, Lomax watches the Mountie raise his rifle, which is nearly too heavy for him to lift. Then he aims the dark barrel in the general direction of the cabin, shuts his eyes, and fires.

BULLETS

THEY SEEM TO erupt from within every object in the room. They pop and ping through the windows and put to bits the porcelain jug of goat's milk that Everett keeps on the night table for Willow. They claw through the room's cedar-panelled walls and blow out the wall-mounted kerosene lamp. They chew up Willow's crib and dismember the sawdust-stuffed rabbit that the Irishman had brought for her, sending the shreds of its corpse flying like confetti.

"I've got a child in here!" Everett hollers into the hail of plaster chunks and wood splinters, scooping Willow from the bed and crashing to the floor, encasing her tiny body with his own. Still the room is alight with muzzle flashes, and the roar of gunfire and shattered crockery and the whipping stutter of ballistic perforation swallows his words.

A man outside hollers for them to quit shooting.

But nothing quits.

The sound is a dozen thunderstorms happening in unison. Feathers escape pillows, pictures fly from nails, and suddenly he's back in the War, pinned under the deafening barrage of German artillery. A bullet comes through the panelling behind him with a kind of *whistle-pop* sound, and instantly he wonders if he's torn his shirt because his back feels slightly cool. But the coolness intensifies, and soon turns searing hot. He coughs, two hacks as dry as paper, then one sopping wet, and in an effort to unhitch his lung he bangs at his breast with his fist like an ape. After he recaptures some of his breath, he drags Willow—who is mute with terror and quivers against him—toward the bedroom door. As he reaches for the knob, he realizes that men who fire so freely on a cabin with a baby inside surely intend to never let them leave it.

HER VOICE

AFTER THE YOUNG Mountie unleashes his first shot, the others follow suit, all tumbling into a collective trigger-pulling mania. They evacuate the cartridges of their large-bore repeating rifles in the general direction of the timber-frame cabin, some mute with eyes clenched, others whooping like schoolboys in June—all despite Lomax's shouts for them to stop. But they cannot hear him, and he watches the structure splinter and shatter from the barrage. In the chaos, a vision descends upon him: bullets hitting his own house back in Saint John with his seven children inside, cowering beneath their beds, trembling in their nightclothes, calling out for their father.

The shots last for what seems an eternity, and the guns' reports echo in Lomax's eardrums long after the ammunition is spent and the muzzle flashes cease and the blackness rushes back in. Amid the stench of cordite, blue smoke hangs low at their knees, and hot brass casings pepper the earth. A few blades of window glass dangle and release to smash inside their frames.

The gasping boys return to themselves and a strained silence descends. An irate McSorley, who'd been screaming the whole time for them to quit firing, reassumes control, saving his most berating words concerning their lack of discipline and general stupidity for later. He first orders them to search behind the woodshed where the boy had gone to relieve himself. They find him, unconscious from shock, pants caught around his ankles, his shin bent grotesquely in the grip of a jagged-jawed animal trap, his face as white as the dagger of bone that juts from his leg.

While the Mounties work to free him, Lomax slips unnoticed to the cabin's bullet-pocked front door and nudges it open. The last thing he needs is McSorley reading the authentic journal before he can get his hands on it. Inside, he treats himself to a generous snuff of laudanum to steady his nerve, while pleading to God that if anyone upstairs is hurt, let it not be the child. Let it be Everett Greenwood, a man who didn't matter to anyone—not even to his own brother—before he stumbled upon that bundle of cloth hanging in those woods.

On the wall at the bottom of the stairs is a splash of fresh blood. Lomax wonders if this is Euphemia's blood. Except Euphemia isn't here, he reminds himself. Though with so much laudanum burbling in his head, who can say for certain that she's not? As he begins to climb the stairs to the second floor, he feels as though his weight has been doubled, like he's carrying an identical copy of his own body draped unconscious across his shoulders. Suddenly, he's back in the forest where he found Euphemia against that maple tree, and in the bark of the surrounding trees are captured thousands of contorting faces. People known to him and not. The faces of his father and his mother. The faces of his own children and the destitute families on his milk collection route. Those he's chased down and those he's beaten. The infirm. The broken. The dead. All of them tortured with anguish.

Did you bring me my coat and shoes? a woman's despairing voice asks.

"Tomorrow," Lomax answers softly, with no way of knowing for sure if he's speaking aloud. "I'll bring them tomorrow."

I can't go through with this.

"With what?"

This.

"Euphemia, this isn't the sort of thing you can back out of," Lomax says, reaching the top of the stairs to find a bedroom door shut before him.

But I can't let her go, she pleads. *Isn't that enough?*

"Don't be foolish," Lomax says, setting his shoulder and preparing to burst through the door. "There's nothing you can't let go."

THE TIME MACHINE

DURING THE WAR, Everett had witnessed soldiers get shot and then immediately start to run, as fast as their legs could carry them, as though trying to beat death in a foot race. Others he saw quietly sit down, as though preparing for tea. Everett Greenwood's response, however, is somewhere in between.

When the shooting stops, he opens the bedroom door and slithers down the stairs with Willow clutched to his chest until he reaches the landing, where he rises and spurts a mouthful of blood on the wall. He takes a deep breath, then crashes through the crookedly constructed rear door, his arms sheltering the child as best he can, braced to charge or punch or die in the crack of the rifles that he knows await him.

But not a soul is there to greet them.

That is, of course, if you discount the trees.

With the baby pinned against the half of his shirt that isn't pasted to his side with blood, he blunders into the surrounding forest. He staggers west, along the seam where the burned section of the forest meets the old-growth, trying to minimize his footprints by stepping root to root and, where there are no roots, keeping to areas springy with moss.

Now that the shooting has stopped, Willow's senses are returning and she's beginning to whimper. So from the pocket of his mackinaw, he pulls the bottle of goat's milk, into which he'd mixed some Mother Bailey's Quieting Syrup. She drains it greedily, without drawing a breath. When the drug takes effect, Willow snores rudely at his chest.

While the sky is moonlit, the moon itself is hidden some-where in the canopy, and his blood glistens black as oil in the stark silver light. When Everett draws a breath only half of his chest expands, which pulls his gait to the right, and he hopes he isn't walking in circles. The bullet entered his back, slipping between the ribs on his left side, but it also came through the cabin's cedar siding, so it lacked the power to exit him and now rattles around in his lung like a pick lost in the body of a guitar. While the wound won't kill him soon, it's a bleeder, and he feels several tributaries of warmth slip down his legs and pool in his boots. With each step comes an accompanying squelch.

He passes an old logging camp and considers hiding in the rotten bunkhouse to rest, or perhaps die. But it could be hours before the Mounties find him, and though Everett is not cold, he can see the vapour of Willow's breath and knows she wouldn't last long on her own after he'd gone. He limps on, avoiding the predictability of deer paths, pushing through brush that rakes his eyes and tears at his clothes. He stops only to catch his ragged breath and to dump the blood from his boots. His blood smells earthy, metallic, like the stones he and Harris had used to sharpen axes when they were boys. Still, his sole thought is that he must keep walking—he's already carried her so far; what's a little farther?

As his shock subsides, it's as if doors open into whole rooms of pain, and the only way he can continue to move forward is with his eyelids half shut, peering through his eyelashes as though through a dream. Soon the baby becomes like a rock and his legs are planks that his hips can scarcely lift.

His thoughts eddy and stray. Shapes dart at the fringes of his vision. For a good while he's in Belgium, dragging a blood-soaked stretcher that contains the tatters of some doomed soul through the mud. Then he's sprinting for a train with Blank, being chased by some thick-necked bulls outside of Oakland. Then he's a child again, mute with fright, running with his brother at his side, their pockets jammed with raided carrots and onions, while the people of the township pelt them with small stones from their porches.

It isn't long before Everett smells the brine of the ocean and the kelpy beach where he and Willow have passed so many lazy afternoons, and the scent revives him. He limps farther and the brush opens to reveal the sucking rocks and sloping sandstone of the shore, and he rests for a moment near the jetty. Sitting on a fallen log and examining Willow's sleeping face, it dawns on him that since that first night he heard her cry, she has remade him into a new kind of creature entirely. Not a good man. Nor one worthy of any respect or adulation. But one who values the life of another over his own. And this transformation has closed a wound that had long festered and seeped inside him.

But there's still one last transformation left for him to make.

After he's sure the jetty hasn't been discovered by the Mounties, he limps over to the big cedar near the water and spots the insulated box hanging from it. The Irishman leaves their weekly supplies in this box—though he isn't due to return with the skiff until the morning, if he's returning at all. Because no doubt it was Harris who gave up their location here on the island, after Lomax threatened to expose his relationship with the Irishman, leaving him with no choice. But despite his betrayal, Everett still believes in his brother, and believes he'll do the right thing in the end.

He'd planned on someday bringing Willow to visit his old sugarbush on R.J. Holt's land outside of Saint John, the place where this all began. He'd planned on showing her the tree he'd found her hanging from. *I bet I can still find it*, he whispers to her now, leaning close to her ear. *I bet the nail is still there*. While in truth, he knows there will be no such opportunity, and that he and Willow likely won't meet again. The thought ruins something inside him that he knows will never be fixed.

He limps over to the supply box and, as a hint of dawn fringes the horizon with pink, removes his woollen mackinaw, twisting as much blood from it as he can before using it to bundle Willow up. His drifting, blood-starved mind returns to Temple's library, its rough shelves of encyclopedias and curious volumes originating from all corners of the world. During his days with Temple on her farm, she described to him a book called *The Time Machine*. The story centred on a mechanical box that could carry a person away from their own time and off into another one, and it put Everett in mind of the places he's known that a person can enter and then emerge from into a different time altogether. A boxcar is one of them. So is a forest. So is a single tree. So is a library. So is a battlefield. And so is—though Everett will only realize this later, after occupying one for so long—a prison cell. *And so is this supply box*, he says, with his throat clenching like a fist. He brushes his lips against Willow's sweet head and lifts the latch.

TO THE TREE

FOLLOWING THE FUGITIVE Everett Greenwood's successful capture and arrest on Greenwood Island, Harvey Lomax returns to the New Sun Wah Hotel, which, after its proprietors submitted a generous political donation to city officials, has re-opened its doors. While the boy with the thick glasses is gone—some say he was deported, others say he was killed in a robbery—another has taken his place, one just as considerate and professional, a boy whom Lomax comes to adore and admire just as much as his predecessor.

In the end, it isn't the pull of the drug itself that sends Lomax crawling back into the opium dens, where he will abandon all hope of returning to his family and his brick bungalow in West Saint John. Instead it's the inhumanity of what Everett Greenwood had done to the child, worse than any depravity Lomax had witnessed in all his decades of debt collection.

"She wouldn't stop crying, so I crushed her neck and buried her and the journal in the ground where you'll never find them," Everett told Lomax with unthinkable coldness after the Mounties spotted him early the next morning, out of his mind and stumbling through the woods bathed in blood with a bullet-punctured lung. It was an act that Lomax could not wholly absorb until weeks later, not until McSorley had gone over the cabin as well as every inch of Greenwood Island's towering forests with a team of bloodhounds and found nothing: no child's remains, no journal.

Not that Lomax had put much faith in the innate goodness of his fellow human beings previously, but Everett's grim disposal of the child convinces him that man is a vile, unknowable creature.

A creature geared for nothing other than evil and mindless waste. And as far as Lomax is concerned, the only cure for this disease called humanity is best administered intravenously.

Here, in the womb of the New Sun Wah, and later, after it's shut down for good, in various dens just like it—a time interspersed by jail sentences after forays into petty theft when his money runs dry— the years will heap themselves upon him. He will learn that in the aftermath of the child's death, R.J. Holt basked in the publicity that the tragedy afforded him, offering countless interviews in his own newspapers in which he fashioned himself as the Canadian Charles Lindbergh, which translated into a boon for his businesses. Lomax will also gather, from a fellow vagrant newly arrived from Saint John, that after Lomax had been absent for two years, Lavern consulted their parish priest, annulled their union, and has since remarried. Eventually, his children will forget their father entirely—all except his eldest, Harvey Jr., who will send countless letters to Vancouver homeless shelters, retaining a steadfast belief that some sinister bit of foul play has robbed him of his good and noble patriarch.

But through all his days of poverty and squalor, Lomax will keep the journal's slipcase in his possession until the day he dies—which will come two decades later when, alone in a skid row hotel, an unexpectedly potent shot of heroin will still his heart. The slipcase will be the only artifact from his previous life that he has managed to hold on to. And while the journal that fits inside it will have long been buried, the deeds of Harvey Lomax will not. Despite laudanum's— and then heroin's—gradual erasure of his mind and body, over the years certain truths will visit him, the parts of the story he'd for so long managed to omit. And often, in his drug-clouded state, he will envision a gathering of his seven children—the children he abandoned, just as his father had abandoned him. Clothed in tatters, their teeth flecked with decay, the unruly crowd will assemble beside his mat, or his jail cot, or the patch of earth upon which he's run aground for the night. They'll be shoeless, crying, hungry. And he will count them.

And then he will count them again.

Not seven.

Eight.

Then he'll search out the youngest among them, with emerald eyes like Euphemia's. A girl. The same girl who Everett Greenwood buried somewhere on the island. The same girl who Euphemia hung from a nail she'd found driven into a tree after she could no longer carry her. And again and again, Lomax will return to the night he visited Euphemia just before she fled the Holt estate, when she told him that she'd changed her mind and had decided to keep the baby instead of giving it to Mr. Holt, and how she intended to tell Holt that it was Lomax's child—even though they'd been together just once, during one of his visits to her apartment. And since Lomax could risk neither tearing apart his own family nor falling out of Mr. Holt's favour, he loomed over her and threatened to take the child away and to never let her lay eyes on it again. The abandoned look she gave him in return is one that will haunt him forever.

It was a bluff. Made to protect his job and his home and his family—but also to protect Euphemia. To keep her from squandering her life like he and Lavern had so early in their lives. Euphemia was smart, ambitious; he imagined she'd use Mr. Holt's money to move to New York like she'd planned and leave her old life behind. He never thought his actions would drive her out into the woods that night with no coat or shoes, or that her child would then be snatched up by a demon in the form of a man.

And always, to conclude these visions, Lomax will beg forgiveness—for his infidelity, for his abandonment of his wife and children, for the undeserved fates that befell both Euphemia and her child. But forgiveness will be refused him. And his torments will be without end.

Preachers and politicians often contend that hardship knits us together. That some great calamity like the Crash brings out the best and most noble in us. Yet in his long, tortured, and grasping life, Harvey Bennett Lomax will have witnessed only the opposite. In his experience, the harder things get, the worse we treat one another. And the worst things we'll ever do, we save for our families.

BIRDS

IN THE AFTERMATH of the cyclone, Temple lives for months in
the basement of the Knox Presbyterian Church in Estevan. And after
hundreds of shoeboxes filled with grubby bills and coins and jewellery and silver tableware have been delivered to its doorstep, brought
from far and wide by the lowest people, Temple will have saved
enough to rebuild her farm.

In the summer of 1935, she will return to her land for the first
time since the cyclone to clear it of debris. Amid the ruins of her
former life, buried under rubble and flung out into her wheat fields
for miles around, she will discover thousands of flapped-open books,
marooned and rotting in the dust. For years to come, farmers in the
area will be pulling her books from their trees and their haystacks,
from the eaves of their barns and the bottoms of their wells, forever
digging them out from between the rows of their fields.

Throughout the following year, Temple will work with a crew of
men and women who once stayed at her farm when they were down
on their luck, and with their help she'll frame a new house and barn,
raising the tall timber bones with a team of borrowed horses. The
crew will accept no pay for their labours, only meals, which Temple
and Gertie will set out under the covered porch that they'll rebuild
first, out near the willow, which has already filled in the hole that the
cyclone left in its canopy.

Long after the work is done and her farm is rebuilt, she'll chance
to run into Detective McSorley at the railway station in Estevan. It
will be their first meeting since the cyclone, and he'll take his hat in
his hands and inform her that he's truly sorry for all her trouble and

all that she's lost. The cyclone was most particularly cruel to Temple's property, and the more judgmental citizens of Estevan will speak of this wanton destruction as a kind of proper comeuppance, given the sinful, unwholesome types she harboured. Thankfully, McSorley will spare her any such insinuations.

Just as they're about to part ways, he'll inquire: "I trust that baby of your sister's recovered all right from her illness?"

Temple will search the detective's face for any lingering traces of suspicion, but will find none. "She came through just fine," she'll reply, stifling a hot rush of sadness, a feeling that can sneak up on her at any moment of the day, as quick as a duster. "The child is living in the east now with my sister, who was able to secure a good job. Thanks for asking. So long, Detective."

"Oh, I'm not a detective anymore, Miss Temple," he'll declare proudly, stretching his suspenders with his thumbs. "After that business out West, I've been promoted to a prominent position in the CN Railway Company."

She'll offer her best congratulations, and they'll part ways with no need for further explanation of what that "business out West" was. By this point, everyone in Estevan will have been held rapt by the series of splashy headlines concerning the baby stolen from the nursery of wealthy New Brunswick industrialist R.J. Holt. They'll have read in gory detail about how the kidnapper—a tramp who demanded a ransom so outrageous that even a millionaire couldn't pay it—had gone berserk and done away with the child on a remote island somewhere on the coast of British Columbia; a crime he confessed to, but only after firing on brave Detective Art McSorley and his intrepid Mounties.

It's the kind of knowledge that can split a person's mind right in half if they even allow it in the door. What about that story Everett had told her, about finding the child hanging there in the woods? Could he have possibly invented it? A man so gentle, committing an act so gruesome—how could that be? But it's the indisputable fact of Everett's confession, which Temple will confirm on numerous occasions in numerous different newspapers, that will extinguish her doubts and seal off any compassion that might have remained for him. She'd thought that he couldn't possibly be the worst person to ever seek refuge on her farm, and only now will she admit that she was wrong.

Over the years, the cyclone that destroyed her farm will often return to her in her daydreams. First she'll see the gangrenous light fall across her property, then she'll watch the coal-black funnel cut across her farm, swallowing her library and sucking its contents into the air. At times she'll imagine that the cyclone had assembled an entirely new book up there in the sky, if only for a fleeting instant— pages of Dickens, Austen, Dante, Eliot, Tolstoy all mingling freely, forming the greatest book the world has ever known.

Whenever she retells the story of the cyclone, as she does at countless livestock auctions and over meals eaten with itinerant men at her newly reconstructed table on the porch, she will puzzle over how to properly describe the sound it made as it ate through her library. She'll grapple with how one could possibly capture precisely the sound of ten thousand books drawn up into the air and scattered for hundreds of miles. And it won't be until years later—long after the Depression ends and poor people stop riding the rails and Gertie dies of the flu on her ninetieth birthday. And long after the smooth hillocks of Everett's shoulders and his thick, dark hair and his odd, earnest demeanour fade from Temple's memory. And long after she's able to again venture into that section of her field where they planted that windbreak of maples together, trees that have only thrived ever since. And long after the void he left in her life entirely heals over— only then will she arrive at a suitable answer: they sounded like birds.

1974

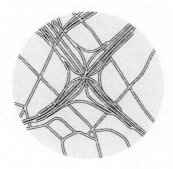

BLACK CARS

SHE'S SUPPOSED TO be sleeping while her baby is off with the sitter for a few hours before the memorial. But instead Willow perches at the window of her childhood bedroom, watching black cars draw to a stop in the mansion's curved driveway. Those who emerge are mostly timber men, straight from the toxin-spewing mills and the cancerous clear-cuts of North America, ranging from the greatest tycoons and mill managers to the lowliest swampers, choppers, tally-men, high-riggers, and chokers. Even the poor souls whose bodies Greenwood Timber's saws and machines have mangled over the years have come—with their crutches, plastic limbs, and wheeled oxygen tanks—to pay their respects. From a pewter-coloured Bentley steps John P. Weyerhaeuser to meet the cool December drizzle, a man Willow recognizes, from the radical environmentalist pamphlets she's distributed, as the son of deceased lumber king Frederick Weyerhaeuser. Earlier she spotted the pug-faced H.R. MacMillan of MacMillan Bloedel, her father's fiercest rival, the very man whose million-dollar feller bunchers Willow ruined just nine months ago with three bags of sugar. A man who Harris would never have allowed in his neighbourhood, let alone in his mansion. Whether they've come to honour her father, gawk at his estate, secretly celebrate his passing, commemorate the fortunes he made them or the pittances he paid them, or simply to salute the great fugue of destructive insanity that was Harris Greenwood's seventy-five-year existence, Willow can't guess.

The funeral hasn't even begun and already she's exhausted to a depth that only a newborn can plunge you. She lies down and shuts her eyes, but the sleep she so desperately needs still won't come. Much to her surprise, the flutter of the future that she'd first detected while fetching her uncle Everett from prison persisted, and to terminate such a miracle at her age seemed to her the very definition of bad karma, so she kept it. Her son arrived last month, though it already seems an eternity ago. She left word for Sage, his likely father, with the Earth Now! Collective, but doesn't expect to hear from him anytime soon. Willow still hasn't named her child. If anyone asks, she says it's because she can't make up her mind. The truth is that she can think of no word that's suitable as a name for her Earth child, her improbable gift—no sound utterable by the human mouth that can possibly contain his glittery eyes, his strange, feline yowl, and his disproportionately fat legs that make him look like he's wearing tiny pants made of blubber.

She spent the entirety of her pregnancy hiding out from the Mounties on Greenwood Island, though she now realizes that she was being paranoid about the black sedan following her. The cops have better things to do than chase down small-time eco-vandals like her, and she's since learned that three feller bunchers are nothing to a company like MacMillan Bloedel. Plus, there are thousands of Westfalias in Canada's hippie capital of Vancouver, many of them driven by women who look identical to her.

When the birth was imminent, she brought a midwife over to help out, and everything went smoothly. In those first euphoric days, she was shocked by her son's greed for her, the clutching and suckling and irrational, blue-faced screaming. Nobody told her how immediate and intense her longing to escape him would be, or how taxing an endeavour motherhood truly is. Given her history of miscarriages, she kept the pregnancy secret from her father, and was preparing to surprise him by showing up at the Shaughnessy mansion with his grandson as soon as her sleep routine had re-established itself. Then, three days ago, she received a distress signal over the cabin's shortwave from Terrance Milner, her father's accountant and house manager, requesting she come see him at once. When she arrived, Milner informed her in the mansion's entranceway that her father had recently travelled to Northern California for his yearly visit to the redwoods to bird-watch (or, in his case, bird-*listen*). Following his usual hike through the trees, he had apparently instructed his guide to leave him, claiming that another guide was scheduled to pick him up. But no one was coming. After that, it seems her father wandered off, deeper and deeper into the sequoias. He was discovered a week later by some hikers in a remote section of the park. The autopsy found a large and inoperable cancerous mass in his brain, about which he had, with characteristic stoicism, said nothing. When Milner finished speaking, Willow sat down next to a rack of her father's rubber overshoes, mired in a kind of floating numbness that hasn't left her since, and wept softly with her oblivious child sleeping in her arms, trying not to wake him.

Milner made funeral arrangements and hired the babysitters, who came and whisked her son from her side for the first time in his life. And even the Marxist in Willow must admit there are certain undeniable advantages to wealth, because what a relief it was to get some time to herself.

Now she burns a bowl of indica in her one-hitter, blowing the smoke from the tiffany window that overlooks the drive. On the few occasions she returned to this house after *Our Plundered Planet* kicked off her environmental awakening, she saw it for what it truly was: a vile shrine to the gruesome violence that her bloodline had inflicted upon the planet, which included slaughtering thousands of ancient and defenseless creatures for no purpose other than gaudy decoration. Lying here now in her bedroom, where the branches of the pin oak still rub against the slate roof, the floor still creaks in front of the closet, and the pen-smeared desk where she wrote her uncle countless letters still sits beside the door, Willow feels as though she's been thrust back in time.

With the reception set to begin at noon, she drags herself to the dusty mirror to appraise her outfit, which even she realizes can only be described as inappropriate: a batik-printed skirt and a faded blouse dotted with tree sap, long baked into the fabric by its monthly tumble in a laundromat dryer. "Clothes don't signify grief," she tells herself. "Grief does." And she is grieving, isn't she? Of course she is. Yet Harris had been such a puzzle of a father, forever occupied, forever out of reach, forever unknown. When she was a girl, this house was a place of empty silences and secrets, with its pianos that nobody played and books that nobody read. With its bronze busts and oil portraits of English frigates and Italian scenery. With its cages of exotic birds, its black mahogany cabinetry buffed to a high gloss, and its antique logging equipment hung everywhere like the weaponry of some noble war. And her father, with his routines and schedules: the same meals eaten at the same times each day, the same records of poetry on the same turntable in his study during the evenings. And the way he would scold her for even the smallest disturbance of these routines: her tendency to walk thumpingly on her heels, or her stomach's habit of gurgling at the dining table.

She did her best to liven things up, though. She remembers roller-skating down the lanes of the mansion's private bowling alley until Harris burst in to yell at her for marring the woodwork (marks which, she never failed to point out, *he couldn't even see*). And once playing a trick on the house staff by hanging the freshly polished silver like ornaments from the garden's perfectly manicured trees. Then there was the sign she pasted to the door of her bedroom that read *KEEP OUT, ENCHANTED FOREST INSIDE*, and the hundred branches she nailed directly to her walls to complete the effect, and the hundred holes left in the plaster after Harris had ordered the gardener to rip them all down.

Even if her clothes are passable, at a minimum her bodily grime needs to go, so she scrubs her armpits and neck at the washbasin, staining forever a white washcloth that she guiltily flings directly into the trash. She brushes, centre-parts, and braids her hair, then glides down the grand mahogany staircase whose steps she counted with her skips so many times as a girl, her hand skating down its spiralling redwood banister hewn from a single tree.

Downstairs, guests clot together in the great room, a cavern of thirty-foot-high oak ceilings, where many round tables are set out and draped with fine white tablecloths. Harris never wanted a formal funeral, but he hadn't explicitly outlawed one, either. So with Willow's approval, Milner arranged the catering and hired the string quartet—though Harris loathed music, and always maintained that it is nothing more than a perversion of the singular perfection of the human voice.

Huddled on silver platters are steamed lobsters flown three thousand miles from New Brunswick and piles of roasted meats heaped high, ninety per cent of which will surely go to waste. A six-foot Douglas fir, sculpted entirely of butter, stands near the bay window, while pomaded bartenders wait behind crystal decanters of fine Canadian whiskies and cases of sake ordered for the occasion. Many out-of-town guests are rooming here at the estate, and she's heard that an entire floor of the Hotel Vancouver was required to accommodate the overflow. Counting journalists and gawkers, it's nearly four hundred people in total, and while it cheers her to see the old mansion teem with life like it never did in her childhood, she's pierced with the urge to throw them all out on their ears.

A tuxedoed server presses a glass into her hand and it shames her how easily she slips into the role of the tycoon's daughter. But after so many grimy months spent in her father's rustic cabin on Greenwood Island, washing the tar-like meconium from her son's diapers at the hand-pumped well, what a relief it is to have people present her with food and wash her clothes and turn down her bed and soothe her child.

She stands near the fieldstone hearth, smoking a menthol and nipping her sake—the only alcohol her father could ever stomach—hoping to pass unnoticed. She scans the room for her uncle Everett, who Milner had tried to invite through his parole officer, though he had yet to reply. Despite the fact that Willow has heard nothing from her uncle since she dropped him off at the Vancouver airport nine months ago, she's reread some of the letters they'd exchanged, and has come to reconsider her harsh judgment of him. Surely it was disorienting to emerge like that into her custody after so long an incarceration, to pass between entire decades as though they were adjacent rooms. It was a troubled time for her, too: haywire estrogen levels and too much weed and too many pills—factors that surely contributed to her paranoid imagining of that mysterious black sedan that had seemed to follow her everywhere. But especially now, with Harris gone, she feels an acute desire to see her uncle again. Who cares about his invented stories of the time they shared together when she was a baby, and his odd nickname for her (*Pod*, was it?). He might be a little crazy, but he's harmless. And she's often wondered how his reunion with that woman in Saskatchewan went, and whether he found that book he was willing to risk violating his parole conditions to track down.

"Miss Greenwood!" calls out a short barrel of a man, leaning on a hand-carved cane and striding through the crowd toward her. Willow hears his knees click as he draws close. "Name's Mort Baumgartner. I founded Greenwood Timber with your father and was there from the very beginning," he says, as though this explains a great deal, before he expounds further upon her father's merits as an employer.

A baby is a vulnerable thing, yet it can also provide a kind of armour, and suddenly she wishes for her child back in her arms, if only to have something substantial to put between herself and this man eyeing her clothes, appraising the gap between the father's success and the daughter's failure.

"We parted ways years ago on account of certain disagreements," Baumgartner jabbers on, "but I'm here to offer my condolences on his passing. Harris was a hell of a lumberman. That's why I was so surprised when I learned of the . . . circumstances. Despite his handicap, Harris Greenwood knew his way around a forest."

"He got lost," she says firmly, unwilling to stoke the wildfire of rumour concerning his possible suicide. "Could happen to anyone."

"I heard they found quite a tumour in his head. Size of a softball, someone said. He must have known. Did he tell you?"

Willow considers the last time she saw her father, in Stanley Park, when he convinced her to fetch Everett from prison. She remembers his wobbly gait, his whitened hair, and how at the time she'd attributed all this to his recent retirement. Though his uncharacteristic sentimentality and the embrace he offered her can now be explained by the fact that he knew he was fading. *Then why didn't he just fucking tell me?* she almost yells in Baumgartner's face. Instead, she says, "In his way, yes."

"At least he had the chance to meet his grandchild," the man goes on. "I have fourteen myself, and it cheers me to know that the Baumgartner line will surely continue."

"Yes," Willow says, though of course Harris never met her son, and the thought nearly undoes her. He'd contacted her twice over the shortwave radio while she was living on Greenwood Island. "I detest talking on this contraption," Harris had said. "But I'm happy you're finding the retreat suitable. Is there anything you need?" Never once, however, did he mention his health or suggest a visit. If she'd known he was sick, she could have helped him. And she would have told him about her pregnancy. They may even have managed to say some things they needed to say. Instead he chose secrecy. Instead he chose solitude and stoicism. Instead he died alone, in the trees. And she hates how much sense it makes.

"Well, that child of yours stands to inherit a fortune," Baumgartner says, raising his glass with an ugly grin. "As do you."

Willow shakes her head and sips her drink without returning his toast. "My father wrote me out of his will long ago, Mr. Baumgartner. And I'd prefer not to talk about it, if you don't mind. I'm a little brittle today."

To her relief, he lets the subject drop, and the two fall into a full-mouthed silence after accepting canapés and salmon cakes—fancy bites her father would have sneered at. "Just mix it all up in a bowl and give it to me," he'd declare whenever the chef got too fussy. "What do I care how it looks?"

With the memorial set to begin shortly, Willow collects her baby and nurses him in a staff water closet. The child, with its mouthful of areola, grunts like a football lineman. Then she and the baby rejoin the crowd on the grounds behind the mansion, standing among the rose gardens and statues and the retaining walls overgrown with ivy. Nearby are the sacred Haida totem poles that her father had stolen from the Native lands he'd logged and kept as the centrepieces of his collection of plundered curiosities. As a girl, she'd often escape into the greenery back here, and today it's as though her very childhood is being invaded.

One after another, men approach the carved podium to speak. The premier of British Columbia. The minister of Forestry. Baumgartner relays a tiresome anecdote about some mill machinery that Harris fixed with only a box of paperclips. Milner extols Harris's powers of estimation concerning the board-foot yield of a forest. "Sight unseen," he adds, which commands a good chortle. Of course her father's conviction for the treasonous act of selling timber to the Japanese before the Second World War goes completely unmentioned. If Willow can only get her hands on another sake, perhaps she'll gather the courage to go up to the podium and correct this narrative oversight herself.

Though they haven't cashed a Greenwood Timber paycheque in years, the workingmen in attendance appear lost and distraught, like whipped dogs, unsure of who'll feed or beat them now that their master is gone. While none of the workers brave the podium, the speeches from the managers drone on. They recount Harris's great character traits: his pithy honesty and his insatiable industriousness. Upon an easel behind them is a giant blown-up photograph of her father as a young man, standing before a mountain of cut logs that fill the entire frame—there must be a thousand rounds, each one twice the size of his head. *Behold the conqueror of trees!* Willow nearly calls out. *Both visually and spiritually blind to the massacre in his wake!* Again she wonders how he could have encountered beings of such unimpeachable grace and beauty and felt the urge (not to mention *the right!*) to destroy them. *How brave,* she murmurs into the tiny cockle of her son's ear. *Your grandfather hired men to cut down defenseless giants, and paid them like rats to do it.*

The old saying goes that the apple doesn't fall far from the tree. But in Willow's experience, the opposite is more likely true. An apple is nothing but a seed's escape vehicle, just one of the ingenious ways they hitch rides—in the bellies of animals, or by taking to the wind—all to get as far away from their parents as they possibly can. So is it any wonder the daughters of dentists open candy stores, the sons of accountants become gambling addicts, the children of couch potatoes run marathons? She's always believed that most people's lives are lived as one great refutation of the ones that came before them.

As the service wraps up at last, Willow notices a man, near the front, with an air of untouchability about him, as though the others have made an unspoken pact to shun him. Though the day is chilly, he's dressed in a fine linen suit that looks European in cut—not one of those brown Dacron jobs popular among the lumbermen. A grey sadness hovers over him, and his eyes are hollow, like a place where an owl might find refuge. While guests begin filing back to the house to tuck into their lobster, the well-dressed man slips to the podium and, without any introduction, commences reading from a small book pulled from his jacket pocket. His musical, Irish-accented voice cuts like a scalpel through the general murmur and the guests turn to face him. It's a poem he's reading, she realizes, something old and lyrical about trees and time. And strangely, the sound of his voice is familiar to her, powerfully so, though his face is one she doesn't recognize in the slightest. And just as he's building steam, his reading gaining in passion and exactness, Mort Baumgartner canes his way to the front and sets a thick hand on the man's shoulder. When the man doesn't stop, Mort leans in close to whisper something in his ear. The man closes his hollow eyes and vents a long, slow breath. Then he returns the book to the pocket of his jacket, steps away from the podium, and vanishes into the crowd.

WHO DO WE HAVE HERE?

THE CONVOY OF limousines arrives later that afternoon to take the mourners to Mountain View Cemetery. Willow rides on the leather seats with her sleeping child draped in her arms, craving a menthol, staring out the window. In a shell-shocked state, she watches the power lines cross and uncross, racing one another through their world above the street.

The drizzle is gone, and as people begin to assemble at the graveside, the sky clears to a smudged, milky blue just as the sun begins its slow tumble into the ocean. To bury Harris Greenwood in such a serene and lushly treed place strikes Willow as both a poignant homage and a laughable irony. His mahogany coffin sits suspended across two plain sawhorses. And before it is lowered into the hole, a saw blade the size of a wagon wheel is placed atop the lid, along with a few boughs of fresh-cut Douglas fir. At the sight of his coffin and the saw blade and the branches sinking into the earth like the root ball of a tree about to be planted, true sorrow punctures Willow for the first time. A hot glob of longing for her father rises in her throat, and she fights to choke it down. Not a longing that he'll return to the world—it wouldn't do anyone much good if he did, including him—but a great incurable regret that an understanding couldn't have been brokered between them before his exit. If he'd only reached out to her, maybe they could have forged some kind of agreement. Because if anything certain could be said of Harris it would be this: he was always good at negotiating agreements.

The lumbermen take turns shovelling soil black as cake over her father's coffin, while Willow half expects the ground to spit him back out. If it's true that the United States was born of slavery and revolutionary violence, she muses while watching them work, then surely her own country was born of a cruel, grasping indifference to its indigenous peoples and the natural world. *We who rip out the Earth's most irreplaceable resources, sell them cheap to anyone with a nickel in their pocket, then wake up and do it all over again*—that could well serve as the Greenwood motto, and perhaps even for her nation itself.

With the burial done, her head is churning with a mix of grief, bewilderment, and relief when Terrance Milner approaches to console her. And once the floodgates open, hand after conciliatory hand wags in her direction. It seems they all want to touch her—on the shoulder, the elbow, the back. They want to taste her sadness, to pity her baby, to ask how she's "holding up," as though the bereaved are poorly constructed buildings facing a windstorm. Already she's frantic to escape them, to break into a run and fly across the cemetery to the limousine—then to her Westfalia and on to a remote forest where none of these people could ever find her. That is, until a figure limps in her direction from the very end of the line.

"Sorry I'm late," he says, this time with his back held straight and with no difficulty meeting her eyes. "It took the accountant's letter some time to find me on the farm. But I came right away when I heard."

He's grown a beard that hits his chest—also an intermixed black and grey, the same as his hair—though his lined face is still recognizable beneath it. There's a woman at his side with shoulder-length, steel-coloured hair, and the weather-burnished skin of someone who's spent more days outside than in.

"May I introduce Temple Van Horne," Everett says. "My personal driver."

Temple whacks Everett's shoulder lightly with the back of her wrist while shaking her head. She holds out her hand to Willow. "I'm very sorry for your loss," she says, squeezing Willow's fingers gently. Then Temple turns her attention to the sleeping baby in Willow's arms. "That's a fine child you've got there. A boy?"

"He is," Willow says, shooting a quick glance at Everett, who has yet to acknowledge her son, probably because men of that generation never much concerned themselves with babies.

"I'm going to take a walk and let you two catch up," Temple says after they exchange a few more pleasantries about the funeral service and the improved weather.

"That must be who you were in such a hurry to get to," Willow says, as they both watch Temple work her way down the cemetery path, pausing occasionally to examine half-rotten flowers or to read gravestone inscriptions.

"We're still figuring it out," Everett says. "But I had my probation transferred to Saskatchewan. And she's letting me stay at her place while I help out with farm work, for now anyway." He grins nervously. "Unfortunately," he goes on, "the book I was hoping to recover for you. The one I mentioned? It seems that a cyclone intervened."

"It's fine, Everett. I've got plenty to read. Still, I'm happy to know that you found yourself a new life after losing so much time. And how was your first airplane ride?"

"I didn't care for it much," he says. "I made it, though. Faster than the train, too, which was nice. I'm lucky Temple was kind enough to drive me all the way back here." He removes his hat and holds it in his hands. "And I'm real sorry for your loss, Willow."

"It's your loss, too," she says, touching his shoulder. "Harris would be happy to know you came, even if he couldn't say it. Now I have my own confession to make: he paid me a quarter for every letter I sent you while you were in prison. I always thought it was because he was too self-absorbed to write you himself. Yet lately I've been thinking that it was very important to him for us to know one another."

"He telephoned me at the farm a few months ago," Everett says, fidgeting with his hat. "He didn't say he was dying, but I think he knew. We didn't talk about much. Just some things from our childhood. The wood we chopped together. The old log cabin we built. I appreciated it, though. I knew how hard it was for him." Everett casts his gaze across the treed cemetery. "And before we hung up, I told him I forgave him. He didn't say anything back, but I know he heard me. He did some selfish things in his time, that's for sure, but he redeemed himself and then some by taking such proper care of you, Willow. And I'm very sorry he's gone."

It's the way he says it—an unvarnished expression of sorrow, with no agenda or requirement for her to perform grief in any particular way—that impels her to fall into his arms, pressing her child against his beard and his shabby sports coat. Half-smothered, her nameless baby lets out an anguished cry and Willow draws back.

"Who do we have here?" Everett asks.

Willow wipes at her eyes with her sleeve. "He's a month old today," she says, unhitching her son from the wraparound carrier. "He doesn't have a name quite yet."

"You should ask Temple. She's read a whole bunch of books and she's really good with names," he says. "You know, if you ever want to visit, you two are always welcome at her place. Just show up anytime and we'll be happy to have you."

"That's generous of you," Willow says, then holds her baby out by his armpits, gravity stretching his wriggling body much longer than you'd expect, like a cat. "Do you want to meet him?"

"Oh, no, that's okay," Everett says, smoothing his cheap work pants with his palms. "I think he's better off with you."

Perhaps it's because her father never had the opportunity to hold her child, or because she wants to atone for how she berated Everett in her Westfalia when he innocently called her Pod, or because she wants to prove to her uncle that everyone deserves forgiveness in this world—but it's suddenly unspeakably important to her for Everett to hold her son.

"Please," Willow says. "I've been carrying him all day. And I'm dying for a cigarette."

"I'm sure we could find someone else—"

"I'm going to drop him . . ." she says with teasing menace, while pretending to loosen her grip on his drool-soggy creeper.

Everett's eyes widen and he reaches out and grasps the baby's armpits, then draws his small body awkwardly against his chest. Willow lights a menthol and watches her son squirm in her uncle's arms. Against the forest of his beard, the baby looks like an impossibly tiny organism, barely anything at all. And when he begins to fuss and grunt a little, Everett commences a jiggling bounce on his toes.

"It's been a while," he says.

After a few seconds spent scowling defiantly up at Everett's bushy eyebrows and his brambly, bearded face, the baby finally settles, if begrudgingly.

"Don't worry," Willow says. "You'll get the hang of it."

THE READER

WHEN YOU GROW up as the daughter of a blind man, you become adept at both stealth and stealth's opposite. From an early age, Willow mastered not only how to sneak like a prowler, but also how to reassure with sound—to produce the ideal quantity of it to avoid startling or embarrassing her father without belittling him. Perhaps this explains why, despite witnessing the burial of his coffin earlier this afternoon, she finds herself whistling and scraping her feet on the hallway's floorboards as she approaches his study, just as she has always done.

It was never a room she entered without good reason. Her father would blockade himself behind its heavy oak door for days or even weeks at a time. Inside, everything is just as she remembers it: the old-fashioned inkwell bolted to his desk, the coal-black telephone; no photographs or pictures, just his stuffed birds and his record player and his classics of literature lining the walls. She runs her hand over the leather writing surface of his desk, feeling the faint imprint of the thousands of documents he signed, the millions of trees condemned to death by the mere stroke of his pen.

She can almost see her father canted back in his chair, eyes shut, one of his LPs of poetry turning on the mantle. If ever he suspected anything in his office had been moved or disturbed, he'd launch into a rage, first directed at the housekeepers, and then at Willow. One time, he ordered her into his study to berate her for stepping on one of his precious poetry records, snapping it in half. She remembers sneaking around behind him so that he scolded an empty chair for five minutes, and how comedic it all was, and how deliciously pathetic he seemed, and yet how wicked she felt afterwards.

Now Willow leans back in her father's chair, testing its springs, soaking up its sensations, as if it might have something secret to tell her about her father, and shuts her eyes. Though the heroic sitter took her baby after dinner so Willow could nap before yet another memorial service later this evening, she finds she can't sleep without his gentle huffing against her, or the pasty ticking of saliva in his mouth. Still, the chair is a sanctuary, its cool leather a welcome antidote to her overheated attic room, and her wakefulness starts to slip.

"Ms. Greenwood?" a man's voice sounds out sometime later.

Willow pushes herself upright to discover the well-dressed Irishman from earlier standing on the other side of the desk. "Sorry, I must have nodded off," she confesses groggily, as though the fact isn't already plain to him.

"I wouldn't have disturbed you," he says, and again his voice is uncannily familiar to her ear, "but my cab is waiting, and there's something I'd like to give you." He's wearing a wool topcoat and his alligator case waits near the door. From his pocket he produces a small book, which he places on the desk in front of her.

"Is this what you read at the service?" she asks, picking it up.

He nods. "Wordsworth. One of your father's favourites. He kept a copy with him always." Despite his brisk, cheerful tone, there's a heaviness about him, as though he's just dragged an anchor across the floor in order to stand before her.

"That was a fine reading you gave earlier," she says. "I was sorry you didn't continue."

"Oh, it doesn't matter," the Irishman says. "Normally I detest such ceremonies. But I thought those crusty old arseholes could do with a bit of verse in their lives. I'm happy you enjoyed it, though." He rubs his hands together briskly, as though warming them. "Well, I should be off." He turns and starts for the door.

"You knew him well, my father?"

"I worked for him for a time," he says, pausing at the door without turning around. "If you'll excuse me, I need to be—"

"He fired you?"

"No, he did not," he snaps, his voice rising then coming under his control again. He turns to face her. "I resigned, then moved back to Dublin. I adore Canada, particularly its natural wonders, but living so far from home proved wearisome for me in the end."

"In what capacity did you work for him, then? I've never heard of you before."

He reaches down and picks up his alligator case. "I assisted him for a time with certain negotiations. Mostly I was his describer and his reader. I read him business briefs, correspondences, newspapers—things like that."

And with that a realization snaps like a deadbolt in Willow's mind. "Now I know why your voice is so familiar," she says, pointing to the collection of records set on the shelf beneath her father's turntable, records she was never allowed to touch under penalty of a two-hour lecture. "Those are your recordings."

The man sighs, as though her realization has disappointed him profoundly. "It gave your father great joy to be read to, and a friend of mine in Dublin produces music," he says wearily. "So each year my friend helped me record an album of poetry for your father for his birthday, just a smattering of verses he liked best." A melancholy expression overtakes him. "He was very kind to me, your father."

"Well, that must've been nice," she quips. "Because he enjoyed listening to your voice more than he did mine."

"It wasn't easy for him, you know," the man continues, and the more he speaks, the more his eyes seem to fill with hurt. "This world is designed to pit us against one another. Brother against brother. Mother against son. Father against daughter. Friend against friend. But it was especially unkind to your father."

"Maybe he deserved it? You ever think about that? Maybe he brought it on himself."

The man shakes his head. "He knew he couldn't be an ideal guardian for you. That it just wasn't in him. But he did the best he could."

"Yeah, well, tell that to the trees he cut down."

The man drops his case to the wooden floor with a neat bang. "Oh, would you quit your whining about the goddamned trees!" he snarls, the restraint he'd so far been practising now completely cast aside. "You aren't the only person in the world who ever lost anything, my dear. For a while I was close to something. Something wonderful. And then I couldn't be close to it ever again. I doubt you've lived long enough to know what that means."

"I've lost plenty," she says, feeling her face grow hot. "Believe me."

He fixes a hard glare upon her, and for a moment she's afraid he might jump across the desk and strangle her. "It's a crime to burden the young with the sorrows of the old," he says, and she feels an odd sense of secret history, as though he's speaking about many things at once. And for a moment she's a child again, wandering this cavernous mansion, picking over the fragments of her father's story, like she'd been given a jigsaw puzzle with pieces already missing long before the box was opened.

"But you should know that many people sacrificed for you to be here in this study today, Willow," he adds with an irritated sneer. "And you'd be best fucking served to remember it."

"I enjoyed your poem, sir," she says, undaunted. "And I appreciate the book of poetry. But I'll remember Harris as who he was, not as the self-sacrificing saint that some ex-employee claims him to be, thank you very much."

For nearly an entire minute they face one another in deadlocked silence across her father's desk, while the black shadows of trees darken the windows and stuffed birds observe them with their glass eyes.

And though she expects the Irishman to commence scolding her anew, he assumes an unexpected calm. "Before I go, I'd like to tell you a little story, Willow. And I'd like it even better if you didn't interrupt me while I do. You see, you and I took a boat ride once. Just the two of us. You were quite little, so of course you wouldn't remember it. But there was nowhere to put you in the boat, so you rode alongside me in an insulated box, sort of a cooler used to transport food—we didn't have car seats or anything like that in those days. It wasn't much for me to do, to take you on this ride; I was a capable seaman then, and you seemed to enjoy yourself quite a lot. After our ride I brought you here to your father's estate, and left you with his housekeeper. I think it's fair to speculate that Harris was surprised to see you that night. He wasn't exactly ready for you to be living with him here in his house. Still, he did the right thing and accepted you anyway. So please, Willow, before you judge him too harshly, just remember that his bit was much more than merely taking you for a boat ride. His bit was to care for you every day of your life. A duty he performed to the best of his ability, despite all he'd already lost. So know this: your father loved you with everything he had. He just didn't have much left."

BEQUEATHMENT

WILLOW STAYS ON at the Shaughnessy mansion for a week after the funeral, helping Milner tie up loose ends, dreading her return to the overcrowded Earth Now! Collective house in Vancouver, the only place left for her to go now that the mansion will likely be sold and Greenwood Island will be auctioned off to a competing timber company, and she'll never be able to return to either place again.

The prospect of an inheritance has rarely occurred to her over the years, since Harris made it so explicitly clear that he'd written her out of his will. And even when the idea did briefly infiltrate her thoughts—usually on nights after she ran out of money and her belly was cramping from the half-rotten food that she and the Earth Now! Collective had pulled from a Dumpster, nights when she would've mowed down a handful of old-growth redwoods for just a few days lost in the impossible whiteness of clean sheets in a four-star hotel room—she saw zero chance of her father ever changing his mind. So she is baffled when she's summoned by Milner, who's been named executor of the Greenwood estate, to a meeting the next morning with her father's attorneys in downtown Vancouver.

As she nurses her son in Harris's limousine, she examines his pinched face for flickers of the Greenwood bloodline, for Everett's wild hair or Harris's crisply handsome cheekbones, but finds no trace. He still retains that generic, gelatinous quality of the newly birthed, and could as well be anyone's child. What does it matter, she reminds herself, as she rides an elevator up to an office on the fortieth floor of a tall, mirrored building. The "family line" is all just capitalist, colonialist brainwashing anyway, designed to sequester power in the hands of the few. A single child has no fewer than sixteen different great-great-grandparents, each with their own separate family traits and stories, and yet we idiotically focus on the single surname that survives. Are not the other fifteen equally important? And what is her son really, but a bundle of flesh and cells and tissue animated by the same sacred energy that impels trees to stretch upward for the sun? No, her son is not hers alone. He descends from many blood-lines. Or, more precisely, he descends from the one, great bloodline: born of the Earth and the cosmos and all the wondrous green things that allow us life.

"Despite your father's setbacks," the lead lawyer says to com-mence the meeting, "he was still in a strong financial position when he died. And it is my duty to inform you that he named you the majority beneficiary of his estate. It's a substantial bequeathment that includes the Shaughnessy mansion as well as his sizeable art collec-tion, his Indian relics, his remaining sawmills, pulp and paper inter-ests, and lumber operations, his schooner, as well as his holdings, securities, and their related dividends."

Though she hears the words and tracks their surface meaning, it's as though she's been blasted by a great, deafening noise, broadcasted at a frequency that only she can hear. With her child sleeping in her arms, she averts her gaze to the window: the sky over the ocean is dolloped with cloud, and the great trees of Stanley Park shimmy far below in an otherwise imperceptible breeze.

"Ms. Greenwood?" says the gruff second lawyer who sits next to Milner.

"Does this include," she manages to get out. "The island?"

The second lawyer flips open a manila folder and scans the docu-ments inside. "That's correct, Greenwood Island in its entirety."

She knows she ought to look at them, but she can't bring herself to do so. She lifts her swaddled child to her nose and breathes in his scent. She and her son will have the means to live together on the island, free and untroubled among its tall trees, for the rest of their days, never needing to worry about money again. She'll beachcomb and garden while he climbs the trees like a monkey and builds forts from windfall branches. And perhaps she'll even invite a few other likeminded people from the Earth Now! Collective to join them. They'll establish a self-sufficient community, far away from the world's soul-killing inhumanity, from its Nixons and Kissingers, from its cancers and robotized, brain-dead conformists.

The lead lawyer clears his throat roughly. "The second, and lesser, beneficiary who's been named is your uncle, Everett Greenwood. I trust this doesn't come as a surprise, despite the fact that the two were estranged," he says, clearing his throat again. "There *is* one slight anomaly, however, which I'd like to draw to your attention. It seems your father left another individual a not insignificant share, smaller than yours or your uncle's, certainly, yet a sizeable one regardless. A man named Liam Feeney."

Hearing this name it's as though she's ripped from a dream. "Is he Irish?" she says. "This man?"

The lead lawyer turns to the other lawyer, who nods. "We have a Dublin address, so probably, yes. But this amendment is unusual, made late in your father's life, possibly under the duress of his illness. So it's our recommendation that you dispute it."

In an instant, so much about her childhood and her father's life comes smashing into focus. The silences. The brooding depressions. The self-enforced solitude. The anti-social veneer. The iron-clad routines. Why did he never confide in her? Did he judge her too antagonistic or too flighty to entrust with the truth? She could've helped him, or at least eased his burden. Perhaps she could have even reached out to Liam Feeney on his behalf. And suddenly an image comes over her: Harris in his study, listening to Feeney's voice each night for all those hours over all those years—not to escape his daughter, but to be close to the one person denied him.

She remembers Harris once fetching her from the Vancouver lockup in his chauffeured Bentley, after she was taken into custody for occupying the offices of a mining company that was poisoning a vital watershed with heavy metals. During the ride home he told her, to her surprise, that he'd like to see the old-growth and the watersheds preserved, too. "But we rarely get what we want in life," he said. "There isn't enough room for it all to fit." At the time, she was convinced he was talking about his blindness, or the Inquiry, or the necessity of environmental destruction in the name of industry and prosperity. Now she's certain he wasn't.

"Please give this man whatever my father wished," Willow says.

The lawyers shift in their seats and shoot glances at one another, reluctant to press the issue, no doubt questioning her sanity.

"Certainly," the lead lawyer says, scribbling a note on his yellow pad. "Well then, barring any unknown claimants, cousins, or other offspring, this process will be predominantly cut and dry. You'll hear from us shortly."

As Willow is whisked back to the mansion in a limousine that she'll soon own, she finally decides upon a name for her son: *Liam New Dawn*. The invented surname will free him from the freight of the tainted Greenwood legacy and provide him with a fresh beginning—something she never had. And the given name is a small gesture she can offer Mr. Feeney on her father's behalf. Even if he'll never know he'd received it, it's still worth giving.

She spends the remainder of the afternoon packing up her Westfalia before they return to live permanently on Greenwood Island. She boxes up the poetry records that Mr. Feeney made for her father, as well as the book of Wordsworth he gave her, along with a few other books of Harris's that Liam might like when he's older. She's nearly giddy at the thought of what a wonderful, forest-defending, nature-attuned soul her son will become after he grows up on that island. Though why is it, she wonders casually as she stacks the boxes in her van, that we expect our children to be the ones to halt deforestation and species extinction and to rescue our planet tomorrow, when we are the ones overseeing its destruction today? There's a Chinese proverb Willow has always loved: *The best time to plant a tree is always twenty years ago. And the second-best time is always now.*

And the same goes for saving the ecosystem.

She could use her father's money to start an environmental foundation, but she's no paper-pusher, and if his tragic life has taught her anything, it's that a person must live in accordance with their deepest-held principles, or else suffer a kind of death of the soul. Who might Harris have become if he was able to be who he truly was? Would he have been the man she'd only glimpsed during their rare visits to Greenwood Island, relaxed and contented? Would he have joyfully waltzed her around the room, like that blind father she once saw on television, laughing while shouldering lamps to the ground and bumping into furniture?

So who, then, will *she* become if she also fails to live according to her deepest self? And it's at this precise moment that she decides upon another path—a more difficult one, admittedly, yet also the path of connectedness, of principle and authenticity. One that will lead her and Liam away from the traps of capitalism and all that's easy and predictable in life, while bringing them closer to the land and its forests and rivers and its wild, incalculable treasures.

But to do that, she must sacrifice even what she most loves. Not only must she give away all the wealth that her poor, lonely father destroyed himself to amass and preserve; she'll also have to surrender Greenwood Island itself to a forest protection group. Because what kind of hypocrite would she be if she kept it? Who is she to deserve her own private island? What makes her entitled to such unlimited comfort and peace and abundance of resources while others starve and suffer?

It's the only way.

If she was dedicated to the environment before, she'll be twice as dedicated now. No more bunking with the Earth Now! Collective during the winter months: Willow and Liam will live year-round in her Westfalia. They'll be rootless, self-reliant, free. She'll do more solo direct actions—nothing radical or violent, just more bags of sugar dumped into more gas tanks. She'll protest, blockade, obstruct. She'll teach Liam to be strong, to live symbiotically with nature. He'll learn to be a warrior. A defender of the Earth. Together they'll consume as few resources as possible, and work toward repairing a tiny portion of the harm that Harris has inflicted upon the forests of the Earth. And someday, her son will thank her for it.

Why is it that people are engineered to live just long enough to pile up a lifetime of mistakes, but not long enough to fix them? If only we were like trees, she thinks, as she pilots her Westfalia through the iron gates of her father's mansion for the last time, with Liam strapped into the passenger seat beside her. If only we had centuries. Maybe then there'd be time enough for us to mend all the harm we have done.

2008

A SPINE

WHAT ELSE COULD it be, he thinks—with its gently curving trunk of bone, its limbs and branches and tributaries of nerve tissue, its flexibility and delicacy and elegant perfection—other than a kind of tree, buried in our backs, standing us up?

And if all this is true, then it would be reasonable for Liam Greenwood to finally admit that plunging from a height of twenty-seven feet and five-eighths of an inch to a polished concrete floor has cut his own tree down, felled it, severing its trunk just above his tailbone. And it will never stand him upright again.

NOTHING IS TRUE

HE WAKES.

Then he wakes a second time, unaware of having blacked out.

He straightens himself up in the driver's seat of his van as best he can manage. It's still dark, but the radiance of morning is brewing somewhere out there behind the house and beneath the sea. His pain has ceased; even the vise cranking in his lower back has ceded its grip. Liam checks his gas gauge: an eighth of a tank left. It was stupid to let himself black out with the engine running, but there's still more than enough gas to get him to help. Instinctively, he tries to reach the brake pedal with his right foot, but though the pain has passed, his lower half feels even farther gone, lost in a kind of emptiness. In frustration, he extends the baseball bat down near his useless legs to depress the brake pedal, then nudges the gearshift into drive, while becoming suddenly aware that even the prickling sensation in his hamstrings has disappeared completely.

If he'd cracked his pelvis or broken his tailbone, wouldn't some sensation have returned to his legs by now? Shouldn't he be able to move them, even slightly? Liam returns the van to park, drops the baseball bat, yanks the key from the ignition, and flings it onto the passenger seat. *No*, he thinks. He's been deluding himself. His legs haven't come back because they are no longer his own. And won't be ever again.

Where is he planning to drive to, anyway? A private hospital? Ever since moving to Brooklyn he's been working in the U.S. illegally. His clients are happy to pay cash, and though he carried contractor's insurance for a time, it was pricey, and once the adjusters discovered he was working without a visa he'd be denied a claim anyway, so he'd let it lapse.

The scans, the rehab, the catheters; the wheelchairs, lifts, and ramps. Not to mention the pain medication they'll offer him like candy. He'll be hooked all over again, with no reason to ever get clean. Paying out of pocket, his injury will cost him everything he has, and then some. And what kind of life will he find for himself at the bottom of such a pit of debt? Unable to properly swing his hammer or push his skill-saw through a piece of lumber? Unable to pilot his van to the next job or install a ceiling or finish a counter-top? There are states he's always feared more profoundly than death: abandonment, helplessness, dependence on others. But it's uselessness that terrifies him most of all.

Liam hooks his arm behind his seat and finds his cooler, from which he grabs as many Red Bulls as he can stuff into the pockets of his Carhartts. Next, he pops open the door and uses the seat belt like a rappelling line to lower himself down to the frosty driveway that he thought he'd left forever.

It's dawn by the time he reaches the house, after a long, gruelling crawl through the leaf mulch, now frozen in rigid mounds. Orange filaments of light angle through the surrounding trees. He slithers onto the floor of the entryway and shoves the front door shut behind him. He puts his frostbitten cheek to the relatively warm porcelain tile. This time around he can better recognize the appeal of the house's minimalist decor. The austere polished concrete. The white walls. The lack of books and clutter. It's a liberation from things, and from history. *The person who lives here is afraid of the past*, Liam thinks. *Join the club*.

He remembers meeting with the owner at his office in midtown Manhattan to plan the project. The man was a descendant of the Rockefeller family but worked for Holtcorp. For their meeting, he'd worn carpenter's jeans and a work shirt, and seemed vaguely embarrassed for needing Liam's help with the renovation at all. He made a point of offering Liam a Budweiser, and as they both drank he mentioned that Holtcorp had recently acquired Greenwood Island. "Any relation?" he asked, to which Liam simply shook his head.

Mercifully, Willow didn't live long enough to see her beloved island sold to a corporation. His mother once claimed that they'd lived there on the island when Liam was a newborn. But she'd already given it away well before his memory kicked in, so let them have it. These corporations will own everything in the end anyway.

Liam begins his crawl back down the wide stairs to the sunken living room. After descending six steps, he's forced to flip himself belly-up on the intermediate landing to rest his arms. He lets his eyes wander along the huge fir beams that support the vaulted ceiling high above. He can tell, even from here, that they aren't square—not deadly, anyway. Over his years as a woodworker, Liam has learned that even the finest-built, most expensive houses have their flaws and deficiencies, and this one is no different.

This is the carpenter's painful truth: nothing is true.

By *true* he means level, plumb, perfect. Every room you've ever entered has been off by at least a sixteenth of an inch—more probably an eighth. Guaranteed. We think we live in boxes until we look closer and find we're in fact living in irregular shapes, in big, misshapen accidents.

Which makes carpenters the high priests of living with mistakes. And while sloppiness is the most grievous insult you could throw at another carpenter, true perfection is maddeningly unattainable, which is why it's never spoken of. Because even after you cut a piece of wood and lay it straight, it lives on after you're finished, soaking up moisture, twisting, bowing, and warping into unintended forms. Our lives are no different.

He shuts his eyes and feels a long-stifled sob finally escape him. He's left behind more than his fair share of mistakes, that's for certain. The night he dragged the replica Stradivarius viola that he built for Meena behind his van; the homes he flooded and ruined with his leaky skylights; all the years he squandered, high as a satellite on Oxycontin; all the parts of his story he's left out, all the things he refuses to think about. But while he'll never be able to atone for all his mistakes, there might still be a few left for him to repair. And there might still be parts of the story left for him to tell. *So let the memories come*, he thinks. *What does it matter now?*

MAPLES

HOLDING HIS MOTHER's hand, Liam exits the parking garage where they've left their Westfalia and walks through downtown Vancouver in a misting, invisible rain. It's the first time in his young life he's seen Willow in regular clothes—a black skirt and a plain green blouse—and he feels an odd pride to be walking beside a mother who doesn't have twigs in her hair or look like she lives in a van. When they reach the provincial courthouse, she chain-smokes three menthols out front before they go inside.

While Willow attends her hearing, Liam waits in the hall, staring wide-eyed at the holstered gun of the policeman sitting across from him. Two months earlier, while Liam sat in the van, Willow disabled some expensive MacMillan Bloedel logging machinery up near Clayoquot Sound. But as they were fleeing the cut block, a group of Mounties riding ATVs pulled the Westfalia over and found Willow's enormous bags of white sugar stashed beneath the seats.

"I'm going to need to go away for a while, honey," she says, after the hearing is over and they've made their way back past the court building's metal detectors. "Just three months." Next, she drives to a phone booth and spends an hour there, calling friends and acquaintances, growling with frustration, and occasionally whacking the receiver against its cradle. When she returns to the van, she informs Liam that he's going to spend the summer with his great-aunt and great-uncle on their farm in Estevan, Saskatchewan.

"I've never even met them," he protests, which of course she ignores. While she's always spoken fondly of Temple and Everett, she's never managed to find the time in her busy sabotage schedule to make the drive out to visit them. But it isn't their unfamiliarity that makes Liam uneasy; it's more that he can count the number of times he's slept indoors on two hands, and he's anxious about the expectations of staying in a proper home.

"You think I want this?" his mother snaps after he's kept complaining throughout the day. "Maybe you'd rather go to a foster home instead?"

Liam shuts his mouth, crosses his arms, gives her his blackest look, and refuses to help her pack.

At daybreak the following morning, she drives the van east from Vancouver and up into the mountains. All through the trip she's jumpy and quick to snap at him, sipping white wine from a Thermos and smoking her menthols non-stop. She grinds the van's tired gears on the drastically pitched slopes as everything inside the van slides to the back where Liam sits. He spends the entirety of the two-day drive whittling in silence, a further punishment for her terrorizing threat of putting him in foster care the day before.

"Can you promise me one thing?" Willow says, stopping the van as they approach the farm around dinnertime the following day. "This is probably never going to happen, and I'm almost certain that I'm wrong. But if Everett ever comes near you . . . like, I don't know, if he touches you, or does anything that makes you feel uncomfortable—you go ahead and tell your Aunt Temple. Okay?"

"Whatever," Liam says, breaking his monumental streak of silence by uttering this powerful new word that he picked up from some teenagers at a convenience store when Willow stopped to gas up.

When they pull up to the farmhouse, Temple and Everett are both reading at a wooden table on the enormous covered porch. On first inspection, even without his mother's cryptic warning, Liam finds his great-uncle off-putting: the cords in Everett's neck are root-like, and his voice is a metal bucket of gravel dragged across the floor. He also walks with a creepy limp, stinks like sawdust, and leaves a trail of it behind him wherever he goes. But his partner, Temple—Willow scolds

Liam when he asks his great-aunt: "Why aren't you married?"—is kind and smells like detergent and has an easy, welcoming way about her. If the pair were trees, she'd be a tall, silvery birch, and Everett a crooked old oak.

That first night at the farm, Temple reads to Liam from an antique book pulled from a shelf that spans their entire living room, while Everett mutely cooks dinner and Willow organizes Liam's things in his new room. After they eat, Liam has three slices of rhubarb pie and then plays checkers with Everett in mutual silence, as Willow and Temple sit up late out on the porch, drinking wine and speaking in low voices.

Temple gently rouses Liam at dawn the next morning and informs him that since he'll be staying on the farm, he'll need to learn how to slop the pigs and feed the chickens and goats.

"Fine," he says, rubbing his eyes, worried she may dump him in the nearest orphanage if he doesn't comply.

"This used to be a proper farm, one where hungry people with nowhere else to go could come and work," she says, handing him a pitchfork. "But ever since we paid it off with that inheritance from your grandfather, Everett and I decided that our efforts would be better spent elsewhere." Temple goes on to say that she volunteers as a book buyer at the public library in Estevan, and Everett makes furniture that he sells, the proceeds of which they donate to charity. "There are still hungry people out there," Temple says, "but they're hungry for different things now. Sometimes I feel like I haven't the faintest idea what it is they need."

When the chores, which Liam enjoys slightly more than expected, are completed, Everett has lunch waiting for them: egg salad sandwiches on real wheat bread and soup with actual chicken in it. Already, Liam has started to secretly pretend that Temple is his true and rightful mother, and that her farm is his true and rightful home.

"Remember that stuff I said about Everett?" Willow tells Liam that afternoon, while he's helping her pack the van before she returns to Vancouver. "You should forget it. Temple and I straightened it all out. It was just a big misunderstanding. You have nothing to worry about. Okay?"

"I never believed you anyway," he says.

Liam doesn't cry when his mother drives off, perhaps because after less than a full day on the farm, he's already flushed with the guilty hope that she'll never come back, that she'll simply forget about him and leave him behind, just like she does everyone else.

Through the hot and dusty days of June, after his morning chores are complete, Liam spends hours exploring the farmhouse and the barn. He gives the goats and chickens funny names and chases them around the wheat fields. He spits fat globs into the black void of the well and climbs almost to the very top of the big weeping willow near the porch, the one that's like a great, green room when you go inside it; the one with the swing that Everett has hung for him, though Liam is nearly twelve and has outgrown swings. Nightly, Liam listens to the radio while his great-uncle cooks dinner and Temple sets the table. She refers to Everett as either "the Help," "the House Carpenter," or "the Resident Arborist," depending on what is to be done that day. And sometimes Everett gets her back by calling the farm "this God-forsaken, treeless patch of dust," which initially strikes Liam as a betrayal, except Everett's eyes glint when he says it, so Liam isn't sure.

He loves the predictability of farm life: waking up each day in the same place to eat the same food at the same table with the same people who say mostly the same things. The only ritual he doesn't appreciate is when each night, just before they're about to turn in, Everett always asks Temple, "You think I can stay here awhile?" and she replies, "Just until we get these trees in," as though Everett is some drifter just passing through. Liam knows it's just another of their jokes, but he despises it anyway. The farm is the one permanent thing he's found in his life, and the thought of Everett leaving or it all coming apart threatens everything he's come to cherish.

By July, Liam has befriended a local boy named Orin, who is Liam's age and lives up the road near the abandoned railroad tracks. When Liam invites him over to climb the willow tree and spit down into the well, Orin claims his parents won't allow it.

"Why not?" Liam asks, recalling his mother once mentioning that some kids don't do certain things because they hold strange religious beliefs, not with respect to Nature, but about a magical person they called God.

Orin glances around, leans in close, and squints. "Everyone knows your uncle was in prison. And that's why no one in Estevan will hire him." Then he drops his voice to a harsh whisper, an expression of half wonderment and half horror on his face: "People say he killed a baby."

Later in bed, Liam mulls this over. While he's gruff, his great-uncle doesn't seem capable of harming a baby, or even an adult for that matter. Everett spends his days in his woodshop out behind the barn, building desks and beds and cribs and tables and chairs, as well as sets of intricate chess pieces made of fine maple, all of which Temple drives into town in her pickup on the first Monday of the month to sell because Everett doesn't have a driver's licence. Willow herself had admitted before she left that she'd been wrong about him. But how, Liam wonders, could a whole town believe something if it isn't true?

Beginning the next day, Liam spies on Everett as he turns wood on his lathe, watching for signs of violence or insanity. While Everett never gets frustrated by a mistake and never makes any quick movements, he curses quietly and constantly. There's an odd tenderness to his curses, as though they are the one power that can coax the pieces of wood into agreement.

To Liam, the woodshop—with its forest-like stillness—is a quiet realm of exactitude, discipline, and possibility. His great-uncle isn't destroying trees at all; he's transforming them, into useful things that will endure. And once Liam is brave enough to alert Everett to his presence, he sits in the wood shavings beneath the table saw like a boy-sized gerbil, watching his great-uncle work. When he finally builds up the nerve, he pesters Everett to teach him how to operate the fearsome tools.

Everett shakes his head. "Your mother forbid it."

"She's not even here."

"She won't have you cutting up wood. And her wishes go around here, at least with respect to you."

"Well, she's a bitch," Liam says, the words slipping out like he's dropped someone's gold watch down the well. He sets his feet firmly on the floor and waits to taste his great-uncle's murderous fury—in fact, he nearly craves it.

But Everett's eyes only soften. He returns to his lathe and resets the guide that braces his chisel. "It's not simple, you know, raising a child. Your mother is doing what she believes is right. And there isn't just one way to do it. You'll come around to that someday."

Suddenly, Liam's cheeks are wet and he can feel his heartbeat in his ears. "I don't want to live in a van anymore," he says. "I want a normal life. And I want to live in a normal place. With normal food."

Everett turns back to regard him and places his hand on Liam's head. "There aren't any normal lives, son. That's the lie that hurts us most."

The following Monday, while Everett and Temple are away in Estevan for the day, buying animal feed and books, selling Everett's furniture, and taking in their monthly movie at the theatre there, Liam sneaks into the woodshop. He flips the table saw's switch and watches the naked blade roar and disappear into a fearsome blur like an airplane propeller. He swallows hard and sets a knotty board on the table and starts gliding it into the saw. He's only cut a foot into the wood when it pinches the blade and there's a loud bang and the board jumps from the table and strikes his chin with the force of a baseball bat.

When they return that night, Everett and Temple leave unmentioned the swollen yellow bruises on Liam's face—his jaw will click for weeks afterward—and following supper they all sit on the porch to watch the wide prairie horizon churn with skyborne vapour and light. Temple reads from the *Odyssey* as they sip their drinks: Everett a seltzer, Temple a white wine mixed with Sprite, and Liam the root beer they brought back from town.

While Temple is constantly reading aloud from her many books, never does she tell Liam any of her own stories. Forever unmentioned is the cyclone that he knows destroyed the farm around the time Willow was born. Or why exactly Everett went to prison (Liam has found letters tucked away in his woodshop that Willow had written to him there as a girl). Or anything concerning Liam's grandfather, Harris Greenwood, and his fallen timber empire or the inheritance he'd left them. Throughout that summer, whenever Liam questions her about these omissions, Temple's stock reply is to select a new book from her shelves and say: "How about this one?" And it's from her, perhaps, that Liam first learns the necessary power of willed forgetting.

When his mother returns in early September, she's speaking a mile a minute and overflowing with so much pent-up energy after her three-month incarceration that she scarcely notices Liam at all.

"Miss me?" she says while distractedly ruffling his hair as they all sit down to the great meal that Everett has set out on the porch to mark her return.

"Not really," Liam murmurs, too quietly for her to hear.

"To Liam," Temple says, raising her glass when the meal is assembled. "Who's been an invigorating presence for two old crustaceans over these past three months. And who might be the best worker this farm has ever seen." Liam raises his glass and feels his chest bulge with pride. And for a moment he's able to forget the brutal, unalterable fact that, like a prisoner slated for execution, he's leaving the farm behind tomorrow.

Early the next morning, while Willow is packing up their things for the drive back to British Columbia, Liam sneaks into the woodshop and steals one of Everett's ballpeen hammers. He goes out to the driveway and whacks a deep dent in the Westfalia's side panel, then knocks an even bigger one in the hood of Temple's weathered pickup truck. When Everett emerges in his long underwear from the house with a shocked look, Liam is certain that after what he's done, they will never let him come back. In truth, he'd rather they didn't. Already he knows that leaving this place once will crush something inside him forever, and he couldn't possibly survive a repetition. Or maybe he'll get off easy and Orin's rumours will be true, and his grizzled uncle will kill Liam right where he stands.

With an ashen, slack expression, Everett limps over to Liam, who is fixed in place with fright, and rests his big, callused hands on both of Liam's shoulders.

His great-uncle shakes his head. "I don't care about the truck, son," he says. Then he lifts his gaze to the impossibly wide prairie sky, which is a tepid blue, laced with just hints of cloud. He sniffs a few times, then clears his throat, as though he's trying to free up the tangled words. "Temple didn't manage to wake up this morning."

Liam feels the ballpeen hammer slip from his fingers. He lets Everett's heavy hands weigh him down to the swirling dust and comes to rest on his knees beside the tire of Temple's truck, his mind blank, his ears ringing. Eventually, Everett turns away, his wizened face a stone mask, and limps off to his woodshop, latching the door behind him.

Some time later, Willow emerges from the house with reddened eyes and the back of her wrist pressed to her lips. When she tries to approach Liam, he leaps up and runs into the barn, where he furiously begins slopping the pigs and feeding the chickens and goats.

He's still working when his mother comes to him a while later. "It was kidney failure," she says from the rail of the pen. "She's been sick with it for a while, Liam. She told me the night we first arrived here. But it was good you had this summer together."

"You should've told me," he says, then bangs a gate shut and begins forking straw into the trough.

"Look," she says, her tone sharp. "That was her choice, not mine. She didn't want to worry you. You're not entitled to every scrap of information around here. That's not how it works. So you can quit this rebellious teenager crap right now, because I need you back on my team. Because now that I'm out it's just you and me again, whether you like it or not." She pauses for her point to sink in, as if he doesn't know it. "We'll stick around until the funeral," she adds. "Then we're gone. If we don't get some chanterelles picked this fall, we'll be Dumpster diving all winter."

After lunch, some neighbouring farmers come and carry Temple's body down into the storm cellar so it will stay cool in the September heat. Everett stays in his workshop all that day. In the evening Liam hears him in the kitchen, quietly phoning up a man in Estevan, who delivers a case of rye whiskey to the house a few hours later.

In all the time Liam has been on the farm, he has never once seen his great-uncle drink, but in the days after Temple's death, it's all Everett does. It doesn't make him unpredictable and loopy like it does Willow; instead, it seems to seal his lips and amplify his weariness. When he's drunk, it's as though his very structural integrity has been removed. He stoops and his limp worsens. He starts drinking when he wakes and doesn't quit until he pisses himself and passes out on a bedroll laid on the floor of his woodshop.

Occasionally Liam eavesdrops from beneath the porch while Willow sits with Everett as they drink rye and smoke her weed late into the night. But they speak little, and when they do, it's only about the lack of rain, or the coming of rain, or how the few trees on the property are doing—never about Temple or anything of importance, which is, he's come to learn, perhaps their most distinguishing family trait.

"Get up, son," Everett says to Liam early one morning after a week has passed. "There's something I need to do, and I can't do it myself."

He coaxes Liam out to the shed, where they fetch some axes and a two-man bucksaw, and then they load them into Temple's dented truck. Clumsily, the old man drives, further denting it by clipping fence posts and running aground in drainage ditches, out to where a long line of mature maples were planted to provide shelter on the edge of the wheat field.

"Temple and I put these in together," he says, tossing the saws from the truck to the foot of the first tree. "She never let me put taps in them. She worried it might do them harm. She wasn't sentimental about many things. Except these trees."

Over the next few hours, the two swing their axes and bring down three of the stoutest maples. Then they buck the trunks into long segments which they load into the truck. Everett spends the entire afternoon chainsawing the maple segments into crude boards. And for the first time, he ignores Willow's wishes and teaches Liam how to properly operate the woodshop's tools. All day Everett and Liam saw and dress the boards until they are the finest, clearest, and straightest maple planks that Liam has ever seen.

It isn't until his great-uncle is putting on the final touches— hand-carving a delicate wreath of leaves and ornate blossoms into the lid—that Liam realizes what they've built.

CLEAR

WOOD IS TIME captured. A map. A cellular memory. A record. This is why, Liam believes, carpenters like himself will never go out of business. Because people will always keep wood close: in our houses and on our floors, ceilings, and walls; in our trusted canes and our finest musical instruments; in our heirloom tables and old rocking chairs; and, most tellingly, in the very capsules that ease our journey into the ground.

When carpenters call a piece of wood *clear*, they mean it is free of knots and wanes and blemishes. And during his many years of fussing over wood, cutting it to exact lengths and lovingly fitting it together just right, all before buffing it to a soul-warming shine, Liam Greenwood has often thought that people like clear wood best because they need to see time stacked together. Years pressed against years, all orderly and clean. Free from obstruction or blemish. The way our own lives never are.

GROUND ZERO

WITH NEARLY FLESHLESS fingertips, he's clawed his way back
down into the sunken living room, back to the foot of the scaffolding that he and Alvarez put up what seems like a lifetime ago.
Judging by the light, it's already mid-morning, and Alvarez would
be here by now if he were returning to work today. Though Liam
hadn't really expected he would, that spark of possibility is now extinguished for good.

If there must be a story told about this whole mess, he'd rather
it be that Liam Greenwood died while working, and not frozen to
death in his van like some vagrant. But he needs to put things in
order first, before he's incapable of doing so. Though his personal life
has always been a constant chaos, he's never once left a job site in
such a sorry state, and he isn't about to start now. He drags himself
over to the tool belt he'd removed yesterday so he could crawl to his
van, stuffs the brad nails that spilled out back into its pouch, then
re-buckles it around his waist. Next, he goes to his air compressor,
switches it off, and bleeds the tank of pressure with a deafening hiss.
Then he puts his jig saw back in its case and goes about collecting
the offcuts of reclaimed boards that came from Temple's farm, the
ones that Alvarez had been wasting. Next, Liam sets about arranging the boards themselves in a neat stack, while reflecting on the
unfairness of how few pieces of wood get reclaimed, and how many
end up rotting out in a field somewhere. He attempts to sweep as
much sawdust as possible with his hands onto the drop cloth, which
he then folds up neatly like a present. There's no hope of taking down
the scaffolding or packing up his mitre saw, so he comes to rest on

the concrete floor, in the exact spot where he fell, marked by the chip his titanium hammer made when it struck the ground.

Chasing his breath, he examines the room's floor-to-ceiling windows and the way they frame the seal-grey Atlantic like a painting, like it's part of the decor itself—the owner's own private ocean. He wonders how long death will take and how it will feel. And then whether it will feel like anything at all. Whether *feel* is a word that could possibly apply. Willow always believed that during our last moments, our spirit dissipates and we become part of the great Greenness. That we live on in some kind of chlorophyll energy field, at one with the trees, the soil, and the rain.

Yet in truth, death came to her cruel and quick.

His mind returns him to the day he was flown to Vancouver from Brooklyn, hired to do a touch-up job on an expensive installation he'd built for the University of British Columbia's forestry department. Since he's in town, he arranges to meet Willow later that day at the gates of Stanley Park. It's been years since he visited, and when she first steps from her Westfalia, he worries that her environmental fervour has finally consumed her to the point that she's stopped eating altogether for fear of harming plant life. Her once voluminous hair is now flat and thin, and her once relentlessly robust body is withered and frail.

"You've looked better, Willow," Liam says. "You want me to drive?"

"It's okay," she says, her skull like a hard-edged sculpture that her skin can barely hide. "I can drive this old beast with my eyes closed."

Willow steers her van, which Liam still knows with the intimacy of a childhood home, deep into the park, back to the site where it appears she's been camping secretly for some time. The day is breezy with a grey sky, and the smaller trees that camouflage her campsite wave in small circles. To get some food in her, Liam insists on cooking her favourite chickpea and tahini dish, which she takes outside to eat in the company of the trees, because, she claims, the van's persistent musty odour and close confines make it difficult for her to get the food down. When Liam comments on the dwindling state of her food supply, she remarks, "I wasn't able to get any chanterelles this year. Just didn't have the energy for it. So things have been a little tighter than usual."

It isn't until later that night that she tells him about her treatments: how she's been driving herself to chemotherapy each day and then camping out in this downtown park, which is a relatively short drive from the hospital. Along with the crush of pity, he can't help but feel a scorch of anger.

"When were you planning on telling me?" he says, his head lowered and his hands in his hair.

"Soon, I suppose," she says weakly. "I didn't want to bother you. You're so busy. I know how well you're doing out there."

His mother has always tried to leave as light an imprint upon the ecosystem as she possibly could, and to his great annoyance, this has also included him. Despite her protestations for him to return to New York, he cancels his carpentry job at the university, buys a sleeping bag, and moves into her van. When he picks her up from her treatments each afternoon, there's a strong toxicity to her breath, like she's spent the entire morning huffing spar varnish, the thick, noxious finish he puts only on his outdoor wooden installations.

He stays with his mother for three weeks, camping like they used to, falling into their old harmony. He buys groceries at the food co-op she still belongs to, makes her tea, keeps track of her medications, and helps her remove the bits of fluff that accumulate in her eyes after her eyelashes fall out. He watches her wither and hears her moan and cough through the night up there in the rooftop tent that she loves so much. And soon she grows so feeble he has to break the childproofing off her lighter so she can light her menthols and her weed.

When she's too sapped to talk, he plays for her the same records that she played for him when he was detoxing: the man reading poetry in a soothing Irish accent. While Liam still doesn't really comprehend the antiquated words he recites, his mother coughs less frequently and with less discomfort whenever the records are spinning on the turntable. So he plays them constantly at a low volume, even though after the tenth time he's flipped the record, the mere sound of the man's voice has begun to rub against his nerves like 40-grit sandpaper.

SUPPLIES

1 Ten-Pound Sack Organic Brown Rice
1 Ten-Pound Sack Organic Chickpeas
1 Ten-Pound Sack Organic Soybeans
200 ml Nystatin Solution
Dexamethasone 4 mg
Senokot 8.6 mg
Soflax 100 mg
Metoclopramide 10 mg
Diltiazem 180 mg
Tarceva 150 mg
Morphine Sulphate 5 mg

WHAT THEY DID

ONCE, NEAR THE end—and ignoring her oncologist's warnings—Liam and Willow get drunk on chardonnay in her Westfalia, in an ancient forest in the middle of a shining city of glass and steel. To mark the occasion, Liam digs his fingers into the slit in the driver's seat, pulls out her secret bottle of Chanel No. 5, and spritzes the van.

"Not too much," Willow says, before she closes her eyes and draws the citrusy scent deep into her tumour-constricted lungs.

The perfume seems to perk her up, however, and they sit drinking and chatting into the evening: about his work in Brooklyn (he leaves out the meeting-room tables he's done for Holtcorp, Shell, and Weyerhaeuser), and about the various environmental causes that she's still managing to champion, even in her diminished state.

"I don't suppose you're in the market for a Westfallia?" she says with a thin smile, after she grows tired and he's lifting her impossibly light body up into the rooftop tent.

Liam shakes his head. "Actually, I hate this thing."

She laughs softly, though he can tell the remark wounds her. "I know you think I've been selfish in my life," she says, as Liam wraps her in three quilts. "But I made a choice just after you were born. A choice to take the difficult path. I wanted to give you a different kind of upbringing, a real one, not like the one I had."

"My upbringing was great, Willow. But it was different, all right," he says, snapping off the flashlight. "Mission accomplished."

She closes her eyes and takes a long painful breath. "I was trying to teach you something."

"What's that?"

"To look upon Nature with reverence."

What is Nature, exactly, Willow? he wants to ask. *Is one of my reclaimed wood tables Nature? How about me, am I Nature? How come you never looked upon me with any reverence? How come trees are the only part of Nature that you ever cared about?*

Instead he kisses her forehead and says, "I try to look upon everything with reverence, Willow. And it was you who taught me that."

"You know," she says, "sometimes I've looked at the things you've made, on the computer at the library."

Liam can't believe his ears. "Remember when I first got my carpentry ticket, and you called me a 'certified forest killer'?"

"I never loved the idea of you wasting defenseless trees," she says, shaking her head. "But this reclaimed work you do makes sense to me. You've made some truly wondrous things, Liam. So yes, you do look upon things with reverence, and it makes me proud."

He sits up for hours in the van beneath her bunk, finishing the wine while listening to her cough—a low, grinding churn that comes on like a thunderstorm and leaves her gasping. He regrets that he can't offer her a morphine pill after she's been drinking—lately morphine seems to be the only thing that can keep the cough from waking her. Though he'd rather handle the morphine as little as possible, especially while he's drunk.

The drunker he gets, the clearer it becomes to him that his mother has lived her life fleeing a brokenness, one passed down to her by the broken people who came before her, and that she's passed some of this same brokenness down to him, like coals pulled from one fire and used to start another. And that he would do the same to his own child, if he ever had one.

"Can you promise me one thing?" she says later, her breath coming in gulping, tortured gasps. "That you'll visit Everett, if you can. I worry about him out there all on his own."

After Liam makes his promise, he sits vigil while she coughs and rants incoherently in a half-somnolent state—sending free-associative dispatches from inside the chemical swamp of cancer medication and booze and weed that floods her brain. It's all nonsense to Liam, just more of her New Age philosophy and conspiratorial ranting, until suddenly, sometime near dawn, just as he's dozing off himself, her burning green eyes appear above him in the entrance to the rooftop tent. "People can save you, Liam," she says with startling clarity. "Always remember that. They do it all the time. Except it's usually in ways we'll never understand. But that doesn't change what they did."

The next morning, when Liam returns from the co-op and the pharmacy with their supplies, he discovers his mother's body stretched out up there in the tent, her long grey hair tied back with a thin bough of cedar. A tree-swirled breeze sweeps crosswise through the mesh screens of the walls. A quiet green caress, passing her from one forest she'd loved to another.

Liam sits for a long time in the driver's seat of his mother's van, watching the trees, wondering if they can somehow perceive what they've just lost.

YOU'RE STILL HERE

HOURS SLIP BY in the sunken living room. Another night comes, spilling its shadows across the concrete floor. Then a new day replaces it. Liam watches the yolky sun seep in and then drain out again as though someone pulled a plug.

When a roaring thirst comes upon him, he opens the last of the Red Bulls that he brought back from the van. The taste is chemically comforting, like it's the pure distillation of all those coveted unnatural products that Willow denied him as a boy. The bombardment of sugar and caffeine restores his senses enough for him to know that with his last Red Bull now gone, he hasn't much longer to wait.

He recalls how Everett's life had likewise devolved into a waiting game after Temple's death. He drank steadily, though not as pitifully as he had in the weeks after she died. Liam honoured his promise to Willow and visited him intermittently over the years. Because upstate New York is full of broken-down structures perfect for his purposes, Liam never actually *needed* to go all the way to Saskatchewan for reclaimed wood; but it was a good excuse. He'd pay his great-uncle a small amount for carting away his fence boards, and though he'd never say it, Everett seemed to appreciate the company.

The last time Liam visits, he pulls up at eleven in the morning to find his great-uncle on the porch, where he sits in all seasons except the brutal prairie winter, with a pair of bifocals on the tip of his nose, a book in his lap, and a bottle of rye beside him like a trusted dog.

"You're still here," Liam says as he walks up to the house.

Everett glances around with eyes as cloudy as milk, as though confirming the fact for himself. "Seems like it."

"I thought you hated this place," Liam says, removing his baseball cap and joining Everett on the bench.

"Oh, I do," says Everett, who still smells of linseed oil and sharpened chisels. "Except I'm too old to go anywhere else."

"Well, I always liked it here. It was a good place for me to come as a kid."

"I plan on leaving it to your mother," Everett says, and Liam has to stifle a cough. After witnessing what Temple's death had done to Everett, Liam doesn't have the heart to tell him about Willow. "So I guess it will come to you, eventually. Can't say the land is worth much, though. Don't tell Temple, but this ground was never good for growing anything in the first place. You want a drink?"

Liam doesn't, because drinking hard liquor makes him crave oxys, but he says, "Sure."

Everett finds another glass, pours two fingers of rye, then adds water to it from a pewter pitcher. "The well here's still wet," he says. "Which is a minor miracle."

"I always loved this water," Liam says, taking a sip. "It never changes. You been in the woodshop much lately?"

Everett holds up his hands and makes two quaking fists. "I'm no good for joinery or chess pieces anymore. I'm building big, ugly picnic tables now. Just some old two-by-fours and some red paint. I give them to parks and public schools in Estevan. I think they might already have all the picnic tables they need and probably just burn them all somewhere behind city hall. Still, they're kind to accept them. It gives me something to do.

"But maybe I'll come out to New York and be your helper," he continues. "You sure those people pay good money for these weathered old boards? You aren't conning them somehow? And also: do you think they might be in the market for some picnic tables?"

Liam laughs and shakes his head. "People like old wood. It comforts them, I guess. Still, I like my work. It fills the days."

"Living is just a whole bunch of work," Everett says, nodding his head. "The trick is finding some that you don't hate."

Liam takes another drink and feels the cheap rye flare in his mouth.

"And how's your mother?" Everett asks. "I haven't heard from her in a while."

According to her wishes, Liam had Willow cremated, and dispersed her ashes in one of her favourite faerie farms, deep in central British Columbia.

"She's good," Liam says, nodding his head. "Off in some forest somewhere saving the world. Don't ask me which one."

"You never know where that one is, do you?" Everett says, shaking his head as he takes a drink.

After their glasses are empty, Liam spends a few hours filling his van with boards pulled from a perimeter fence. All that afternoon, he helps Everett build a picnic table from start to finish, then cooks him dinner and leaves by daybreak the next morning.

Three months later, a lawyer in Estevan calls Liam and tells him that Everett has died of heart failure and left Willow the farm. "So it goes to you," the lawyer says. When Liam returns to the property a week later, he finds a fine maple coffin—its joinery and intricately carved decoration as flawless as the one they'd built for Temple years ago—stretched across the table in Everett's woodshop. Liam buries Everett among the maples out near the lot line, where Temple's grave is, though it was never marked.

How his great-uncle had managed to fashion so beautiful a piece of woodwork with his gnarled, tremulous hands is still a mystery to Liam. But envisioning the coffin's fine craftsmanship now recalls to him the viola he made for Meena and then destroyed. His one genuinely beautiful thing.

Two, actually.

Two beautiful things.

Liam has made two beautiful things in his life.

And with this admission rushes in what he's long ignored, what he's been willing himself to push out of his thoughts. Because so close to the end of his life, Liam Greenwood is finally ready to fill in the gaps, to undo the knots, to make things true and clear—even if it's only for a short time.

JACINDA GREENWOOD

ON THE DAY of her birth, he's working with his phone set to silent, a particulate mask strapped over his face and hearing protection clamped tight over his ears. He's sanding a slab of expensive Douglas fir that he'll install in some Brooklyn yoga studio or some corporate office in Manhattan, the drone of his orbital sander nearly erasing the oddly similar drone of guilt in his head.

A week later, Liam still hasn't replied to Meena's initial text, sent to announce their child's existence, when he receives another of her texts, this one telling him that she's selected a name: *Jacinda*, after a kind girl Meena once knew in school. She also surprises Liam by revealing that she's given their child *Greenwood* as a surname. Meena says she has a few male cousins already carrying the Bhattacharya name forward, and she found it too tragic and unfair that Liam's surname should die off completely. Even when performing a musical piece, Liam thinks, Meena has always hated endings.

Despite his efforts to banish his daughter's very existence from his mind through constant toil and a strict regimen of deliberate forgetting, Meena often texts him pictures documenting Jacinda's early years. A little black-haired girl grabbing at her feet or smearing paint or chasing pigeons, images that Liam always views with half-averted eyes, the way one might glance at an eclipse. He keeps the photos on his phone, though he never prints them out. And now that his phone has been smashed, those photos are gone.

She must be three by now.

Which means she's already lived a thousand days without him. A thousand days he could have come home with his hands full of splinters, but not too many to prevent him from picking her up and swinging her high enough to brush the ceiling. A thousand mornings his daughter has woken and he hasn't been there to witness those thick lashes open like wildflowers; a thousand nights he's failed to read her a story and then watch them close once more.

Liam remembers George Nakashima once writing about how in a traditional Japanese family, a paulownia tree is planted immediately after the birth of a daughter. It's a species that grows rapidly, and by the time the girl has matured and is ready to leave home, the tree is likewise ready to be harvested for its wood. The handsome, fine-grained boards that it yields are shaped into an ornate chest, inside which the grown girl will store her kimono. For this reason, the paulownia is known as the empress tree, and the most shameful mistake he's made in all his life, Liam now admits bitterly, is that he never planted one for Jacinda.

He pulls a three-inch woodscrew from the pocket of his Carhartts and begins to scratch some letters into the concrete floor beside him. When was the last time he'd written anything that wasn't with his thumbs on his phone, something that wasn't spelling-assisted? He takes great care to get the words down right and arranged in the correct order.

To reduce the chance of making a mistake, he keeps it brief:

> *EVERYTHING I OWN TO JACINDA GREENWOOD.*
> *WITH LOVE, YOUR FATHER*

He takes his time, retracing the words again and again with the screw's tip to carve them deep and ensure their legibility. He wishes *everything* meant more than it does: his meagre cash savings, a plot of worthless farmland in Saskatchewan, a stack of poetry records, his arsenal of tools, and his work van, all of which must total something in the neighbourhood of fifty grand.

In one of Meena's most recent texts, she mentioned that Jacinda is bright, and can already identify letters and animals, and that she loves trees most of all. So perhaps she'll use his money for her education—which is no empress tree, but it's something.

I'm not ready to die, he first thinks, then whispers aloud, then shouts, the words reverberating in the sparsely decorated room without a scrap of carpet to dampen them. The sound makes him feel minuscule, no bigger and no more consequential than the screw clutched in his fist. And after that, a series of doors begin to close in his head. Never will he know the stories that Temple and his mother whispered about on the porch. Never again will he taste the bitterness of oxycodone or watch fresh wood shavings fly from a lathe or smell a rhubarb pie baking. Never will he ride with his mother in her van, or walk with her through the tall trees. Never will he hear Meena play her viola while she's wearing pajamas in the kitchen. Never will he feel his daughter's warmth against his chest. And never will the story be told in full.

Time, Liam has learned, is not an arrow. Neither is it a road. It goes in no particular direction. It simply accumulates—in the body, in the world—like wood does. Layer upon layer. Light then dark. Each one dependent upon the last. Each year impossible without the one preceding it. Each triumph and each disaster written forever in its structure. His own life, he can admit now, will never be clear, will never be unblemished, will never be reclaimed. Because it is impossible to ungrow what has already grown, to undo what is already done. Still, people trust the things he's built. And there is something to that. It's not enough. But it's what he'll take with him.

Through the ensuing dim and delirious hours, he consoles himself with hazy imaginings of people sitting with their coffees at his counters to talk and complain about those they love. People leaning against his bars to drink beer after beer, confiding desperately into one another's ears. A little black-haired girl with thick lashes sitting at one of his tables, eating a piece of carrot cake as her mother looks on, the girl's muddy shoes swinging beneath her as she talks about trees.

2038

PROPORTEE OF WILLO GREENWUD

ON THIS FOGGY Monday morning, Jake's group of Pilgrims consists of a Dubai-based solar panel tycoon, a celebrity chef hailing from what remains of Las Vegas, two teenage girls from China, thin as sheaves of grass, and the entire Toronto Maple Leafs hockey team. Jake is already halfway through her tour, but they have yet to ask a single question, and their eyes have been glued to their phones with greater fixation than usual. Jake doesn't blame them: even she can tell that her speeches so far have been flat and uninspiring, perhaps because she stayed up late again last night. But if she doesn't turn things around, and quickly, the Pilgrims will give her poor ratings, and if her average dips below three leaves out of five, Davidoff will have no choice but to fire her.

"You're currently standing among the highest concentration of biomass anywhere on the planet," Jake says with renewed enthusiasm, desperate to win them back. "Each tree is its own symphony of cellular perfection, one of the most magnificent and elegant creatures that has ever graced the biosphere. Deserving of all the mythology and the faerie tales and the holy buildings. Not to mention all that godawful poetry," she says, relieved to see her joke momentarily pry their eyes from their phones. A few of them even smile. "Over time," she goes on, "the lateral roots of these Douglas firs fuse together. And this is how these trees share resources and chemical weapons among their neighbours. There are no individuals in a forest. In fact, it behaves more like a family."

That last bit about family appears to genuinely move them (particularly the hockey players). Eager to keep the momentum going,

Jake leads the group into a nearby riparian area, while carefully avoiding the boundary where the true old-growth ends and the lesser trees of the once-burned half of the island begins. Here she expounds upon the importance of water to all life, which invites a few questions that Jake answers easily. When the celebrity chef claims he's hypoglycemic and needs to eat or he'll pass out, Jake coaxes the Pilgrims to the picnic area where their catered lunches await. As they dig into their handmade clay bowls of artisanal pork and beans, Jake wolfs down a granola bar and uses the lull in activity to pull the paperbook from her pack. She is calmed instantly by the familiar purple-stained cracks in its cover and the fine dust that continues to shake from its binding, even after weeks of her constant handling.

Though the journal's cursive script was initially difficult for Jake to decipher, she finally made her way through to the end after two weeks of trying. And once she got the hang of the looping hand and the antiquated punctuation, Jake's immediate second and third readings required mere days each. And now, after her tenth time through, she can read it with such fluency that it's almost as if she'd written it herself.

Contrary to what the misspelled inscription suggests, the journal's entries weren't written by her grandmother Willow Greenwood, but by an unnamed pregnant woman during the Great Depression. The woman was being kept by a rich man she refers to only as "RJ," who had agreed to adopt her baby once it was born. Though she wrote mostly about simple things—the walks that she took among the snowy maples, the fine meals that the cook prepared for her— woven into her descriptions are moving observations on many subjects, mostly concerning her fears. Her fear that the economy will never recover from the Crash, and that people are too short-sighted and selfish to survive. Her fear that the Dust Bowl will make its way to where she is, and harm her baby once it's born. Her fear of RJ and how he'll ruin her life if she somehow displeases him. Her fear of wasting her intellectual gifts at a meaningless, underpaid janitorial job. But despite all her fears, Jake hears hopeful whispers in the spaces between her words. *Take heart,* she seems to say. *The world has been on the brink of ending before. The dust has always been waiting to swallow us. People have always struggled and suffered. Your poverty is not shameful. It is not a failure of your character. Life, by its very nature, is precarious. And your struggles are never for nothing.*

Like the author of the journal, Jake knows what it means to struggle and to be afraid: she fears her ever-ballooning student debt, her plummeting Forest Guide approval rating, and the fact that her period is late. Her stomach has been cramping lately, even though she's been careful to avoid dairy—especially the dining yurt's infamous Creamy Potato Stew. Yesterday, she asked one of the younger female Forest Guides what she knew about the Cathedral-supplied IUDs, only to learn that they stop emitting hormones around year four: the exact vintage of Jake's. So she should probably admit that her night with Corbyn Gallant was more consequential than intended and add an unwanted pregnancy to her heap of worries. Except she can't risk getting tested by the Holtcorp doctor, because a positive result will mean her temporary banishment from the island, at least until she has her child. Then she'll have to somehow scrounge up the money to pay someone to care for her baby when she returns to work, which will set her debt-repayment plan back years. And that's assuming they'll hold her job for her and not give it to the next eager Forest Guide recruit waiting in line.

Her last remaining hope is that Silas is right, and she is legally entitled to lay claim to Greenwood Island. But whether his scheme works or not, at least she's had the chance to read the journal, along with the index card outlining her family history that Silas's researchers prepared. She keeps both of these in the cardboard box of her father's inexplicable heirlooms, along with his unlabelled poetry records, his woodworking tools, and his work gloves. Prior to Silas's visit, the idea of studying one's family history always seemed to Jake like the favoured pastime of narcissists, people seeking to either establish or shore up their own self-perceived greatness. She'd grown so accustomed to living with no family wisdom to consult, no stories to recount, no memories to share, no legacy to carry on. She'd spent an entire life in this drifting state, floating as a seed does. But only now is she starting to understand how good it can feel to be rooted.

"What about those trees over there?" says one of the hockey players as Jake leads them past the old-growth after lunch. "They look huge."

"Oh," Jake says briskly. "Well, those trees are equally significant as the stands I showed you earlier."

In the month since she first spotted the two firs with browned needles, Jake has made several after-hours attempts to study them, only to be turned back by a patrol of Rangers each time. It wasn't until two weeks ago that she finally managed to reach the afflicted firs, set her rainfall meters, and take a series of soil samples from around the trees. And since her findings indicated that the rainfall has been adequate and the surrounding soil is rich with nutrients, the only potential cause left to consider is something biotic. But she found no evidence of bacterial pathogens or fungal infestations in the tissue. Still, she's been avoiding the trees during her tours, just in case one of the more observant Pilgrims spots the browning and sounds the alarm.

"Excuse me, we're here to see the big, beautiful trees?" one of the Chinese girls interrupts with painful politeness, pointing at God's Middle Finger. "And those trees are biggest?"

"We want them," her companion adds, nodding solemnly.

"Sure," Jake says. "Of course."

Jake escorts the group along the bark-mulched trail, her eyes cast downward, watching her thighs alternately rise and fall inside her Cathedral-issue shorts. She brings them to a halt, and when the time comes for her canned speech, she's forced to lift her gaze. "This 230-foot titan was already 150 feet tall when Shakespeare sat down and dipped his quill to begin writing *Hamlet*," she says with all the enthusiasm she can muster, as the other half of her mind examines the diseased trees. While the needle-browning hasn't changed, it's immediately clear that the soggy bark has spread, and now afflicts five trees in total. Even God's Middle Finger appears compromised. She notes several places where the colossal tree's bark has pulled away, revealing something growing on the tree's nutrient-rich cambium, its tissue as slick and deep black as a dog's gums. And higher up, pileated woodpeckers have punched numerous holes in the softened bark, around which beetles and ants are swarming. The tree is being plundered, Jake realizes with horror, like a thousand-year-old museum with all its precious antiquities flying out the door.

Thankfully, none of the Pilgrims notice, and after concluding her speech, Jake hastily sends them back up the trail and takes a quick tissue sample from the afflicted area of God's Middle Finger. With a sick, sinking feeling, she rejoins the Pilgrims a minute later, and as they set off for the Villas, she strains to dispel the swirling globs of panic that now hinder her every breath.

She stops to pour water over her neck, scrubbing her sweaty face with her hand, watching a duo of ravens dogfight through the branches above. She's reminded of a story Knut once told her of a region in northern Minnesota that was particularly hard hit by the Withering, where people woke late one night to the sound of hundreds of blunt objects striking the shingles of their roofs. When they ran outside, they saw that it was birds, of every size and species imaginable, falling from the sky like hail. It was later discovered that they'd been flying for months straight, and had flown themselves to death, searching in vain for somewhere to nest.

THEIR EQUAL

IT TAKES JAKE an hour of examining the latest samples under a microscope before she sees it. And even then, she isn't exactly sure what it is she's seeing: a haze of ghostly filaments that have woven between the xylem cells she took from God's Middle Finger, replacing the lignin that normally gives them their structure. On closer inspection, and only after she strategically stains the tissue, she identifies the filaments as the fruiting bodies of a new species of fungus, one that's flourishing between the cell walls. Whatever it is, the fungus is aggressive, and if the tree can't make enough tannins to fight it off and the fungus manages to penetrate through the sapwood and into the heartwood, God's Middle Finger won't stand a chance.

Jake leans back in her chair and emits a pained sigh as despair courses through her body. What she's dreaded for so long has finally occurred: the island's local microclimate, which has shielded the Cathedral's trees from the Great Withering, has shifted enough that the trees have become stressed and can no longer properly defend themselves against intruders. And if this follows the same epidemiology of other fungal blights brought about by the Withering, the fungus will spread, and all the island's ancient trees, some of which have survived for a thousand springs and a thousand autumns, will perish.

If there were ever a time for bourbon, it would be now; but instead Jake brews a pot of mint tea and buries her head under a pile of blankets on the ratty loveseat that commands most of her staff cabin's floor space. Sometime later there's a knock at the door. When she opens it, Knut is standing there with a large bottle of peppermint schnapps dangling from his fist.

"You've been so busy lately, Jacinda," he says as she invites him inside. "I've missed our evening conversations. You're the only sane person on this island, you know."

"Sorry, I quit drinking. And I haven't really felt up to socializing lately," she says, giving him a hug. "But I think you're going to need one."

After she pours Knut a glass of schnapps and herself a mug of lukewarm tea, she points to the microscope. "That slide is a sample of tissue I took from the trunk of God's Middle Finger this afternoon."

Knut grooms his mustache with his fingers and bends to the eyepiece with his other wrinkled lid pinched shut. While he looks, Jake relates the story of how she first noticed the browned needles and the soggy bark during one of her tours, and how she's sorry that she kept it from him for so long. "But now I need your help," she says in a tight, hopeless voice.

After another minute at the lens, Knut grimaces, straightens up, and drains his glass. "We will do something," he says, his eyes fiery with conviction. "Tonight. Before it's too late. Even though it may already be too late."

"We'll tell Davidoff," she suggests, attempting to steer his usually rash thinking toward reason. "Management will launch an official investigation. They could shut the Cathedral down and let us do more tests."

"Those Corporate snakes are only interested in protecting their investment, Jake," Knut says with a sneer. "And Davidoff couldn't even keep a Christmas tree alive past Boxing Day, let alone some of the most significant life forms remaining on this planet. No, these poor, sick trees must be brought down and then burned. Immediately. It's the only hope to halt the spread of the fungus. And we need to do it ourselves."

"Now?" Jake says. "Knut, the Rangers will hear our chainsaws."

"We can do it together," Knut says, putting his hands on her shoulders.

She feels her gaze sink downward. "I can't lose this job," she says, her voice wavering. "I'm too deep in debt. And I think I might be pregnant. So can we just press pause until we understand it a little better? We'll do more experiments. Perhaps there's an antifungal treatment we can prepare." She doesn't say that she's terrified of getting banished to the Mainland, even with Knut at her side. He's been at the Cathedral from the very beginning, and has no idea what it's like out there: the dust, the firestorms, the squalor, the children choking with rib retch.

He hesitates, gears turning somewhere behind his eyes; then he reaches out to touch her chin, nodding solemnly. "You have a lot going on right now, Jake. I can understand that. We'll do some more research. And when we're done, we'll decide on a proper course of action."

After this is agreed, they sit on the loveseat and visit for a while longer. But their conversation is stilted, and Knut's mind is elsewhere. Oddly, he hugs her a second time before he leaves, which is something he never does.

The next day, over lunch, she learns from the housekeepers that immediately after Knut left her cabin last night he snuck over to the Maintenance Shed where he forced the door, triggering the alarm. From the shed he took a long, tree-felling chainsaw and marched out with it into the dark forest like some knight off to vanquish a dragon. But a squad of Rangers rushed him before he even reached the old-growth. As they dragged him past the Pilgrims' Villas, Knut unleashed his greatest jeremiad, a scathing critique of the Cathedral and its inherent absurdity and perversion, all while referring to himself as a "Tree Barista," an incident that two Pilgrims recorded on their phones and posted widely.

Davidoff's justice was swift and severe. The wharf workers say that Knut wept and tore at his hair when he was informed of his banishment. The Rangers dumped him along with all the recycling and compost bins on the very next Mainland-bound supply barge. They wouldn't even let him take his collection of paperbooks, including his beloved first editions of Linnaeus and Muir, which Jake narrowly managed to rescue from his cabin before they were confiscated and burned along with the rest of his belongings.

Now it's early Monday morning, and as she lies awake, listening to the groggy pre-dawn chatter of red crossbills and juncos, she fights to halt her alarm clock's advancing digits with her mind. She isn't sure she can stand another numbing day of Forest Guiding—especially now that she's facing a possible pregnancy, and all the Cathedral's trees are quite likely dying, and her only friend is gone.

When her alarm sounds, Jake rises and shuffles sluggishly to the locker where she keeps her uniform. Inside, she finds a note taped to the interior of the door. Knut must have put it there the night of his visit, while she went to the bathroom to check yet again if she'd got her period:

> *They stand. They reach. They climb. They thirst. They drop their leaves. They fall. You see, Jake? We __make__ them human. With our verbs. But really, we shouldn't. Because they're our betters. Our kings and queens. (We gave them __crowns__, didn't we?) And they are the closest things we have to gods.*
>
> *You, however, Jacinda Greenwood, are their equal. – Knut*

CONSANGUINITY

FOUR DAYS LATER, Jake hears from one of the maintenance guys that "her lawyer friend" has returned to the Cathedral. Silas invites her for drinks that evening at Villa Twelve, the very same Villa where she'd spent the night with Corbyn Gallant. Again, Jake dons her Pilgrim disguise and sneaks to the Villas through the cover of the trees.

Silas greets her at the door wearing an untucked dress shirt and a wide smile. "I forgot to mention last time that your great-grandfather Harris Greenwood built this cabin," he says, leading her inside. "It was the first permanent dwelling ever constructed on Greenwood Island. Some claim he built it as a retreat for himself and his lover, a man in his employ named Feeney—though all of this remains unconfirmed by my researchers. The cabin has been redone since, of course, a remodel performed by Holtcorp, which I'm told involved extracting numerous high-calibre bullets from the priceless timber beams."

Though the name *Harris Greenwood* remains foreign to her ear, Jake allows herself a twinge of pride as she again examines the fineness of the cabin's woodwork, with its beautiful, honey-coloured fir beams, its great shelf of paperbooks, and its sense of oneness with the forest.

"Sorry I didn't book you for another private this time," Silas says. "But I figured it would be better if we spoke without the wonders of nature to distract us."

He pours her some wine as thick as blackberry juice at the kitchen island, then brings it over to the coffee table. She can almost feel a magnetic pull between the edge of the glass and her lips, but leaves it untouched. Instead she sits on the sofa and extracts the battered journal from her pack and sets it on the coffee table.

"So you *did* manage to have a look at it?" Silas asks.

"I read it," she says, nodding her head noncommittally, reluctant to let on how much the book has already come to mean to her, the depth to which it has taken root. "But I doubt *you* have. Because it definitely wasn't written by my grandmother."

Silas gives a wriggling smile, and she's reminded of how he always hated to be told he'd made a mistake. "I never made any such claim!" he declares, joking unconvincingly. "Though now that you've familiarized yourself with it, I'll tell you how the journal came to us. My firm specializes in intestate litigation—unresolved estates and unclaimed inheritances that have languished in trust accounts for years. For this purpose, we routinely acquire rare paperbooks from private collections: journals, ledgers, diaries, that kind of thing. This particular one came to us in the sixties—way before my time—from a rare book collector in North Dakota, who bought it from a farmer who claimed he found it one day out in his wheat field. Apparently, the book was discovered spread open in the dirt, just lying there, as though some fieldworker had been reading it and set it down for a moment. In fact, the collector who initially acquired it considered the journal a lost work of fiction—a precursor to *The Bell Jar*. After my firm purchased it, the journal sat in our collection for decades. Even though it was digitized in the 2000s, the phonetic spelling of your grandmother's name inside the front cover didn't trigger any of our search algorithms, which are primed for names of interest like *Greenwood* or *Holt*. It wasn't until last year that an articling student of mine, who was conducting an inventory of our holdings, discovered this reference to your grandmother. Although the inscription was clearly added after the journal was completed, a deeper analysis of the text gave us good indication that the entries were made in Saint John, New Brunswick, which led us to speculate that the "RJ" named in the paperbook could in fact be R.J. *Holt*, the founder of Holtcorp. Our investigation stalled there, however, without concrete evidence to tie the file to any living person.

"That is, until the book was united with *this*," he says, reaching into a carbon-fibre briefcase that looks bombproof and producing a slim, clothbound box, open on one side, into which he snugly slides the journal. "And then things got interesting."

He holds up its spine for Jake to see:

THE SECRET & PRIVATE THINKINGS & DOINGS
OF EUPHEMIA BAXTER

Jake feels a galloping thrill at finally learning the woman's name.

"This slipcase is the missing piece of the puzzle that I spoke about last time," he continues. "We succeeded in borrowing it from an amateur researcher named Harvey Lomax III, who for years has been trying to track down information about his grandfather, Harvey Lomax Sr., a man who was once employed as R.J. Holt's driver until he inexplicably went missing sometime in 1935. Harvey III made it his life's project to locate his grandfather, a search which eventually led him to an archivist who'd collected artifacts from the Vancouver skid row hotels that were being bought up and gentrified during the great condo boom of the early 2000s."

"Is that who owns the journal now?" Jake asks, already eager to get the journal safely back into her hands. "This Harvey Lomax III?"

"The slipcase, yes. The book, however, remains the property of our firm. Though we've reached an understanding with Mr. Lomax that if certain eventualities occur, he'll be fairly compensated for providing this important piece of the puzzle."

"Those 'eventualities' of yours still seem like a long shot to me," Jake says skeptically, "even with the slipcase."

"Well, here's where it gets *really* interesting: Officially, in the spring of 1935, around the same time Harvey Lomax Sr. went missing, R.J. Holt's infant daughter was kidnapped from his estate by your great-uncle, Everett Greenwood, a known vagrant and criminal who claimed to be a veteran of the First World War, although there's zero record of his service. After an unsuccessful plot to milk Holt for the ransom money, and with the authorities closing in—this was all established in court—Everett holed up with the child right here on his brother Harris's private island, in this *very cabin*. And after a firefight with Mountie officers—hence the bullets—he was captured, and subsequently admitted to disposing of the infant somewhere in this forest, a crime for which he would serve a thirty-eight-year prison sentence."

"Charming," Jake says. "No wonder the Cathedral never puts the island's history on its brochures. But you said 'officially.' What about *un*officially?"

"On closer examination, the whole story gets iffy. R.J. Holt was a known philanderer, and we can find no confirmation he ever had a child with his lawful wife. After further digging, my people found that a woman named Euphemia Baxter *did* work as a cleaner in one of Holt's banks. We believe that Ms. Baxter had an affair with Holt, and that once she became pregnant, they made a deal for him to adopt her child. Yet there are no hospital records of the birth, and shortly after, Ms. Baxter's body was found in the woods near the Holt estate. The cause of death was listed as suicide, except there was no formal investigation—because of Holt's far-reaching influence, is our guess."

Tears blur Jake's eyes. For some reason, the news of Euphemia's possible suicide hits her like an axe. She'd seemed so hopeful while writing her final journal entry. So alive and dedicated to her future.

"Coincidentally," Silas goes on, oblivious to the story's emotional impact on Jake, "she died the very same year that your grandmother, Willow Greenwood, was born to your great-grandfather Harris and an unnamed washwoman at one of his remote logging camps. Given his rumoured, and quite probable, homosexuality, I had my team pull Willow Greenwood's birth certificate, and they discovered it contains many characteristics of a forgery, including a different typeface and paper stock than all others printed in British Columbia during that year. Leading us to suspect that the child was not Harris Greenwood's at all, but the Holt infant your great-uncle Everett kidnapped and confessed to having disposed of in the woods. We believe that the child was adopted secretly by Harris Greenwood, who, to keep up appearances, claimed it was born to a washwoman who'd died during labour while in his employ."

"Then why the hell would Everett Greenwood say he killed the child and spend forty years in prison for a crime he didn't commit?"

"Our only theory is that because Everett was reportedly illiterate and seriously shell-shocked, his wealthy brother—who was, by all accounts, as shrewd as he was ruthless—wanted a child to carry on his legacy, and duped his simple-minded brother into fetching him one."

"What you're saying is that my noble Greenwood ancestors were hobos, forest-destroyers, eco-terrorists, slave traders, *and* kidnappers—but *not* child murderers. That's great, Silas. I feel so much better now that I have a 'story to tell,' as you put it."

"It all matters more than you think, Jake. If this theory proves true, and your grandmother Willow Greenwood was the biological daughter of R.J. Holt—whether she arose from a lawful relationship or not—it means we could reasonably establish your own consanguinity with the Holt family tree. You see, R.J. Holt was predeceased by his spouse and siblings, and was survived by no immediate family. A genealogical search conducted at the time of his death found no viable heirs, and his intestate estate has since been held in a trust controlled by the province of New Brunswick."

"So?" she says with mounting impatience.

"So all we have to do is file a legal challenge attesting your ancestral relationship to the decedent," he says. "We'll need to prove this connection to a judge, of course, but with the journal and slipcase united and entered together as evidence, we'll have a more than robust case. Once you are established as the estate's beneficiary, a number of related dividends and trusts, which have been accruing interest in Crown accounts for years, would flow to you. Your debt will be a thing of the past, Jake. You'll be free."

Suddenly, her great-grandfather's cabin feels oppressively small and a slight pain has begun to pulse behind her eyes. "I'm still getting used to the idea of even *having* a family," she says, rising from the sofa. "And now you're hitting me with all this. It's a bit much, Silas. I need to go for a walk to clear my head."

"If it worked," he says, standing beside her and clasping her hand, "along with unimaginable wealth, you'd also gain a controlling interest in Holtcorp, which has been rudderless for years. Of course we expect the board will put up a fight, but even they will agree that a strong leadership presence could only enhance the company's long-term stability. Plus, your educational qualifications are stellar, and your name alone will lend Holtcorp's many eco-entertainment assets an added air of authenticity. You could do so much more than pay off your debt, Jake. Greenwood Island would be yours to do with as you please. Perhaps you could even save it."

"From what?" she asks suspiciously. She doubts Knut alerted management to the fungus in his final rant, or that they would have believed him if he had. In the days since his banishment, Jake has been covertly applying an antifungal solution she prepared to the afflicted trees each afternoon during her tours, even though there's been little sign of improvement.

"From further exploitation," Silas says. "From the Pilgrims. From the Withering. From people like me. You could make things more equitable for everyone. Set up a proper laboratory. You could do *research* again. I know how much this place matters to you, Jake. Just think how much more it will mean to you once it's yours."

"But what if this plan fails and we're denied our claim? I doubt Holtcorp will keep me on here after I've made a gambit like that. I'll be banished."

"I do this for a living, Jake," Silas says, taking both her hands in his and fixing her with wide, imploring eyes. "And, like you, I'm good at what I do."

"I'll consider it," she says, dropping his hands and heading for the door.

"What's to consider?" he says, following her. "Do you know how much of the world Holtcorp *controls*? Its last valuation was two trillion. That's tourism, security and firefighting services, solar, mining, desalination, resource development, and even asthma medication. You don't need to play the noble, selfless scientist anymore. Not with wealth like that on the table."

Freedom from her crushing debt. A possible cure for the fungus. A viable future for the child she might be carrying. A *laboratory*. "I said I'll think about it. In the meantime, I'm holding on to this." Jake dashes back to pluck the journal, still in its slipcase, from the coffee table.

"I'm not sure my firm will like that," Silas says tersely.

"Well, I need to read it again before I make my final decision."

A pained grimace comes over him, and in an instant she realizes just how valuable the paperbook actually is. Then he raises his palms in surrender. "Fine, take it," he says with forced mirth. "More than anyone, I know better than to pressure you. The last time I did you moved to Utrecht and blocked my number."

"I have one last question," she says from the Villa's doorway. "Why are you doing this? The research. The time investment. For money?"

"Yes—well, partly. There'll be some for my firm, I admit it. But there'll be an ocean for you. And you can well understand that making a company like Holtcorp happy is good for us, long term."

"And here I thought you were trying to help me."

"That's exactly what I'm doing, Jake. Life is getting crueller with each passing day. Not even Canada is the oasis it once was. And if this Cathedral ever goes under, you'll be cast out there to retch on dust in some treeless, sunbaked snakepit along with everyone else. And I don't want to see that. We can't change the world anymore, but if we're smart, maybe we can preserve the best of it. And who better than you to do the preserving? So let me know. I'm booked in here all week. My door is always open."

THE TREE
ENTERTAINMENT
BUSINESS

MIDWAY THROUGH DINNER the next day, Jake is summoned from the dining yurt to Davidoff's office, where in a stern, exasperated tone he goes over the raft of online complaints about her that he's received from Pilgrims over the past month. "It's alleged that you've been *deliberately* ignoring certain sections of old-growth during your tours and that you've been delivering muddled and unenthusiastic speeches about the Cathedral's natural features.

"*And*," he continues, shaking his head and closing his dim eyes, "last night, you were observed by our security staff exiting one of the Villas after hours. Number Twelve of all places."

My great-grandfather Harris Greenwood built that cabin so I can go there whenever I please, she wants to yell, but instead says: "I'm sorry, sir. I was meeting with a Holtcorp representative, and I forgot to clear it with—"

"I know it was that lawyer from Corporate who asked you over there, Jake, so I'm not going to punish you. But from now on, if he wants to meet with you he needs to schedule a private like everyone else. Is that clear?"

She nods and prepares to get up.

"But that's not all," he says with a grave expression, motioning for her to stay seated. "You've now officially dropped below a three-leaf online approval rating. So I'm going to need a very good reason for why I shouldn't fire you."

Jake feels her eyes pinch shut. "I've been having some family trouble, sir."

Davidoff's squat face takes on an unexpectedly sympathetic look.

"Jake, with the exception of our young, trust-funded Forest Guides, all the Cathedral's employees have us transfer a large portion of their paycheques home to families living in the various slums of the world—all except you and Knut. So I'm sorry, but the fact is you don't have any people out there. Look, I know that you and the German were close. Honestly, I didn't want to banish him, but he punched his own ticket with that stunt of his. Still, his leaving has nothing to do with why you of all people have been giving substandard tours. So I'm going to need a better explanation, or you can start thinking about joining him."

For a moment, she indulges in imagining herself sitting behind Davidoff's desk in his web-backed chair. First, she'll shut the Cathedral down and send the Pilgrims home, let all the hiking paths grow over and allow the forest to regenerate properly. Then she'll claim Villa Twelve for herself and her child. As Greenwood Island's steward, she'll renew her commitment to the study and protection of trees. No more mandatory selfies or inane Pilgrim questions. No more being grateful to Holtcorp for her job and her dismal staff cabin. She'll be her own person again, with real, attainable hopes and dreams, just like a Pilgrim. And, most important of all, she'll establish a lab in this very office and hire Knut back, along with the world's brightest minds in dendrology, and together they'll discover a cure for the Withering that will save the trees not only here, but everywhere.

"Remember that unusual browning I told you I noticed in some of the Douglas firs?" she says, feeling emboldened by her fantasy. "The ones you let me sign out research equipment to study? Well, it's a fungus. One I've never seen before. And there are more affected trees now. Five in total. Including the island's largest tree. This is the section I've been avoiding during my tours, for fear of the Pilgrims noticing."

Davidoff holds her eyes as his face blanches. "And this could be Withering-related?" he says. "Potentially?"

"Given the current epidemiology, yes, I believe it is."

He furrows his brow and massages his thick cheeks with his hands. "What do you propose we do?"

"I've already tried an anti-fungal preparation, and it didn't make a dent. Our only option is to cut the diseased trees down and burn them. Immediately. That's exactly what Knut was attempting to do—and he was right. It's the only action we can take to stop the fungus and prevent, or at least slow, its spread across the entire island."

Davidoff laughs. Then he sits there blinking at her, looking horrified once more. "The Greenwood Arboreal Cathedral is in the tree *entertainment* business, Jake. Can you imagine what Corporate would say? The chainsaws roaring at breakfast? Cathedral staff *willingly* cutting down and burning *ancient trees* just because some needles have browned and some bark has chipped off? All while Pilgrims take videos? *With their phones?* The publicity would be a disaster. We'd have to empty the resort—we're talking millions in lost revenue. Corporate would crucify us."

"If we don't," she says, "there will be nothing left within five years."

Her boss sits silent for a moment, staring at the pens on his desk. "You know," he begins in a confidential tone, his voice husky with emotion. "I have two little girls. Nine and five. Back in Oklahoma. There, the dust comes in through the window casings and under the doors, no matter what my wife does to keep it out. Both my daughters wheeze so bad from asthma they need daily steroid injections—injections that cost me half of what I earn here. We can't afford visas for them to come to Canada, even though I've been in the country for years. And make no mistake: if we tell Corporate about this fungus, Jake, you and I will lose our jobs, and I don't know what will happen to my daughters then. So what we're going to do is keep this between us, and we're going to ride this out. Like you said, these things spread slowly. Five years is a long time. Who knows if the Cathedral will even be around by then? Either you agree to keep this a secret, or I'm banishing you right now. Is that clear?"

"Perfectly clear, sir," she says, before Davidoff dismisses her.

As Jake starts back to her cabin through the forested dark, her thoughts circle what is now her only option: to claim Greenwood Island for herself, with Silas's help. But she can't keep herself from recalling Euphemia's numerous mentions of a mysterious visitor, a large, hulking man she refers to only as "HBL". She was fond of him, this man, who visited her throughout her pregnancy, and brought her paperbooks and the special pickles she was craving, and was the only one who ever encouraged her to become a writer.

So how can Silas be so sure that R.J. Holt is her great-grandfather, Jake wonders, when this HBL could also be? It's as she's flipping through the journal once more that she realizes Silas had read Euphemia's entries as a lawyer, searching only for seams of opportunity and lines of attack, too blinded by self-interest to detect the complexities and undercurrents present in her words. Still, Jake has no choice now but to go through with it—whether she believes she's related to R.J. Holt or not.

Just after she's made her decision, she's surprised by the faint ache she feels at the thought of shedding her father's name, this curious word she's worn so uncomfortably her whole life, with so little connection to those who'd borne it before her. A name that to her fellow Cathedral employees has been nothing more than a symbol of her family's fall from grace. But she'll grit her teeth and cast it off and declare herself a Holt, and take command of this island and its trees. Though in the back of her mind she knows they can't possibly belong to anyone. Not really.

BRUSH CLEARANCE

THERE IS NOTHING more quieting than an ancient tree.

It commands reverence, the way a tightrope walker stills an audience far below; the way a church soothes even the non-believers who venture within it. And here at the foot of God's Middle Finger, Jake Greenwood removes the Husqvarna chainsaw from its orange plastic case, reverently, as she imagines her mother might have once produced her viola, or her father one of his more refined woodworking tools. She handled her share of chainsaws during her research days, taking core samples in northern Sweden, felling fire-scorched black spruce in Northern Ontario, though she's never before brought down a gargantuan tree like this, especially not on her own.

At the Maintenance Shed that morning, Jake was relieved to discover that she was still cleared by Davidoff to sign out equipment. After she signed her name and selected the Husqvarna and some other tree-falling supplies, in the box labelled "Purpose of Use" she wrote: BRUSH CLEARANCE.

Two hundred and thirty feet tall and thirteen feet wide at its base, God's Middle Finger is a tree that her great-grandfather Harris Greenwood would have sent a small army of men to bring down. If they were logging it by hand, they would have first sunk springboards into its trunk to support them before they whacked at it for days with their sharp, double-bitted axes. But today, through the miracles of modern engineering, it's a job that Jake and the Husqvarna can perform in thirty minutes, tops. Whether this is progress, she cannot say.

It's Sunday, her day off, and the only day there aren't any Pilgrims tromping through the old-growth groves. Sundays are also when the

Cathedral's groundskeeping crews start up dozens of leaf blowers to clear away the carpet of fir needles that have fallen throughout the week on the resort, and with all those engines roaring, hopefully the Rangers won't hear what Jake is up to out in the forest. Still, she needs to be quick.

When her period came late last night, she was half relieved and half desolated to learn that there would be no new Greenwood to inflict upon this ruined world. That it would be just the holy trinity of Jake, the trees, and her debt, forever, as it's always been. Perhaps her debt will be the closest she'll ever get to having a family, the only entity that cares about her whereabouts and sticks with her through everything. But if there's to be any hope for the future at all, she can't cower and protect her security and her job like Davidoff suggested; nor can she wait the years that Silas's scheme would take to play out in court. Knut was right: something must be done. Even if it's just to buy the Cathedral's trees a little more time before the Withering takes them.

So once again, Jake chooses trees above all else.

The wide-spreading roots of God's Middle Finger support its mammoth trunk like the buttresses of a castle wall, so Jake needs to get herself above them, to where the trunk is narrower, if she's going to have any chance of making her cut. Wearing her father's unused work gloves, which seem fitting for such a task, she takes out a hammer and bangs in several iron spikes, four feet off the ground, to create numerous footholds for herself around the tree. With each strike, hundreds of wood-boring beetles and carpenter ants scurry from the cavities that the woodpeckers have drilled into the tree. While God's Middle Finger has fought bravely to close its wounds, building up bark tissue around its many intrusions, the fungus has worked quickly and has eaten through the cambium and gnawed fatally deep into the layers of the tree's heartwood. Now, all the cellulose and lignin it has stored over the centuries will be devoured from the inside, and though the tree may stand for a while longer, it can't possibly survive.

When she gets her feet set on two of the spikes, she starts the saw, which catches on her second pull and roars like a jaguar, sending a tide of numbness up her arms that chatters her molars. She guns the engine and brings the long bar near the tree. Just before she lets the blur of the chain bite into the lichenous bark, she nearly yells out an apology. The scientist in her knows that the very moment she cuts into it, the doomed tree will begin transferring its chemical wealth into the soil for its neighbours to absorb. All its precious pesticides and antifungal compounds, all its nitrogen and phosphorous—donated by way of the fungal network that the forest shares, offered up as a kind of family inheritance, a final act of charity in the purest sense of the word.

This tree is older than the language I'm thinking in, she says to herself as she watches the saw split the bark, which is a foot thick. Still, she manages to detach a section about the size of a picnic table, revealing wood that is wet and black with fungus and teeming with bugs. She revs the saw and presses the chain into the trunk, plunging it in as deep as it will go. A blizzard of sawdust flies up into her face as the motor screams. It takes all her strength to keep the heavy machine from leaping out of her hands. After making two similar cuts, she kills the saw, then uses her sledgehammer to knock away from the trunk a piece of wood the size and shape of a small canoe. She leans back from the tree to admire her work, realizing that the tree appears to have cracked a massive grin. "You've always been a joker, haven't you," she says, marvelling at the hundreds of intricate rings of heartwood now made visible inside it.

But if she cuts any farther into the grin, the wood could give way and pinch the chain, and the saw could kick back and kill her. So she steps gingerly on the spikes around to the back of the tree, then restarts the saw and makes her felling cut, leaving only a hinge of wood between this cut and the grin at the front. Into the new cut she hammers a plastic felling wedge. And after driving in a few more wedges, each one bigger than the last, she glances up to see the tree's needled crown shiver, twenty storeys above the forest floor—four-hundred tons of wood balanced precariously above her, all of which grew from a nearly weightless seed.

"Come on, honey," she says. "You're sick. And it's time to lie down."

She hammers in her last and largest felling wedge; immediately there is a shattering crack, and the tree shudders all over like a dog that's just climbed out of a lake. With agonizing slowness, it begins to tilt forward toward the grin, and she hears long wood fibres pulling then snapping like guitar strings through the trunk's length with a series of shrill screeches. She jumps to the ground and backpedals as the great tree begins to crash faster and faster through the branches of its neighbours. It hits the earth with the force of a comet strike, and the ground rumbles beneath her boots and she nearly loses her footing. A blast of air flings the cap from her head and swirls her hair into her eyes. After the tree comes to its final rest, the forest rains needles and branches for a whole minute.

When the cascade stops, a silence like nothing she's ever experienced replaces it. It's as though the fallen tree has swallowed all sound, and she's overcome by the feeling that something of great significance has just transpired, that an entire era has come to an end. After the feeling passes, she climbs atop the fresh stump to catch her breath. She still has four smaller trees to take down and already it hurts to lift her arms. The stump is large enough that she can lie at its centre with limbs spread like a starfish and still not touch its outer rings.

She rests and drinks some water, then crawls over to the stump's edge, removes her gloves, and touches just a few of its 1,200 rings, which are already weeping a rich sap, thick as tar. She begins at this year's growth, the cambium, and counts backward to the ring that grew the year she first arrived at the Cathedral, which is not even an inch from edge. Next, she finds the year the Great Withering began. Then the year she earned her Ph.D. Then she indexes back an inch to the year her mother died. Then her father. Next, she finds her own birth year. Then, at least according to Silas's researchers, the year her grandmother Willow and Everett Greenwood both died. Then Harris Greenwood. She passes over the drought of the thirties, easily identified by five rings thinner and darker than the others surrounding them, until she arrives at the charred ring of the great fire on Greenwood Island, which was also the year Willow was born and the same year Euphemia Baxter wrote the last entry in her journal. Here Jake stops. She hasn't even moved eight inches from the edge, and there are still about six feet left before she reaches the centre.

Even when a tree is at its most vital, only ten per cent of its tissue—the outermost rings, its sapwood—can be called *alive*. All the rings of inner heartwood are essentially dead, just lignin-reinforced cellulose built up year after year, stacked layer upon layer, through droughts and storms, diseases and stresses, everything that the tree has lived through preserved and recorded within its own body. Every tree is held up by its own history, the very bones of its ancestors. And since the journal came to her, Jake has gained a new awareness of how her own life is being held up by unseen layers, girded by lives that came before her own. And by a series of crimes and miracles, accidents and choices, sacrifices and mistakes, all of which have landed her in this particular body and delivered her to this day.

She's always secretly believed that everything we do is somewhere recorded—whether this record could ever be read does not really matter. Just that it is kept is enough. And here, perhaps, in this stump, she's found it.

While preparing to cut down the next diseased tree, she spots a fir sapling growing on the north side of the stump, a seedling that is quite probably the child of the giant she just felled. Jake scoops up the tiny tree in a handful of dirt and re-plants it in the most opportune spot: dead centre in the patch of sunlight that is now reaching the forest floor for the first time in almost a thousand years, all thanks to the gaping hole that God's Middle Finger has left in the canopy. And for a moment Jake stands perfectly still, envisioning the towering juggernaut of timber that the seedling might become, in a mere five hundred years or so.

"Good luck," she says.

HBL

WITH HER FOREST Guide uniform furry with sawdust, Jake arrives at the door of Villa Twelve. When her knocks go answered, she tries the door and finds it unlocked. Inside, she hears Silas humming in the shower, and waits for him on the sofa. At rest, she realizes she's still shaking, the chainsaw's vibration caught somehow in her joints and nerves. She'd cut down the remaining four trees and left them where they fell, because the Cathedral staff will surely limb and burn them the second they're discovered, mainly to protect the Pilgrims from being traumatized by the sight. Still, the fire will eradicate the fungus. That's the hope, anyway. But she heard voices calling out from the forest as she was leaving, which means the Rangers must have heard her chainsaw or felt the tremors of the trees coming down. No doubt they're already scouring the Cathedral for the cause of the disturbance, and once they find the stumps and the chainsaw she left behind, a quick check of the logbook will tell them she's responsible. She doesn't have much time.

Jake goes to the kitchen island and pours herself a hefty bourbon. After weeks of restraint during her pregnancy scare, the drink slips easily down her throat. She spots Silas's phone resting on the counter and nearly picks it up. She'd like to call Knut and inform him that she's completed the job he started and the island's trees now have at least a sliver of a chance, but she has no idea where he's gone.

"Tell the truth, Silas," she announces tipsily when he finally steps from the bathroom in a forest-green Cathedral-branded bathrobe. "They're going to do genetic tests, aren't they?"

His eyes widen momentarily. "Once we make our filing," he says, after his shock passes, "you'll likely attend a kinship hearing. A mere formality. But sure, a genetic test could be ordered by the judge. However, old R.J. wasn't quite prescient enough to set aside any genetic samples. So there will be nothing for them to compare yours to. And I can assure you that the last thing our legal team will allow is any kind of excessive or intrusive testing of your genetic material."

"I'm not a Holt, Silas," she says before taking another long drink. "Anyone who has actually read the journal could tell you that."

"I don't really care if you are a Holt, or a Greenwood, or the prime minister's cousin, Jake. This is not a criminal court we'll be facing. All we need to do is prove that you are *plausibly* a descendant of R.J. Holt, and it'll be enough. Just some useful ambiguity is sufficient, and I expect our magnificent journal will create exactly that. These days, a real, authentic paperbook can convince people of almost anything."

"If R.J. was such a serial sleazeball," she continues, "why haven't you discovered other 'accidents'? Why weren't there children with his wife? No doubt they tried. Men like that love an heir. And besides, Euphemia had visitors other than him."

"I thought scientists are supposed to reserve judgment," he says, nudging the bottle of bourbon out of her reach. "And yes, Euphemia mentions other visitors, including this HBL. But let's not cherry-pick facts and rush to any hasty conclusions. Why are you covered in sawdust?"

"I cut down some diseased trees," she says before draining her glass and stretching for the bottle to pour herself another. "It needed to be done."

His forehead crinkles, but he remains unfazed. "I'm sure you were right to do that. You're the expert. Now look, I'm not here to pressure you. If you're not quite ready to go through with it, just return the journal to me, and you can contact us as soon as you'd like to proceed. You did bring it, didn't you?" Silas gives her a frozen, faintly panicked smile, like someone posing for a photo he doesn't want to be in. He holds out his soft hand for the journal, as if she owes it to him, as if it could ever mean more to him and his firm than it does to Jake.

The bourbon has hit Jake hard and things are already happening too fast. Davidoff knows that Jake has visited Silas here at Villa Twelve once before, so the Rangers could burst in at any minute. But at least she's found a way to save Euphemia's journal from vultures like Silas. She takes another belt while holding his eyes. "I burned the journal," she says coldly. "This morning."

A muscle twitches repeatedly somewhere just beyond his mouth, and two red patches appear on his neck. "You did what?"

"It was mine to burn."

"Including the"—he walks over to the sofa and begins pacing around it—"slipcase?"

She nods. Then she laughs nervously, a single burst, a noise she realizes might come across as insane.

For a man who specializes in adaptation, in poise, in adjusting his beliefs to the shifting circumstances of a shifting world, Silas is rattled. "Okay, you burned it. You burned it?" He rubs his face with both hands. Then he shouts, "Like completely burned it?"

"To a crisp," she says.

"All right," he says, tying and retying his robe while he paces. "That's okay. Of course it's not fucking okay!" he shouts again. "But it happened. We do have scans on file, all verified by notaries, but this still seriously damages our case, Jake. Just the optics are awful. And personally, this hurts because we have a history and I went out on a limb and entrusted the journal to you. I don't know how my firm will react when I tell them. I might not be able to shield you from further litigation, and frankly, I'm not sure I want to."

"The inscription said *Proportee of Willo Greenwud*, Silas—that will show up in all your scans. That means it was *mine*, legally. And if your firm has a problem with that, they can sue me. I've got tons of money," she says sarcastically, setting down her empty glass.

At this, Silas seems to collect himself, and begins to speak with the false, parental empathy she always loathed: "Jake, you've had a long day and too much to drink. All of this can be worked out tomorrow." He goes to the kitchen and picks up his phone from the counter. "Here, I'll have them make up the Villa's guest room." As he thumbs the screen, she creeps up behind him and sees him call up the button that summons the Rangers in case of an emergency.

She bats the phone from his grip and it clatters to the tile floor. Then she stomps on it with the heel of her boot and makes for the door. And for the final time, Jake Greenwood abandons Silas for the trees.

CATHEDRAL PROPERTY

THEY FIND HER at dawn the next morning, tucked behind a decomposing nurse log, among the lesser stands of the once-burned trees that surround the staff cabins. Her face is pasted with dropped cedar needles that smell of grapefruit when crushed against her cheekbone.

Jake's dehydrated skull pounds with each tug and jostle as the Rangers lift her from the ground and lead her through the Cathedral, past trunks garlanded with moss, over thick black roots that surface from the ground like eels. Each of the five Rangers carries a small, snub-nosed machine gun that appears all the more terrifying for its diminutive size. At her staff cabin they stand sentry by the door while she removes her Forest Guide uniform and hangs it in her locker for the last time. Then she digs into the locker's deepest recesses to unearth a garbage bag that contains the tattered pants and shirt she wore when she first arrived on Greenwood Island, dusty, starving, and broke. When she's dressed she begins to pack Knut's paperbooks, tucking the first-edition Muir and Linnaeus into her father's cardboard box, along with the woodworking tools and the records of poetry that he left her.

But the lead Ranger enters and speaks just as she's about to lift the box. "This one is Greenwood Property," he says, his accent from somewhere Jake can't place. "You must leave it."

"No, no—'*Liam* Greenwood'," Jake says, running her finger along the words, trying to keep her tone under control. "It's my father's name, and it has absolutely nothing to do with the Cathedral."

With the barrel of his gun he points to the word *Greenwood* and says, "Cathedral property. You are allowed only what is yours."

It's then Jake realizes that like so many of the Rangers—mostly war-ravaged souls flown in from the various dusty hellscapes around the world—this man likely can't read, and can only recognize the *G* because he's seen it so many times here at the Cathedral.

Jake knows better than to embarrass him or make a scene, especially after what she's done, so she clenches her jaw and kisses the box goodbye. Knut can get more books, and her father's tools and strange records never held much significance for her anyway. She draws her hair back then pulls on her Leafskin jacket.

"Also Cathedral property," the Ranger says, now pointing at her coat with his gun.

"The wind will cut right through me out on the open water," she pleads. "Please, sir. It's the only coat I have."

The Ranger glances at his comrades standing outside the door, none of whom are listening closely. He tightens his lips in what seems like a flash of pity and nods affirmatively. "Go," he says.

Outside they parade her past the row of staff cabins, then past the dining yurt, while being careful to avoid the Villas. Soon they reach the trailhead, where a small group of eager Pilgrims have already assembled to look at their phones and await their morning tours.

Just as they reach the wharf, Jake spies a yellow paste floating on the surface of the waterfront hot tubs. At first she assumes it's algae, a common flare-up at the Cathedral, brought in from other oceans on the bathing suits of their jet-setting guests. But Jake also notices a thin, yellow tint to the air. She's dragged aboard the supply barge, which soon pulls back from the wharf, and it isn't until she's out on the bay that she can glimpse the thick, lemony haze, caught in the highest branches of the Cathedral's trees, like a great yellow curtain drawn around their crowns. The trees are masting, she realizes—releasing their pollen together—more furiously than she's ever seen before, and six months out of season. Most tree species only ever reproduce so vigorously when conditions are dire, when they're stressed by disease or after they've been licked by wildfire or emaciated by drought.

Whether they perform this reproductive gambit because they believe things will get better after the threat subsides, or they believe they have nothing left to lose now that everything has gone to hell, no researcher has been able to say for sure. But Jake can't help but admire their optimism.

She brushes off some of the fine powder that has clung to her coat and rubs it into her hands. After exchanging their genetic material through the wind-blown pollen, the trees will set their seed cones, which will eventually open and send seedpods whirling on single propellers to the forest floor—at the exact time they shouldn't. Even under the best conditions, a minuscule percentage of Douglas fir seeds ever reach adulthood. And at the wrong time of year, the seeds will find the soil muddy and inhospitable. They'll rot long before any can germinate. And after all that's gone amiss for Jake in recent months, only now does her composure shatter at the thought of these trees expending their last reserves to release millions of propellers to the wind out of utter desperation. Tears prickle her face. She lowers herself to the deck so the crew of the barge won't see her weep.

THE GREENWOODS

AN HOUR AFTER Greenwood Island recedes from view and the sub-
sonic hum of the resort's desalinator can no longer be heard from
the barge, Jake stops sobbing. She's dedicated her life to the study of
the world's great trees: the eucalyptus, the banyan, the English oak,
the baobab, the Lebanese cedar, the yakusugi of Japan, the sequoia
of northern California, the Amazonian mahogany—but it is the
coastal Douglas fir of the Pacific Northwest that remains dearest to
her. And since the day she first arrived at the Greenwood Arboreal
Cathedral, she's believed that she couldn't possibly survive without
its forest, or the island that—at least for now—sustains it. Yet of
course she can. People can adapt to anything, as long as it is necessary. And though she's been turned out of her Eden, she's leaving
with a story. Only a partial story, it's true, but as far as she can tell,
that's the only type there is.

Jake finds a secluded nook formed by the crates that the barge
carries, tucking herself behind some bins of recycling and compost
stacked head-high. She picks at the lining of her Leafskin coat with
her fingertips, and from the hole she's made she pulls the battered
paperbook, nestled inside its slipcase. She removes the journal and sits
leafing through its coal-blackened pages in the bracing sea air, hearing
Euphemia's voice, feeling the faint imprint her pen left in the paper a
hundred years ago, like inverted Braille. *Leafing.* Why this expression,
always? *We make them human,* Knut wrote. *With our verbs.*

As she so often does, Jake lands on the journal's final entry, the
one in which Euphemia addresses her newborn child directly for
the first time, and describes her decision to keep her, despite the

Great Depression, her impoverished circumstances, and her previous agreement to give her up. And though Jake now knows that Euphemia may have inexplicably taken her own life soon after, the passage still offers Jake a tenuous strength with which to face her new life on the Mainland.

After a few more hours, the barge nears Vancouver, and Jake lifts her eyes from the journal to behold the city. She remembers the excitement of first seeing this landscape after arriving from Delhi— this convergence of mountains and trees and ocean that charged her with such energy she couldn't sleep for days. But so many of its great trees are gone now, replaced with climate-controlled towers of glass and steel. Even Stanley Park's ancient cedars and firs have succumbed, just a few of them left to stand like green sentries beside the high-end housing developments that crowd the shoreline.

The barge chugs into a ramshackle service wharf where other ships of industry are moored. The air is dusty and pungent and toxic, and already Jake yearns for the island's soothing, coniferous scent. The barge captain approaches her and says that since they're short on crew, they'll pay her a small sum to help unload the cargo. Now that she's lost her job, she'll soon be defaulting on her student loans, so it would be good to have some cash in her pocket.

Jake and some other crewmembers take up some plastic bins of recycling and carry them down the gangplank to the landing. For her next load, she's about to pick up a large bucket of rank-smelling compost when the captain tells her to wait, before he quickly douses its contents with a jug of bleach.

"Why do they do that? Add the bleach?" Jake asks one of the crew as they're walking back up to the ship to fetch another load.

The man grimaces at a large group of beggars, all children, huddled near the base of the ramp. "To keep those ones out of it," he says warily.

A half hour later the unloading is done and Jake receives her paltry payment. She pulls two empty wine bottles—perhaps one of them was the very bottle she shared with Corbyn, or the one she watched Silas drink—from the recycling bins, which are placed to await pick-up in a chain-link enclosure where the beggars can't get them. Jake walks over to the group of children and shoves the bottles into one of the scuzzy plastic bags that dangle at their sides.

"Thank you, Miss," a child says in a raspy, dust-scoured voice, removing the bottles from the bag to carefully appraise their value. With the rags wrapped over the child's face, Jake can't accurately discern its gender or ethnicity. Indonesian perhaps, maybe Pakistani. The child's exposed forehead is the same faint brown as her own.

"How much can you get for those?" Jake asks.

"Not too much," the child says protectively, clutching the bottles to its chest, as though worried that Jake is having second thoughts and may snatch them back.

"Don't worry, they're yours," Jake says, then glances at the bucket of bleached compost sitting nearby, which one of the ragged boys is now prodding with a coat hanger. "Maybe you can buy something to eat?"

"We are lucky," the child proclaims proudly. "The bleach does not soak all the way down. And the Greenwoods throw out many good things, Miss. They are very generous."

"You're right, they throw out many things," Jake says, and for a moment she recalls Silas speaking of the downtrodden masses who'll butcher your family and loot your home without first asking you for a handout. "But I wouldn't exactly call them generous."

"You are generous and you are one," the child says, pointing to the Cathedral's stylized logo on Jake's Leafskin jacket.

Jake touches the silkscreened logo with her fingers and smiles. "Not anymore. Still, you're right. I was a Greenwood once," she says. "But do you have anyone here? A family? Or if not here, then somewhere?"

"No, Miss," the child says with downcast eyes, then points to the other beggars with a brightened expression. "But I have them."

In an instant, Jake pictures herself enfolding this child in her arms and carrying it away from this squalid wharf—though the sudden desperation of the urge also frightens her. Because what child could possibly want Jake to rescue it? And how could she ever hope to care for another human being properly? She's broke. With no family support-network and no partner. She drinks too much. And once she declares bankruptcy, her life will downshift into a whole new gear of squalor.

The child's life with Jake would be a painful and low existence: hunger, dust, and discomfort, maybe even rib retch. In truth, she'd be a terrible guardian, and would probably leave the child worse off than it is now.

And yet. If she did take the child in, maybe they could track down Knut. He of all people would know whether there's an arboretum somewhere, a sanctuary where at least some of the Earth's great tree species have been preserved—probably funded by some tech magnate with a God complex, no doubt, but still. There, Jake could watch the child marvel at the banyan, the eucalyptus, the oak, the monkey puzzle, and the sequoia. And over time, after they'd put together the shards of the child's own story as best they could—including how the child had ended up here on this wharf, eating bleached food and picking through refuse—Jake would tell the child the story of the Greenwoods, at least what little of it she knows. She'd speak of her great-grandfather the lumber tycoon. Her great-uncle the kidnapper. Her grandmother, who'd given away a fortune on principle. Her father, who'd built beautiful things for the richest people in the land. And when the child was old enough, Jake could even let it read Euphemia's journal, which would be like their family album, the text that bound them together.

And someday, when things got a little better and they had saved up some money, Jake would return with the child to this wharf to show it where they first met. And from here they'd hire passage to Greenwood Island, if it hadn't yet been swallowed by the rising sea, and they'd stay in the cabin Harris built. And even if the Withering had already killed off all the island's Douglas firs, Jake would teach the child about them anyway.

If history were itself a book, this era would surely be the last chapter, wouldn't it? Or have all ages believed this? That life can't possibly go on and that these are the end times? At the height of the Great Depression, Euphemia wrote about a society that couldn't possibly continue. Still, things did go on. And on. And on. Years piling on years. Layers upon layers. Light and dark. Sapwood over heartwood.

"Would you like me to buy you something to eat?" Jake asks.

"Yes, Miss," the child replies skeptically. "But please, I need to be back soon for the next barge."

Jake agrees and takes the child's soot-blackened hand in hers, which is still dusted with lemony fir pollen, and they start out from the wharf to make their way into the city. *What if a family isn't a tree at all?* Jake thinks as they walk in silence. What if it's more like a forest? A collection of individuals pooling their resources through intertwined roots, sheltering one another from wind and weather and drought—just like Greenwood Island's trees have done for centuries. And even if Euphemia Baxter isn't Jake's great-grandmother, and Harris Greenwood isn't her great-grandfather, and even though she's never even laid eyes on her father Liam or her grandmother Willow—they're all Greenwoods. And they're all with her, embedded in her cellular structure; if not a part of her family tree, then part of her family forest. And no one knows better than a dendrologist that it's the forests that matter.

What are families other than fictions? Stories told about a particular cluster of people for a particular reason? And like all stories, families are not born, they're invented, pieced together from love and lies and nothing else. And through these messy means, so too might this poor, destitute child become—for good and for ill—a Greenwood.

THE SECRET & PRIVATE THINKINGS & DOINGS OF EUPHEMIA BAXTER

TODAY, DURING MY WALK, I *saw a man in the trees.*

The doctor advised against leaving my bed, but I felt strong enough & I left you sleeping in your crib & ventured alone into the maple forest that surrounds the estate. The woods were locked with frost & the spring air was frigid & because RJ won't allow me a jacket or shoes, I borrowed the housekeeper's. It was my first outing as a mother & even the ground felt altered beneath my feet, a little more wondrous, yet also a little less forgiving. But the forest seemed to welcome me & I was soon filled with cheer.

If the man in the trees hadn't been tapping a nail into one of the maples, I would never have noticed him. He was bearded & looked destitute & almost half-tree himself. But I saw goodness in the careful way he hung a bucket from the nail & in the gentle pace with which he moved. He didn't appear much of a talker, so I left him undisturbed.

RJ would be furious if he knew someone was living on his property, so of course I'll say nothing. He's visiting tomorrow & will meet you for the first time. I must remember to hide this journal before he arrives. To him, its very existence is an affront. He mistrusts books. & private journals he mistrusts even more.

Though it embarrasses me to say it, I want to be a writer like Virginia Woolf. What would that sort of rapture feel like? To have words overtake you? To have them run in your veins like quicksilver, faster than your own blood? Unlike RJ, HBL likes my writing. Often he tells me that I can do whatever I set my mind to & I hope he's right. I've asked him to bring me shoes & a coat tonight when he visits & he said he would. He's an anguished soul, but he's also kind. He's like me, in many hidden ways. A person with more burdens than choices, with more love than places to put it.

For so long I've felt as though my life were a seed that the soil of the world refuses. The Crash is to blame, at least partially anyway. Everything is fraying & falling apart. It's all everyone at the bank used to talk about. None know why the Crash happened, just that it suffocates & disfigures. & though people are prepared to work, there is no work. & even here, so near to the ocean, the sky occasionally clouds with dust. I worry that the green & growing things have abandoned us for good & that the dust is all that we deserve.

In my time, I have worked & worked & worked & still I've got nowhere. Even when I was a girl, hope was something I've always been short on.

But somehow, you've afforded me some. Perhaps because a world with you in it feels fundamentally richer. Though it's you who will face the bleakness of the future, not me. A future that's no longer better than the past. So I suppose this is also an apology.

Still, there's a cherry tree in full blossom outside my window & I talk to it. During your birth, I counted the blossoms while the doctor wore that worried expression & I was losing blood & felt my body creeping towards death. & now every time the wind blows through its blossoms I see you in the shimmer.

After I left the man in the trees, I decided something: I'm going to keep you.

I thought I couldn't. But that has changed.

I don't care how little money I have. I don't care how bleak things look. I don't care who your father is. I don't even care that I'm your mother. I do not want you because you are mine. I want you because I am yours.

RJ will be livid & I will certainly lose my apartment & my job & maybe worse. But HBL will help me. I can be stubborn when I make up my mind. Just ask your grandparents, if they are still alive when you read this.

You are sleeping now. You've sapped my energies, though this is to be expected. What are our energies for, except to be sapped? I've rolled you in a bolt of brocade cloth that I bought in a charity shop. & though I always *hated needlework, tonight I will suffer some hours on your behalf & stitch you a blanket from the cloth myself. You should have at least one thing that RJ hasn't bought.*

I must lay down my pen for now. I am still light-headed & sore from your birth & from walking & can sit no longer. I promise to take the pen up again tomorrow & finish these thoughts, if they can be finished. My only hope is that this journal will explain things. & that you, when you are old enough, will read this & perhaps grasp my truest, guiding intentions. That my principal aim is to be worthy of you. As soon as I'm ready, we're going to leave this place. Together. If they attempt to stop us, we will flee into the forest. It will be a long walk from here into town. But I am strong & you give me courage & a forest has always been the best place for a person to escape into.

ACKNOWLEDGMENTS

MY THANKS TO Bill Clegg, whose belief in this book was the scaffolding that made its construction possible.

My deep gratitude to Alexis Washam and Jillian Buckley at Hogarth for their insight and their dedication. And a special thanks to Anita Chong at McClelland & Stewart, who has been my champion for so long and who helped me tell this story, ring by ring, branch by branch, and leaf by leaf.

Thanks also to Jared Bland, Joe Lee, Ruta Liormonas, Melanie Little, Jennifer Griffiths, Shaun Oakey, Francis Geffard, Simon Toop, David Kambhu, Marion Duvert, Henry Rabinowitz, Griffin Irvine, Lilly Sandberg, Molly Slight, Henry Rosenbloom, Marika Webb-Pullman, Alexander MacLeod, Benji Wagner, Alex Craig, Arnie Bell, Jackie Bowers, Naomi Brown, and Claire and Martha Christie.

Greenwood owes its inspiration to many other books. Here are some of them: *The Tree* by John Fowles; *The Wretched of Canada: Letters to R.B. Bennett, 1930–1935*, edited by Linda M. Grayson and Michael Bliss; *The Great Depression* by Pierre Berton; *The Worst Hard Time* by Timothy Egan; *Hard Times* by Studs Terkel; *You Can't Win* by Jack Black; *Beggars of Life* by Jim Tully; *Riding Toward Everywhere* by William T. Vollmann; *H.R.: A Biography of H.R. MacMillan* by Ken Drushka; *Let Us Now Praise Famous Men* by James Agee and Walker Evans; *Cabbagetown* by Hugh Garner; *Confessions of an English Opium-Eater* by Thomas De Quincey; *The Hidden Life of Trees* by Peter Wohlleben; *Tree: A Life Story* by David Suzuki and Wayne Grady; *Unchopping a Tree* by W.S. Merwin; *The Wars* by Timothy Findley; *How to Live in the New America* by William

Kaysing; *Woodsmen of the West* by Martin Allerdale Grainger; *The Return of the Soldier* by Rebecca West; *The Journal of Private Fraser* by Donald Fraser, edited by Reginald H. Roy; *The Soul of a Tree* by George Nakashima.

Much of this big novel was written in a little cabin on Galiano Island, and I would like to thank the people of this community for supporting me throughout. I'd also like to record my debt of gratitude to the Canada Council for the Arts for their financial support.

Thanks to my parents, who each left this world too early, and whose unsung sacrifices I'm only beginning to fathom. And to Jason Christie, the greatest brother and table tennis opponent I could ever ask for.

And lastly, thanks to Lake and August, whose lives have regenerated my own. And to Cedar Bowers, for what it would require an entire forest's worth of paper to describe.